Liberty's Call

Shadows of the Appalachians

Book 1

Patricia Reece

Outta the Holler Publishing

First Printing, 2017

ISBN 978-0-9992952-0-5

Outta the Holler Publishing   PO Box 1278   Bridgeport, WA 98813

www.patriciafayreece.com

Dedication

This book is dedicated to Christ Jesus, my Savior.

I have never had a better friend, in all my life, than the Son of God. To Him goes the credit for anything I complete, now and in the future. He leads me through the therapy of writing I so desperately need, to regain my sense of usefulness after losing much.

As I take my place among the Lord's writers, I want to thank each of them for the hard work and the suffering they sometimes endure, to craft words helpful to the souls of a fallen world. They use words as swords, fighting on the front lines, as they intercede in the pages of their books for us. They stand in the gap for others who desperately need a light shined on the path that leads to Christ.

Acknowledgements

My heartfelt thanks go to my husband, Ken, and our family, who encouraged me as I wrote.

Thank you to ACFW's critique group members who used gracious words and soft suggestions to help me shape my story: Marti Chabot, Celeste Charlene, Nike Chillemi, Shirley Connolly, Connie Cortright, Jean Kinsey, Terri Wangard and Betty Thomason Owens.

Thank you Ane Mulligan for guidance I needed.

I want to congratulate Ginger Aster, my beta reader, for finding what I needed to rewrite.

Pam Umberger, who made our lunches productive, I appreciate your personal input and emphasis on important details that may have slipped by.

CHAPTER ONE

Baltimore County, Maryland
Thursday, April 10 1755

Thomas wiped his brow with a sleeve, walking toward the shed. The sun blazed down on the open area around the blacksmith's forge, adding more heat. He preferred the milder spring days, before summertime began.

Peering into the sky, his mind on something besides all the hard work they just finished, Thomas bent down, reaching for a back leg on the last animal he readied for Simon to shoe. He ducked the skittish new farm horse's kick, not sure what had warned him.

"Look out!" Simon called.

Jumping back to avoid the other hind leg, the eight hundred pound animal's hoof sliced the air, landing a glancing blow on his shoulder. Knocked off balance, he pivoted at the waist, leaning away as he managed to catch himself.

Simon moved into the space by Thomas. "You all right, then?"

"I think so." Thomas gingerly worked his shoulder. "Powerful hind legs. Too close for me."

The servant nodded as he reached for tongs to grasp a horseshoe. Thomas came at the animal again. They moved from hoof to hoof, finally getting him shod. Thomas sucked in a deep breath as he turned the horse out to pasture. He knew better than let his mind wander, working with a strange animal.

After they finished, he left Simon at the anvil as he moved toward the door, hand rubbing his shoulder.

"Let me know if you need more help, Simon."

He started toward the house, thinking about God, Who had just smiled on him. If bent a little closer toward the ground, the horse's powerful hoof may have kicked out his brains. He had seen a few men not so fortunate, never able to hold a job or think clearly after that. The dangers surrounding a new workhorse should always come first. Here on out, he must be more careful.

His thoughts now, though, drifted to eyes the color of a clear sky, dark curls billowing around delicate shoulders.

He entered the house, a firm hand pressed to his lower back. Strolling to the common room, he poured a drink, taking a swallow. The cool water refreshed him. Setting down the mug, he started toward the front room, when a knock sounded at the door.

He turned the knob, pulling hard.

A man stood on the porch, fist poised for another rap. Dressed in a butternut colored jacket over a white shirt, dark brown breeches labored to contain his rotund stomach.

"Good day, sir. How may I help you?"

"Please, young man, call me Mr. Greene."

Thomas nodded as he shook the man's extended hand.

"Now, who shall I speak with about freighting services?" The man blinked, as his bulging gray eyes swept over Thomas.

"My father's the proprietor, Cyrus Craighead." Thomas widened the doorway, stepping back. "Come in. You may wait for him in the front room."

His brother looked on from across the room. "Isaac, inform Father we have a visitor."

"Straight away," Isaac replied.

Showing Mr. Greene to the front room, Thomas gestured toward a camel-back sofa. Their visitor took a seat.

"Would you care for something to drink?"

"No, thank you." The man shifted his ample weight.

Thomas sat at the opposite end of the sofa, standing when Father entered the room.

"Mr. Greene wishes to speak with you."

Father stepped in the man's direction. "What can I help you with today?"

Mr. Greene rocked twice to gain his feet. Accepting Father's hand, he returned to sink down on the sofa. Father took a chair just opposite.

"Sir, I represent William Franklin, Benjamin's son, in a matter concerning General Braddock and the British troops."

Father nodded. "Well then, I'm acquainted with Benjamin." He gazed toward the ceiling, before continuing. "I'm not a great admirer of the British general, or his troops." Rubbing a hand across his chin, Father muttered something unintelligible. "But tell me, what's this to do with me?"

Thomas shifted position, his neck muscles tightening as he looked down. Father must carefully watch everything he said about King George's general, especially to this visitor. Who knew how that might be received? He breathed easier when Mr. Greene continued.

"Mr. Craighead, you have a good reputation. We need reliable men, such as yourself, to deliver supplies to Wills Creek here in Maryland. We'll require a pledge that you'll finish the job." The man blew a sharp breath as he shifted position. "If you're interested in hauling for the Crown, how many wagons can we count on?"

Father leaned forward, head slightly tilted. "How many freighters has Mr. Franklin committed from Pennsylvania?"

Mr. Greene's eyes narrowed. "At the present time, we're sending sixty, filled with oats and corn. We've contracted with other freighters to accompany the military to the forks of the Ohio." His face grew serious. "You'll deliver the goods through Maryland. You'll pick up a shipment at the Port of Deposit on the Susquehanna, delivering it to the new Fort Cumberland."

"I don't favor this employment, sir, but if necessary I'll spare two wagons." Father leaned back, crossing his arms. "My horses are hitched to our wagons only, going and coming. They won't do any other work."

Mr. Greene cleared his throat. "I see."

Placing a hand on his knee, Father continued. "We run a business. We haul by the hundredweight, and payment's expected promptly unless other arrangements are made."

The visitor squinted into the distance, eyes moist, rosy cheeks perched high on a broad face. "Very well, Cyrus. I'll deliver your concerns to William Franklin."

Inching closer to the sofa's edge, Mr. Greene angled a leg out, rising. "You may hear from me again."

Thomas stood in the entryway as his father escorted the man out the door. They returned to the front room.

"Da, what do you think about the agent's proposal?"

"This isn't likely to happen if I have a say. My mind's made up."

He probed his father's eyes—something done since childhood to determine Father's true thoughts. Thomas knew their family would not help unless forced into it.

"I've offered assistance to Gerald this evening." Thomas glanced at his father, then away. "I'll go there directly after supper."

"Seems like you're over at the Hacketts more than Gerald's here, working for me. Sophrona have anything to do with your visits?"

Thomas met his father's smile. "It's six months I'm keeping company with her. I now visit Gerald to see her."

Father grunted, his smile deepening.

"What was it like with Mother?"

A shadow flickered across his widowed father's face. Why did he ask such a question? Hurting Father like that?

4

"You'll know soon enough that she's the one. If you feel the urge to wed her, speak to her father."

"Is that what happened with Mother? Did you ask Granda Wallace for her hand?"

"Yes, I did." Unusual softness drove the shadow away, leaving Father's face looking younger.

"Did he agree to the marriage?"

"Not at first."

Thomas leaned closer. "What changed his mind?"

"Well then, after he'd worked me clean into the ground clearing rock from his field—him with a mule, me using my back—he agreed. In the family's presence, he gave us his blessing."

Thomas glanced at his mother's portrait on the wall. "When it's time, I'll ask Mr. Hackett for his daughter's hand."

"I'll give you and your lovely lass my blessing. After you've learned all the trade, we'll enter into a partnership. Perhaps God will bless me with descendants."

Thomas's chest swelled, pressing tight against his shirt, as Father's smile pushed the wrinkles clear off his weathered face.

After supper, he started the six mile ride along the Patapsco River toward the Hackett house in Baltimore Town. The small Narragansett pacer, with its well-shaped body and comfortable gait, picked the way by moonlight while he thought about Sophrona.

She smelled like roses warmed under the sun. Occasionally, she preened her dark curls with her fingertips. Other times she stood with hands clasped behind her, or shoved into her apron pockets. He liked her hands—the delicate way God touched her littlest fingers. Thomas wanted to keep her close to him.

The Hackett residence sat on the edge of town. The two-story whitewashed frame gave the house a soothing appearance, its peaked roof sloping to one story in back. At first glimpse, the candlelight glowing through the windows warmed him like a welcome harbor

5

from the darkness. After he loosened the reins, the pacer took him the last quarter mile in less than a minute.

He tied his horse to a post. Rushing up the steps to the large porch, past two Windsor rocking chairs, he rapped on the front door.

Sophrona peered around Gerald, as he opened the door wide.

Thomas squared his shoulders to enter the house.

* * *

Late April

Thomas hurried toward the front door, answering a persistent knock.

"A post for Cyrus Craighead," the messenger said.

"Thank you." Thomas took the letter and closed the door.

He strode to the office. "This came for you."

Father looked up, reaching for the correspondence. Breaking the wax seal, he unfolded the leaf.

"Hmmm. I had hoped they'd forgotten us." Father rubbed his temple with a knuckle, lips moving as he looked over the page.

"What, Da?" Thomas said.

"Want it or not, we have employment. Governor Sharpe threatens to follow the Pennsylvania governor, who is already pressing freighters to transport for the British." He drummed his fingers on the desk.

"Must we work for Maryland?" Thomas said.

Father nodded.

"Next Monday, the fifth, we'll pick up flour in Bladensburg, then beef casks near Watkins Ferry at the Potomac, freighting it all to the fort at Wills Creek. We'll haul, earning some money. If we refuse, they'll take all our horses and wagons at the Crown's behest."

Craighead Freighting owned five wagons, along with twenty-six well-tended horses. Father trained Simon, an indentured Scotsman shipped over by the English as punishment for thievery, to shoe and care for their animals.

6

"Da, which wagons are you taking?"

Father scratched an ear. "We'll drive the smallest and one of the largest reinforced Dutch wagons. Then hitch them to our best horses."

"Must I drive one?" Thomas said.

"Usually you want to travel with me. I value your good judgment more than you think, Lad."

"I planned to visit the Hacketts on Monday, maybe ask for Sophrona's hand."

"Why not ride over there today, and let them know we'll both call tomorrow? It's time I renew our contract with Peter Hackett."

* * *

The following afternoon, Thomas dressed in his best beechnut colored breeches, hose and square-toed gentleman's riding boots. He slipped into a black velvet short-coat, snug at the waist, with a row of silver buttons. Simon saddled their horses.

They tied up their mounts at the Hacketts', strode up the path, crossing the porch. Thomas cleared his throat before knocking.

"Mr. Craighead—Thomas—come in." Gerald moved aside to allow them entry.

Peter stepped across the room toward them, his hand outstretched. "I'm pleased to see you again, Cyrus. Come, take a seat."

Moving past the staircase to the sitting room, Thomas sat by Gerald on a stuffed sofa. Peter gestured for Cyrus to take the first of two easy chairs. Across the room, a servant worked at a cavernous rock fireplace. Behind her sat a chair-back settee, flanked by wingback chairs.

Thomas stood when Sophrona entered the room. Her skirt glided over the floor as she came to sit between him and her brother.

Father tapped his fingers against a knee, listening as Gerald spoke.

7

Peter cast a piercing glance at the three, briefly settling on Thomas before turning to Father.

"This meeting on our freighting agreement is timely, Cyrus. The contracts are all drawn up."

"Yes, let's do that while I'm here."

"Shall we move to my office, then?" Peter turned to Sophrona. "This shouldn't take long."

Thomas rose, following the men down a hallway. Peter sat at his desk. Thomas and his father took the pair of chairs opposite.

"Cyrus, I've prepared a new three year contract, worded as the last one. You'll transport pig iron from my furnace on the Gunpowder River, over to my brother's forge on the Chesapeake." Peter scratched his neck. "Providing Gerald continues to drive for you, at his current wage."

"Well, Lad, shall we sign for three more years, then?" Father turned toward Thomas, and he nodded.

Lifting two sheets of parchment at his left, Peter placed them side by side, offering Father a quill. After they signed, Peter sprinkled sand on the ink, leaving them on the desk to dry.

Father folded his arms. "To ease any fear I intended to raise my prices, I assure you they would have stayed the same."

"That's a relief, considering the military's out contracting with every freighter possible."

Father took a letter from his pocket. "I received this from Governor Sharpe." He stood, handing it to Peter before taking his seat. "They took the right to refuse away from me."

Peter tapped his desk with a finger as he read. After finishing, he handed it back to Father. "I see what you mean."

Reaching for the contracts, Peter shook off the sand. "Well, then, it's done."

He handed a copy to Father, who folded his before slipping it into a jacket pocket.

8

Thomas followed his father and Peter back to the front room. He joined Sophrona on the sofa, where she talked with Gerald.

"Shall we sit, Cyrus, while Fronnie helps her mother ready the table?" Peter stared hard at his daughter.

Rising from the sofa, Sophrona clutched her skirt. Thomas caught a brief glimpse of her face turning pink as she dashed from the room, likely the result from her tender feelings getting squeezed.

"Now, tell me your reason for coming tonight, young man, other than the contract."

"Mr. Hackett, I'm here to ask for your daughter's hand in marriage." Thomas glanced at his father. "Even discuss posting our first marriage banns."

Cyrus leaned over, clasping Peter's shoulder. "A good day for the Scots when my son weds your daughter, eh, Peter?"

"Well then, he's decided on marriage." Peter turned to Thomas. "No doubt you've discussed this with her."

"Yes, sir, I have."

The four waited as Sophrona helped her mother, Fenella, set out slices of apple cake on a table near the entrance to the common room. After that, she retrieved cups for tea or coffee.

When his wife called for him, Peter rose. "Cyrus, Thomas, please join our family in refreshments."

They stood at the table, waiting until the two ladies were seated. After the men joined them, the group began to eat and drink as though the two families had already become one.

"Are you sure about marriage?" Peter's voice carried a trace of Highlander brogue.

Thomas glanced at Sophrona, so beautiful in a bright blue dress with her chestnut hair.

"Yes, sir, I'm sure, if you two will agree to this."

"We are pleased to welcome you into our family," Peter said, as Fenella nodded.

"Thank you, sir."

"Cyrus, we shall post the first banns at Saint Paul's Church. You two must be married there."

Thomas' breathing slowed. He looked toward his father.

"Where did you say, Mr. Hackett?"

"We'll post the banns at Saint Paul's Church, of course, where we attend."

"Our marriage banns must be posted at the Church of England, sir, as required by the Maryland statutes. But we don't attend there." A small voice inside whispered, "Careful", but Thomas could not stop. "Our family must tithe to the Anglicans, but we're dissenters all our lives. We attend the Presbyterian meeting house on the Lower Crossroads, three miles from the Susquehanna."

"Yes, I know where it is." Creases deepened on Peter's face. "You attended the Garrison Forest Chapel, part of our parish, for several years. What in the world's wrong with our church, Thomas?"

"It's true. I did attend the Garrison, but only to get an education from Reverend Craddock. Not to worship."

Peter's face deepened to a red hue.

"Not to offend you, sir, but I learned about my Lord in the Presbyterian Church, where we shall marry." Thomas glanced at Father, who nodded ever-so-slightly.

* * *

Sophrona clutched her hands, looking toward her mother. Fear almost consumed her. What if Thomas did not want her now? Somehow she must change her father's mind.

"But Father, what's the difference which church w…"

"Stay quiet while your father and Thomas discuss this matter." Mother reached for her hands, but Sophrona shoved them under the table.

Her father cleared his throat, in that authoritative manner he used.

10

"I don't want problems with you, who my daughter seems to love. However, I feel strongly about Sophrona being married in any church other than ours."

Thomas did not argue with her father. "Let us consider our words tonight, sir, though I cannot see changing my position."

"I need help serving tea and more cake," Mrs. Hackett said.

Sophrona rose. Jaws clamped together, she shook out her skirt before following her mother. How could they decide her life as though she were not even in the room? Thomas must not let Father keep them from marriage. It did not matter to her where they took their vows.

* * *

Thomas unclenched his fists, his shoulders relaxing. He forced a smile when Sophrona offered him more cake. He thanked her parents before leading her to the front porch. There they sat in rockers looking out at the trees, shrouded by silvery moonlight.

"Will we still marry, after such a contentious discussion?" Sophrona's voice quivered.

"I love you, Sophrona, but no one else shall tell us where to hold our wedding." He took her hand, so soft he almost kissed it. "We've encountered some unexpected freighting that needs done immediately. After that, we'll speak about marriage again."

He rose, helping her to her feet. Bending his head, he kissed her cheek.

"We'll settle this disagreement to everyone's satisfaction, before we get married. Then, contented, we'll grow old together." He drew her close.

She pulled away. "But, Thomas, what if Father doesn't..."

11

CHAPTER TWO

Thursday, May 4, 1755
Baltimore Town, Maryland

Sophrona rolled onto her back. The smell of fresh bread started a complaint in her stomach. She yawned, stiffening her legs. The last time Thomas had called on her, when he refused marriage in their family's church, he indicated they would wed. But what if they did not? What if she never saw him again?

She was grateful their fathers signed a new contract that night. At the least, she might hear about him through her brother, Gerald.

Lying in the bed, with the smell of lilac on the covers, her thoughts roamed.

Around Baltimore Town, people considered her father an ambitious man. His ore furnace sat on the Gunpowder River's edge. Once, she and Mother had stopped by with Gerald, who occasionally worked alongside Father's hired men. Father spoke with Mother, then rushed them out before the heat, and stares from his workers, became unbearable.

Discussions around their supper table had included smelting crude ore down to pig iron. One evening Mother remarked, as she passed Father the bread, "Peter, you must encourage Gerald to work for Cyrus Craighead, hauling to your brother's forge on the Chesapeake." She stopped to dab a finger at her eye. "That's the better job. He mustn't take a chance on getting scalded or injured at your furnace."

While their parents talked, Sophrona glanced at Gerald, neither one willing to enter the conversation.

"I won't tell the boy what to do, Fenella. You shouldn't, either. One day, when he takes over for me, he must make all his own decisions."

"Yes, Peter, but by then he'll be the owner. Someone else will do those dangerous tasks." Mother pinched her lips closed after that, ending the conversation. Discussions during supper about Gerald's work seemed to end after that.

Sophrona rose, choosing a dress to slip on. She glanced in the mirror before sitting at the dressing table. The pale blue material almost matched her eyes. Brush in hand, she gave her dark curls twenty-five strokes, then hurried downstairs to the front room.

She glanced back toward the common room. Mother stepped through the door, no doubt coming to roust her from bed. Approaching, she smiled as she reached out to pat Sophrona's arm. "Later, I'd like your help in the common room, but now you must eat something to keep up your strength."

"Mother, can a servant help you later?"

"Fronnie, you won't learn how to cook well unless you do it. How can you be someone's wife and run a house if you don't learn how?"

"Not *someone's* wife, Mother. I'm going to be Thomas's wife." Sophrona followed her back into the common room, mumbling, "I thought you already knew this."

"Be careful what you say, daughter. I'll not take anything from you today. Besides, it's not good to be contentious on an empty stomach. Now, get some breakfast."

"Yes, Mother." She took a plate from the cupboard, going to the cook-place to fill it.

Mother cleared her throat. "Now tell me, how do you know Thomas is the one for you?"

13

Mother dipped a wooden spoon into a black iron pot hanging from a trammel hook, bringing the contents up to blow on before tasting. Her eyes remained fixed on Sophrona.

"Forgive me, Mother. It's just that…well…I like the way Thomas smiles at me. How he makes me feel when I'm standing near him."

Laying her spoon aside, Mother sighed. "He's just one boy, child. Don't you know your father wants your wedding in our own church? Since that disagreement with Thomas, he's decided to invite young people from our parish to mingle with you and Gerald."

"Oh. When are these visitors coming?" She pushed loose hair from her face.

The sharp look returned to her mother's eyes.

"We'll receive company tomorrow evening. You must be a gracious lady toward our guests. Now, after you eat, go start the servants on their work. Then when you've finished the house, come back to help me."

"Yes, Mother." A servant could do that, but Mother insisted she learn how to become a wife. Not just any wife, either, but a "good" one.

She went to the front room, where two servants straightened up.

"We need to prepare the house." She clasped her hands. "Guests are coming tomorrow evening."

Thomas crept into her thoughts as she started to polish a table, leaning over to use smooth strokes. He stood almost as tall as Father, with thick, honey-brown hair swept away from his face and gathered at his neck. His eyes matched a cobalt medicine bottle at the apothecary, only so full of light. When he smiled at her, his eyes smiled. Lids fringed with deep brown lashes that swept his cheeks almost made him pretty.

Would he return to marry her? If only Father had not become so stubborn about where they said their vows, then…

14

"Miss Sophrona, I…"

She looked up to find a servant twisting her cleaning cloth between her fingers.

She sucked in her breath. "Please say that again. I didn't hear you."

"Uh…well, I only wondered what to do now."

"The stair steps need scrubbing. After that, wipe down the baluster before you polish it."

"Is there anything else?" The servant chewed her bottom lip.

"Yes. The front room carpets must go outside. Beat them thoroughly before you leave them to hang in the sunshine."

"Yes, Miss Sophrona."

"Get what you need from the scrub room. Hurry, there's so much to do."

"Right away, Miss Sophrona." The young woman moved toward the common room.

Later, she sent the servants out to gather the carpets. As the last rug went down on the floor, Gerald walked through the front door. She reached out to grasp his sleeve before he got past.

"Is Thomas still home? We're having company tomorrow evening. Perhaps he'd like to come."

"I don't think so. He's leaving with his father early tomorrow morning. Hauling supplies for the General's army could take some time." Gerald reached over to pat her hand. "Father may not want him here. What if he invites a young man to visit? Thomas will take up all your time."

Sophrona searched her brother's eyes. "I wouldn't want Father angry enough to stop our wedding." She tightened her grip on his sleeve. "You must let me know when Thomas returns."

"Yes, I'll tell you when I know." Her brother turned, strolling toward the common room.

15

Instructing the servants to continue their work, she went to help with supper, but somehow Mother already finished.

After setting plates and glasses on the table, she filled a pitcher with water. Mother's scolding eyes followed her movements. She just finished as Father arrived home.

"I'm sorry," she whispered, passing Mother as the family gathered at the table. "Next time, I'll come help you sooner,"

"God, we're grateful for this provision." Father lifted his eyes, looking around the table.

He took a slice of beef off the warming plate, cutting it up before spooning gravy over the pieces. "Pass the bread Fenella."

Father looked at her brother. "I spoke to Assemblyman Walter Tolley, Gerald. He just returned from the assembly session in Annapolis, where they debated paying for troops or supplies. He's already discussed this several times with Governor Sharpe."

"How long before they run the French out of British territory?" Gerald poured some milk as he slowly chewed a bite of beef, before continuing. "General Braddock the man to do this?"

"They expect the British to possess Fort Duquesne no later than summer's end. His Majesty has placed General Braddock over all the British forces in North America."

Father took a slice of bread then reached again for the beef. "Good gravy on the meat, Fenella."

Mother's face softened. "Thank you, Peter."

"Son, it's said the king has great trust in the General." Father scratched his jaw as he slowly shook his head.

Sophrona understood her father's thoughts. No matter what, those two little movements meant he did not agree.

Gerald wiped his mouth with a napkin. "How many soldiers fight under General Braddock?"

"Right now, twenty-five hundred are gathering at Wills Creek. The Assembly passed an act keeping the ordinaries, taverns, and inns from raising the troops' prices on necessities as they travel to engage the French." Father shook his head.

"Why would that affect the assembly?"

Father pursed his lips. "Well, the assembly's tasked with raising the funds for the war. It takes more money to pay for higher expenses." Father placed his napkin on the table. "Why charge them two or three times more than anyone else? Not fair, even if it is the Crown's war."

"Sophrona, please get your father a bowl of that vanilla pudding." Mother smiled at her.

"Bring me a bowl as well, dear sister." Gerald winked at her.

"Father, he should get his own pudding. I've worked all day, too."

Father took another bite before motioning his head toward the common room.

Sophrona sighed as she rose from the table to do his will. Gathering four pudding bowls to place on a tray, she decided a woman did not fare as well in today's world. She served the dessert, placing the tray on a sideboard. Taking her seat, she tasted the pudding. Sweet and smooth on her tongue, she finished it.

"Mother, I'm so exhausted. May I retire?"

"Yes, dear," Mother said, as lines settled between her eyebrows before smoothing out.

Father cleared his throat. "We're having company tomorrow evening." He glanced at Mother, then to her. "I want you looking beautiful and well rested for our guests."

"Who's coming?" Gerald said.

"Well, now." Father absently rubbed his forehead with a middle knuckle. "There's young Richard Hale with his twin cousins, Mary and Sarah Sanborn, from our parish. I also expect Samuel to stop by, a most remarkable young man. He's the newest addition to my furnace crew."

Something about the look on her father's face troubled Sophrona. Surely he had not taken a shine to this Samuel. A gnawing began in her stomach. Father employed young men determined to succeed, possessing only their wits and a strong back. She must not slight this man Father had invited. Something inside told her it must be for him she look beautiful.

Richard was handsome, mannerly, and quite witty. He came from a large, prosperous family. Perhaps she could stay close to him, instead of her father's furnace worker.

She stood, shaking out her skirt before moving around to the head of the table. She leaned over, placing a kiss high on Father's cheek before going to Mother. She passed her brother, ignoring the finger pointing to his cheek.

Reaching the front room, she started upstairs, inspecting each step to the second floor landing. The staircase looked clean. She moved on to her bedroom.

Once inside, she closed the door. After slipping into a loose cotton shift, she undid the knot that bound her hair, catching a glimpse in the mirror of her curls cascading past her shoulders in disarray. She brushed her tresses and then looked into the mirror again, nodding. Much better.

She set the brush aside when a soft knock sounded at the door.

"Come in."

Estelle entered. "Do you want your gown shook out for tomorrow evening, Miss?"

"No, I don't think so. But when I get ready for our guests, I'd like you to dress my hair."

"Then I'll just turn down your covers." The girl moved toward the bed.

"No, I'll take care of that." When she smiled, the girl shyly ducked her head before turning to leave.

Sophrona smoothed a hand across the quilt's fine stitching before she folded it back. Blowing out the candle lamp, she crawled in between the cool covers. After finding a comfortable position, thoughts of the following evening's guests swirled through her mind. Soon she drifted in and out of sleep, thinking about Thomas. Did he miss her tonight?

Sometime before dawn she awoke from a dark, confusing dream, her hands still aching as though she had clung to something important, wrenched away in the struggle. Wiping her eyes, she slipped back into sleep, not recalling the details that brought on her tears.

CHAPTER THREE

Thursday, May 5th, 1755

Thomas's teeth almost rattled in his head after Simon shook him once more, in the pitch-dark hours before dawn, broken by the smallest flicker of candlelight.

"Get up, sir. The day's almost here. Your father needs some help."

Thomas leapt from bed, his mind still foggy with dreams. He shook his head in an attempt to dispel the image of Sophrona's pale blue eyes, her dark curls spilling over ivory white shoulders, soft pink lips waiting for him.

"Good morning, Simon."

He cleared her from his mind, purging out the thoughts her father would flog him for—and rightly so.

"What time is it? The wagons ready yet?" Thomas scrambled into his homespuns as Simon handed him a shirt.

"Very early, sir. Your father sent me back to wake you before I get the morning meal." Simon started toward the door. "Hurry, Master Thomas. Daybreak comes faster than you think."

Thomas hopped around the floor as he yanked on worn boots. He ran fingers through his hair as he clung to the staircase railing, banging down the steps to the landing below, then out the door. Stars speckled a velvet black sky, glittering in their brilliance. In the east, a smudge of light told him the sun was on its way.

He glanced back at the two-story framed house that had evoked such warmth back to his childhood, before Mother had died. Then, when darkness chased him from the barn to the common room, she would embrace him as the aroma of good food beckoned from the table.

Her death invaded his thoughts. He wanted to cover his ears, block out her screams like he did that night, long ago, when Father's tear-strangled voice had pleaded, "Fight, Viola Wallace. Fight fer your life an' our babe. I don't know how ta go on without ya!"

Now a man, though, Thomas could only pick up his step, rushing the distance to the barn. He needed to hear Father's voice, be reassured by his presence and strength.

"What's left to do?" he called, as he collapsed against the door to catch his breath.

"I've fed the stock. Gerald's gonna take that load to Joppa today. He'll arrive soon to hitch his team." Father wiped his hands on his shirt. "Expected him earlier, but—well, that sounds like him now."

Thomas strained to hear Gerald's horse.

"After hitching the teams, bring him to the house for breakfast. Don't take the whole day. That load's waiting in Bladensburg, and it's just the start of our journey."

"Yes, sir. We'll work fast as we can."

His father started out toward the house. Thomas moved quickly to greet Gerald.

"Glad to see you this morning. Think you can handle it while we're gone?"

Gerald smiled at him. "I can handle anything. Just name me one time I didn't."

Thomas opened his mouth to recall Gerald needing help, but that wasn't what came out.

"How is Sophrona?"

21

Gerald blinked twice before he said, "She misses you. She's lonely. Confused. Thought you'd see her again before you started to Will's Creek. Poor little thing hasn't been the same since your dispute with Father."

Pain tightened around his heart. How he longed to visit her, but there was not enough time. Nor did he want to face Peter, since his own decision remained the same. He stood there unable to take his eyes off Gerald, who spoke so honestly about his sister, Thomas' love.

Gerald shook his head. "Father has invited Samuel, who works for him, and Richard Hale from our parish, over for refreshments. The Hale family controls many land holdings. Mother and Father know Richard's parents well."

Thomas swallowed, looking for moisture, as he parted his feet. "I'd rather not speak about this just yet. Let's get started. We'll use the best teams for the wagons."

"That's understandable." Gerald said. "I'll still be here to take a fresh team from the stable each day."

Thomas corralled the horses. His stomach quivered as he questioned his actions again. Was he right to postpone their marriage banns, rather than agree to take their vows in Peter's Anglican Church? Something he could not agree to.

When Gerald returned from the barn with the gear, the two readied the teams for the wagons. Almost through, Thomas cleared his throat, eyes fixed on the harnesses he tightened.

"Will Richard accept the invitation?"

Gerald said, "Yes, I think so. Our families attend the same church."

Thomas studied Gerald's face but did not reply.

"Thomas, my sister may ignore Richard, but no one in our family ignores Father's wishes for long." Gerald went back to work.

After hitching the teams, they walked to the house. Father and Isaac waited at the table. After prayer, the men ate.

Gerald brushed crumbs from his shirt front and rose from the table, crossing the room to the back door. "I'm off then, sir."

Isaac dug his fingers through his long, neatly-clipped hair, vigorously scratching his head. He turned to Father, "When will I ever go with you to learn about freighting? I'd rather be on the road than sitting in a chair, studying."

Father set down his mug. "Where are your manners, Isaac? Don't scratch at the eating table."

"Why not allow Isaac to ride along some with Gerald, after we return?" Thomas said.

"Your brother's suggestion is all right for now, Isaac, but you'll get your education." Father jutted out his chin. "Expect to work only on occasion, until you've finished your learning."

"Yes, sir," Isaac said. He glanced sideways at Thomas, smiling, a gleam in his eyes.

Father took another piece of bread as Simon refilled his mug.

The sun reached the horizon, shining through the window to compete with the light from their cook fireplace and strategically placed candle lamps.

"I expect you're going for several weeks, sir," Simon said. "Will you two need more than one more day's spare clothes?"

"Yes. Add something warm for cold nights on the ground." Father rose from the table.

Simon nodded as he walked away.

"Help Simon load our possessions, Thomas. It's time we get on the road."

Laying his napkin on the table, Thomas stood. Walking through the dining room they seldom used, he hurried past his late mother's Welsh cupboard that held her rose-covered plates. He was careful not to glance in that direction. They all preferred to eat off wooden or pewter chargers at the mahogany trestle table in the common room.

Entering the front room, he turned right, climbing the staircase to the second floor. He placed more covers on Simon's outstretched arms before filling his own. They hurried down the steps to outside.

Simon returned to the house for a water cask. Tipping it side-to-side, he walked it out to a wagon. Isaac followed with the food box, going back for cooking utensils.

"You'll deliver any short hauls that come in unexpectedly, Simon. You may take Isaac with you if the haul doesn't interfere with his education. Remember, Gerald always uses the big fortified wagon for the heavy ore." Father took a few steps before he turned back toward Simon.

"Young John Alexander should arrive home tomorrow, soon finishing at The College of New Jersey." A look of pride seemed to settle on Father's face. "Try to tempt him with good food. There are instructions in my office that will work him hard." Father glanced away. "Young men training for ministry don't always sweat enough, nor burn with desire for food like they do the Lord's Word."

Simon nodded. "Yes, sir."

Father hoisted himself up onto his left wheel horse. "Come on, Lad. We're wasting time."

"I'll follow behind you."

Thomas climbed on his freighter's lazy board, the only place to sit other than the left wheel horse. Taking the reins, he talked softly to his team.

Father's wagon lurched forward as he snapped the leather straps. Thomas gave his father distance before he clicked his tongue while tugging on the lines, as he guided his team in a half circle. They both turned right, traveling the first five miles on the Patapsco Road. Freighting empty, the wagons picked up speed. Once they loaded the flour-filled kegs, Thomas expected slower travel.

Father guided his team over to the side of the narrow, hard-packed dirt road. Thomas just moved over when a wagon going their direction rolled past, moving fast. He angled his team back on the road, gaining speed. They traveled just under two hours on Annapolis Road, before taking a right fork headed toward Bladensburg.

The sun stood almost overhead when Father pulled his wagon off the road, alongside some trees, Thomas behind him. The two men stepped down, walking to stretch their legs.

"It's good weather for hauling, unlike some trips I've made. I'm about ready to eat something, Lad. See what Simon packed for us."

Thomas walked to the wooden food box. His stomach rumbled as he unfolded napkins holding crusty slabs of bread filled between with beef, and the soft pale cheese Simon learned to make. Their mid-day meal included molasses cookies tied up in a cloth.

"Would you care to thank the Good Lord, Lad?"

Food gripped in cotton napkins, they sat down on an old log before they lowered their heads. "We thank You, Almighty God, for these provisions. In Lord Jesus' name."

Unfolding the napkin, Thomas stared at his meal, his mind absorbed with the blue-eyed girl he left in Baltimore Town. He took a bite and slowly chewed. Barely able to swallow the food, he sought Father's face, looking for relief.

"Am I doing the right thing by refusing marriage in their church? I didn't know any other way except to tell the truth about my contempt for the Church of England." Thomas slowly shook his head. "I'm afraid I'll lose her over this."

"It's too early to think about fixing what happened, Lad. How could you do anything else but speak yer heart. Just give it some time." Father shifted position. "The answer will come," he brushed off a crumb, "but maybe not today."

Thomas nodded as he took a bite.

"Peter's a good man. Just stubborn about wanting his only daughter's wedding his way. He believes he's right. That puts you in a risky position. You'd do well ta tread light with him."

Thomas considered his father's words as he finished eating. They traveled about two miles before reaching a shallow stream overflowing the road. He waited until Father's team finished, before urging his horses up to the water. After the animals had enough water, he crawled onto the left wheel horse to ride.

The sounds soothed him, as the warm May sun shone down from a pale sky. He grew drowsy from the sway of the team.

Almost to their destination, several wagons filled the wider road. Most traveled in their direction. One sturdy looking wagon came up from behind, six horses pulling fast. The driver almost pushed Thomas's wagon off the road as he sped around him. Thomas wrestled his team back under control when another wagon came from behind, horses neighing as they struggled to gain speed.

"Look out, Da. He'll roll you over."

A tall young man came off his seat, legs spread wide as he leaned forward, whipping the reins. He passed Thomas, then his father.

The last man caught up with the first wagon, forcing it to the road's edge. The first wagoner jumped down, fist in the air. When the second driver jumped off his wagon moving toward him, the first man's fists dropped as he remounted his seat, cracking his whip.

The young aggressor returned to his wagon, chasing after the first man. Arm muscles tense, Thomas shook his head.

What happened to provoke such anger? Would he find himself in conflict from someone's rage before they reached Wills Creek?

CHAPTER FOUR

Thomas followed his father through Bladensburg, stopping their wagons at the public landing by the river. He stepped down from the wheel horse and crossed the road, approaching a British military officer who shouted at a soldier.

"You'd bloody well start moving faster than that."

"Yes, sir." The soldier grasped a wooden cask, practically dragging the supplies into a log-built storehouse.

"We're here to pick up a load for Braddock's military going to Wills Creek," Thomas said, when the officer looked at him.

"That's *General* Braddock." The officer frowned as he reached for a roster. "Who's doing the hauling?"

"Cyrus Craighead."

"Yes, here it is. Cyrus Craighead's hauling flour, fourteen hundredweight, to Wills Creek." The officer made a notation on the list, handing Thomas a document. He nodded toward a grey building.

"Go to the storehouse's furthest entrance. Show this to the corporal. He'll set out your casks. Fill your wagon fast; before someone else takes off with part of the load, leaving you to replace it. Turn in the document at Wills Creek, if you want to get paid for your work."

Thomas strode to Father's wagon. "The grey building's where we pick up the goods."

"Well then, Lad, we'd best get to it." Father loosened the reins.

They pulled to the farthest side of the warehouse. He took the document to a corporal who directed soldiers where to place casks.

27

"We're setting out several orders." The soldier gestured toward a man who seemed vaguely familiar to Thomas. "There's two more loads after his. Then I'll start yours. Where are your wagons at?"

Thomas indicated their position.

"When it's your load, get your wagons here quick as you can."

"Yes, sir." Thomas went to join Father.

"If we help them, Lad, our load will come faster—maybe get on the road sooner."

Studying the man the soldier indicated, Thomas recognized him as the angry young driver who earlier chased down another wagon. In his black shirt, the man seemed more like a bear as he bent over to pluck up the casks. Depositing them in his wagon, he moved faster than anyone else. The 'bear' was almost done when they approached him. He refused their help. They worked to fill the next two wagons. The second wagoner barely mumbled thanks.

The corporal waved them forward when the casks began to appear. "This is your load. Better get started. It's coming fast."

"We'll use both wagons. Spread the load equally, Lad."

They hurried, but the casks came quicker than their ability to wrestle them into the wagon bed. Thomas wiped sweat off his upper lip with a shirt sleeve, as he looked back to see other wagoners lining up.

"How about some help?" The words uttered in the manner of a common working man, not the British military.

Thomas turned to face the very person with the bad temper, someone about his age. The man's face looked well-seasoned. Earlier, he refused their help. Why did he stay around? Just to help them?

Father moved the casks closer, as they wrestled the containers into a wagon. The work almost finished, Thomas turned to the man.

"My name's Thomas Craighead. Say, wasn't that you passing us up, hot after another wagoner?"

"Yeah. He'd have something more to think about than he already did if he hadn't outrun me." He balled his hands several times, his face growing red. "That clod cut in too close going around me, spooked my team. He almost ran my wagon into the river."

Color faded from his face as he wiped a hand on his breeches, offering it to Thomas. "I'm Daniel Morgan."

Thomas noticed the breadth of the man's hand as they shook, similar to a paw, with a solid finger-numbing grip. Having strength like that, no telling the damage a man might do.

"Looks like this is the last cask. We sure appreciate your help." Daniel flinched when Thomas clapped him on the shoulder.

Climbing down, Thomas introduced Daniel to his father. They shook hands.

"I'm getting behind." Daniel started toward his wagon. "I'll see you freighters up the road."

"Let's go, Lad. After we put a few miles behind us, we'll look for a place to camp."

Crawling onto the lazy board, Thomas kept his soft voice as he snapped the reins. "Let's go, now."

The horses moved forward, adjusting their pull to a heavier load. He guided the wagon in behind Father's as they headed toward Frederick.

Shading his eyes, Thomas looked at white clouds strewn through the afternoon sky. The sun dipped toward the horizon, still leaving some time before sundown.

Thoughts of Sophrona brought dread. What would life be like without her? He had called on girls before, but no one like her. Each time he found it easy to walk away, never visit them again.

Last October, when he went to help Gerald, Sophrona came out to sit with them. Her tinkling laughter brought memories from before his mother died. Long lashes fluttered over her blue eyes when she grew excited, talking. The first time it happened, something constricted in his chest. After that, Thomas could not decide why he went to their house—to visit Gerald, or see her again. It would not be easy to walk away from Sophrona, now. He was sure of that.

The wagon lurched as a wheel hit a rock, startling him and driving the thoughts away. The sun began to slip behind the mountains, its rays laying down a pattern against the grove of trees in the distance. Sunlight squeezed through the foliage to reflect streaks of gold off the river's shimmering surface.

"Over there, Da. There." Thomas gestured.

Father guided his team off the road toward some trees. Thomas followed. He jumped down, alongside Father, walking to ease the leg cramps.

"We need fuel, Lad. Let's go see what we can find before the light goes."

"I'll drag up the wood, Da," He arched his back, stretching. "Let's save our kindling. I'll gather some up."

Thomas struck out through the grass and tall brush, going deeper into a thick forest. Spotting a fallen log, he grabbed the nub from a broken branch, yanking the wood free from debris. The fading light hastened his steps. Before long, a supply of fuel lay on the ground. He bent down, filling his arms with the first load.

"Ya did good, Lad." Father's speech slipped into the familiar Scottish brogue as he fed dried vegetation, then twigs, to a small flame. He smiled up at Thomas, patting the ground next to where he knelt.

Thomas put down the load. "I'd better get the rest while it's still light enough to see."

He returned, placing an armful on the pile. Father had the fire built up, the food pulled out, and the spider pan next to it.

"After we eat, I'll fill a bucket from the stream for cleanup."

Father nodded as he filled the tin pot from the water cask. Throwing in a knotted cloth of coffee grounds, he placed the pot on the embers.

"I'll do the cooking, Lad." Father sliced pork with his folding knife, layering the pieces into the pan, setting it over an ember bed to fry.

Soon Father handed him a wooden mug of coffee. The good aroma filled his nostrils.

After turning the meat with a three-tined fork, Father filled wooden plates, handing one to him.

"The feed's almost gone. There's barely enough for morning." Thomas sipped his coffee.

"We'll stop at Lawrence Owen's ordinary and purchase feed, along with fodder." Father grunted. "Could stop at a tavern, but they're mostly for local folk. We'll get a better hot meal at the ordinary, if Braddock's military hasn't used up their supplies."

Later, Thomas pulled out their blankets, along with linsey-woolsey shirts. The coarse homespun would keep them warm from the cold ground.

He threw a few more sticks on the fire. Placing his father's pistol next to the food box, an arm's length away, he stretched out on his back. Pulling the blanket up on his chest, Thomas crossed his hands behind his head. He picked out the North Star in the night sky, hanging low on the horizon.

"Do the stars shine bright in Scotland, Da, like here?"

Father's voice carried a tremor. "Nothing's more beautiful than the stars shining on the homeland. Scotland's always my home—but here in the new land lies our hope."

Thomas swallowed at the emotion in his father's voice. "Then why'd our family leave Scotland?"

"We wanted to pursue our faith and our fortunes in Ulster. When our fortunes changed in Ireland, we sought a new land with better prospects. I needed ta find some peace for my soul." Father's voice deepened. "Lad, A flame burned hot for liberty. Something we could only find in this new land. I wanted to worship Almighty God—the Scot's way—still own some land."

The stars captured Thomas' attention again. He sighed, growing drowsy. His father soon snored. Thomas rose from his blanket to mound up the coals over the log. He hurried back under the covers and rolled over on his side, pulling a blanket up close around his ears.

Before dawn, he woke to the noise of a forest creature's scream, and the sound of beating wings, as something large passed over between him and the moon.

He rose and clutched a blanket around his shoulders, while he made his way to the fire. Breaking up small branches, he scraped aside the cold ashes down to live coals, then built a new fire. Afterward, he filled a bucket at the stream as light grew in the eastern sky. When he returned to the fire, his father stirred.

"I'll take care of the horses, Da." Afterward, Thomas checked the harnesses before looking over their wagons' hitches. Something he did each time. When through, Father poured coffee before serving their food.

They snaked their way onto the road just as the new day broke. Thomas breathed in the mingled smells from new flowers, dirt, and pine, when a cool breeze blew past. The road grew busy as soldiers, then riders, passed them on horseback in both directions. The wind picked up, kicking up dirt. When the blowing died down, the sun's warmth settled on him.

* * *

They traveled the Monocacy Road after leaving Bladensburg. Almost evening now, they grew closer to the Philadelphia Road.

He glanced toward the roadside, at a house with a barn, stable, and smaller buildings in back. His father pointed before guiding his team onto a short trace going in that direction.

32

Completely built with logs, wooden boards partially covered the ordinary. Three men walked around in front. In the field, on the far side, several freight wagons rested. Father pulled in, leaving space between his and the last one. Thomas did the same. They intended to sleep between their wagons later, after he hobbled the horses.

"Unhitch the teams, Lad, while I purchase some feed."

When Father returned, Thomas stored the food on his wagon.

"I'm hungry, Da."

"Turn the horses loose in the enclosure, Lad. I've paid for hay tonight, then grain in the morning. We'll go eat, maybe hear some news about Braddock's army."

They sat at a table in the dining room. A stout, dark-haired woman with flour on her sleeves came to their table.

"What'll I get for you two?"

"I'll have a tankard of ale ta fight off the night cold. Bring it for the lad, too. We'd also like something to eat."

"There's minced meat pie with rice pudding. It ain't fancy—just an ordinary meal, but there's plenty."

When his father looked at him, Thomas nodded.

Brushing his hands together, Father said, "Could ya show us where to clean up?"

She directed them to the water room. Thomas splashed his face, drying off with a reasonably clean cloth. While he combed his hair, Father forked fingers through stiff reddish-brown curls.

The ale sat on the table when they reached their seats. It wasn't long until the woman returned with a tray. She set out two plates, along with bowls of rice pudding. She lay down forks on clean, worn napkins. Father said the blessing.

Thomas raised his head. Picking up a fork, he broke through the stiff crust for some minced beef with fruit bits. "I like the meat pie. She's almost as good a cook as Simon."

33

Father ordered another tankard for them. They listened as the ordinary's proprietor talked with some wagoners grouped around a table.

"Say," a man said, "how about the first English regiment that came through in April. Did the men give you any trouble?"

"Surprised me. The soldiers seemed almost too well-behaved. Course, quite a few officers accompanied them." The proprietor shook his head. "When the second regiment came through, they almost wiped out all our goods."

"I'm guessing that left you in a bad way," the man said.

"We hardly replaced our supplies, when here comes Braddock with a small company. It did get busy in here, I tell you."

"Just wait 'til General Braddock's army runs them French out of the Ohio country," the missus said, looking to her husband. "British settlers out here'll bring more business than we can handle."

His frown sent her scurrying.

"Just passing through, or hauling for the General?" a freighter called to Father.

Father tapped Thomas' shoulder. "My son and me are headed for a load at the ferry, then on to Wills Creek. We're independent haulers for the Maryland governor."

After the talk died down, they rose to leave. "We need some wood," Father told the proprietor, when he settled the bill.

"You'll find plenty out back by the shed. Take what you can use."

Thomas carried enough sticks back to their camp for the morning fire. He brought out their bedding. Shaking his out, he dropped to the ground, rolling up in a blanket. His head felt like it would roll off his neck. He wasn't accustomed to strong ale. It put him fast asleep.

Before dawn, Father shook him from a dream about Sophrona. "Get up, Lad."

Thomas stood, shaking his head before he reached for a bucket. "I'll get water."

He returned to find Father setting the coffee-making pot on the coals.

Rinsing out his mouth, he spit out the water. Then Thomas drank a cup, hoping the sweet spring water would restore his mouth. He poured some over his head, raking his hair away from his forehead. They finished breakfast by the time the sun rose.

Back on the Monocacy Road, they rolled up to a crossroad, turning right toward the Great Road. It must have been Braddock's troops, passing through earlier, that flattened the surface like a dried-out mud pie. Thomas sucked dust through his nose until he spit it out at every turn of the wheels it seemed. When the sun reached high overhead, they stopped at a level place to drink some water. In the early evening, they stopped for the night, built a small fire, but only ate cold food.

"We'll get on the road at daybreak. By late afternoon, we'll be at Fredrick, Lad."

They rolled up in their blankets by the fire. Thomas barely remembered to bank the coals before he fell asleep.

Well before dawn, in the flickering candlelight, Father brought the banked coals to a flame. He soon poured them a cup of coffee. Before dawn broke, they guided their wagons back on the road.

The sun perched high up in a grey-blue sky when some freighters passed, accompanied by a troop of British soldiers. They left dust swirling in the air as they passed, shouting, "Get out of the way! King's men coming through!"

Thomas pulled his shirt up over his nose, as much for the dirt as the bad taste their words left in his mouth.

He and Father just started traveling. What else might they encounter on their journey?

CHAPTER FIVE

Sophrona awoke to her mother's voice as she pulled back the curtains. "We have a busy morning in front of us, child. Now get up."

"But it's still dark out. Must I?" She moaned and rubbed her eyes, peering out the window. A few faint stars remained in the sky.

"Right away, while I rouse Gerald." Mother bustled out the door, pulling it closed behind her.

Sophrona sat up on the bedside. Yawning, she fought to keep her eyes open as she thought about the evening. Were her concerns all for nothing?

Mother rapped on the door, no doubt back from waking Gerald. "Sophrona, don't make me send your father up here after you. Breakfast is almost ready."

"I'm coming." Did Mother hear her? Getting out of bed, she dressed, brushed her hair, and twisted it into a knot at the base of her head. Smoothing out the bed covers, she left the room.

Gerald met her in the hall. They descended the stairs together.

"Are you working for Mr. Craighead today?"

Gerald gave a small grin. "Yes, wee lass, just about every day from here on, if I'm not assisting Father."

"What about Thomas?" she whispered. "Will he ever come home?"

"He's barely gone. I said he may be away for a while, but I don't know how long that is. When he returns, you'll know. Alexander, his brother who attends seminary, is coming home in the next few days.

He may be here for a while." He touched her arm when they came off the bottom step, ending the conversation before they reached Father.

A small orange flame sputtered in the sitting room fireplace. Their father sat in one of the wingbacks.

"Good morning to you, Father. I trust you rested well." Gerald moved on toward the common room.

Sophrona stopped humming as she bent to kiss her father's cheek. "It's quite a lovely day."

He stood, taking her arm. "Fronnie, let's hurry. Your brother may not leave us much to eat. You know how his appetite improves in the spring."

Father smiled when he peered down at her. She kept up with his long stride toward the back. He was right about Gerald. Thankfully, Mother made plenty of food.

She stepped into their newer common room, moving toward the stone cook-fireplace taking up one wall. Katherine, their older servant, stooped over a three-legged frying pan turning meat, then pivoted around to a Dutch oven to check on the shortbread.

"Sophrona, set this on the table with some apple butter." Mother handed her a crusty brown loaf, still warm.

Her mouth watered as the bread's fragrance filled her nostrils. Sophrona placed the loaf on a slicing board alongside a knife before filling a dish with apple butter.

The previous evening, Mother placed loaves of dough on the hearth to rise while a fire built with maple sticks heated the oven walls. When the oven grew hot, a servant scraped out the embers. Using a wooden board, Mother moved the loaves into the oven before closing it up tight, where the bread baked during the night. Twice a week, her mother mixed the dough. Sometimes Sophrona readied the oven. Last night she had begged off.

Gerald took a seat at the trestle table with their father. After they set the food on the table, Sophrona and her mother joined them. Father said the prayer.

"Got an early load," Gerald said between bites, as he consumed food faster than Sophrona thought possible. Then he excused himself.

Father finished his coffee, coming around the table to kiss Mother's cheek before he left.

Sophrona spread some bread with apple butter. Eating the last crumb, she stood to assist Mother. There were things to do before the evening's guests arrived.

She looked out the window to their garden. Black-capped chickadees, dark throats against a grey-white body, squabbled with each other over seeds. Thoughts about Thomas swelled her heart with joy. Despite their struggles with Father, surely they would marry by August.

"Mother, I'll polish the table in the sitting room. Later, I'll come back and help you." She left through the door.

After finishing the table, she used the morning to tidy what had been their common room before Father added on the new one.

The old cook-fireplace gave up its cooking utensils to the new common room hearth. This left a large uncluttered fireplace sufficient for a sitting room to receive their guests. During cold evenings the heat from the fire rose, warming the sleeping rooms on the second floor. Sophrona found this a source of comfort, since she easily grew cold.

She took a critical look at the fireplace stones. They never received a cleaning, removing cooking soot, once Mother changed to the new common room. Sophrona gathered materials to scrub down the fireplace and hearth. The room must look perfect before she went to help Mother. How had that task eluded her yesterday?

Shadows soon streamed across the front of the house. She had used too much time, thinking about Thomas as she worked. She hurried to the common room, where both servants assisted Mother, one with supper, the other preparing a lighter fare for entertainment later.

Sophrona set out glasses and plates. Once Father and Gerald arrived home, a servant placed supper on the table. When they sat down to eat, Father said the prayer.

After filling her plate, Sophrona only pushed her food, occasionally taking a bite. Sighing, she shifted her position. Eating seemed such a bother anymore. Why make the effort?

Mother took another helping as she fixed her gaze on Sophrona's plate.

"Don't dawdle, child. There's still the kitchen to do. After that, you need to get dressed for the evening. Now hurry."

"Yes, Mother—right away." She took another bite before she stood.

Along with Estelle, the younger servant, Sophrona helped her mother ready the kitchen. "I'm going upstairs now, Estelle."

"May I help you with your hair, Miss Sophrona?"

"Yes, I'd like that."

In her room, Sophrona undid the knot, running her fingertips through her hair to loosen the ends. She took a seat, handing the brush to Estelle, who began at her hairline. Using long strokes, she pulled the brush through Sophrona's hair several times, before gathering it in a red ribbon at the base of her head.

"Please help me into this."

With the servant's assistance, Sophrona slipped into a deep red dress, ivory lace stitched around the curved neckline.

"Miss Sophrona, this color gives your white skin a beautiful glow."

"That's a lovely compliment."

When Estelle left, Sophrona looked in the mirror. Wide blue eyes looked back at her, framed by lustrous dark hair drawn away from her cheekbones. She guided a few loose hairs into place before arranging shorter front curls to frame her face. Satisfied with the results, she hurried out the door to descend the stairs.

Reaching the common room, she picked out six bayberry candles. Using the brass extinguisher to snuff out the sitting room candles' flames, she replaced them with the lovely-smelling bayberries.

After lighting a wax taper at the fireplace, touching the fire to the new wicks, she let the candles burn briefly before using the cone to extinguish the flames.

Now if only the guests didn't come until the candles' scent filled the room. Did she hear someone out front?

"Ooh, not yet. I need time," she whispered, gently tapping together her finger tips.

She forced patience as the smoke dissipated and the candles' pleasant odor filled the room. A few minutes later she relit them. She did not know why putting out the candles worked, only that each time they released a pleasant smell.

A horse snorted outside. When someone rapped, Gerald went to the front door. She moved to the entranceway just behind him.

"Good evening Mary, Sarah. What a lovely picture you ladies do make. Come in Richard. Close the door, if you will." Gerald took an arm of each young lady, walking them toward the camelback sofa.

"Oh, Gerald, you are so charming," Sarah arranged her skirt as she sat.

"You're handsome, too." Mary took her seat.

Sarah giggled uncontrollably until Mary reached out and shook her.

"Hello, Richard." Sophrona touched his arm. "I'm so pleased you came."

40

She found him easy to be around, so charming. She needed his friendship tonight.

Richard grasped her elbow, following behind his two golden-haired cousins. He gracefully guided her to one of the two easy chairs opposite the sofa. His eyes were the same pale blue as the twins'. His hair bordered on a silvery white more than gold, gathered at the nape of his neck and hanging almost to his shoulders.

"Are you attending services this Sunday, Sophrona?" Voice husky, Richard smiled with perfect white teeth.

"All our family shall be there—Gerald and me included."

"Let's all sit together during services," Sarah said, joining their conversation.

Mary clapped her hands together. "Oh, what a grand thing to do. Then we'll enjoy small tea cakes afterward at our house. We shall all sit on the balcony while we enjoy each other's company." Sophrona glanced across the room at their parents on the settee. When a knock sounded, Father rose to answer the door.

"Good evening, Mr. Hackett. I hope I'm not late."

"Nonsense, Samuel, you are right on time. Do come in." He stepped back.

Sophrona strained to hear her father as she watched to see who entered. A young man about Gerald's age stepped into the front room. He reached to shake Father's hand, before following him toward the sitting room. He strode with surety, moving up alongside Father.

"Samuel, meet my wife Fenella, my daughter Sophrona, and you know my son Gerald. I'd also like you to meet Richard Hale, as well as his cousins, Mary and Sarah Sanborn."

"Hello." Samuel bowed at the shoulders. "I'm pleased to meet everyone."

"You're just in time to join us for dessert," Father said.

41

Gathered at the sitting room table, Sophrona found herself seated between Richard and Samuel. A servant placed glasses, along with two pitchers of spring water, on the table. Then, filling cups with coffee, she passed out saucers holding currant cake slices. Sophrona studied Samuel from the corner of her eye. With his thick dark hair he resembled Father. Confidence seemed to pervade his every move. Did she just feel her resistance waver?

They ate slowly, speaking in low tones, until Father said, "Would you care to attend services with us this Sabbath, Samuel?"

The table grew quiet.

Samuel took a sip from his coffee. "Usually, I attend Saint John's Parish at Joppa Town, sir, but I would enjoy services with your family."

"Well then, young Samuel, you must come to our house. We'll travel to services together. Gerald and Sophrona shall introduce you around."

"We're planning to sit together during services," Mary said, as she smiled toward Samuel. "Away from our parents. Afterward, everyone's going to our house. How delightful if you joined us."

Sophrona's mouth went dry. She drained her cup before pouring some water, unable to believe Father—right away—invited this stranger to accompany them to church. When he had mentioned Samuel coming tonight, something in her stomach rebelled. A warning, she thought. Now, though, she felt worse. Dropping an arm below the table, she leaned forward to press a hand against her queasy stomach.

Mary had no right to invite him along, or ask him over—not without discussing it beforehand. Sophrona thought about offering an excuse, but she could not do that now, not after her father extended the invitation.

How long could she endure Samuel? His near presence already suffocated her.

If only Thomas returned before Sunday to help her.

CHAPTER SIX

Thomas arrived on the edge of Frederick with nothing on his mind after a meal but a good night's sleep. Following his father's wagon in the late afternoon sun, he turned onto a side road just off the main road. They traveled toward Mr. Owen's small ordinary, which usually entertained freighters. Ordinaries had a reputation for providing a plain, ordinary meal—exactly what he needed right now.

He reached low, grasping the reins tighter, then leaned back, pulling hard.

"Whoa. Slow down, now."

Pulling alongside the other wagon, he brought the horses to a halt. Stepping down, he walked alongside Father, stretching his legs.

"I'm hungry enough to eat a chicken with its feathers." Father combed fingers through his hair.

"Me too, Da." Thomas smiled as he unhooked their teams. "I'll water the horses before I lay out their feed."

He finished, joining Father, who walked toward the log building that housed the ordinary. Once inside, they took a seat.

A woman, most likely the proprietor's wife, set a pitcher on the table. "Ya look a little thirsty to me."

Thomas filled a wooden mug. He knew from the first sip the cool, sweet water came from a spring. He drank enough to wash down some of the dust.

"I'll have the ordinary's meal," Father said.

The woman looked much older to Thomas than himself. Her large dark eyes stared at him from a plump face.

44

"You may bring me the same," he said.

She returned with a tray, setting two plates of pork roast with stuffing, generously covered in gravy, on the table.

Thomas swallowed hard from the smell of the bread plate, as the woman pulled her red, cracked hands away. She thrust them into her work-soiled apron, leaving her shoulders and dimpled arms visible.

"Is there anything else ya care for?"

"This'll do it for now," Father replied.

Bowing his head, Thomas asked blessing then lifted his eyes. He reached for one of the large slabs of soft, crusty-topped bread to go with his supper. After he finished, he had baked apple pudding for dessert.

"It was so good, Da."

"Well then, if you're full, Lad, let's go."

After Father settled the charges, the two returned to their wagons, anxious to ready their bedding. His father yawned, lying down before the small, tight fire Thomas built. Soon, Father's snores echoed through the cool night air.

Sophrona passed through Thomas' mind, but he wasn't awake long enough to dwell on his thoughts.

Before daybreak, after consuming nothing but bread purchased the night before, they were soon ready to travel.

Father bent down and pulled out chunks of wood, wedged under the front wheels as brakes, tossing them into his wagon.

Thomas settled down on the lazy board to guide his team back onto the main road.

"How far is the Potomac crossing, Da?"

"If things go well, we'll be close to the ferry sometime tomorrow."

* * *

The next afternoon they followed the Frederick road up above the Potomac River toward the ferry. The road intersected with the

45

Great Philadelphia Wagon Road, which they took. Wagons crowded the way, some traveling in the opposite direction.

After they arrived at Conococheague Creek, the pair made their way to the Commissary of Provisions.

Thomas addressed a man with a rolled paper in his hand. "I'd like to speak with Mr. Cresap."

"That's me, young man. I'm the agent in charge of supplies. What is it you want?"

Thomas straightened. "We're here to load up some Maryland beef."

"Who're you driving for?" the agent said.

"Craighead Freighting, for both wagons."

The man looked over a list making a mark on the paper. "Move on through. Get loaded quick. There's plenty more wagons that'll need filling."

Thomas followed his father to the loading area. After hoisting the beef casks on their wagons, the two continued a short distance down the road.

Once they arrived at Evan Watkins's ferry, Thomas climbed down to stretch before he mingled with others—some from as far away as Philadelphia. His father walked toward a younger man who stood at the river's edge, looking out over the water. A little later Father turned, motioning him toward the wagon.

Thomas hurried over. "What is it Da?"

"Our turn's coming up. We may cross sooner than expected. Let's get ready ta go, Lad."

Thomas positioned himself on the wheel horse, reins in hand. Then, as if Father knew something he did not, the ferry landed, and a man motioned them ahead of other men running to mount their wagons.

"The Lord bless ya, John Fleming." As Father rolled past, he saluted the young man who had waved them forward.

Among the confusion of barking orders, Thomas lined up his wagon next to his father's. The ferry lurched away from the landing while men hurriedly cranked up the ramp with a windlass. When they reached the other side, the ramp on the opposite end dropped down. They departed equally as fast.

After traveling up the Philadelphia Wagon Road a few miles, Father pulled over. Thomas edged his team to the side, jumping down.

"Why did we stop, Da?"

"Let's travel until the sun's almost gone. Tomorrow afternoon we'll make the turn on Braddock's Road."

Thomas nodded before he hurried back to the lazy board.

"Let's go, now." He snapped the reins.

The two men drove their wagons through a valley filled with woods, occasionally passing a farm, until almost dark.

"Over there, Da." Thomas pointed toward a shallow stream just up ahead. They stopped their wagons close to several others.

"I'll get the teams," Thomas jumped to the ground.

They ate a cold supper before settling down for the night.

Before sunrise they jostled for position ahead of slower teams, reaching the turnoff for Braddock's Road by day's end. Most wagons turned with them going toward Will's Creek, while the main road continued a short distance to Winchester, then on to Carolina.

A few miles up Braddock's Road, they found a place for the night, fitting their wagons in among others.

"Here's your bedding, Da."

After Thomas found a place on the ground to sleep, he rolled over to face his father.

"Phew! Did you smell that stench coming from our load, Da?"

"Yeah, I got ah whiff—and it ain't the flour. Mighty putrid—must be the beef. All ya need to think about right now is sleep. Don't worry about any problems. They'll find us early enough."

Soon Father snored.

Before the crack of dawn, wagons, as well as military detachments, travelled the road in both directions.

* * *

On May the nineteenth, Thomas pulled his wagon to the water's edge beside his father's. He looked across Wills Creek to the fort on the upper embankment.

"Will ya take a look at that sight?" Father rubbed his jaw.

When wagons rumbled from behind, Father snapped the reins to urge his team into the shallow creek. Thomas followed. Their wagons reached the small hilltop, where a crude, rectangular wooden palisade sat to the right, opposite row after orderly row of white military tents.

Off to the side, men unloaded a freighter under an officer's direction, while another waited.

After the men finished, Father urged his team forward. Thomas followed him. Father started to unload, when a sergeant approached with several men.

"Halt your unloading. My men will handle that. Did these casks come from Frederick?" He stood ramrod straight, an arm crossed to grasp his gold-braided red lapel as he questioned Father.

Looking back at him, Father struggled not to smile. Thomas also questioned the man's ability to smell.

"No. We picked them up from Cresap at Conococheague. We loaded the flour in Bladensburg, but nothing from Fredrick."

"Very well, then. It's more of Cresap's Maryland rot. When my men are finished unloading, move your wagons to a place for the night. There's fodder in the woods roundabout, but best keep your eyes on your horses. They've spotted unfriendly Delaware savages."

The sergeant spoke to a man unloading their wagons. "Bury this batch of beef rot Cresap neglected to brine." He turned back to face them.

48

"We don't have much provision, but you're welcome to the salt pork tonight. Again in the morning, before you head out for a load at Winchester. There are thirty wagons going, with a detachment."

"I'm Cyrus Craighead. This here's my son, Thomas. Where's the Maryland paymaster? We'd like to collect."

"The Maryland paymaster's not here anymore. You must travel to Frederick to collect your pay." The sergeant went to turn away, then swerved back to them. "From now on, you'll collect from the paymaster here, now that you're hauling for General Braddock. Maryland does not cover runs made from Fort Cumberland."

After the sergeant moved away from earshot, Thomas asked, "What about collecting?"

"That'll need to wait till we travel through Frederick going home. Don't like it a bit, Lad, but there's not much we can do if the paymaster's moved."

Thomas climbed up on his lazy board to wait. He recognized Daniel Morgan's exceptional height and gait, approaching Father. The two spoke briefly before Morgan hurried away. Father mounted his left wheel horse urging his team on behind Daniel. Thomas followed, as the sounds from a city teeming with people closed in around him.

Adjacent to the fort, on the close-cropped parade ground, soldiers marched in flashing red and white uniforms. At the side, accompanying the soldier's maneuvers, a brace of uniformed musicians with fifes and drums played "The King Enjoys His Own."

The lilting melody saturated the encampment, gently stirring Thomas.

He did not expect so many women at the fort. Some had men at their sides, while others carried clothes or utensils for preparing food. Among the crowd, Thomas passed red-brown faced Indian men, women, and their children. He followed his father back behind the military tents into the vicinity of the other wagons. Father pulled his wagon next to Daniel's, out the farthest. Thomas pulled in beside his father, stepping down.

"Our horses will get to the fodder easier with our wagons so close to the woods." Daniel lightly slapped his hands on his chest in a quick rhythm, before dropping his arms.

Thomas took in Daniel's appearance again, grateful they became friends the first time they met. He could not imagine having to quarrel with someone this big.

"We're back on the road to Winchester tomorrow." Father slapped Daniel on the back. Quick as Daniel's color drained, it returned. He nodded his head, as the cords in his thick neck disappeared.

"I'm in that train as well." Daniel slung his head, flicking hair from his face. "There's nothing for regulars or drivers to eat, except salt-pork, but it'll keep your stomach from cleaving to your backbone."

Thomas clamped his teeth, attempting to head off a smile, but something gave him away. Daniel laughed, perhaps at Thomas's appreciation for his choice of words.

"We'll do better than that, Daniel." Cyrus turned toward his wagon. "We still have provisions. One is ham. I'll cook supper after we gather wood."

"Never mind the wood. I know where there's building scraps. We'll get some for tonight and tomorrow, Cyrus."

Thomas followed Daniel.

Gathering armloads, both carried their wood back to the site. While Father cooked, they watered the teams before hobbling them to graze. Thomas must watch their animals, so close to the encampment's edge, with unfriendly Indians traveling through.

After eating, the three men grabbed their bedding, quickly choosing spots around the fire. Sleep came fast.

Father rose before dawn, setting the coffee-making pot over hot coals. Thomas helped Daniel hitch up the teams. Once finished, they drank coffee until Father filled three wooden plates. Later, Daniel took his blankets to his wagon.

A corporal walked around to alert the drivers, approaching their wagons at the group's far end. "It's time to form up for the run to Winchester."

"How much time we have?" Father said.

"Hardly any. I wouldn't advise holding up the supply train. Too many men doing without the good food they expected this morning."

His father emptied the last coffee into their mugs. Thomas gulped his down as he eyed the overcast sky, hinting at rain. Then he loaded up the bedding. Daniel pulled his wagon onto the packed-down road leading behind the soldiers' camp. Father rolled in behind Daniel. Thomas urged his team out, managing to go next when a wagoner slowed to let him in.

They crossed the creek to join the other wagons. Thomas stepped down to stand by his father. Nearby, a detachment of twenty-five Virginia militia waited under their lieutenant's command. A British captain accompanied them, in his crisp red and white uniform, a silver gorget suspended below his neck.

The militia wore black tricorn hats trimmed in white. Their red vests hung mid-thigh, over white shirts. Blue coats matched the blue pantaloons. Their uniforms stood out against the British captain's in color as well as design.

After the wagons lined up, the eight militiamen on horseback split up. The lieutenant, along with three young men, rode toward the front with the captain. The other four horsemen rode toward the back. It seemed to Thomas the men acted as one moving to opposite ends of the train.

"I'd better get back to my wagon, Da." Thomas started away when rain sprinkled his face. He reached his wagon, mounting the left wheel horse to wait.

When the lieutenant shouted an order, seventeen men on foot dispersed themselves into wagons at the front, middle and back of the train. The lieutenant rode out beside the front wagon, raising his arm. He circled his hand in the air before bringing it down, pointing forward with his forefinger. Thomas, along with the other drivers, watched. When he dropped his hand, the wagons rolled forward.

Rain fell softly as Thomas' thoughts went to Sophrona. Would she continue to think about him, while he traveled so far away from her?

CHAPTER SEVEN

May 27th, 1755
Fort Cumberland, Maryland

Thomas, Cyrus and Daniel arrived back at Wills Creek in the late afternoon, their wagons loaded with goods from the military stores in Winchester. The weight slowed down their return, adding an extra day to the three-day trip.

Thomas looked around, not seeing many Indians. The few squaws still there remained outside the encampment. He wasn't sure what changed after they left, but something seemed different about the men they encountered. They appeared quieter; their boisterous spirit more subdued.

Several drivers raised their hands as the three passed by, probably meant for Daniel, who many wagoners and militia seemed to respect. The three men rolled through to find their old places unoccupied, as if waiting for them. They had just settled in when a man made his way to their camp.

"I'm Mr. Scott, Wagonmaster General. Who's driving the smaller wagon, here?"

Thomas stepped forward. "That's me, sir, Thomas Craighead."

"We need wagons this size for hauling to the forks of the Ohio. If you attach your wagon to the military, we'll pay you well." The man held a journal in his hand.

"Cyrus Craighead, my father, owns this wagon. You should speak with him." Thomas nodded toward his father.

"Cyrus, may we use your wagon to haul goods for our soldiers journeying to fight the French? We've lost wagons due to their poor condition—could greatly use yours. It's just the right size to travel over that rough trail they've cut."

"Mr. Scott, that's a decision for my son. Since I own the freighter, I certainly won't encourage what might cost me a wagon. But I'll not stop him from using it, if he wants to drive for you."

"We'll leave early Friday morning," Scott said. "Morgan, here, will bring you along if you decide that you're interested. We'll provide extra funds if you help us out, beyond what you'll receive for the work." The man shifted his glance from Thomas to his father before he turned to leave.

He took a few steps before turning back to address Thomas. "If you decide not to drive for us on the twenty-ninth, get ready to haul tomorrow with your father. In the morning there's a train headed out for Conococheague." He walked away.

"You two care to come along with me?" Cyrus stretched his arms. "I have some business with a sutler."

"Need something, Da?"

"Coffee. We're almost out. Hope it's a reasonable price." Father turned to Daniel. "I'd be pleased if you joined us for supper. We sure do enjoy your company."

Daniel nodded.

The three struck out for the middle of the encampment, where they found several sutlers displaying their wares, from personal items to foodstuffs. A few private suppliers even carried wagon parts, along with gear for horses.

Father approached one to make his purchase, while Thomas stood on the side with Daniel. A man passing by motioned for Daniel to follow him.

"I'll meet you back at the campsite, Thomas. There's something I need to take care of." Daniel followed the man.

Thomas turned toward the large crowd of people around him. They appeared to ebb and flow, somewhat like the tide on the Chesapeake. Soon Father returned with a package.

"Daniel's going to catch up with us at the wagons, Da."

"Let's go, then. I'm ready for some supper." Thomas tried to stay up with his father.

Daniel arrived at their campsite later. He handed Father a bundle.

"This is for us tonight. You've treated me like kinfolk since we first met and, well, that feels pretty good to me."

Thomas stood close when his father opened the cloth. A faint smoky odor rose from the herring. The biscuits looked freshly baked. Father unfolded a second, smaller bundle tucked in, containing cookies. Thomas's stomach growled at the smell of molasses. How he missed Simon's cooking.

"Where'd you get the fish, Daniel?" Father glanced down. "It's been a while since I tasted any."

"Several wagons, along with packhorses loaded with supplies, arrived here the day we left for Winchester. A while back, two drunken infantry caught a sutler away from his wagon. I jumped in to help out when the two over-ran him."

Daniel looked into the distance, a smile on his face, almost as if he watched it again.

"The sutler sent that man to get me. I told him he didn't owe me anything for my help, that I kinda enjoyed the fight. But he insisted I take the food—said he won't be indebted to me. And, well, I thought him right about that."

As they talked, Father laid the shavings for a fire. He brought out the tinder box, with a socket on top of the lid holding a candle stub. Removing the lid, he struck a steel and flint spark over the tinder box, igniting the charred linen inside. Transferring the fire to the candle wick, he snuffed out the tinder and lit the shavings. Quickly he

55

fed twigs and dried debris to the small wispy flame until it grew, then threw on a few sticks.

"I'll get some water, Da." Thomas grabbed a bucket.

Daniel said, "I'll find enough wood for the night, Cyrus."

Thomas returned, to find Daniel already back.

Father filled wooden plates with food. After he finished, Thomas grabbed three mugs to pour the coffee. Daniel selected a few more pieces of wood, placing them on the fire.

After they finished eating, Thomas reached for some molasses cookies, washing them down with his coffee. "Haven't tasted cookies any better than these, Da, except what Simon makes."

"Supper was mighty fine, Daniel." Father took a sip from his coffee. "A man might travel a long way down the road before he eats this good again." He set the mug down. "I hope you two don't mind if I lie down, now. I'm worn out from that haul."

"I'll get our bedding." Thomas quickly returned from their wagons.

Father rolled up in his blankets close to the fire. "Have a peaceful night, then. I'm going ta sleep."

Daniel walked away, to return with his bedding. "If you don't mind, Thomas, I'll join you and your father again tonight. Using the same camp fire cuts down on the need for wood, considerably."

"You're always welcome to join us. Stake out your place." Did he hear Father snore?

He placed pieces of wood in close proximity to tighten the fire, which ensured live coals for morning, then added a second layer. Less air would produce smaller flames—not burn up the wood as fast.

He rolled up in his blanket as Daniel worked his back up against a wagon wheel across from him.

"I've thought about what Mr. Scott wanted, Daniel, hauling their goods to Fort Duquesne. It's a hard decision. Why did you agree to haul for the military, rather than staying independent?" Thomas propped an arm up under his head.

Daniel's eyes gleamed in the firelight. "Well, I'm all alone—without a family to worry whether I come back. I'd rather be in the action than not, to tell you the truth."

Thomas heard the lonesome sound in Daniel's voice. He never wanted to feel like that.

Daniel continued. "There's a bunch of Indians who back the French. Almost none want to fight alongside the British. You've noticed most have left the fort?"

"That's true." Thomas sighed. Daniel sure knew a thing or two about people.

"Make no mistake about this," Daniel's eyes brightened. "The British are in for a fight when they go to run the French off that land they've claimed. I hope I'm in the middle of that." Daniel scratched his head, first, then moved down to his shoulder. "What's at home for you, Thomas—anything worthwhile?"

"Two brothers. Alexander's just completed seminary, soon to become a minister. My youngest brother's pursuing the education Father insisted each of us get before we work."

"Is that it for you?"

"There's Sophrona back in Baltimore Town. We may get married. Eventually I'll learn the freight business, become partners with my father."

"Well, it sounds like you want to make it back home. But what do you mean, may get married? Do you love her, Thomas?"

"Yes, I do. But like other freighters, we had little choice but to make this trip. It sure interrupted my plans."

"Does she feel the same?" Daniel rolled to his side.

"She says she does—but her father insisted we get married in his English church. That's something I cannot bear to do. Last thing I heard, he invited two young men over to spend time with the family, one from their church." Thomas glanced at the fire. "I haven't seen her since he issued those invitations—don't know for sure if she still feels the same."

"It does no good ta get stubborn, sometimes, with so much to lose. Now, if it's easy to replace her, what do you care what happens?" Daniel sat up, looking at him. "But say you want only her. Well then, I could see ya bending just a little for her father's wishes."

"Huh, think so?" Thomas cleared his throat.

"Better think about this before you make a decision. I wouldn't head toward the battle if I had a woman on my mind." He lay down flat. "Talk with your father about this."

Thomas added a large chunk of wood to the fire, before tucking an arm behind his head to stare up at the night sky. The low background noise from several thousand people in the encampment pressed in on him. He grew drowsy. Thoughts about Sophrona drifted through. The way she looked at him with her pretty blue eyes. Her tinkling laughter, sounding like Conestoga bells on a proud lead horse. He couldn't remember exactly when she crossed over from a friend's sister to become more than he wanted to lose. It came so subtly. One thing he did know—he couldn't do without her now.

Soon his eyelids grew heavy and he drifted to sleep.

Thomas chased Sophrona through a deep green forest sprinkled with little yellow, blue and purple wildflowers. She grew smaller in the distance.

"Sophrona, don't go."

He ran faster but she shrank before his eyes, to almost disappear. Too tired, he stopped to slump down under a tree.

"Help me, Thomas…can't run anymore…"

Horses snorted in the distance, disturbing Thomas. The sounds from stomping hooves dragged him from sleep.

He rubbed his eyes as Sophrona's plea still echoed in his mind. Dread overcame him as he drew up his knees to pull his covers closer, barely aware Daniel shifted position across from him.

Later, hearing footsteps, he blinked his eyes. His father stood over him. He shifted his gaze to see grey streaks plowing through the dark sky.

"I heard you cry out in yer sleep last night. Then, are ya doing alright this morning, Lad?"

"Just a bad dream." A nightmare, more like it, but he wouldn't tell Father. He unwound his blankets to pull himself up from the ground. Daniel had left his spot by the fire.

"Have you made a decision, then?" His father's intense look caused Thomas to blink. "Will I travel alone this morning while you go to the French fort with Daniel and that British general?"

Thomas stretched, reaching for a mug to scoop out water from the bucket.

"I won't haul for the British out to Fort Duquesne. I want to finish what we started, then get home fast as we can. I know Sophrona's waiting for me."

"We'd better work fast. We're expected to head out to Watkins Ferry." Father stooped to add wood before he filled the coffee-making pot. "We'll haul back more provisions from Governor Sharpe for the Maryland Assembly."

Thomas emptied the water bucket over his head, stripping off his shirt to wipe his face. After he slipped into something dry and pushed back his wet hair, he went after more water. The cask in the wagon brimmed, but Father had taught him to reserve that water for hard times.

After he returned, Daniel showed up with biscuits. He stayed long enough to drink some coffee.

"I need to go somewhere else this morning. Guess you'll join Cyrus headed to the Potomac."

Thomas nodded. "I made up my mind last night."

"I'll strike out for Fort Duquesne tomorrow with the British." Daniel flicked his thick wrist, and the dregs of coffee hissed on the still-hot embers. "Don't rightly know what'll happen after that, but I hope to see you both again."

"Watch how you fight the French, Daniel Morgan. Be careful." Father reached out for Daniel's mug.

Thomas felt odd when he clasped Daniel's shoulder as he shook his hand. Daniel seemed much older, maybe because of harsh circumstances that came from being alone in the world, without family around.

"I won't forget you, Daniel. You're always welcome in our family."

Jamming fingers through his hair, Daniel pushed the hanging mass off his forehead straight back to his crown. A few strands broke loose to settle on each side of his wide cheekbones.

"I'll see you again, Thomas." He pivoted away from their campfire.

Thomas thought about the brief glitter in Daniel's eyes before he turned away. He wondered about the man's family, what separated the Morgans. Just as quick, though, he determined it was not his business. He'd leave it there.

He hurried to his wagon, bedding in his arms, looking back as Father poured water on the fire and used a boot to scatter the coals.

Thomas climbed onto his lazy board to wait. What was Sophrona doing just now at home? How long must he wait before he held her in his arms again? How long could he wait?

Father mounted his left wheel horse, talking to his team as he urged them forward. Thomas pulled in behind him, the new morning breaking golden red in the sky.

They joined the other four wagons, on their way to pick up Maryland supplies, a pungent smell of horses filling the morning air.

The teams rolled into position to form a line, accompanied by a militia detachment of five.

A sergeant rode to the front. He raised an arm over his head, then dropped it shoulder level. Pointing straight ahead he shouted, "Move out."

Two from the militia rode with the sergeant in front, while the other two militiamen brought up the rear.

Thomas had no doubt he and his father were in for long days before they saw Baltimore Town again. Eager to return and marry Sophrona, he wondered if this trip would ever end.

CHAPTER EIGHT

Sophrona returned home from services. She changed into a plain green linen gown, before shaking out curly hair to flow down her back. She rubbed her throbbing temples with her fingertips. Samuel sat in their pew again today. Fighting off his attention left her exhausted.

She should say something to Samuel about Thomas, but she didn't dare. She brought up Thomas's name once before, in Samuel's company. Father immediately turned the conversation in a different direction after giving her a stern look. Her stomach flipped just thinking about it.

It was time to speak with Father about his favorite replacement for Thomas.

Making her way downstairs, Sophrona found him sitting with Mother on the settee. "Must Samuel sit beside me next Sabbath, like he did today, Father? I've grown weary of him always being with our family at worship."

Silence filled the room.

Sophrona ran a hand across her brow to follow a curl down to the tip, turning it up. The ends looked dry, lusterless, like the straw broom used for sweeping the floor.

"My hair's beginning to fall out, Mother. I need rain water to wash it, that'll soften the ends." A thin sigh escaped her lips after realizing she whined, something she rarely did.

Mother's eyes darted toward Father. He looked away.

"Nothing can help your hair until you take in more food. You've barely eaten enough in the last month to stay alive." Mother clasped together her hands. "What's wrong with your appetite, child?"

Sophrona stared at her parents in silence.

"What do you mean, Sophrona isn't eating?" Father said.

Mother cleared her throat. "I mentioned this to you, Peter. Don't you ever listen to anything I say?"

"Yes, but I thought that passed. Since she's not up when I have breakfast, then surely she must eat after I'm gone. Regardless, Fenella, when Sophrona gets hungry she'll eat."

He turned to her. "Won't you, Fronnie?"

Sophrona nodded, trying to remember the last time she had wanted to clean her plate.

Father's voice grew sharp. "What's wrong with Samuel? He's honest as can be. No one works harder. Several young ladies now want their family to attend our parish because he does."

A sharp twitch in her stomach brought a sour taste to her mouth.

Father's voice deepened. His face settled like stone. "Now, don't you complain to me about Samuel, ever again. Do you hear me, daughter?"

"It's nothing, Father. Nothing." She fought back the desire to vomit.

Loneliness for Thomas filled her.

Throat tightening, Sophrona felt trapped. She thought Samuel a handsome young man with a strong presence. When Father forced her to sit between them, she lost a little of her resolve to wait for Thomas. Father, the man with the most control over her life, actively worked pushing her closer to a man she wondered if she could resist.

Even Richard respected Samuel enough not to pursue her. *Traitor.* To think she had planned on using him to keep Samuel at bay.

Then there were Richard's cousins, the Sanborn twins. What a disgrace. Sarah and Mary practically tripped over themselves trying to sit by Samuel during services. Yet, each time, Samuel reached Father in the pew first, taking the seat next to him.

If she thought to sit nearer someone else, shifting away from Samuel, her father pointed toward the seat as he said, "Sophrona, come sit next to me."

Father required her to change positions with Samuel, which placed her between the two. When Samuel leaned her way, she moved toward Father, sometimes almost lying on him.

"Move over, Sophrona. I need some room," Father would whisper, as he struck out at the air with both elbows, freeing a shoulder. That's when she felt suffocated, to where she almost couldn't breathe.

"Please excuse me. I want to lie down for a nap."

"Yes, child." Mother's voice softened. "I'll send someone up for you later."

Sophrona nodded as she started toward the stairs. Once in her room she changed from her dress into a shift, crawling under the covers, shivering and tired. She must remember to tell a servant about her gown.

God in heaven, please bring Thomas home to me. Sophrona pictured his blue eyes; almost heard his laughter, as she drifted into sleep.

It seemed she barely closed her eyes when she awoke to a rap on the door.

"Miss Sophrona," Estelle called before she opened the door. "It's time to come down for supper. Do you want me to help you dress or brush your hair?"

"No, I can manage. But do come up before bedtime. You must measure my dress. It doesn't fit like it should. May need a few tucks around the waist to fix that."

"Yes, Miss Sophrona."

64

When the servant closed the door, Sophrona threw the covers back, rising from bed. She chose a simple drab green dress to slip on, brushing her hair as she recalled her prayer asking God to send Thomas back to her. Thomas said God answered prayers. Would his God answer this important one for her, even though she did not know Him like Thomas did?

There came another rap at the door. "Let's go now, little sister. I'm starved to death. Mother may not hold the food until we're at the table."

Sophrona opened the door, smiling at Gerald's remark. "I'm ready."

She took his arm as they descended the stairs.

After they finished supper, a servant removed the plates. She brought in coffee. Mother rose to fill their cups with a drink Father seemed to enjoy as much as tea.

"I've discussed another celebration with your mother." He raised his cup to take a sip.

"Why so soon?" Dread spread through Sophrona. "We just entertained guests."

Mother smiled. "It's a summer party, Sophrona. We'll wear beautiful clothes; enjoy the sun, forget about the cold winter. You'll receive a new gown." Mother's eyes misted. "You'll be the prettiest girl...What's wrong, child? Did you forget how to enjoy a party?"

"Of course not." Father softly drummed his fingers, staring at her. "You remember how to enjoy yourself, don't you?"

"No, I haven't forgotten." She glanced at him, then down.

Gerald cleared his throat. "When will that be, Father?"

"Your mother shall decide the exact date, but most likely toward the month's end, sometime around the twenty-fifth. Is that right, Fenella?"

"Yes, Peter, that's close to the date I have in mind. Today's June the first. If the party's on the twenty-sixth, we'll have more than three weeks to prepare for it. That's time to clean the house, get the yard ready—even bring in a seamstress for new clothing." Mother sighed as contentment settled on her face.

Sophrona knew from previous festivities that her mother enjoyed the challenge. No doubt Mother had already started a guest list. She expected Samuel's name on the list, as well as Richard's.

Mother pushed back her chair to stand. Sophrona rose, also. Time to clear the bowls. They moved to the common room where one servant worked on the spinning wheel while another strained milk through a fine cloth.

"Mother, is Samuel attending the party?" She rubbed her upper arms with her hands.

A look settled on her mother's face, her eyes narrowing in what reminded Sophrona of a raven going after a sparrow.

"Yes, Sophrona, he is invited—and he's welcome here. There's many a young lady looking for a man handsome as him. A mannerly person, too." Mother shook her head. "Why do you object to him receiving an invitation? Well, I won't hear any more about this from you tonight."

"Yes, Mother. It's only that I feel like he's being shoved on me." She pushed her curls back.

"If you don't like him, Daughter, just politely ignore him."

If only it were that easy. She could not tell Mother he reminded her so much of Father, she had difficulty ignoring his presence. That if Thomas did not return soon, she might get dragged in too deep to ever get away. Instead, she said, "May I go to my room, Mother? I'm tired."

"You do look a bit peaked."

She gave her mother a kiss before going to look for Father.

Sophrona found him in his office. When she tapped on the doorframe he looked up, motioning her in.

"Come sit down, Fronnie. It's such a long time since we talked." He moved from his desk to one of the two wingback chairs upholstered in deep green brocade. She took the other.

"Do you feel well? What with you having no appetite, sleeping so much, I'm worried about you." His eyes glistened. She regretted her harsh thoughts over him inviting Samuel into the family like he had.

"Oh, Father, before going upstairs I came to say I love you." She felt better when his brow smoothed out, his face softening.

"Then there's nothing else you wish to speak about?" He placed his hands in his lap, lacing his fingers together.

She glanced down, then up at him. "Well, there's something troubling me. Why don't you get along as well with Thomas as you do with Samuel? You've known Thomas and his family much longer. I thought you liked him." She gulped, pressing her lips together, afraid she had already said too much.

Her father's face paled.

"Daughter, he doesn't even respect me enough to marry you in the church you've attended your entire life. Do you expect me to be satisfied with that? Why are you agreeable to such a thing?"

"Father, I…. Well, I know you want that—but I want to marry Thomas. I love him. If he doesn't want the wedding in our church, then I should agree with him. You've always insisted Mother do things your way. It seems she always has." She looked away before placing a hand on his arm "At least I can't remember her ever not doing what you wanted."

Father shifted position, and her hand fell away.

"I don't love Thomas more than you or our family, but I do love him. I'll just stay miserable as long as I live if we aren't together."

Tears filled the corners of her eyes. She waited for him to speak, but he didn't. When the silence grew long, she rose.

"I'm going to bed."

She kissed him on the cheek and left the room. Blinking away the tears, she stumbled upstairs through her bedroom door, into the place that belonged to her. It was the only safe place to think about Thomas without too much interruption.

A tap on the door reminded her Estelle had come to pin her dress for alterations, as she requested earlier.

"Please, not now. I don't feel well. We'll do this tomorrow, Estelle."

"Yes, Miss Sophrona, I'll come back in the morning."

She took out a heavier linen shift, readied herself for bed, crawling under the covers. Hot tears rolled down her face. She wiped them with the back of her hand before she whispered, "Lord God, I want to marry Thomas. If this is Your will, then please tell me what I should do."

She closed her eyes to listen for God's answer. All she heard was the silent night around her before doubt set in.

CHAPTER NINE

Cool, sweet air blew past Thomas, as his wagon rolled toward Watkins Ferry, giving a hint of near perfect weather conditions for the day's travel. Regardless, Thomas had difficulty keeping his thoughts on anything but Sophrona.

The dust from an approaching group yanked him back from her soft dark hair, reminding Thomas to keep his mind on controlling the animals.

They arrived at the Potomac River, where the ferry bobbed against the blue-green current. Thomas managed to get his wagon onto the large ferry next to his father's. Once across, they waited with the other men until all the drivers gathered together. Thomas smiled. The storehouse was less than a mile away.

He knocked the dust off his clothes before tipping the water keg to get a drink. Just then a British sergeant rode up to Father. Thomas listened.

"The Commissary will show you men where the Maryland supplies are stored. He's on his way." The soldier urged his horse past them toward other drivers.

"There's Cresap now." Father shrugged a shoulder toward a rider. "Better get ready to roll, Lad."

The Commissary directed Father to form a new line, going in another direction. Thomas followed. Before long, another team pulled in behind his, ready to follow. A private from the militia detachment rode up next to Cresap, commanding their attention.

"Sergeant says to load your wagons fast," the private said. "He wants a quick turnaround, crossing back over the river today." The man spit and scratched his neck. "He'll get real unhappy if wagons belonging to his train are still on this side ah the Potomac, come nightfall."

A few hours later, Thomas drove off the ferry; his thoughts on the orderly way they loaded the wagons, despite the dust, confused animals, and angry drivers. After the train stopped for the night, he joined Father around a common campfire, where they briefly socialized with the others before returning to their wagons.

"How long before this job's finally over, Da? I'm worried about Sophrona."

Father uttered a sympathetic grunt. "This may be the last trip, Lad."

Thomas nodded as he gathered their bedding. He handed over some blankets to Father, who found a place to lie down.

Thomas dropped to the ground, arranging his covers. "Then, do you think we'll return home, soon?"

"Don't know, Lad. Maybe we'll find out more back at the fort." Father yawned, rolling over.

Satisfied with the answer, Thomas turned on his side to sleep. Tired as he was, he thought about Sophrona. *Almighty God, keep her safe while I'm gone.*

The day's activities soon caught up with him, sending him into a deep slumber.

* * *

They arrived back at Wills Creek on the eleventh. Many from Braddock's military, including the Provincials, were already gone. All the Pennsylvanians, along with most of the other wagoners, had left, too. No doubt on their way to the Big Meadow encampment, putting them closer to the French fort.

Colonel Innis, along with the hospital staff, remained behind to care for the sick or injured soldiers. Compared to the way the camp crawled with life when they first arrived, Fort Cumberland now looked like a deserted town.

They went back where they'd camped with Daniel. Loneliness reminded Thomas that he missed his friend. He hoped Daniel found safe passage through the war with the French.

His father found a small wood pile some wagoners left when they followed General Braddock's road-builders.

"I'll get some water." Thomas grabbed a bucket. On his way back with the water, he picked up some kindling, then returned for a large log that somehow got overlooked earlier.

He arrived at their wagons to find Father had a small fire going. He added a few sticks to the blaze, his mind mostly on Sophrona. He could not get past the thought something had happened.

"Have some coffee, Thomas. It'll help fix what ails ya." Father handed him a mug filled with hot drink, then went back to the cook-fire.

Thomas found a place to sit and drink his coffee, thankful for the time to rest. It seemed they stayed busy constantly since leaving home in May. They were almost half through June, now.

After they finished eating, his father poured them another cup before dropping down beside him. Thomas added the big log to the fire, situated between their wagons, to offset the cool night. They had traveled right up to dusk the evening before, and today, were almost that late arriving at Wills Creek. He took a sip, staring at the liquid he swirled around in his mug.

"I woke up several times last night with bad dreams. I couldn't seem to get any relief from worry about things back home."

"Is that what's on your mind, Lad?" Father's eyes bored into his.

71

Thomas withered under the intense stare. "It's more about Sophrona. I'm troubled in my spirit, Da. Don't know why—can't find out all the way out here. I must get back to her soon."

"No doubt it's possible to know something's wrong, especially coming from your mother's side. The Wallace family's known for their keen instincts on such matters as loyalty, commerce, even love. Our Craigheads always grow close to the Lord. Ministers..." His voice grew hoarse. "Certain men in our family, such as your great-grandfather, had dreams about dangers to come. Course, that was the Lord God warning them, I'd say."

Father added, "An officer came by when you went for the water—said we fulfilled our obligations. Settled our pay, too, except what Maryland owes us."

Thomas breathed deep as the weight from his arms tugged on his shoulders. His lids rolled back and his eyes looked beyond the sky. Finally, free to go home. *I'm grateful, Lord.*

Father continued, "Tomorrow, after we go over our wagons we'll mend the gear. There's still a sutler here that carries the materials we may need."

Thomas blinked. "What possesses such a man to travel from place to place, selling goods from his wagon, Da?"

"I don't rightly know." Father scratched at his neck before shifting position. "Seems some men wander from town to town, but a sutler wanders where there is no town. He goes from forts to encampments to battlefields—always close to the action, but never quite a part of it."

He gazed into the distance. "No store to sit in to sell their wares. No land to work. Some men just seem born to wander. Craving the excitement from waking up in a new world each day."

Thomas lifted his eyes. Did he see envy flicker across Father's face—his eyes briefly cloud up with unfamiliar emotion as he spoke?

Then, just as quick, Father added, "Why, Lad? That kinda life something yer interested in?"

Thomas shook his head. "I only want to put down some roots fast as I can."

"Just as well. Tomorrow we work. The next morning we start for home. We'll stop in Fredrick at the Maryland paymaster to collect for that first haul we made. Maybe enjoy an ordinary meal—stay the night in their field. We'll purchase some provisions, then travel home fast. No, sir. Grass won't sprout under our feet, Lad."

Thomas' heart beat faster at the thought. Finally going home to his family, holding the woman he intended to marry, looking in her pretty face.

His father moved around the campfire putting away essentials. Thomas went for their covers. The stars came out before he finally grew drowsy, but he slept the sleep of the dead.

He awoke before the night's black sky melded with the dawn's red-gold light and reached out for the strong hot drink Father poured him. Before long, his father handed him a wooden charger filled with food. Thankful for their fare, Thomas bowed his head in earnest prayer.

"Almighty God, thank You for this food. Stay with us, Lord, as we get ready to travel."

Thomas wiped his brow through the day, as they worked readying their wagons. They looked over each horse in their teams, checking hooves. When evening came, they finally slowed down for food.

His father lay down to sleep, snoring louder than usual.

Thomas stretched out on the ground, rolled up in his blankets, not awake for long. Sophrona haunted his sleep. Abruptly waking, he blocked out the sound of her voice, falling back into an exhausted sleep—only to dream about her again.

The last time he lurched awake, running from her muffled sobs, he couldn't convince himself to go back to sleep. He lay there, drawn up in his blanket in the cool air, his eyes on the stars bright in the night sky. A powerful need to understand what his dreams meant descended on him. Sophrona's beautiful face filled his mind as he recalled her words that last night.

"But Thomas, what if Father doesn't…"

He jumped when Father stirred, then rose to start a fire. The small orange-red flames licked the wood in the dark night. Thomas stood, folded the blankets, then returned them to a wagon. After splashing his face, he ran fingers through his hair. He chased Sophrona in his dreams through the night. Today he intended to chase his memories of her all the way home.

Light swirled in the charcoal grey dawn as Thomas cared for the horses, while his father put on the coffee-making pot. They stood as they ate. Thomas doused the fire before he climbed up on his left wheel horse.

Father mounted. "Are you ready then, Lad?"

"Yes, sir."

Snapping the reins, Father drove his team out along the trees, slowly descending down the gently-sloped embankment. Thomas followed close behind. Sunlight flashed golden across the sky as his wagon reached the halfway point in the creek, the horses' powerful legs spraying the air with glittering water drops.

They traveled part way accompanied by a small New Jersey militia, headed home. With all the unrest, talk about renegade Indians, even unsavory men out for no good, Thomas had no doubt they were safer getting accompanied to the Watkins Ferry over the Potomac.

The horses surged forward, pulling hard, as if they, too, realized home lay up ahead. The days ran into nights and, before long, they arrived at Fredrick, where Father took care of his affairs. Stopping at the same ordinary they visited in May, Father purchased provisions for themselves as well as for their teams.

After seeing to the animals, they went inside for a hot meal. Roasted beef with cabbage, along with thick slices of warm bread. Thomas chose cider, not ale, this time. After they finished, the two men returned to their wagons. They lay down to sleep without a fire, too exhausted to build one.

"Wake up, Lad, you're dreaming."

Father's voice pulled him from a nightmare, where again he ran after Sophrona. Thomas heaved a sigh, thankful he was awake.

He lay there awhile, listening to the animals' snorts before he rose. He breathed deeply, filling his lungs so full he thought they might burst. He reached for a mug to get some water, the back of his neck tingling from the thought that today's ride took him closer to Baltimore Town.

What waited for him there? That question had haunted his mind a dozen times. He didn't know if he wanted the answer, or just what he must do to keep Sophrona.

"Let's get our teams ready." Father's voice startled him. "We'll eat breakfast at the ordinary—with plenty of strong coffee to wash it down."

"Yes, sir. Right away."

Thomas went down to the fenced pasture where the horses already received grain. He led one team to the spring's overflow tub to drink. When he took the horses to their camp, his father hitched them to the wagon while he went for the second team.

They walked through the pale dawn to the ordinary. The clear light from a whale-oil lamp shone through the windows. Thomas followed Father to a table in the dining area where he took a chair.

It wasn't long until the proprietor's wife brought them a pitcher of water.

"We're pleased to see you back." She dipped her stout little body in a curtsey, going deep, flour-covered arms soon beginning to flail. When she rose, her bent knee gave off a cracking sound. "What'll you have this morning, gentlemen?"

"Bring two mugs ah coffee fer me and the lad. I'll take a stack of the Queen's pancakes, ham...uh, some stewed apples."

She turned toward Thomas.

"Give me everything he said, only make it plenty."

"All right, I'll hurry." Before she turned toward the cook room, Thomas spotted a little smile on her thick, bow-shaped lips.

When the food came they ate quickly, gulping down their coffee. While his father paid for the meal, Thomas checked on their horses. Now ready to leave, he pulled his team in behind his father's wagon.

The gray-black sky thrust out red bolts as the sun rose. The day had barely started when Thomas' mind slipped to Sophrona. How her chestnut curls spilled over her shoulders when she occasionally loosened the ribbon from her hair.

The two drove their wagons with few stops, rising early the next morning to start again, eating when they found time.

They had been on the road ten days now, traveling hard. If they continued without problems, day after tomorrow they would be home.

Thomas felt downtrodden, tired. His father must feel just as bad. He wished for one of Simon's roast pork suppers. The man knew how to prepare food almost as good as a woman. He just wasn't nearly as easy to look at. The memory of warm, crusty bread watered Thomas's mouth. They had no good food left over from their scraps.

He must keep his thoughts on getting home. He leaned forward, snapping the reins, as he urged his team on.

He had to get just a little bit closer to Baltimore Town, and his love, before nightfall.

CHAPTER TEN

Tuesday
June 24th, 1755

Sophrona sat up in bed, startled awake from a confusing dream. She pulled the quilt close around her neck, tracing the ivory-stitches on the pale blue cover with her finger. Just after midnight she found herself at the window, pulling back the drapes to stare at the full silvery moon, her thoughts a jumble. She sensed, more than knew, a storm gathered. How would she survive the outcome without something to hold on to? She went back to bed, eventually falling asleep.

A knock roused her. Estelle, their servant, opened the door a crack to stick her head in.

"Mistress says you need a final measure for your new clothes, Miss Sophrona." Her eyes swept the room. "Should I bring you some coffee or tea?"

"No. I don't want anything just yet." After Estelle left, she gazed toward the light that seeped through the drapes.

Only two days remained before the party. The servants already worked preparing the house. At Mother's insistence, Father brought in several boys to clean up the grounds. Gerald supervised them when he could.

As the affair drew closer, Sophrona needed someone to guide her through this. Thomas, the only one strong enough to withstand those forces threatening to tear her from his arms, could not help.

* * *

77

"Hold still, Sophrona. I thought that seamstress measured your new gown correctly."

Mother's ability to talk from one side of her mouth, with sharp little pins clenched between clamped lips on the opposite side, caused Sophrona to smile. One day that might be her.

"She measured precisely, Mother. Her measurements are correct."

The smell from her mother's rosewater teased Sophrona's nostrils, as she sucked in her stomach to avoid being stuck by a pin. The fragrance reminded her of years ago when she was four. She poured a whole container of Mother's sweet smell on herself and her little dog, Beauty. That day Father saved her from Mother's wrath, while Gerald jumped with laughter.

Her mother's shoulders dipped down as she worked—first tuck, then pin. "Nonsense, girl. Did you give her a difficult time, or pooch out your belly?"

"Stop. You're pulling me over." Sophrona slid her feet apart, bent her knees slightly, pulling back to keep from pitching forward.

"Never mind the discomfort. I must fix that waistline." Mother folded in one last tuck, setting it with pins. "Your father insists you look beautiful when your friends arrive."

He really means Samuel. Her stomach almost emptied out, right there. Not as much from her waistband pulled tight, but at the thought Samuel was coming after her.

"It doesn't matter. I may need new tucks in a day or two."

"Go on, now, remove the dress—while I thank you to watch that mouth. A servant will take care of this. I already have enough to do."

As Mother straightened up, sunlight touched her loosely knotted hair, giving the top the appearance of golden strands weaved through.

Father called up the stairway. "Fenella, come down here. I need breakfast before I leave."

78

Mother snatched the dress completely over Sophrona's head. "Hurry! Your father's so generous with money for your pretty clothes. He needs calming. He's hungry."

"Yes, ma'am." She pulled on an older dress, almost stepping on Mother's heels as she hurried down the stairs behind her.

"Oh my, Peter. Time just got away from me." Mother smoothed the back of a hand across her brow. "I'll have fried ham with apple pancakes on the table before you know it."

Her mother started toward the common room.

Sophrona stepped toward Father, giving a little swirl before dipping in a graceful curtsey, like she greeted him as a child. She grasped his arm, standing on her tiptoes to kiss his cheek.

"That's a good daughter, Fronnie. Now, go help your mother by bringing me coffee. I'll take it by the fire." He turned toward the settee.

She went to the common room, where a servant, Katherine, cooked at the fireplace. Young Estelle turned the spinning wheel until Mother called her to mix batter. Sophrona filled Father's pewter mug, carrying the hot drink to him.

Tomorrow she would help with the cooking for the following day's party. She blinked back moisture. What about Thomas? Had he already forgotten her?

* * *

Thomas traveled behind his father through the day, stopping only to water the horses. Near evening time they found a place by a creek where Thomas made a fire. The piercing song from an oriole in the distance caught his attention. Looking up, he spotted an orange belly flittering between the branches of tall trees, bathed in golden light from the setting sun.

"There's enough food in the box for tonight, Lad. Some's little more than crumbs, but we'll eat. I'll make coffee."

After Thomas finished the meal, he stretched out to sleep. An owl's screech echoed through the trees, the moon splashing its silvery rays over the forest. He rolled over to bury his face in the covers, avoiding the empty spot growing inside him. The sound from water rushing through the creek's shallow bedrock lulled him to sleep.

He rose as Father placed the coffee pot on coals near the flames. Thomas wanted a mug of coffee before getting on their way. Satisfaction swelled inside him. This was their last day on the road. Before long he would straighten out that problem he had with Peter Hackett.

After traveling so many miles he ached all over, feeling like someone sneaked up on him with a tree limb. Searching for a way to keep his mind off the soreness, thoughts of the woman he loved replaced it. The first time he had kissed her, his heart hammered so hard, he thought it might pop from his chest. He did not want to turn her loose.

"Thomas, you mustn't do that. Mother or Father may walk out here." She pushed back on his chest, slipping from his grasp to hurry toward the porch's edge, tilting her face up toward the sky.

He went after her. This time she did not resist when he pulled her to him. Her skin felt soft to his touch, like velvet. Within a matter of moments he stepped back, mindful of the danger in his uncontrolled emotions. He never allowed himself that situation again, unsure of what might happen.

Shading his eyes with a hand, he peered at the sun, gauging its position in the sky. If they made it home early enough, he could go see her.

"Whoa," Father called, as he guided the team over to the side.

Thomas followed him. "What is it, Da?"

"Got a cracked wheel, Lad. Wanta give me a hand to lighten my load? We'll transfer what's in my wagon to yours.

"Will we still make it home today?"

"I don't know, Lad. Once we get started again, it should be slow going or I'll bust it apart."

Thomas grunted as he helped move the contents of the wagon into his.

"The spare wheel's cracked too. Don't make much sense to switch them out." Father scratched his head. "Here, help me move the water cask."

Thomas grabbed hold. "I wanted to go see Sophrona tonight, but I don't know, now."

Father nodded. "Once off the ferry, we'll have two hours to travel the last miles, unless we're slowed down more." He shook his head. "The moon will still be mostly full. Otherwise we'd face a dark ride from the Patapsco."

Thomas guided his wagon in behind Father's, traveling at a slower pace. Reaching the ferry at the Patapsco River, they waited their turn for the ride over. Once on the other bank, they pointed their wagons toward home. Still, disappointment tugged at Thomas. There was no time to see Sophrona, even if they arrived tonight.

The sun set as his father pushed on, now driving the team much harder than Thomas expected. He stayed up, hoping the bad wheel lasted, not wanting to stay away from home another night.

The moon rose, its silvery light flooding the night as he guided his team through their yard on down to the barn. Father stepped down from his wagon. Thomas thought he heard him groan.

Simon hurried down from the house, breathing hard, Isaac right behind him.

"I'll get that, sir."

"I'll help Thomas," Isaac said

They unhitched the horses, corralling them in the barn.

"Looks like you gave the animals a workout, sir." Simon reached for a cloth. "I'll rub them down."

Thomas jabbed Isaac on the arm with his fist. "Have you earned your keep since we've been gone?"

"Hey. Better watch out, if you know what's good for you." Isaac punched back, smiling.

Thomas threw his arms around his little brother's shoulder. Feeling for Isaac warmed him. "What's to eat? I'm about starved."

"Simon made a good supper, Thomas. There might be a bite or two left over for you." Isaac ducked Thomas's right fist as he took off running toward the house.

Thomas loped behind his little brother toward the front door. For the first time since their departure in May, he truly felt free to be himself. *Thank you Lord for getting us home.*

"Gotcha, Craighead." A voice rumbled as a hand snaked out from the shadows, clasping him by the shoulder.

Thomas spun around, breaking the man's grip. He threw a fist at the face he did not clearly see. The man ducked, laughing. Isaac laughed along with him.

He spun on Isaac, not understanding why his youngest brother laughed. Something was just not right. "What are you doing? Laughing while a stranger tries to…"

"Whoa, there. Don't you know your own brother?" Alexander stepped from the shadows, the disguise gone from his voice.

Thomas took in his new height, his solid build. "I half expected you not to be here. Our little brother didn't mention you were. I must say, you've grown some in the last six months."

Thomas shook Alex's hand, gripping it tight, then quickly moved behind him while slightly twisting his arm.

"You're in trouble, Alex, if you ever do that to me again."

"All right! We shouldn't have. Now turn me loose."

After Thomas stepped away, Alex worked his shoulder with a hand.

82

The three started laughing and, finally, Thomas caught his breath to say, "Your voice did change—I didn't recognize you. Is your arm all right?"

"Yes, but if you had wrenched my shoulder I couldn't assist the reverend."

Thomas nodded toward Isaac. "Then you'd use the one who helped you cook this up, to do the reverend's writing."

The three turned around, hearing Father's low laughter. He had obviously observed them, on the pathway from the barn. Thomas waited as Alex embraced Father, before he walked with Isaac toward the common room.

Later, Thomas followed Alex out to the front porch. They took seats in straight-back chairs, where Thomas admired the moon in a star-speckled sky.

"It's good to have you home, Alex. I've missed you. Did your studies go well?" He turned toward his brother, who smiled. That angelic look on Alex's face made Thomas more certain his brother should be a pastor.

"Yes, I'm through now. I'll assist at our church until I'm sent to a position somewhere else. Not exactly sure where, but I'll assist there, too, until appointed to my own position."

Alexander chewed the edge of his lip. "What about Sophrona, Thomas? You want to marry her, like Isaac said?"

"Of course. Why do you ask?" What a strange thing to say. Dread hovered over him as he waited for an answer.

"Well, Gerald talked to me about his sister the other day. He said their father is pushing her toward someone who attends their church."

"Yes, I know. Richard."

Alexander shook his head. "No, I don't think so. Gerald said the man interested in her is named Samuel."

"What does Gerald say about how she feels?" Thomas said.

"He didn't say anything about that."

Thomas pursed his lips. Her father pushing her toward another man—and not Richard, the one Gerald spoke about?

Thomas rubbed his chin. "I'll ask him tomorrow when he comes to pick up the wagon."

"He's not coming. The family's giving a party. He's staying home for the festivities."

"When are they receiving guests?"

"Gerald said early in the afternoon. It's my opinion you should arrive early if you can. Eat a good breakfast, Thomas. He's a Scots lad."

Alex rose, going inside the house. Thomas sat there in the quiet night. He must not lose Sophrona, tomorrow. No matter what.

A little later Father stepped out on the porch, taking the chair Alexander vacated.

"I hear there's a celebration tomorrow at the Hackett house."

"Yes, sir." Thomas filled his lungs, then slowly released the air.

"Did you get an invitation, Lad?"

"No." Thomas turned to face him. "I'm still going. If Sophrona knew I had returned, she'd expect me there."

"Well then, Laddie, I shall accompany you to your intended bride. I'll enjoy getting socially acquainted with Peter, since our interaction only takes place during business transactions." He nodded before continuing. "One day we'll share grandchildren, if all goes well. We should know each other's shortcomings."

Uncertainty settled inside Thomas.

"I don't know what's best to do, Da. I just don't. While I want marriage, I cannot take those vows in a church where God belongs to England. I owe loyalty to Sophrona, but I owe my salvation to the Lord. I cannot turn my back to Him."

"It's not easy being a man. Especially when you must choose between God or your bride. If it means anything to ya, Lad, I always put the Lord first."

They sat there in silence. Thomas drew strength from his father's acknowledgment that God came first in his life, too.

"It's my opinion there's a compromise there, somewhere, between you, Peter Hackett, and his daughter. It's knowing what you're willing to accept—or not." Father tapped fingers on his knee. "Trust the Lord will make you a way to Sophrona. Alex holds a firm position in the Lord's work. Perhaps take him along, as well."

"Yes. I'll ask him."

"Well then, Lad, I need some relief from that hard ground we slept on so many nights." Father rose from his chair, making his way inside.

Thomas remained on the porch. How could he approach Mr. Hackett? One thing he knew for sure, he did not put anyone before God. After a while, the weariness in his bones set in. He barely made it up the staircase to the bed, where he collapsed.

Using his last conscious breath before sleep, Thomas fervently prayed.

"Don't let him kill me, Lord, when I come to take Sophrona back."

CHAPTER ELEVEN

"Good morning, Sophrona." Mother gently shook her shoulder. "Everyone's working on your party. Come get some breakfast before you begin."

She fluttered her lashes as Mother bent over the bed, shaking her again. Eyelids open wide, excitement caught at her like the sticky candy she helped make the evening before.

"Is Thomas coming today? I dreamed about him last night."

"Another dream you say? Hmm. I hardly think he'll show up here today, or anytime soon. Get up, now, Sophrona. Samuel's coming early to assist Gerald with placing tables and seats around the back yard."

"All right, Mother. Just give me time to wake up before I get dressed. I'll come down soon, honestly I will."

"I'll be back if you don't hurry." Mother left the room, wagging her finger.

Sophrona closed her eyes as she thought about the day. Maybe Samuel wasn't so bad. At least they'd leave her alone if she gave in. He was a handsome man, someone Father liked.

That's it. They've finally driven me where I'm almost ready to give in.

Shuddering, Sophrona shook her head to drive away thoughts of Samuel. Throwing back the covers, she crawled out of bed to sit on the side. Mother could return at any time. She rose, choosing a plain dress to wear.

Creeping slowly down the stairs into the sitting room, she came up behind Father, seated on the green sofa with Mother. Bending, she kissed him on the cheek before hurrying around to sit on his other side.

"You shouldn't sneak up on an old man, daughter. You might frighten me to death one day."

"I don't think so. You're not nearly the old man you want me to believe." She laughed as her father smiled, patting her arm.

"That's my dear Fronnie, laughing, so happy like you used to be." He stopped talking to clutch her arm, pulling it closer.

"What, Father? You're staring. Is something wrong with my arm?" She pulled back.

Mother cleared her throat. "Sophrona, go pour your father some coffee."

With a nod, she hurried toward the common room door, hearing Mother whisper, "Peter, we must do something."

The two entered into the common room as Sophrona filled a mug. When Father sat down at the table, she placed the coffee in front of him.

"You're a good daughter, Fronnie."

Breakfast had ended. Sophrona pushed her food around, occasionally taking a bite, when she heard her brother enter from the common room door.

"Let's get Father," Gerald entered the room with Samuel beside him.

Samuel stopped in front of her. "Good morning, Sophrona."

"Good morning." She pushed aside a warm feeling, barely looking at him.

Father came around to kiss Mother's cheek before he left with Gerald and Samuel.

Mother brought her a cup of tea. "Eat something, Sophrona. When you're through, we'll take a final look at your new dress."

"I'm not hungry." Sophrona took a sip of the tea and stood up. "I'll eat later."

"You don't eat enough to stay alive. Whatever must I do with you? Soon as we're through, you put something in your stomach."

"Yes, soon as we're through." She followed Mother to the sitting room.

* * *

The sun rose as Thomas joined his family at the table. Simon filled a platter with slices of fried ham. A loaf of bread sat on the breadboard, a knife beside it.

"Here's something to drink, Thomas." Simon set steaming coffee in front of him before turning to fill Father's and Alexander's mugs.

"And how'd ya sleep, Lad, seeing you're the last one outta bed today? Even Isaac got up first." Father took measure of him as Thomas scratched his head, still a little groggy.

"It's the best night's rest in a while. How about you, Da? Feel all right this morning?"

Father nodded.

Today he would see Sophrona. She awaited him. Thomas' heart fluttered, producing an outpouring of joy. He had no thoughts on working things out with her father, but he must. He mumbled a quick prayer as he fell asleep last night, then another when he awoke. Would the Lord God show him a way?

"I'll ask the blessing, Da." Thomas said. The family lowered their heads. "We thank You for this provision, Lord Jesus."

Afterward, Thomas accompanied his father to the barn where Simon waited. They intended to look over the animals, then, given enough time, the freight wagons.

"What about the young ox, sir? It looks about time he's shod. Maybe the other one, too," Simon waited.

Father stepped to a room off the barn that held the special stanchion for shoeing oxen. He turned the windlass, studying the pulley that raised and lowered the sling which lifted the animal off its feet.

"The pulley's in working order. We'd better do the shoeing in the next few days." Father scratched the back of his head. "I'll look at both animals tomorrow. Right now, Alexander needs the young ox in the field. He must finish up before we leave for Peter's house."

"Yes, sir."

"Look over the belly slings, Simon. See if they're frayed. Don't want ta drop that ox." Father shook his head as if at the thought.

After they finished with the horses, Thomas walked out to the field. "Accompanying us to Sophrona's house, Alexander?"

"Soon as I'm through, here, I'll turn my beast over to Simon. I'll come along if you want me there."

"You ask if you're wanted? You're an ordained minister. I need you there."

Alex pursed his lips. "So then, you still want to marry Sophrona? If you do, brother, please make sure it's a recognized marriage."

"I won't take the easy way out, Alex. I'll have our marriage banns posted in the Church of England. Otherwise, my children won't be recognized by England as legitimate." Resolve surged through Thomas. He would straighten this out with Peter, but not marry in their church.

* * *

"Take a girl upstairs to dress your hair. Now, hurry." Mother turned the gown right side out, inspecting the tucks she'd deepened in the waistband, before starting on the opposite side.

She raised her eyes to Sophrona. "Go on, child. I'll have this dress done before you know it."

"Yes, Mother." Sophrona moved toward the staircase. Estelle hurried behind her.

Arriving at her room, Sophrona sat on a carved maple chair fashioned for her room years earlier. She picked up a brush from the matching table, handing it to the young servant who began brushing her hair. Mother soon arrived carrying the blue satin gown, with a package clutched in her other hand.

"This shade is perfect for your complexion."

After Estelle took the gown, Mother removed a pair of slippers, the same material as the gown, with small heels.

"Oh, Mother, they're lovely." Sophrona kissed her mother's smooth cheek.

Undressing, she stepped into her petticoats, then her stays. Estelle laced her from behind while Mother stood in front, observing the results.

"Tighter, Estelle, pull tighter. Her form isn't showing through like it should."

The girl grunted as she pulled harder, then laced her up. Sophrona thought she'd pop right out of the stays. Mother helped her into the gown she was sure cost Father more money than he cared to spend, along with the slippers. She glanced in the mirror, gasping at the bodice of her gown. Only a ridge of stiff ivory lace, encircling the neckline, kept her bosom from being indecent.

The servant held a mirror as she swayed her hips, looking at the skirt's effect when walking. The blue set off her dark curls. The bodice ended in a snug "V" at her waist, the gown falling straight to swirl around her ankles. She slipped into the matching cloth slippers.

Mother took a square of white cloth from her apron, unfolding the material to expose a necklace of glossy white pearls, which she hung around Sophrona's neck.

"You're beautiful. So lovely." Tears glistened in Mother's eyes. "Now, I must finish what still needs done." She hurried out, Estelle behind her.

Sophrona used the wood-framed mirror to look at the pearls circling her neck. Mother wore them at important times, such as weddings, special Sabbath's or infants' sprinklings. The pale ivory of the lace offset the white luster of the necklace.

She replaced the mirror and left the room. Father met her part way down the stairs, taking her arm.

"You're much too lovely to descend the stairs alone, my daughter."

When they reached the bottom, he turned toward her. "Fronnie, I'd like you to socialize with Samuel during the party. Would you satisfy an old man's request?"

"Yes, if you only require this from me today—you don't look like an old man. You are very handsome."

Father patted her arm. He turned toward the common room, when Gerald walked in.

"Everything's in place, Father. Samuel left to dress for the festivities. He'll return soon."

Father continued through the house as Gerald turned toward Sophrona.

"That color's most becoming." He took her by the elbow, guiding her toward the sofa, where they sat.

She shifted toward him. "It's been so long since I've seen Thomas. I hope nothing happened to him."

"I don't think anything's wrong." He crossed a knee.

"I assured Father I'd socialize with Samuel, but 'be friendly' is what Father really wants me to do. What do you think about Samuel?"

Gerald sighed. "The truth is, there aren't many better men than Samuel. I like him more than I expected when he first attended our parish."

"Better than you like Thomas? Oh, Gerald, I'm so confused."

"Do you love Thomas?"

"Yes, but he's not here. Father prefers Samuel. I just don't know what to do." She blinked, holding back tears.

Gerald took her hand. "Yes, you do. You must choose the man who'll make you happy."

Samuel entered the room. He took a seat on the other side of her. Thick, dark hair touched with curls, he looked most handsome in his burgundy jacket, grey waistcoat, with dark blue pantaloons.

"It's lovely outside, Sophrona. Come stroll with me on the back lawn. Take a look at what your brother and I accomplished." He took her hand. She rose before fully deciding she wanted to walk with him.

"Gerald, please let us know when the guests start arriving," Samuel said.

Strangely enough, Sophrona felt secure when he took her elbow guiding her toward the back yard. The trees were trimmed neatly, the grass clipped. Her mother's prized rose bushes, some from England, filled the air with a delicate tea fragrance. He guided her to a whitewashed love seat, where she sat with him.

"Sophrona—a lovely name. Now tell me, what must I do to call on you after today?" He reached over, stroking her hand with a forefinger.

Her head started to spin. Did she really want to escape, run far away from him? Samuel possessed mannerisms much like her father. He resembled Father in other ways, like his dark hair and well-muscled physique. A spicy male scent tugged at her.

Gerald started across the yard toward them. Richard and his Sanborn cousins, with two other young women from their parish, walked behind Gerald. Her uncle, who owned the foundry, came with his wife. Sophrona rose, with Samuel, to greet her relatives before meeting other guests as they arrived.

A light breeze rippled through the trees, past the rose bushes, scenting the air with their sweet smell. The back yard soon filled with her friends, all eager to meet Samuel, who charmed the ladies no matter their age.

Sophrona's senses cleared. Somehow, she had let down her resistance to Samuel, now seen as her suitor. The young men, along with the older gentlemen, gravitated toward him making conversation, while she shared pleasantries with their ladies.

She stopped to look around, admiring her friends in their summer gowns of blue, green, and pink—the men so dashing in their finest jackets. High upon a branch, a bird trilled its sweet song, so strong, so clear. It seemed almost a warning for her, alone.

Then she remembered.

Something must happen soon, or she might never return to the way things were before Samuel entered her life. When it was only her and Thomas.

CHAPTER TWELVE

Thomas expected Alex to join him at the house. Finally, he went looking for him. Alex was in the barn, where he'd led the young ox, still helping Simon go over the stanchion.

Alex rose. "I didn't mean to take so long, Thomas." He turned to hand Simon a rope. "It's just that…"

"It's grown so late, I may not arrive there during the celebration." Thomas rubbed his face. "I must go."

He strode toward the house, with his brother trying to stay up.

"I'm not ready to appear in public, yet." Alex pointed toward his clothing. "Someone will think I just stepped out of a peat bog. I can't allow that. I…Wait!"

Thomas spun around. "Wait. Wait. You've done that all morning. Now what is it?"

"A man just…well…never knows where he'll meet his bride. I may find her at this gathering, brother."

"There's not much time left to get dressed." Thomas did not want to arrive after the festivities started. His mind grew cloudy over his brother's self-centered attitude. He pawed the ground for smooth little pebbles, as Alex made a run for the house.

A stone found its mark. "That stung. Now leave me alone or I'm telling Father." Alexander leaped in the air, legs moving fast as he hurried away.

The humor of his brother running for cover, like when they were kids, sobered Thomas. He must not act like a child as he prepared to take a bride, but as a man. He dropped the remaining pebbles, regretting his act, as he continued on.

"What happened out there, Lad? Your brother's state of mind didn't sound good to me."

Thomas dusted off his breeches. "I may need to dress him if he doesn't hurry. If only Alex offered to help Simon with that ox tomorrow, not today."

"Let's take a seat on the porch while your brother settles down." Father moved toward the door. "It makes no sense going into a situation with your thoughts already troubled."

Thomas followed his father outside, where they waited on Alexander, who finished sooner than he expected. Before long, the three rode toward Sophrona's house.

Arriving, Thomas dismounted, tying up his horse. Father and Alexander did the same, following him up the steps. A servant answered Thomas' knock, holding open the door.

After they entered, Thomas looked around before asking, "Where's the festivity being held?"

The middle-aged woman smiled, as she pointed toward the open door leading to the back yard.

The three men crossed the room. Thomas' hand trembled as he straightened his jacket.

Ladies in bright summer gowns, their men in jackets almost as colorful, were present. Some sat at tables or on benches, while couples strolled among the flowers.

Stepping through the doorway, Thomas took heart at his family's presence.

"Careful, Lad. Don't lose your head over nothing," Father said.

Thomas looked over the group. He thought he'd found Sophrona, but the young woman seemed far too thin for his intended. A husky, dark haired man about his age clasped her arm as she leaned in toward him. Thomas turned slightly, looking past the two. His father grunted as he tapped Thomas' shoulder and nodded his head toward the woman.

His head spinning, Thomas realized the emaciated young woman was her. Then every muscle in his body worked together, like a well-greased wheel, propelling him toward Sophrona.

Thomas paused for his thoughts to clear, but could not tolerate another man standing so close, as if he belonged with her.

"Take your hands off the woman I love, or I'll move them for you."

The man faced Thomas. "Are you speaking to me?"

"You're the only one I see with hands on Sophrona."

"No." The muscular, intimidating man patted Sophrona's arm. "I've been courting her for some time. If you put your hands on me, I'll not take it lightly."

"Don't do this, Lad. Talk it out."

Thomas heard his father speak, but had trouble grasping his words.

"We're planning on marriage soon." Thomas looked toward Sophrona. "Tell him, Sophrona."

Her eyes grew big, as she muttered, "I...don't...Thomas you've come back?"

Hearing that, Thomas stepped toward the man.

"I told you to turn her loose."

"No. She doesn't belong with you."

The man's lips thinned, as he lifted his chin, his face still as a glassy stream on a calm day. Instinct told Thomas to slow down, but he could not. He threw a right fist that fell on empty air.

The stranger moved toward him. They fell into position, fists out front. The crowd backed up. Someone shouted encouragement to the man, Samuel.

Peter Hackett moved quickly across the yard, several men beside him, anger on his face.

Thomas backed up when his father, then his brother, shucked their jackets. Time seemed to stop. Then in a thicker brogue, Father spoke.

"If it has to happen this way, then it'll be a fair one, Peter, or I'll personally hold you responsible."

"That's not my intention, Cyrus, but your son interrupted our day, to provoke the man our daughter's seeing. Thomas wasn't invited."

Peter's words hung in the air.

"Stop it! Stop it now!" Sophrona pushed past Samuel to face her father. "He would have the invitation, had I known he was back at home." Sophrona's body shook, the lines deepening around her once plump, pink cheeks.

No one moved except Fenella, who came to stand beside her daughter.

The roaring in Thomas's head stopped. Looking at Peter, he finally spoke.

"I apologize, sir, for disrupting your good time. I only came to see Sophrona." He glanced down, and then met Peter's eyes. "It's such a long time since I left. I lost my head finding her so thin, with another man next to her."

"Ohhh," a woman in the crowd said, joined by others.

Close to Thomas, a trace of a smile appeared on an older woman's face as she nudged her male escort. "No wonder he's fighting mad. He didn't know…and loves her, too."

"Please, excuse us everyone, but do continue with the festivities." Peter pointed to the largest table, draped with a white cloth. "They'll set out supper, soon."

As the guests began to move around, talk resumed.

"Will you see that our guests enjoy themselves, son? Make sure they get plenty to eat."

Gerald nodded. "Yes, Father."

"Sophrona, bring Thomas and his brother to the sitting room. Alex—you are Alex?—it's awhile since we last met."

"Yes, sir, I'm his brother." Alex put out his hand, but Peter already turned toward Father.

"Cyrus, you like to be present for this affair?" Peter immediately whirled around, marching toward the house.

Father and Alex trailed Peter. Thomas fell back beside Sophrona, her mother walking behind them. Sophrona smiled up at him when he took her hand, looking more like his intended bride.

After gathering in the front room, Thomas spoke.

"I love your Sophrona, Mr. Hackett. I want to marry her."

"I'm not so sure you'll take good care of my daughter, Thomas. You won't consider our feelings over the small matter of her being married in our church." Peter folded his arms.

Thomas cleared his throat. "If you'll forgive my saying so, I don't think you've taken very good care of your daughter either, sir."

Face growing red, Peter gasped for air. "How dare you say such an outrageous thing to me."

Briefly, Thomas thought her father might strike him.

"Will you take a good look at Sophrona, sir? I hardly recognized her. She's practically skin and bones. Don't tell me you haven't noticed she's a mere shadow."

"Don't concern yourself about my daughter..." Peter widened his stance.

"Peter, I'd like a private word with you."

"Very well, Cyrus, but that'll end your family's intrusions into my day."

The two men disappeared.

While Alex rose to take a cookie from the tray a servant placed on a table, Thomas sat on the sofa next to Sophrona.

* * *

Cyrus followed Peter, feeling driven to reach the conscience of a man holding the key to his son's happiness.

When the two men entered the office, Peter turned to Cyrus.

"What do you want? What's so bloody important you must interrupt me during my most important discussion about who shall marry my daughter?"

"Your daughter, Peter!" Cyrus met his gaze. "It's your daughter, herself, that's important. You fail to see the danger she's in."

Peter stepped back. "What's wrong with Fronnie?"

"Take a look at her. She's lost so much weight, a person could almost see through her." Cyrus tossed his head in contempt. "Peter, you might lose her before it's over. Don't you know she'll die if her weight keeps dropping?"

"She's grown a little thinner, but that will change as her relationship with Samuel grows."

Cyrus moved toward the two easy chairs. Dropping down on one, he leaned forward and said, "Let's sit down, discuss this like sensible men, shall we?"

Peter took the other chair, turning toward him.

"You can't tell her who to marry, any more than someone could tell you not to marry Fenella. You'll lose her." Cyrus rubbed a hand over his chin. "I don't think Thomas will give her up. And, it's me opinion she doesn't want him to."

Peter's face waxed gray as the lines on his brow deepened.

"There's no other recourse left, Cyrus. Thomas won't marry my daughter in our church. He doesn't appear concerned the marriage won't be considered legitimate, unless performed in England's official church."

"Says who? The King of England? As if a Scot cares a whit about what he thinks." Cyrus blew a long breath.

"Just watch what you say. I'll not listen to this kind of talk one more minute." Color rose in Peter's face.

99

"Let's not forget why we're here." Cyrus rubbed his hands together. "I can't speak for Thomas, but you shouldn't come to a hasty decision."

"Care to give me a good reason why, Cyrus?"

The look in Peter's eyes spoke of danger.

"Because Thomas loves your daughter and she loves him. He'll take good care of her.

"Hmm." Peter's gaze shifted away from Cyrus then returned.

"Alexander finished seminary studies. He's waiting for a position in one of our Presbyterian churches. Eventually, he'll lead his own flock."

Peter's face softened. "That must make you proud, Cyrus—an upcoming minister in your family."

Cyrus shook his head. "Na, Peter, he isn't upcoming. He's already a minister. He could take a position tomorrow if appointed to lead a church."

Peter stood, turning toward the door. "Well, it's time to put an end to all this foolishness."

Cyrus rose, turning his back to the door. Reaching out, he touched Peter's shoulder. "At least neither of our families is Papists, Peter, and we can thank the Lord for that."

"Perhaps so."

Cyrus's heart yearned for a good ending to his son's struggle as he stepped aside to let Peter pass, following him toward the sitting room.

* * *

While Mrs. Hackett looked on, Thomas enfolded Sophrona's thin little hand in his.

"I thought about you every day. Unfortunately, I couldn't return sooner—to help you." Anger boiled inside him. If Thomas controlled it, maybe he had a chance to wrestle Sophrona from her father.

100

"It's all right now, Thomas. You're home." She smiled, her lips trembling.

Mr. Hackett entered the room, Father behind him. They took the stuffed easy chairs across from him, Sophrona, and Alexander.

Gerald came in from the back yard.

"Are the guests doing alright, son? I hadn't intended to stay away this long. We're still in discussion. Could last a bit longer."

Gerald hesitated. "Some guests have left. Samuel's asking if you want him to stay."

"They must not leave, yet. The day's hardly begun." Peter gritted his teeth.

"Despite the interruption, everyone's enjoying the food. A few are interested in who shall court Sophrona."

"Oh, my!" Mrs. Hackett gasped, struggling from the settee to come stand next to her husband. "I'm mortified, Peter. What shall we do?"

Father stood up, offering her the chair next to her husband. Thomas rose to get a straight-backed chair for his father, placing it on the other side of Peter.

"Would you finish seeing the guests off, Gerald? Tell Samuel he may leave whenever he chooses."

"Yes, sir."

Peter reached over and patted his wife's hand. "Now don't you worry any, Fenella. I'm sure the guests didn't mean any harm. They're only interested in how this is settled."

"Sir, I'm terribly worried about Sophrona." Thomas leaned forward. "Can we work this out somehow?"

Peter's bushy eyebrows shot up, bottom lip curling up to swallow the top. "How, Thomas? How do we come to a decision we'll both welcome? You're so set against marrying her in our church."

Thomas cleared his throat. *Lord, help me tread lightly.*

"Well, sir, I'm only against our marriage in your church. Now, for instance, if we are married here at your house, with your pastor hearing our vows, then that's fine with me. Although I don't find it necessary, our marriage would be considered legitimate in the eyes of your church and the Crown."

Sophrona sat up, still dabbing at her eyes.

Fenella reached over to clutch her husband's arm. "You should at least hear him out, Peter. Why, imagine our daughter getting married in our own home. We'd open our front lawn as well as the back. Her father escorting her down the staircase so she doesn't trip over her gown…"

"Silence, Fenella. It's hard enough for a man to think during all this turmoil." Peter smoothed his hair back. Then, almost as an afterthought, he reached over, patting his wife's arm. "I'm not quite through discussing this matter, yet."

"What do you mean 'our pastor hearing the vows'?" he turned back to Thomas.

"If you'll pardon my brother, sir," Alex spoke up. "He means both the pastor from your church and I shall perform the wedding together, right here. With spiritual representation from both sides, no one need feel slighted. Did you mean that, brother?"

Father's cheeks bulged as if suppressing a smile, as Mr. Hackett's sharp little eyes bore down on Alex.

"Why, yes, Alexander, that's what I meant to say." Thomas swallowed hard. "It's a splendid idea, if only you'll allow it—Mother and Father Hackett."

"Yes, Father. Oh please. It'll make me happier than I've been in such a long time." Sophrona swooped from the sofa, landing in her father's lap, planting a kiss on his cheek.

"Get up, Fronnie. The chair's too small; you'll topple us both onto the floor." Sophrona returned to her seat on the sofa.

Peter pulled vigorously at his chin.

"If Thomas is serious, then Cyrus and I shall post the banns. After that, I'll make arrangements for our pastor to come perform the vows."

"Thank you, sir. I am most serious. I'm also determined my brother must be included in performing our marriage."

Thomas held his breath as he prayed, *Please, Lord, don't let him change his mind.*

Peter's face turned beet red as he stood. "It seems to me you've been determined before, Thomas. I'm trying hard not to let..."

Father jumped up and, with a deep laugh, grabbed Peter by the shoulder from behind.

"It's a good day for the Scots, eh Peter? My son soon to wed your daughter!"

Finally! Father really meant finally his son could marry Peter's daughter.

Sophrona moved close, smiling. "I love you Thomas. I just knew you'd come back for me."

He shrugged his shoulder, leaning in to smell her hair. How could he do anything else but claim her love. He must while he could; who knew just what might happen to them next?

CHAPTER THIRTEEN

Thomas finished the slice of spice cake Sophrona's mother placed on a saucer. He enjoyed her food. If Sophrona cooked half that good, he'd be home for supper every night. He looked forward to eating at her table, good cook or not.

"With your appetite, daughter, I'll be letting out the clothes I just took in." Her mother slid another cookie onto Sophrona's plate as she smiled at Thomas.

Finishing his milk, he stood. "I'll join your father in the sitting room. When you're through, we'll enjoy the breeze on the front porch."

"Wait. I'm ready now." Sophrona pushed the cookie into her mouth as she rose.

Thomas smelled molasses as he took her arm, guiding her through the sitting room to the front door. He pulled the Windsor rockers together, holding hers steady as she gathered her skirt.

The twenty-third of July turned a bit warmer. The full moon rose as stars shone clear in the evening sky. He reached for her hand, rubbing her fingers. His breath caught at the feel of her soft skin.

"I love you, Sophrona Hackett. One day soon I'll call you Mrs. Thomas Craighead."

"Oh, Thomas, I missed you. It's only a month since your return but I'm so happy. Before long we'll become a family."

She let out a throaty little sigh as he squeezed her hand. The sound soothed him.

He almost let her get away from him. Where did he find the courage to go after her, knowing her father disliked him? Peter even plotted to replace him with another man. The Lord heard his prayers, though, sending him over to her house that day. He prevailed against Samuel, a man very much his equal in intelligence, stature, ambition.

"What do you hear about Samuel? Still working for your father?"

"Oh, yes, one of his best men. He stops to see Father about business, but doesn't stay long. He's escorting Mary Sanborn, Richard's cousin, to services." She pushed off, gently rocking. "He laughs easily with her. The community thinks the two made a commitment already. He never laughed so much around me. Now that I think about it, he hardly laughed at all."

Thomas patted her hand.

"Perhaps he wasn't encouraged to laugh. After all, where's the satisfaction in courting a woman who's involved only because of her father?" He breathed deeply.

"Still, he seems more contented around her, in such a short amount of time."

"Sophrona, you never belonged with him. Much as Samuel wanted to marry you; he surely had to know that." He rose, pulling her to him. "Let's not talk about the biggest source of our discontent. Not tonight."

They gazed up at the sky. His arm fit snugly around her shoulder, as he enjoyed her presence in the tranquil night. When her scent clouded his mind, he turned her toward the door, walking her in. He kissed her before he left, looking back to see her hand on the door pane, her face a reflection of his sadness at leaving. He wanted to go back, but did not. After their wedding, he would spend a lifetime with her, God willing.

* * *

August arrived. Thomas dreaded the hot days of summer. Their fathers published the final marriage banns at Saint Paul's Parish.

Preparations for their wedding began in earnest. Every evening he visited his lovely betrothed, where he heard about the women's latest progress.

He wanted a simple wedding, such as his Presbyterian upbringing embraced. However, Sophrona attended the Church of England all those years. If the English monarchs knew anything, they knew about pomp and ceremony.

Once out from under her parents, he would find a way to lead her into a closer walk with the Lord, away from her pretentious ways. It was his duty to see their home, their lives, reflected righteousness.

Tonight, though, he wanted time alone with her. The moon waxed crescent, as the front porch loomed dark, giving Thomas a keener sense of his desire for closeness with Sophrona. He only held her hand, though, as she took a seat in the rocker.

"There's some good news," he said. "Father got word to Aunt Elizabeth and Uncle Jonah quickly enough they can attend our wedding. He just received the answer." Thomas shifted closer.

"How far away do they live?"

"They will travel over three hundred miles, coming from the Appalachian foothills of Virginia." He leaned in, enjoying another whiff of rose water.

"That's a long distance." Sophrona plucked at her sleeve. "They must love you very much."

Thomas nodded. "Family is important to us, especially my aunt and uncle. They have no children of their own."

"I don't remember you talking about them."

"Elizabeth is the youngest of my father's siblings. She married Jonah Shepard."

"Oh, I do want to meet her—I mean, both of them."

"They'll travel with a company of Virginia militia as far as Winchester, coming on alone to Baltimore County. They must stay safe. If something happens to her, Father won't easily get over it."

Sophrona fixed her gaze on him. "What will they do after the wedding?"

"There's a regiment of North Carolina militia going home. They'll travel with the militia through the unprotected territory. After all the Indian massacres, it's the only way Uncle Jonah agreed to bring her."

She clasped her hands, looking down.

"Have you thought about me being the only woman in your father's house?"

"Well, it's not like you're moving in with a company of soldiers. There's Father, two brothers—one of them young, the other looking for a church to lead—our indentured servant, Simon. Actually, that's not many."

"Hearing it put that way, I guess there's not much need to complain."

Thomas rose, taking her arm as she came to her feet. He walked her into the house, where he said, "Good evening", to her parents before he kissed her at the door.

Traveling home, his thoughts turned to their wedding day. He still smelled her womanly scent, almost felt her soft skin, even tasted her lips.

What if Daniel Morgan did not plant the seeds of compromise in his stubborn mind, as first his father, then Alexander, helped ease him over the line? He was not sure what Father said to Peter Hackett while alone with him, before they all discussed the wedding, but Father softened the man, somehow.

He rode his horse to the barn, stripping off the bridle and saddle. After a quick rubdown, Thomas pitched him fodder before starting toward the house.

He must only wait two more weeks for their wedding.

CHAPTER FOURTEEN

Father shook him again, hard. "Wake up, Lad. It's your wedding day."

"All right, all right. I'm getting up."

Thomas rolled to the bedside, knuckles rubbing his eyes as he struggled to push sleep from his drowsy mind. After today, Sophrona belonged with him. His aunt and uncle stayed at the house for over a week. They intended to leave for home the following morning.

Sophrona developed a strong friendship with Aunt Elizabeth in the days since their arrival. When his aunt talked about the Virginia frontier, Sophrona's eyes glowed. The notion she might consider the solitude of country living a pleasure surprised him, since her family continuously resided in town.

* * *

Thomas turned toward the steps Sophrona must descend, his heart pumping hard. Her father stayed with the wedding party, as her mother climbed the stairs. A woman from Mrs. Hackett's church accompanied her, toting a basket.

He put aside thoughts of their marriage as he attempted to draw Gerald away from Peter.

"I'd like a drink of water. Care to accompany me back to the common room, Gerald?"

"Yes. I'd say your throat must be terribly dry, considering you'll soon marry." Gerald slowed his pace. "Before I forget, some of our guests insisted on a wedding posse to bring you and Sophrona back, once you leave. They're determined you'll spend your wedding night in our father's house."

"Oh, and is your name included in that group?" Thomas drummed fingertips on his gold colored sleeve.

"No." Gerald smiled. "I'd have to face my sister, and she's meaner than you think."

His shoulders tensed thinking about their first night together. He cringed at the thought of sleeping in Sophrona's old room, under Peter's roof.

"Alex tried to stop the posse from forming. A guest even asked him for a wager on you being up to the run."

They arrived at the common room, where a servant brought Thomas a cool drink.

Gerald shuffled his feet. "Want to know what Alex said?"

Thomas shook his head. "My brother's not a betting man. I'm sure he declined."

His almost brother-in-law smiled. "He said he wouldn't wager, but he did expect you to beat the posse home with your bride."

* * *

Sophrona turned as her mother entered with Mrs. Margret Holmes, who carried a basket of combs and beauty items she set on the dressing table. After Margret finished with her, she would look perfect standing next to Thomas.

"Oh, Mother, I'm so happy. Now, if only I don't trip going down the stairs."

"You mustn't worry about that. Your father's arm will steady you. We need to hurry. Everyone's waiting."

Mother turned toward Margret, who brushed Sophrona's hair in long strokes. "Did you bring the ribbon?"

"Yes, several colors." She pulled some from a pocket.

Mother selected a length of red ribbon. "This'll do fine. The color's perfect."

Sophrona held still as the woman worked, piling her hair into curls, turning her into a beautiful bride.

"You can finish later, Margret, after you help me get her dressed."

Mother shook out her gown, draping it over an arm, before grasping Sophrona's elbow. "What's wrong with your mind, child? Stand up, if you want this dress on you."

Gathering one side of the skirt as she held the bodice, Mother waited until Margret took hold of her side, before carefully settling the gown over Sophrona's head and guiding her arms through. Mother descended on her, plucking and pulling until the gown fit perfectly.

Sophrona arranged the skirt before sitting. Mrs. Holmes moved in, her fingers back on Sophrona's hair.

"I'm almost done, just need to place this curl." She wove the ribbon through Sophrona's hair. "She's lovely, Fenella."

"I do believe you're right, Margret. She's the prettiest thing I've ever seen."

Sophrona dabbed at her eyes. "I didn't sleep well last night, Mother, thinking about after the wedding. I'll go to my husband's home, but don't know what to expect." She shook her head, lips tight. "I'm out of sorts about this."

"Don't worry about anything, especially tonight." Mother took her hand. "After that, it's all what you make of it."

Mother wiped her nose. "You love Thomas. Women have married for a lot less than that. Besides, if I'm any judge of character, you're getting a man who'll take as good care of you as we ever have."

The significance of loving Thomas stirred her heart. Sadness at leaving her family home seeped through. She batted her lashes holding back the moisture. A sweet ache filled her senses, softening her loss. She stiffened as her heart beat out that age-old rhythm, 'It's time to leave.' Swallowing her fears, she glided past memories of her childhood, in readiness to embrace her womanhood in a home of her own.

She blinked when Mrs. Holmes tucked in a final hair, stepping back.

Mother placed the strand of pearls around Sophrona's neck. "You wear the pearls better than I ever did. Your beauty breaks my heart." Mother sniffed. "Come, Margret, her father's waiting."

Sophrona stood to hug her mother. "I love you."

She sat back down after they left, to wait for Father.

* * *

Thomas looked up as Sophrona's mother motioned at the head of the stairs, the woman standing beside her.

Sophrona's father climbed the steps, gave his wife a kiss on the cheek, then disappeared down the hallway. The woman followed Mrs. Hackett's descent.

Thomas turned to speak with Alexander when he heard a gasp. He pivoted toward the staircase, his breath stopping as he gazed at his bride.

Peter braced Sophrona's left side, as if waiting for some unspoken signal. Then father and daughter extended a leg, taking the first step on their descent from the top.

She wore a royal blue gown, the scooped neckline ringed with pale blue lace, her skirt gently swaying. Dark gleaming hair swept away from her brow, piled high on her head. A cherry red ribbon weaved through, the ends gently bounced.

Thomas's breath caught in his throat—much too beautiful for him to marry. Inadequacy filled his thoughts before air returned to his lungs, bringing back confidence.

Halfway down, at the center landing, where the staircase pivoted right to spill into the room, her father paused. It seemed to last forever. Hairs on his neck tingled. Had Mr. Hackett changed his mind about giving his daughter to wed?

Sophrona shook out her skirt with barely a twitch of her wrist. Taking a fresh hold, she raised it just above her blue slipper for the final descent. Her father guided her down, bringing his lovely daughter to Thomas, who shifted forward.

Gripping the back of Thomas's jacket, to restrain his forward movement, Alexander quickly moved up to one side of him as Reverend Craddock moved to the other.

Her father stopped in front of Thomas, releasing her arm, as the two ministers stepped back. Thomas wiped a hand down his jacket, as he pivoted around to Sophrona's side, her father stepping away. The two faced the ministers, Thomas' heart pounding.

Reverend Craddock held a worn copy of The Common Book of Prayer, cleared his throat, and began. "Dearly beloved friends, we are gathered together here in the sight of God, and in the face of His congregation, to join this man and this woman in holy matrimony."

Mr. Craddock paused, while Thomas' attention focused on Sophrona. Shifting his weight to his left leg, Thomas waited. Surely her father had not set up a cruel joke for him.

Suddenly, he realized the reverend's stern look was directed at him.

"Wilt thou have this woman to thy wedded wife, to live together after God's ordinance in the holy estate of matrimony? Wilt thou love her, comfort her, honor and keep her, in sickness and in health? And forsaking all others, keep thee only to her, as long as you both shall live?"

"I…" Thomas began. He swallowed and tried again. "I will."

He smiled when Sophrona replied, "I will."

Reverend Craddock said, "Who giveth this woman to be married to this man?"

Mr. Hackett replied, "I do."

Alexander moved forward, palm up, and Thomas plucked out a wide golden band gleaming the color of soft butter. A heart shaped ruby, raised just above the metal, glowed red as blood. His hand shook so; he almost dropped the band before he placed it on her finger. It seemed the room took a collective breath, but maybe just him.

Reverend Craddock read more prayer from his book. After ending with, "Amen", he nodded to Alexander, who took the right hands of Thomas and Sophrona, joining them together. Alex said, "Those whom God hath joined together, let no man put asunder."

Reverend Craddock stated, in a loud voice, "I pronounce that Thomas and Sophrona be man and wife, together."

Joy settled over Thomas as he kissed his bride. Immediately the men converged on him—the women on his new wife.

A lone fiddle sounded in the background. The guests moved aside as Thomas, in his gold jacket over white shirt with black pantaloons, grasped his bride in a commanding hold. He guided her around to the music, weaving through the clusters of smiling guests, her skirt swirling with each dip or turn. As the song ended, he kissed her cheek before escorting her to the side.

Musicians joined the fiddle player, bringing "The White Cockade" to a foot-tapping melody. Then they moved to the back yard, playing for those who wished to dance with their ladies, or only to listen.

A group gathered in the sitting room, occupying the settee, sofa, and other seating brought in for the wedding. The Sanborn twins walked toward the table with their escorts. Samuel held Mary's chair for her. When she sat, he turned, crossing the room toward Thomas, who stepped past Sophrona to meet him.

Samuel squared his shoulders.

"Only a blind man would miss Sophrona's state of joy. It's my wish the two of you enjoy many years of happiness together, with an

113

abundance of heirs." Samuel looked down before he again met Thomas's eyes. "I do hope you won't hold anything against me. Affection for Sophrona overpowered my ability to think rationally. I see that now."

Thomas nodded as he reached to shake Samuel's hand. He did not say he understood Samuel's position. That he once thought himself the loser, until the Lord intervened, giving Sophrona to him.

When Sophrona approached, Samuel took her hand. "May the Lord our God bless your union."

Samuel started to turn when she reached out, grasping the sleeve of his blue coat. Moving up, she stood on tiptoes, kissing his cheek.

"It wasn't that you're not handsome enough, or a fine enough gentleman, or any of the other things—you're all of those. I already loved Thomas. No one could replace him."

Samuel nodded as he turned in Mary's direction.

Emotion clutched Thomas's heart. If he had lost her to Samuel, would he be as gracious? He placed an arm around his bride's waist, pulling her close to him, grateful for the privilege of touching her in such a manner.

"I'm thirsty," Thomas said. He led her to the common room, where servants worked hard preparing their wedding feast. A sideboard, along with tables, held several roasted turkeys, platters of vegetables, breads, and sweets. A servant carved sections from a roasted hog. Another turned the spit that held a beef roasting in the cook place.

Thomas discovered their cake. He started to pinch off a small portion when Sophrona smacked his hand. After he groaned, she handed him a morsel of the cake, opening her mouth for the bite he offered.

Sophrona turned to a passing servant. "My husband is thirsty for water."

A new woman, slate-gray tilted eyes and traces of silver in her dark hair, brought him a goblet. He took a sip of cool water, drinking it all.

The woman said, "It's your wedding day, sir. You mustn't neglect your guests."

Thomas took his wife's hand as he moved toward the door, the taste of their cake lingering in his mouth. He thought about the unusual servant's soft voice, almost quivering with hesitation as she dared admonish the master's new son-in-law.

The afternoon passed so fast, Thomas didn't know where it went. Peter came in for his daughter, taking her outside to dance. Just when Thomas thought he might reach her before Gerald did—he stumbled. He looked up to see Sophrona's back moving toward him, her blue gown swaying.

The male seemed familiar, arm stretched up to hold her hand, guiding her, his shoulder working back and forth. When he swung her around, it was Isaac. His head almost came to her neck. He stood by Gerald, watching his youngest brother move faster as he danced Sophrona past.

"What's he doing, Thomas? Doesn't he realize the music stopped?" Gerald heaved a sigh.

"I don't know, but he has to give her up. The next dance belongs to me." When Isaac passed by, Thomas stepped toward them, but his little brother skillfully guided Sophrona around.

"When they come back through, Thomas, you grab Isaac while I take Sophrona. Then you'll get your dance."

"All right, but I'd only do this for my favorite brother-in-law."

"I'm your *only* brother-in-law."

Thomas smiled as he gestured toward Gerald in conversation, as if they didn't see Isaac leading Sophrona around the back yard's circle. When they drew close, Sophrona's laughter filled the air, her arm resting on one of Isaac's shoulders as she said, "Oh, Isaac, you're far too witty for..."

Thomas stepped out, grasping Isaac's arm. At the same time, Gerald tugged Sophrona in the opposite direction, dancing her away.

"You shouldn't do that, Thomas. You're only jealous that Sophrona's having fun with me." Isaac folded his arms, saying "I'm going to marry someone even prettier than your wife, one day."

"Yes, well, until you do, leave my wife alone to finish her wedding responsibilities." Thomas turned to look for Gerald.

His brother-in-law circled around twice before he stopped for Thomas, who took Sophrona's arm.

"These look lovely on you." He stood still, tracing his finger along the pearls she wore, before kissing her cheek. "Did Isaac force you to dance so long?"

Sophrona smiled. "He's charming, Thomas. He certainly knows how to command attention."

When she followed that with laughter, he joined her. They danced until the music ended.

The servants moved from the house to the yard, setting up tables to fill with platters of food. The wedding couple took a seat inside at the big table, but ate very little of their special supper. A servant girl brought the first two pieces of the wedding cake to them, before passing out saucers to the guests. The brown-sugar spice cake, filled with raisins, nuts, and bits of other fruit, tasted too good to leave.

After Thomas finished, he excused himself to go find Alexander.

"It's almost time. Did you saddle her a horse? She doesn't want a side saddle."

"Yes, I know. It's the brown mare next to your pacer. The one with the pink ribbon tied to the bridle."

Thomas laughed under his breath, wondering where his brother got the ribbon.

"I placed the lady-steps on the front porch, between the rockers. With the dress she's wearing, you'll want her to mount the mare using the steps. You should leave even earlier than planned, so she doesn't ride in the dark."

Rubbing his chin, Thomas said, "I'd use a carriage, but the only way we'll beat that posse is taking a short cut almost too narrow for a horse."

Alex nodded. "I understand your difficulty. A carriage means you get caught and brought back here. Riding a horse lets you use those trails you know so well. I say outrun that posse."

"You're a good brother, Alex. After I tell her, I'll leave by the front door." He looked over at Sophrona. "Take her to the back yard, then sneak her around the house. Try to give us time before you tell her father we're gone."

"Rest assured I'll handle this correctly."

Thomas strode back to the table. He stood by his bride, offering his arm when she started to rise. They moved from group to group, making pleasant conversation. When he spotted Alexander, he walked her away from the guests.

He bent to kiss her cheek, whispering "Go with Alex."

Thomas slipped away to the front door. He picked up the lady-steps as he crossed the porch, placing them in position.

Alexander brought Sophrona around, leaning to kiss her cheek. He clapped Thomas on the shoulder before disappearing.

She leaned into Thomas, breathing softly. He kissed her.

"We must hurry, Sophrona."

He guided her to the steps, helping her up as he held the mare. She gathered her skirt to slide across the horse, settling into the saddle. He led both horses away from the house, handing her the mare's reigns before mounting.

"Ride, Sophrona, or that wedding posse will catch us for sure. They'll take us back to your father's house for the night."

She smiled. "Remember what happened to John and Bridgette?"

"Her father managed to keep them three days before they got away." He had laughed at the time, but it was not funny now. "John complained so much, the community decided a 'wedding posse' must be agreed on, beforehand."

The thrill of the chase shot through him as he brought in his knees, spurring his pacer forward.

"Stay close to me," he called.

CHAPTER FIFTEEN

Branches disappeared as Thomas settled into the gait his pacer set, taking his new bride home.

They traveled several miles before Thomas slowed. He looked back. Sophrona held her own, hair breaking free of her wedding curls, skirt fluttering back off the horse's haunches. He reined in, stopping as she drew abreast of him.

"What is it Thomas? Why'd you slow down?"

"The sun's going down. I don't want to chance you getting hurt trying to outride that posse. Nothing's worth that."

"You shouldn't worry about me, with all my riding. Something Mother frowned on."

"I've helped capture some fast brides and grooms before, Sophrona, but this time they're after us."

"Come on, Thomas. I'll give you a good run to the…"

Hooves pounded the ground in the distance as riders grew near. Thomas reached for his wife's hand, searching her face before he made a decision.

"If you want to ride fast enough to stay up with me, let's go. I know a shortcut to get us there first."

"Thomas, you know I'm as good as Gerald, better at times."

As the sound of riders grew louder Thomas dug his knees into his horse. The pacer leaped forward. Could Sophrona really stay up with him? He glanced over his shoulder. Her body bent low, she whipped the reins, her once coifed hair billowing behind, as she

119

gained ground. Spurring his mount, he laughed into the wind. When they drew closer to the short-cut, he slowed his mount to a trot.

"Stay low as we ride through. Watch out for limbs."

The last light faded fast, the woods turning darker as they veered off the path. Shots rang out, hooves pounded the ground, but the sound faded as they rode further into the shortcut. On familiar ground, now, Thomas kneed his mount as he raised an arm, motioning Sophrona forward.

Breaking through the trees, they rode up to the barn door, where Thomas dismounted. He reached up for Sophrona, swinging her to the ground. Placing their horses inside, he took her hand, running up the slope to the house. Voice low, he gave instructions to Simon as they sprinted through the door.

The sound of pounding hooves approached the front. Simon went out to meet them. The door stood slightly ajar—Thomas's eye at the crack.

"What can I do for you, gentlemen?"

"We're waiting for the bride and groom. Gonna take them right back to her father," a man said, as several guffawed, their horses' front hooves pawing the ground.

Simon held the light up high, his feet spread wide.

"The master of the house has already arrived. He won't be disturbed tonight." Simon scraped the porch with a shoe. "I wish you more success with the next wedding." He scratched his head. "I just can't understand this game at all. It seems to me someone could get a mouth full of knuckles if it goes too far."

The lead rider shook his head. "Don't you know anything? We don't interfere with their wedding to provoke trouble. If the couple gets caught, it prolongs the festivities. They even get a head start toward their destination. Although, I must say, Brother Alex bought Thomas some time, fooling us into thinking they hadn't left yet."

Simon shook his head. "Yeah, well I don't know…"

120

"How did they get past us?" someone said. "I still don't understand that."

A heated discussion broke out among the group, until someone else spoke up.

"Never mind that. Let's go back. The evening's still young. There's ladies, music, food—all waiting for us!"

The group roared their approval. Hoof beats, horses neighing, and men's shouts faded into the night.

"Simon, our horses are in the barn, still saddled."

"No need to worry. I'll take care of that. However, Master Cyrus said I must show you to your room when you arrive." Simon started toward the stairs.

"Are you daft? I know where my room is."

"Where's that, Thomas?"

"Same place it's always been."

"No. At your father's insistence, I changed things around. Come see if you approve." This time Simon went up the stairs.

Taking Sophrona's hand, Thomas followed.

They reached the landing at the top, where a stuffed chair sat next to a small table. Thomas made the turn toward his room at the end of the hallway.

"That room now belongs to your father. You and your wife shall reside in the master's old room."

Simon walked the other direction, stopping to push open a door as he spoke. "Is there anything more you wish tonight?"

Thomas gripped the doorframe, leaning in to look. "No, Simon, thank you. I'm grateful for your work. This room's much bigger than my old one."

"Well, then, I shall rub down the horses before pitching some fodder. I do believe everyone's coming home late tonight." Simon turned and left.

"Come see what Father's given us."

Patricia Reece

Sophrona poked her head in next to his. "Oh Thomas, this room's perfect for the rest of our lives."

Thomas laughed as he urged her inside, closing the door with his foot. The bedstead, with four tall posts Father helped him carve from the trunks of yellow pine trees, sat catty-corner in the room.

"This is lovely—the colors so bright. It'll keep us warm, even on the cold winter nights." Sophrona stroked the bed cover. "Who pieced this together, Thomas?"

"Well, I haven't seen it before, but..." He flipped the quilt. "Here's our mark. It's one of Aunt Elizabeth's. She made it. See?" When she leaned in to look at the quilt, he pulled her down to sit on the bed.

"Never mind the Craighead mark on the quilt, my beautiful wife. Look at it later."

He walked over, blew out the candles and returned, sitting down on the bed beside her as she giggled. In their zeal for comfort, the covers landed down at the foot of the bed. Later, Thomas thought he heard horses ride up to the house, then voices, just before he fell asleep.

* * *

His lovely new wife flung open the curtains, as the sun peeked over the horizon. Love flowed through Thomas. Finally they were together. She came to sit by him, taking the other blue, wing-back chair.

A soft knock sounded at the door.

"Come in," he said.

The doorknob turned and the door thrust open, as a woman angled through with a tray in her hand. She set it down on a round table.

"Sir, I've brought your morning coffee."

Thomas blinked his eyes, growing more accustomed to the morning light. He recognized the servant from the previous day in the Hacketts' common room. He looked into her slate grey eyes, stormy as the deep Atlantic in winter.

"Where did you come from? I thought we left you behind."

"Oh, I don't know, sir, except I rode out with Mr. Craighead and your brothers last night." She shifted her feet, much like a young girl in trouble. "Your father indentured me to your family—a wedding surprise for your wife. He said I must take my direction from her."

The servant brought them mugs of coffee from the tray, returning to the door. "Is there anything else you want?"

"No, this will do nicely, Penelope. Thank you," Sophrona said, then looked at Thomas. "I learned her name yesterday, while you admired our wedding cake."

"Yes, Miss Sophrona." She nodded ever so slightly before turning away, pulling the door closed behind her.

"You'll need your clothes. Pretty as you look in that wedding gown, you can't wear it forever." Thomas took her hand.

"I didn't want to ride with a bag. Clothes can always wait—last night couldn't." Sophrona traced his sleeve with a finger. "I'm not the only woman in the house, now. Did you tell your father about my concern?"

Shaking his head, Thomas finished his morning drink. "Let's go down for something to eat. Simon knows how to use a fry pan."

Placing their mugs on the tray, he opened the door. She walked through, and then waited for him to lead the way down the stairs. In the common room, Thomas seated her at the trestle table. He filled their mugs and took a seat, as they waited for breakfast.

Simon finished, then brought a platter of fried ham to the table. He followed up with a plate of sweet breads. Bringing over a bowl of peaches, he addressed Sophrona.

"Your mother sent a carriage with some clothes. Your new servant collected them and she's taking them to your room."

"Well, that settles the clothing for now," Thomas said.

123

Penelope returned, moving to a sideboard, where she sliced up a small cake, while Simon set down pewter plates, with cutlery, before filling coffee mugs. Penelope set the platter on the table along with a stack of saucers. After they filled their plates, Thomas lowered his head.

"Thank You for this food, Lord, and for Sophrona, in Christ Jesus' name."

After they ate, Thomas reached for two saucers, filling them with slices of cake. "Where ever did this come from? I didn't know they had wedding cake left over."

Penelope cleared her voice. "Mrs. Hackett said to make a smaller cake, as well, yesterday morning. She sent it along with me last night."

"Simon. Penelope." Thomas smiled. "Please have some cake with us."

"I must go help your father when I'm finished." Simon took a slice and began to eat.

"I'll walk down to the barn with you, to hitch up the small wagon. I'm moving the rest of Sophrona's things from her father's house to mine." His heart pounded at that thought as he turned toward Sophrona. Her cheeks held a spray of pink as she looked down.

"Go change your clothes while I'm at the barn. Don't want your father to think you're returning home." He gave her his most charming smile.

CHAPTER SIXTEEN

September 1st, 1757
Baltimore County, Maryland

Thomas whipped the reins, pushing his horses hard as he drove the freight wagon up the Patapsco River Road, headed toward home.

He had continued freighting the past two years, preparing for a partnership in his father's business. He would take good care of his wife and their future children, the next generation of Craigheads born in the new world.

After supper one evening, Sophrona took him aside for some news.

"It's possible I'm with child. We must be sure before you say anything."

Thomas pulled her close, his heart hammering in his chest.

"When—how long before you know?"

"I'm not sure, but I hear the midwife, Claudia, is good." She rested her head against his chest.

Several weeks later, she led him out onto the porch. "Tell it now if you like. I'm definitely with child."

"I'll shout it to the world," he said, as his wife laughed softly.

Thomas thought his father might do hand stands around the barn when he told him.

"Finally, Lad. I've longed to hear this good news."

With the coming birth of their first child still on his mind, Thomas guided the freight wagon off the road toward the barn. He spotted Sophrona running from the house, chestnut brown hair streaming in the breeze, her long skirt swaying. He wondered how she kept from tripping. She shouldn't run.

"Thomas," she called, "I'm so happy you're home."

She rushed into his arms as he stepped down from the wagon. Taking her by the waist, he danced her around, skirt swinging as they turned, until he finally stopped to kiss her.

"I love you so much. Every turn of the wagon's wheels I thought about you."

She stood in front of him, his hands still low on her waist.

"You must be hungry." She clutched his arm. "Remember what today is?"

He reached up to scratch his head. "Is it a special day?" He ducked when she swung with her free hand, then grabbed her arm, pulling her close.

"Sophrona, love of my heart. Forget today's our second anniversary? We married the first of September, seventeen fifty-five. I'll never forget that day."

"You'd better treat me nice, Mr. Craighead. I've cleaned all day—even made a special anniversary supper."

A quick hand movement tossed the hair off her neck as she continued. "I meant to say, we shall eat in our room, before you flustered me with a kiss. Think how romantic, Thomas, just the two of us."

Simon approached. "Go on to the house. I'll take care of the team. When Alex returns from church, I'll warm his supper."

Thomas shifted position. "What's he doing at the church?"

"Something to do with discussing his seminary work with the minister traveling through." Simon shrugged. "You'll need to ask him if you want more. I've told you everything I know."

Thomas nodded.

Taking his wife's hand, he pulled her close, placing an arm around her shoulders. They went directly into the common room. His mouth watered at the good smells.

"Hurry up with the food. I missed you while I was away."

"Shush, Thomas, Penelope might hear you." Her face turned a bright pink.

Thomas went to his father's office to check the freighting sheet, still smiling at her modesty. Had she forgotten they were married? When he returned, Sophrona started toward the stairs, her hands full.

"Allow me. I'm going upstairs." After he took the articles she turned away.

Thomas went up to their room, placing the items on the table before he changed shirts. Just as he finished, Penelope arrived.

"Will you help me move the table closer to the window, sir? Sophrona really shouldn't move anything heavy after trip..." The servant dropped her head as she grasped the table.

Taking the other side, Thomas moved the table into position. Then he crossed his arms.

"I want to know what happened to my wife, Penelope."

She looked up at him, her back toward the window still grasping the table edge.

"Miss Sophrona hurried down the stairs this morning, already preparing food for your return. Her skirt caught on her heel, causing her to miss the last step. She fell the rest of the way, landing on her hands and knees." Fear in her eyes, she said, "I beg you, don't tell her I told. She didn't want you to know, since she already felt better."

"Don't worry about getting in trouble for this. If anything else happens, I expect to know about it immediately." He stepped closer, placing a hand on her arm. "Do you understand me?"

"Yes, Master Thomas." She draped the cloth over the table, laying down napkins and cutlery.

127

Sophrona entered the room, setting down their plates as Penelope walked toward the door.

"Penelope, please carve the turkey." Thomas moved away from the window, hands clasped behind him. "When you're through I'd like you to bring it up, along with the rest of our food. We'll also want a pitcher of cold water."

"Yes, Master Thomas," she said, eyes lowered.

After she left, Thomas went to Sophrona, cupping her face in his hand.

"Do you feel all right?" When she nodded, he said, "Don't scold Penelope for telling me—it was a slip of the tongue. Never again encourage a servant to keep anything from me concerning you. You do understand how important you are?"

"Yes, Thomas. I'm sorry. I just didn't want you to worry about anything your first night back home. Please don't get angry with me. I just can't bear the thought of it."

"I'm not angry. I love you so much it troubled me. Do you feel well?" When she nodded, he said, "Let's eat our anniversary supper. Then, I have something for you."

Penelope returned with a tray. His wife sat while the servant placed the platters of food on the table.

Sophrona rose, starting toward the door. He took her arm, leading her back to the chair. "No, Sophrona. You've worked too hard already."

Penelope brought up a water pitcher with glasses. Leaving, she pulled the door closed.

Thomas took Sophrona's hand as he bowed, saying, "We're grateful You provide for all our needs, Lord, in Christ Jesus' name."

Later, Penelope returned to remove the dishes.

After lighting candles, Thomas closed the drapes. He pulled a package from his freighting bag, untied the string and handed it to his wife.

"It's so beautiful." Her eyes gleamed as she stroked the material. "This feels like silk, Thomas. We can't afford that."

"Let me worry about what we can afford. You'll look lovely in that shade of green."

He laid the material aside when she came to him, kissing her before he rose to blow out the candles. Later in the evening, when she lay beside him, breathing softly, he shifted onto one side. Placing an arm under his head, he grew drowsy. Thoughts of his mother invaded that place in his mind protected from intrusion. He felt the sting of her absence.

Our child is coming, Mother. If only you had lived...

CHAPTER SEVENTEEN

Thomas fought the intrusion into his sleep, as a hand shaking him increased in intensity, breaking up the dream of a son running in the fields, through tall stalks of corn growing golden shocks.

A distant voice penetrated his foggy mind, the tone urgent.

"Help me."

He tried to clear his head. He'd dozed off the previous evening, relishing thoughts of being home with his wife, of their celebration together. Even the sadness over his mother missing from their lives...

"Get up, Thomas." Sophrona stood over him, her hand slowing.

In a corner of his mind, the green bolt of cloth he had brought her still billowed. He sat up, shaking out the wisps.

"What's wrong, Sophrona? What is it?"

"Thomas, get the physician—no, Claudia's closer."

In the soft candlelight, Sophrona bent over clutching her middle.

"It's the babe, Thomas. Hurry. Something's wrong."

He stumbled from the bed, slipping in a patch of something wet and sticky. Grabbing at a chair, he crashed to the floor. Throwing on clothes, then shoes, he rushed from the bedroom toward the staircase.

"Da...Da?"

In breeches only, Simon met him halfway up the stairs, a candle-lamp in his hand. "He's not here, Master Thomas. May not get home til day after tomorrow."

Fear swirled in his mind when he remembered. Father took a freight wagon up Patapsco Road to York, for a load of goods. Isaac accompanied him.

"Sophrona needs a physician. Quick, wake up Alex. Tell him to go after Doc Thompson. Hurry! I'm riding for the midwife."

Thomas swerved around Simon, shoes hitting the stairs two steps at a time. Down on the first floor, he hurried to Penelope's room, pounding on the door.

"Go upstairs fast. Sophrona needs you."

He passed through the front door, rushing toward the barn. Bridling the Narragansett in the dark stall, he bare-backed him toward the midwife's dwelling in the light of the approaching full moon.

* * *

Sophrona heard Thomas speaking to Simon, then nothing except the sound of shoes on the staircase. Would Claudia arrive soon enough to stop the bleeding?

She carefully rubbed her stomach, curled up on her side, facing the door. How much more pain could she take?

The door creaked as Penelope entered, face drawn tight with fear.

"Master Thomas sent me up."

Penelope stepped closer, peering into Sophrona's face, then at her bed clothes. She twirled around, hurrying toward the door.

"Don't move, I'll be right back."

She returned with padding she handed to Sophrona, and a bucket of water. After setting the lamp closer, she stooped down, thoroughly cleaning the floor before setting the pail by the door. "I may have cleaned it before it soaked into the wood."

"What if the babe dies, Penelope? What will I do?" She pushed hair away from her face, tears in the corners of her eyes, as she

131

reached for Penelope's hand. "Why didn't I listen yesterday—lay down like you said I should?"

"Don't say that, Sophrona. It's not your fault." Penelope patted her hand. "We don't know what's going to happen, yet."

"But what if my babe dies?" Her stomach hurt so much, Sophrona had trouble thinking. "No! Thomas may never forgive me for my ignorance. He'll leave me."

"It's going to be alright." Penelope spoke softly as she rubbed Sophrona's back. "Women lose babies, but they still continue. Thomas won't leave you for an accident. He loves you." She put her arm around Sophrona's shoulder. "Let's just wait to see what Claudia thinks."

* * *

Thomas reached the midwife's house. Light from the moon reflected off the roof, down the walls, except where the eaves cast a shadow. Sliding off the horse, he ran up the steps onto the porch. Strength surged in his arms as he pounded on the door.

Breath coming in gulps, he pounded the door again, the frame shaking under his fist.

"Who's there?" a voice called out. "It better be important. I just got to sleep."

"Quick, Claudia. Sophrona needs you. It's the babe." Hurrying back down the steps, he mounted to wait for her.

When she got to the horse, he reached out with his right forearm. She grabbed on, jumping in the air as he swung her up. Her hand scrabbled for a hold as her leg crossed over behind him, the birthing bag slamming against his thigh.

When they arrived at the house, he swung a leg over the horse's neck, jumping down. She tossed the bag toward the porch just before he grasped her waist, letting her down.

"Run. Run," he urged her, climbing back on, kneeing the stallion toward the barn, where he removed the bridle. Closing the barn door, he broke toward the house, air cooling the sweat on his brow and under his arms.

* * *

Relief washed over Sophrona when Claudia entered the room. It was going to be all right, now.

"We'll need bedding, Penelope," Claudia said. "Would you get some?"

Sophrona plunged her fists down and gripped the bed-covers, screaming as tears coursed down her cheeks. Writhing in pain, she screamed again. The room went black. She came to as Penelope left, closing the door.

Claudia pushed back the soaked covers. "Did this come on while you slept?"

Sophrona shook her head. "Going down the stairs yesterday, I fell. The pain didn't last long. It didn't feel like I needed to get off my feet."

Penelope returned with the bedding. Claudia touched her shoulder. "We'll need more covers for the bed. Hot water, too. And cups."

Sophrona screamed, holding her stomach.

"Hurry." Claudia opened the door for her helper. "Bring a bucket, too."

"When she returns, Sophrona, I'll fix some tea that'll help." Claudia rummaged in her bag, pulling out packets.

"Am I going to lose the babe?" Sophrona drew her knees up, moaning.

Claudia moved to Sophrona's feet, removing the covers from her legs. "Don't bear down." She gently tugged on Sophrona's legs straightening them out. "I can't tell you the outcome. Just don't know, but I'll do my best."

Penelope returned. Setting the other things down, she placed a teapot with two cups on the table.

Filling a cup, Claudia pinched some herbs from the packets, grinding the substance between her fingers into the hot water.

"Soon as it's cooled, Penelope, hold the cup for her. Be sure she drinks it all."

A few minutes after Sophrona finished her tea, Claudia instructed Penelope to prop up her legs. She barely felt the movement. Their voices sounded far away as cramps slowly knotted her stomach.

* * *

Thomas arrived on the upstairs landing, the midwife already inside their bedroom, no doubt. Sophrona screamed. When she stopped, he heaved a sigh. Maybe it was over. Then she screamed again.

Penelope came around him, headed to the room with a stack of bedding on her arm.

"Don't be troubled, sir. Claudia's the best around."

She continued on inside, closing the bedroom door.

It seemed like hardly any time passed when Penelope rushed out of the room, on past him, down the stairs. She returned with a steaming teapot, the bail of a bucket hooked over the elbow of one arm. She gripped bedding in the crook of the other, with mugs twined on the fingers of her hand.

"What's the bucket for?"

She glanced at him, eyes distant, but did not answer. He turned the latch on the bedroom door for her.

Thomas went back to the landing, taking a seat in the stuffed chair by the table. Unable to just sit there, he stood up, pacing the floor. Tears formed in the corners of his eyes, the bitter taste of dread filling his throat, coating his mouth.

Uncertainty rolled through his soul, like a slow winding stream he swam in as a boy, only deeper and biting cold. What if he lost the child, maybe his wife? Like he lost his mother and baby sister when he was six years old?

He clung to the hope that both would live, as he whispered in the silence of the second floor. "God Almighty, I beseech You for Sophrona's life. For the child's too, if You will."

His brother cleared the stairs, falling in step beside him, talking as they paced.

"It'll be a little while yet, Thomas. The physician wasn't available. He won't know to come until he gets home, but I left word. You know he's doing the work of a doctor most nights. Not like Claudia, who only expects deliveries. Be thankful she's here."

"I am, Alex. It just seems like being more attentive yesterday would have been the right thing to do, after knowing she fell. Instead, I just wanted to celebrate our anniversary and being home with her."

"You can't change what happened before you returned, Thomas. I've asked the Lord for her life as well as the babe's. If only one survives, you'll still receive an abundance of His mercy."

He nodded as Alex walked over to the chair. He needed his brother to stay with him through the trouble. Thomas drew comfort from his presence.

Penelope left the room, rushing down the stairs with an armful of soiled covers. She barely looked at him.

"All that blood doesn't necessarily mean anything," Alex said.

Thomas nodded. He hoped in this instance it was true. Claudia pushed the door open, leaning out as she motioned for him.

"I'll wait for you downstairs." His brother said as he rose.

"Come in, but remember she's been through a rough time." Claudia stepped aside for him.

He went to his wife, a wilted white spot with inflamed eyes. She lay there staring at the ceiling, a mound of straggly, dark hair spread over the pillow. He took her hand as he turned to the midwife.

"Is she going to be all right? Don't keep anything from me, Claudia."

"It didn't look good for a while, especially after the child passed. Then I got some herb tea down her that slowed the blood flow."

Along with tea cups, contents of open packets lay on the table, crushed flecks of dried herbs, obviously from Claudia's birthing bag.

"What about now?" Thomas' stomach muscles tightened.

"If she gets plenty of rest, she'll be all right." Claudia rubbed at her eyes. "I'm sorry I couldn't save the babe. For a while I wondered if your wife would live."

"It's not your fault. She took a fall, remained on her feet instead of going to bed. It wasn't anyone's fault. She just didn't know." Thomas' shoulders drooped. "Could you…I mean…what was…"

"A boy." She wiped her hands down her skirt, looking toward the floor. "When you go, take the bucket. There needs to be a proper burial for what's wrapped in the bedding."

After that, Thomas couldn't concentrate on anything else she said.

The crushing knowledge they lost their child, a son, consumed him. Wailing filled the air. He realized the sounds came from him when the hand that covered his face grew wet. He stopped crying, looking around. Claudia had slipped out of the room, leaving him alone with his wife.

He looked down when she squeezed his hand. Tears streamed down, crisscrossing a tortured face.

"I'm sorry about the babe. It's my fault…"

"You must not blame yourself. I'm so grateful to the Lord you're alive."

One of the cups held liquid. He vaguely remembered being told to hold the drink for her. Wiping her face, he held her head as she sipped the tea. After she went to sleep, he smoothed her covers, and then stooped down to kiss her cheek before leaving the room. He started slowly down the stairs, walking like an old man, each step jarring his body as the bucket clanked between the staircase, his leg and the baluster.

Through the front room window, gray fingers of dawn clawed a dark sky. Out the back door, he set the bucket in a safe place. Once in the common room, he sat with Alexander until Harold Thompson, the Baltimore Town physician, arrived with his medical bag.

"Do you still need me, Thomas? I understand you rode for the midwife."

"Sophrona's upstairs, sleeping. Claudia thinks she'll be alright."

"I was digging out a bullet from someone who almost died. I didn't know Alex came until I arrived home. Did she save the babe?"

Thomas shook his head.

The doctor looked away before he continued.

"Instead of waking her, I'll just go on home, get some sleep. I'll drop around in a day or two. If you need me sooner, come get me."

While Alexander walked the doctor to the door, Thomas sipped his coffee. When his brother returned, Thomas said, "What took you to the church, yesterday?"

"It wasn't anything, yet. At some time I'll be sent to pastor a church. Until I do, they want me to fill in for the reverend traveling to our church, when he can't be here."

"That's a blessing for our congregation, Alex. You were meant to speak about the Lord."

His brother slowly nodded, as if in thought, then left the room.

"Are you ready to eat yet?" Simon said. "There'll be food on the table before long."

Thomas shook his head. "I'm not hungry, but I'll take another mug of this."

While he waited for the coffee, he thought about the babe. It seemed lately, every conversation with Father contained something about his coming grandchild. Thomas must find a way to tell him about this.

* * *

Three days later, after Father and Isaac arrived home, he intended to tell them the news. He tried, but did not gain the courage until after supper.

"Let's go for a walk, Da. Come along with us, Isaac."

They followed him out to an area behind the barn where, in his grief, he put up a wooden fence. Opening the gate, he walked over to a small mound. A wooden spade lay on the ground.

"Sophrona lost the child, Da. That's why she's in bed, ill." Thomas dug his fingers into the palms of his hands, unwilling to show his emotions, just yet. "She suffered so much. Now she's worried that you'll be disappointed, too."

Father nodded, his eyes shining with moisture. "The Lord's decision, Lad—we must move on from here."

"I'm sorry the child died, Thomas. I wanted to be an uncle." Isaac blinked his eyes.

"A boy, Isaac, a son. One day you'll make a fine uncle."

After the three cried together, Father wiped the tears away with gnarled hands. Thomas suspected his father would never speak of it again.

* * *

Fall had returned. Almost a year since the babe died.

Sophrona stopped waking up at night from bad dreams. She no longer cried, either.

Earlier today, Thomas heard her humming while she helped Penelope prepare the oven for bread. He went in to see if she wanted to pick berries, but quietly left them working, his once lonely heart warmed with happiness by the sounds.

She found him later.

"The bread's baking. Would you like to take a stroll? There's something I want to discuss with you."

He nodded. "It's going to be a little cool, so put on something warmer."

He went to get a heavier shirt off a wooden peg. After Thomas returned, he pulled her wrap closer around her shoulders to keep her warm. Taking her hand, he led her out the front door. They walked down toward the barn, where the tall maples and oaks already turned color.

"It's a lovely day, isn't it?" She looked up at him, her face like carved ivory, and a little pink in her lips.

When Thomas nodded, they burst out laughing. At that moment his world felt whole again. He tugged on her hand, pulling her toward him.

"All right, Sophrona Craighead. What would you like, a new dress or lovely bauble? Whatever you want is yours, my lovely wife." He caressed her face with a fingertip.

"Oh, it's not what I want from you at all, Mr. Craighead." Her voice grew husky. "I'm with child, Thomas. You're going to be a father sometime in February or March."

He drew in a sharp breath. "Are you sure…I mean …it's not a mistake or something?" His heart swelling with happiness; he could not breathe as he waited for her answer.

"There's absolutely no mistaking my condition. I'm with child."

* * *

The days whirled past as Sophrona's mood grew brighter, her laughter filling the house. Thomas breathed easier when the first two weeks passed with nothing to change her progress.

One evening Alexander came to the common room, taking a seat at the trestle table where Thomas sat with their father, discussing a new cradle they wanted to build.

"I'm afraid you two must do this without me. The Presbytery in Philadelphia is in discussion over sending me to the Virginia wilderness, to get some experience for the pulpit. I'll travel to

Augusta County, and also Bedford County, to learn under your cousin Alexander, Father."

"Yes, that's where he's at—but you'd better be ready to learn his ways. Our clan came by way of Ireland, but we're Scots through and through. He won't be giving way much, so be prepared to bend like a young sapling before maturity sets in."

Alex nodded. "I'm going near there to visit Aunt Elizabeth and Uncle Jonah, before committing to the Presbytery."

"Well then, better leave before the snow flies, or take a chance on finding yourself in a bit ah trouble." Father rose, draining the coffee from his mug before leaving the room.

Thomas turned toward his brother. "Too bad we're settled here. Sophrona would love to move that way, but Peter will never hear of it. Not with a grandchild on the way. Besides, there'll be no help for Father if both of us leave."

"Thomas, Isaac's coming into young manhood." Alexander shook his head. "Besides, he'd rather be freighting than getting the fine education our father's providing."

"I'm already promised a partnership with Father. I don't see any way to move, Alex. Besides, I don't want to go. I don't want anyone but Father teaching my child those things he needs to know."

"Already know it's a boy, do you, Thomas? Be up early. I'm leaving before dawn."

"I'll be up—but wish I'd known before now."

Alex gave a good natured laugh as he left the table.

Thomas followed him out to the front porch where Father sat. Would this child be a male? Maybe grow into a strong young man to help him in later years?

CHAPTER EIGHTEEN

Baltimore County, Maryland
September, 1758

Thomas answered a knock at the front door. A freighter the family knew handed him a message for Father. Thomas turned it over, recognizing his brother's handwriting. The family eagerly waited to hear from Alex. Father would want this right away.

"Care for something hot to drink—maybe a bite to eat?"

The big man adjusted his cap. "I could use a mug of hot coffee right now. I got on the road at sunup. It's a while since I ate."

"Step inside and close the door. I'll return directly." Thomas moved aside for the man to enter, then went to find his father.

"Da, a post came from Alex." He handed it to Father before returning to lead the freighter to the common room, where he instructed Penelope.

"Be sure to give him the best we have. When he's ready to leave, you may see him out."

She nodded, reaching for the man's coat. "Yes, Master Thomas."

He joined the family in the front room. Father entered, broke the wax seal, and read the correspondence aloud.

"'Dear Father,

You'll be pleased to know I arrived safely. It was a bit of luck meeting up with the Carolina militia. We started before dawn, traveling into the evening.

I arrived at Aunt Elizabeth's hungrier for a good meal than I thought possible, but enough of that.'"

Father paused, nodded, a smile on his lips, then continued.

"'I'm taking the position under your cousin, Alexander. Send your correspondence in care of Jonah Shepard, Near Hale's Ford of the Staunton River, Bedford County, Virginia.

Always your faithful son,

Alexander Craighead.'"

"I don't think he's coming back here for a while." Thomas took Sophrona's hand. "Maybe he'll return after our child's born."

Sophrona nodded. "I can't imagine him staying away."

He turned toward Isaac. "You must take over Alex's chores, like when he attended Seminary."

"You can't tell me what to do, Thomas. I'm all grown up now." Isaac looked toward their father.

"He's right about this, Isaac. You must do as Thomas says."

"Humph. Well, all right. But not because Thomas said—only because you said." Isaac refused the cookie platter Penelope offered, as he pushed away from the table.

* * *

October arrived. Splashes of molten gold, then fiery red, gave Sophrona a hint of the splendor to come. What a fine time to be with child. The trees lit up with shades of orange, then brown, too, as the leaves changed color. The joy of giving Thomas a child overcame other things in her life.

The following week, while she sat outside with Thomas and Cyrus one evening, Sophrona grew tired. She left Thomas with his father while she went up to their bedroom. Her body seemed to ache without reason. Walking to the second floor landing, she slowed at the stuffed chair but continued on to their room. Closing the door, she changed into a night shift. A sudden pain wrenched through her. Bending over, she clutched her belly.

"Ah, that hurts."

She straightened, only to bend back over in agony, tears streaming down her face. Ready to collapse, she lunged toward the nearest wingback chair.

Please Lord, not again. Thomas won't ever get over me losing this child.

One hand on the chair arm, the other on her stomach, her muscles tensed before relaxing. What had she done to herself?

"Thomas...Thomas, help me..."

If only she had not told him about the child coming in the spring. She should have waited to make sure she went past the danger before she said anything. But—he looked so happy that day as he guided her over uneven ground, walking back to the house.

A sharp pain struck deep in her abdomen. Thomas usually visited with his father for a long while. Fear surrounded her mind, squeezing her in its grip.

"Thomas. Help me. Help...help..."

She didn't know how long she continued to scream. It seemed like forever. Did she hear a noise? Straining, she listened for it again.

Please send him, Lord. If I move, I may lose the babe.

"Thomas."

* * *

Thomas sat in the middle chair, between his father's and Sophrona's empty chair. He felt restless, needing to move around.

"Good evening, Da. I'm going up to bed."

He went to the common room to pour a glass of water. What made that noise? He set the mug down, starting toward the stairs. The sound grew louder. Sophrona called for him. Halfway up the stairs she called again. Fear in her voice sent his heart pumping as he bounded the rest of the way. Reaching for the knob, he opened the door.

"What's wrong? What's the matter?" Breathing hard, he hurried across the room, placing a hand on her shoulder. "Your face is white as a snow bank."

"Help me into bed, Thomas, I…"

Grasping her hand with his, he ducked up under her arm. Pulling, he reached his other arm under her legs.

"Hang on to me."

When they reached the bed he laid her down. He stood there, unwilling to leave her alone. Fear caged his mind as his legs buckled. Why was this happening again?

"Quick, Thomas, go get Claudia. Maybe there's time she can do something. This can't—I mean, nothing's happened—not like before, when I fell."

He opened the bedroom door, breaking for the steps. His father stood at the bottom.

"Something wrong, Lad?"

"Da—Da. Send Penelope up to Sophrona. I'm going for Claudia."

The color drained from Father's face. "Right away, Lad." He whipped around, starting toward the common room.

This reminded Thomas of the last time he rode for Claudia.

He was not surprised it ended the same.

"I'm terribly sorry I couldn't stop it." Claudia wrung her hands. "She just hasn't made it past the first four or five months, yet. It's a heart breaking thing."

Thomas nodded that he understood, but losing the child was only the beginning. Her body would heal, but he did not know beyond that. She almost slipped beyond his reach after they lost the first child. Did Sophrona have enough strength to keep her sanity after losing this child?

* * *

144

Strength drained, Sophrona lay exhausted. She only found peace in sleep. Each morning after rising, Thomas came back to the room to wake her.

"Good morning, my love. Let's go down for breakfast before I starve."

Thomas took her hand, but she pulled back.

"I don't feel much like going downstairs. Ask Penelope to bring me a tray. I'll try to eat."

Why did he continue to insist she go downstairs? Didn't he know she wasn't hungry? She couldn't eat—only three weeks had passed since that terrible night. If she went down, the babe might start crying. What if she could not find her?

A strange look crossed her mother's face when Sophrona told her the child was alive. Her mother patted her hand before saying, "It's only two weeks, Sophrona. You shall have other children. You must forget about this."

But how does a mother forget the sound of her crying babe. The child was there somewhere. Sophrona heard her crying.

So tired all the time, she slipped back into an exhausted sleep. Later, after waking up, she wasn't so sure the babe lived.

The painful event haunted her. Like her eyelids springing open to morning's glaring light, she received no relief. She had watched Claudia gather the blood stained blanket, struggling to push it in the bucket. When she looked again, the bucket had disappeared.

Again her mind clouded. She heard the crying—would the babe never stop crying?

* * *

Springtime came, but the love of his life did not seem to notice. When Sophrona's midnight screams woke him, Thomas tried to comfort her. Each time, though, she responded the same, "Bring me the child, she needs me..."

145

Patricia Reece

"Sophrona, the babe didn't live. Remember, Claudia came but you lost the child."

How much longer could he continue to love her—protect her—when the constant reminders started the pain inside him all over again? Somehow, he must find a way to hang on until the Lord made changes, no matter what.

"But—I hear her crying. I look, and she's not there. I search the house over. Each time I enter a room, her crying comes from somewhere different. Why won't someone bring her to me? Why?"

While losing the child, somehow his wife grasped this babe was a daughter.

"The babe isn't here. Don't you remember we prayed about her death?"

"I hate this house! I don't know what to do." She grabbed his arm. "You must help me, Thomas."

The sound of her crying beat hard against his ears, bruising his heart again. He pulled her into his arms, rocking her exhausted body until she finally slept. Like that stray dog's pups born in their barn early last winter, her whimpering sounds continued a while. It took him a bit longer to fall sleep.

A few weeks later, when Sophrona completely stopped taking care of herself, he sought Penelope's help.

"Starting tomorrow morning, you're to help dress your mistress. Comb her hair if needed."

"Yes, Master Thomas. If only I could do something more to help her."

"Getting her ready for the day will help more than you know."

He realized something must change before she did little more than drift through the house, always needing a servant to groom her.

146

CHAPTER NINETEEN

Thomas roamed the house thinking about Sophrona. He must do something to help her, but he did not know what. He left the common room with a mug of coffee, going to the barn, where Simon helped Father.

"I'll finish up with Da."

"Then I'll start breakfast." Simon turned toward the door.

Using the bucket Simon put down, Thomas filled the feeder with grain for the oxen. He pitched fodder to the cattle and horses. Finishing, he turned around as Father pulled up a couple of three-legged stools.

"Come sit down, Lad. Tell me the problem. I see trouble buried deep in the lines a yer face."

"It's Sophrona, Da. I'm worried about her. I don't know if she'll come out of this. She has bad dreams at night."

"Yes, I hear her sometimes. I don't have an answer for you. Lord knows I wish I did." Father wiped his hands on his shirt.

"Sophrona's grown to almost hate this place. Says she hears the babe—that she looks for the child but can't find her. She doesn't understand why no one will bring..." Thomas stopped when a tortured look crossed his father's face.

"Maybe it's time you consider moving from here." Father looked away. "Don't misunderstand me, Lad. I'm not anxious for you to leave, but I don't want you to lose her."

"What do you mean lose her? Is it possible to be any more lost than she already is?" His voice cracked as he spoke the awful truth. "I mean, Sophrona, the woman I married, has not been around here for a while."

"Listen to a story, Lad. A family back in Scotland ran into trouble with a neighbor over their boundary line. The wife wanted to give in, but the husband got stubborn, determining not to let this neighbor have any of their hard earned property. She said fighting over who owned it wasn't worth the bad feelings between their families. The arguing continued. One day, around supper time, he came home to find his wife hanged herself off their front porch beam."

"This is different Da. Sophrona lost her children."

"It's true the circumstances are different, Lad, but serious difficulties can push people into making deadly decisions."

Tendrils of fear worked their way deep into Thomas' mind.

"Is the story true, then?"

Father nodded.

"Sophrona's a daughter to me. I don't want to lose her either. Lord willing, the two a you'll bring other children into the world. But take her away from the memories. Let her forget, first."

"I don't know, Da. I need to be around you—live here in my own home—the one I grew up in."

"You'd get along, Lad."

Thomas chewed on his bottom lip. "We could find a place around here. Even buy. That's what I'll look for."

Sadness crossed Father's face. "If you brought her out when you visit me, she'd hear the crying. Then what'll you do about that?"

"I'll consider moving somewhere, but only a little farther out."

Father heaved a sigh as they rose. "There's your Aunt Elizabeth, in Virginia. Your brother's there, too. You're a man now, Thomas. You must think about your wife. There's nothing to keep you away, if you want to return, but get the lass out of here for now.

"Maybe somewhere around here, Da. That'll have to do."

"Let's talk about this again in a few days, Lad. Right now, I'm hungry." Father reached to clasp his shoulder.

Was Father right? Thomas did not want to move out, but what would it hurt to talk with him some other time?

They rose and Thomas walked beside him to the house. When they entered, the smell of good food chased most other thoughts from his mind. He went upstairs for Sophrona, who had started coming down to the breakfast table some mornings.

Thomas escorted his wife to the table. After they finished eating, he must remember to speak with Penelope, while the day was still young enough for her to prepare his request.

When early evening came, he walked his wife upstairs to their bedroom, pulling out a chair for her at the round table. A few minutes later, Penelope brought a tray, with slices of cake on rose covered saucers and water in heavy glass goblets. She placed them on the table, turning toward the door with the tray in her hand.

"Don't bother coming for the dishes tonight. Pick everything up in the morning, when you arrive to assist your mistress." Thomas held the door open.

"Yes, sir."

He closed the door, going to Sophrona, who sipped water. He hoped she remembered their cake. Maybe some food in her stomach would help her sleep through the night. Sitting down, he moved her saucer closer. Then he took a bite of the cake.

"Umm, this is good. Now you take a bite. It tastes just like the cake your mother made for our wedding. You remember how good it was?" *Help her remember, Lord.*

She nodded, picked up the fork, but then laid it back down.

He took her fork, cut into the cake, bringing the bite to her mouth.

"Will you eat it for me?"

She did.

149

"What do you think about moving away from this house?"

For the first time in a while, he looked into her eyes and found a trace of his wife peering back.

"You mean move away from this house to start over again?"

He nodded.

"Oh yes, Thomas, that's a wonderful thing to do. Tell me where we are going."

"I'm still in discussion with Father about moving to Baltimore Town. He's suggesting we move out to Aunt Elizabeth and Uncle Jonah's, in Virginia. It will take time to arrange, but before the summer is over we may live somewhere else."

"Thomas, the cake's good."

She managed to eat every bite. Reaching for her water she took a big drink, wiped her small fingers across her lips, then her chin to catch what spilled, as she giggled.

"Sophrona, I want our life the way it was when we…"

She stiffened, a shadow crossing her face.

"What's wrong, dearest?"

"It's nothing, really. Just thought I heard a sound…"

He didn't insist she tell him, not really sure he wanted to know. He thought it enough that she came back to him, if only briefly. He stood, offering his arm to assist her as she rose, before going to turn down the covers. Once in bed, he pulled her to him, gently rocking her to sleep.

During the night she woke up screaming. He whispered, "Go back to sleep. Everything's all right."

When she did, he finally slept, too.

* * *

Thomas and Sophrona entered the Hackett residence, standing in the sitting room like strangers. Sophrona's mother and father approached.

"What's wrong, Sophrona? Tell me what it is," her mother said. Fear showed in her eyes.

"I...Mother, we...tell her, Thomas." He took Sophrona's hand as she moved closer to him.

"Peter, Fenella, we've come to tell you we are moving out of my father's house."

Sucking his lower lip, Peter said. "When will that be, Thomas?"

"As soon as we possibly can."

Sophrona began to cry. Her mother dried the tears with a handkerchief before hugging her daughter.

"Do sit down. When I come back, we'll talk."

Mrs. Hackett returned, setting a pitcher of water on the table, with glasses. Minutes later, Estelle brought in a tray of bread, sliced ham, a cake, and their plates.

When Sophrona filled a plate without being encouraged, her father turned toward Thomas.

"What's brought about this change? She hasn't eaten enough since losing the babies."

"Well, Peter, she's feeling better the last few days. Even gotten her appetite back, as you can see."

"Does that mean she's recovered her faculties enough to—get over it?" Peter wiped at his brow.

The surprised looks on their faces reminded Thomas that they worried about her, too.

Without being asked, he lowered his head. "Father, we're grateful for thy bounty, in Lord Jesus' name." He looked up, reaching for a plate.

"Well then, I'm sorry it's necessary to move from your father's house, Thomas." Peter glanced at his wife, then back. "We understand it's for the best. Where will you go?"

Thomas hesitated, realizing Sophrona's father expected them only to move a short distance from the family. In that instant he made a decision that pierced his heart like a blade.

"We're going to Virginia, where my aunt lives. Alex is there, also."

Sadness in his father-in-law's eyes troubled Thomas. He must stay strong, not give in to the desire to stay around their parents, no matter how much he wanted to. If he weakened, they might lose Sophrona.

Peter blinked several times. "When will you make the move?"

"We'll leave in time to reach Virginia before winter."

Looking up, lips pursed, Peter nodded.

"We're not sure about the best way to get there, with the French still in resistance, stirring up the Indians." That had also kept him from considering the move to Virginia. He set down his glass. "Although the hostilities are lessening, it's important not to travel alone. I'll need to find others going our way before we can leave."

"I understand. We do hope our daughter brings her children back for visits. You may come too, Thomas, if you insist." Peter smiled.

Ignoring his father-in-law's attempt at humor, Thomas felt immense relief that Peter did not intend to stop their move. He continued to eat, as he thought about the dangers of traveling. How would they manage to safely move to Virginia?

CHAPTER TWENTY

Before dawn, Thomas awoke to the sound of rain drumming on the shingles, as the heavens opened up, giving the earth a good rinse. The rhythmic sound of the raindrops soon lulled him back to sleep.

After he rose, then dressed, he stepped outside. Breathing deep, Thomas filled his lungs with the sweet smells wafting up from blooms and vines, as the morning sun dried out the night's rain.

After breakfast, he joined his father on an open flat wagon traveling to pick up a load of iron from Peter's brother in Baltimore Town. They not only needed the metal for freighting, but also to forge tools to use on their farm.

"I spoke with Sophrona about moving, Da. After that, she woke up only once with a bad dream."

Father nodded.

"I don't want to leave you, go away from our home, but when Sophrona realized we could move, it seemed to bring her back. You are right about this, Da. We must go. Even her parents agree."

"All right then, Lad."

Thomas cleared his throat. "We won't move to Baltimore Town or anywhere around here. You and Peter helped me realize we must move further away if she's ever to recover."

From the corner of his eye, Thomas watched his father pass a hand over his face.

"If you'll let me borrow a wagon, I'll either return it or replace it after we're settled."

153

"Just like that, you've forgotten about becoming a partner in our business. You'll not borrow a wagon, Lad. You'll take two of the best freighters we have, even two of our best teams to pull them." Father raised his chin. "You have things to move—a long way to travel. I'll not be worried your wagon's broken down on the road."

"But it doesn't make sense to me that…"

"—and, Lad, we'll fill the second wagon with every item you need to start up a new home, as well as a business. You must look at this as an extension of the Craighead freighting name." Father cleared his throat, wiping his face again.

"But we never drew up the papers for a partnership. Your generosity will only leave you shorthanded, Da."

"Well now, I recollect that we shook on it. I didn't put it in writing because we never got around to it. Besides, I planned to leave the entire business to you one day. Now, don't you begin to think I can't make it without you being here." Father pulled hard on the reins.

"No. I'd never say that. I know better." Thomas' chest swelled.

"Isaac's almost through with his education. He's smart, too. Then there's Simon, who'll most likely stay on after his indenture. Don't forget Gerald. He's family now, with you wed to his sister." Father snapped the reins, moving the wagon forward. "Maybe it's time to visit the harbor, purchase the indenture of another poor soul who survived the voyage from England. One who's looking for fairer treatment than he ever got over there."

Thomas touched his father's arm. "You're a man of honor, the way you've raised me, along with my brothers. I love you, Da, respect you. No matter where I go in my lifetime, I'll always remember what you've taught me."

They rode along, almost reaching the Hackett foundry, when he offered his father another thought.

"In the years to come, when the time grows closer for your heather to bloom, I'll want you with me and Sophrona. I know you have other sons, but I'm the eldest. I feel it's my right."

"Well, then, in time I'll expect to come join you."

* * *

They chinked the wagons tighter than their neighbor's rock fence, as everything needed to build a house went in the newest of the smaller wagons, which provided a seat for Sophrona next to the driver. Their furniture from both sides of the family filled the larger Dutch freight wagon. The teams came from the best in their barn, newly shod.

"I insist on eight of our most powerful horses to pull that largest wagon," Father said. "At least two of them will be mares. You'll also need six horses to pull the smaller one. You must include two young brood-mares, for breeding."

"That'll take your stable down considerably." Thomas shook his head.

"The Lord's good to us," Father said. "There's more business than I can handle. Me and Isaac will travel to York. We'll pick up new wagons to replace the ones you're taking. I might order a large Conestoga if they don't have one already built."

"That may take a while to get, Da. What'll you do until then?"

"We'll get along with the smaller wagons until it's built. Business keeps going like this, we may even need more drivers." Father dragged fingers through his hair.

"All right, then, we're all loaded. We'll stay with Aunt Elizabeth for as long as we must, but I still need to earn money to buy land for the spring crop. If that happens, we'll fell the trees for a house, then after that the barn, along with a freighting shed."

"What'll you do if that doesn't happen?" Father said.

155

Thomas scratched his head. "I'll just put out a small crop on their land to raise our own food, at least. Maybe even a small cash crop. I believe Uncle Jonah will let me do that."

"There's still a few days to think about this, Lad. In the meantime, let's go get something to eat."

Thomas walked inside with his father, going directly to the common room. Sophrona helped with the cooking. He took a place at the trestle table where she brought him coffee.

"The days sure are lovely," Sophrona set a mug in front of him. "I can hardly wait till we leave for our new home."

"I'm still looking for a man to drive the smaller wagon." Thomas shifted in his seat as she placed her hand in his. He cupped it with his other hand. "We can't start our journey to the wilderness until that happens, and it may take some time to find that person."

Sophrona removed her hand to grasp his arm. "Gerald came in to see me after you left, when he picked up a load. He said Father got someone who'll drive for you."

"Are you sure you didn't misunderstand him?" Thomas reached for his mug.

"No, I heard him correctly. I'm not daft. Gerald said the man's coming here day after tomorrow. He said we must get ready to leave early that morning." Sophrona took his hand.

He looked up to see Penelope nod her head in agreement.

"Did you hear that, Da?" Thomas said when his father came back in. "It looks like we'll leave in two days. It's good you helped us load the wagons."

Father nodded as he took a seat.

After the food went on the table, Father said, "Isaac, you may ask the blessing."

They bowed their heads as his little brother said, "Lord bless this food, in Jesus' name."

Later, after they'd eaten, Father found Thomas on the porch with Sophrona.

"Lad, come join me in the office. There are a few things I'd like to discuss." Father went inside.

Thomas rose, offered Sophrona his arm, then held the door. "I'll join you upstairs soon as we're finished."

Thomas went into the office, where he took a seat. Father picked up a paper off his desk, handing it to him. Thomas recognized Penelope's indenture.

"What's this, Da?"

"It seems Penelope doesn't want to stay here after Sophrona leaves. She found me after supper to ask if you'd take over her indenture. She may go if you're willing. That's the reason I sought her indenture in the first place—for Sophrona." Father paused to nod. "Now she's so attached to your wife she'd be no use here. Shall you provide for her the next three years, then agree after that to send her off with provision?"

"Yes, I'll see to that, but I must speak with Sophrona. Penelope will easily find work out where we're going."

They sat there for a while until Father finally broke the silence.

"A while back, I sent your aunt a message through some Virginia militia. I thought you'd probably decide to go to Virginia, so I asked your Uncle Jonah to look around for at least a hundred acres of good land, close to them."

"I haven't earned the money, yet, to pay for land." Thomas scratched his head. "I must set up the business and get contracts to haul freight before receiving any pay."

"Let me speak, Lad. I'm aware of the problem. You'll have funds to purchase the land when you arrive. I haven't divided our business equally, or paid anywhere near what you're worth these last few years. You'll get more than enough to secure your future when you leave here. You've rightfully earned it."

157

Thomas nodded, swallowing hard, overcome by his father's generosity.

"I'm tired. Let's go up to bed, Lad. We'll talk again tomorrow."

When they rose, Thomas embraced his father. Blowing out the candles, they walked to the stairs.

The next morning, after breakfast, Thomas found Sophrona in their room folding clothes.

"We're leaving tomorrow," he said. "Make sure you include everything."

"I've gathered what's going. Is there something I've forgotten?" Sophrona moved to a chair.

Thomas cleared his throat. "That depends on whether you want Penelope to go or stay here."

"But Penelope isn't in our servitude, so that's not my decision to make."

"Yes, it is."

Sophrona giggled as she rose from the chair. "Oh me, are you sure?"

As Thomas nodded, he smiled at her laughter—so pure, like sunshine.

"I do want her to move with us. May we tell her?"

Thomas took her arm and they went downstairs, where they found Penelope.

"I've decided to take on your indenture, Penelope, if that's what you want."

Happiness surged through Thomas when Penelope twirled around, a smile on her face.

"Yes. I want to go, sir. Don't know what I'd do without Miss Sophrona." She stepped closer to her mistress.

"Be ready to travel by morning, then. Make sure there's enough provision for you as well. It's a long way to Virginia."

"I'll ready my things and help Simon with the foodstuffs we'll need. The Lord bless you, Master Thomas."

Thomas nodded as he turned toward his wife, suppressing a smile. Penelope patted Sophrona's hand before she hurried away.

He took his wife's hand. "I want you to come outside with me."

"Where, Thomas? Where are we going?"

"Out to our children's graves, Sophrona. We cannot leave without you making at least one visit to their final resting place."

"I don't think so. I'm not ready yet." She attempted to pull away, but he held on as he urged her toward the door.

CHAPTER TWENTY-ONE

Dread settled on Sophrona as she struggled against her husband walking her out toward the graveyard. Her voice barely above a whisper, she asked, "Why today, Thomas? Why? I don't want to see..." She placed a hand on her stomach, her head growing light.

"Because it's the right thing to do. They were our children. We'll soon be gone from here." Thomas tugged on an arm, moving her forward.

"No." She pulled back. "Maybe tomorrow."

He didn't reply, as he urged her on through the gate.

At the far end of the graveyard, near a large white oak, two tombstones marked the final resting place of Thomas's mother and the baby that took her life. A trodden-down path led toward two large rocks on the near side of the tombstones where, off to one side, a maple sapling grew.

The graves in front of those rocks seemed hardly longer than the length of her forearm. The ground in front of the first one had sunken deeper. That must be her son's, the second one her daughter's? Her mind swirled briefly like a cloud moving through before it cleared.

"Turn loose of me. I'm going back." She pulled hard, but Thomas held on.

She had managed to build a safe spot inside her thoughts. She told herself the children went away. That soon she must leave here, too. Now that refuge quivered, threatening to collapse. She could not let that happen—not strong enough yet. Where would she run to hide when the truth shook her mind like a raging storm?

After Thomas turned her loose, she collapsed, falling on her knees in front of her son's grave. She had learned to deny her feelings—even came to embrace the icy sleeve that enveloped her soul.

"God help me, I cannot go on…"

A warm wind blew through, caressing her face and touching her neck. Much time had passed since she allowed herself to feel anything soothing, even from the Lord. The fear that came when reality broke through stunned her.

Before she scrambled to protect that safe refuge, it shattered; much like a carelessly placed foot might crack the first layer of ice on a shallow stream. Golden sunlight now warmed her body as she sobbed into her hands, the pain not quite as bad as she expected.

She rocked back on her heels. "Lord God, You remembered me and I shall always be thankful to You."

Thomas reached down and grasped her hand, helping her up. She brushed tears from her eyes before gathering the skirt of her brick-red dress to shake off the debris. She nestled in her husband's arms, unable to believe the robin's egg blue of the sky overhead. She nearly forgot the sound of a bird singing from a tree, the feel of the wind moving her hair.

"Let's go inside, Sophrona. You need to rest for a while." Thomas leaned down to kiss her.

She took his arm. "Yes. I'll lie down before supper."

* * *

The family gathered at the table for their evening meal. Father lowered his head. "Lord, we're grateful for Your provisions. I ask guidance for Thomas as he moves his family to their new home, in Jesus Christ's name."

Thomas took what he wanted from the roasted turkey platter before passing it on. Part way through the meal he stopped eating. Not only the final evening meal together, but this was the last night with Father in his childhood home. Tomorrow they left his family—Sophrona's, too. She seemed quite content with the decision, even happy. Thomas did not embrace contentment or happiness, but wondered if he would ever find it within himself to do so.

"You'll be at your Aunt Elizabeth's by the middle of August," Father said, "if everything goes alright. That'll give you time to clear a field large enough for yer crop, come spring."

"Soon as we arrive I'll post you a message."

Father grunted as he looked down.

After supper, Thomas went to the porch. Sighing, he slumped into a straight back chair as the red glow from the sunset faded. When the stars twinkled like brilliant bits of jewel scattered through the dark sky, Thomas' chest tightened. Since almost before remembrance, his day ended watching the sun set in the western sky. First from Mother's lap, before she died, then from Father's. Finally, he grew to appreciate the view from his own chair.

"Is it all right then, Lad?" Father clapped a hand on his shoulder.

"I believe it may be, in time." Thomas stood, saying, "I'm ready for the bed. How about you?"

* * *

Knocking on the door to wake him the next morning, Father called, "Get up. The day's almost gone."

"All right, Da, I'm awake. You'll raise the dead with all that pounding."

He felt for his wife next to him, but she wasn't there. Fear shot through him. His thoughts scuttled back to her unstable time. Pushing that aside, he rose, dressed, then made his way toward the staircase.

162

Following the steps down to the first floor, he went on into the common room. Sophrona poured him coffee before helping Penelope finish cooking breakfast. He took his mug to the front room, where he opened the door, looking at the wide swath of morning light spreading through a murky dark sky. What if this turned out to be the last morning to see land he lived on all his life? Thomas blinked his eyes. He would not allow this to change his mind. They had no choice but to go.

Isaac and Simon worked down at the barn, a faint light from a candle lamp shining through a crack in the wall.

Thomas caught a whiff of the rose bush beside the house, as he opened the door wider, stepping outside. He took another look at the sky. Sucking in another breath of the rose scent, he stepped back in, closing the door. He found Father sitting in the office, with a pouch beside two firearms on his desk. Thomas took a seat as the glow of peace, always present in the company of his father, surrounded him.

"It seems like a good day for traveling, Da. There's not a rain cloud in sight. If we don't stop, except for the animals, we'll make our way far down the road by nightfall."

Father pivoted toward the maple desk, gleaming under the candle light, then picked up a pouch and turned back to face him.

"Be mindful about who ya show this gold. Good men have died over considerably less than this."

Thomas reached for the bag, his hand dipping as he adjusted his grasp, making a calculation of what he now held. He collected too many payments over the years for their business, not to know what he just received.

"Are you sure about the amount? I don't want you doing without."

"There's not a lady to squander me coins on, Lad, something not likely to change any time soon. Best use your time preparing for a family. There's another child or two in yer future, yet." Father rubbed

163

the side of his face. "Don't forget the pistols. Keep one of them close to you at all times."

Thomas nodded as they stood. His father blew out the candle lamp before they left for the common room. Once there, Thomas sat down at the trestle table where Sophrona joined him."

"Good morning, my love." She took his hand. "Everything ready?"

He smiled, nodding, as he remembered the foolish fears he dismissed about her that morning.

He turned as Isaac and Simon entered. They washed up at the sideboard, then Isaac poured a glass of water while Simon helped Penelope put dishes of food on the table.

After everyone sat, Father looked around the table before bowing his head. Fingers gripped the hands of loved ones in a circle that included their servants, as he asked the blessing.

Looking up, Father reached for a charger filled with ham. Taking some, he passed it to Thomas, who took a slice before handing it on. The bowls and platters moved around the table as the family filled their pewter plates for one more meal together in Baltimore County. Would he and Sophrona ever return here? More than that, would they ever see Father, Isaac, or Simon again?

Simon helped Penelope wrap the last breads they baked, before loading them in a barrel, which he rolled toward the front porch. He returned for wet barrels of beef, pork, and other foodstuffs, while Thomas sat finishing his coffee.

Sunlight flooded the house as Thomas went to the office to gather his gold pouch and the two firearms, along with ammunition. He secured one pistol on his person, intending to store the other in the Dutch wagon. He helped Simon move the food barrels into the smaller wagon, along with a large cask of water. They left room on top of crates for the women to rest on quilts. He intended to sleep on the ground, along with the other driver.

He turned toward the sound of hoof beats, as four wagons pulled off the road onto their land. A single rider continued up. The man, a few years older than himself, dismounted.

"Where's Thomas?"

"That's me. Who owns these wagons?"

Another smaller wagon rolled up. Peter stepped down, helping Fenella to the ground.

"Thomas, these families are going your direction," his father-in-law announced. "I thought traveling with more people would be safer."

Peter turned, nodding toward the first wagon. "That's Nathaniel Radford and his family. They're going only to Winchester." He pointed individually toward the next three wagons. "John Buckley, Mathias Urquhart, and the last are Reverend McWhirter and his nephew, all of them going to North Carolina"

"Glad we're traveling together. If anyone's thirsty, my father's house is hospitable. We'll be leaving soon."

Thomas turned back as his father-in-law said, "This is Charm Wilson. He'll return to my employment after driving your second wagon to Virginia."

Thomas stepped over to shake Charm's hand. "I'm grateful to have you going."

Peter looked around. "Where's our daughter?"

Thomas shook his head. "I don't know, but she's here somewhere."

* * *

After visiting her children's graves yesterday, a heavy weight came off Sophrona's shoulders. The Lord freed her from the torment of grief. Today, she hurried through breakfast, determined to visit the graveyard again, if she could.

She went upstairs for items needed for the trip, placing them next to Penelope's possessions by the front door. She slipped outside, breathing the sweet morning air as she hurried toward the cemetery. She must again stand in front of those two little graves that held the children she would never know or experience the pleasure of watching grow.

Sophrona glanced back at the house. She did not need to do this—but then she reached for the gate, pushing it open. A sliver from the wood pricked her hand; the pain reminding her she must finish this while she still could.

A breeze played with the short curls around her temples, brushing her face. Lifting the skirt of her beechnut-colored dress, she hurried along the path to the two rocks. Looking down, she remembered the torment of losing her babes.

"I love you both so very much. I'm sorry we'll never know each other."

Not in this world. A tear rolled down her face.

"I'm getting the chance for a new start, somewhere else, but I'll always remember that you two were the beginning of my family. I won't forget that."

She wiped her eyes, not knowing how long she stood at the graves. Urgency in her step, she hurried out. Looking back, she closed the gate, no longer thinking about how it might have been; only that it ended and she must move on.

"Sophrona. Where are you, child?" Mother called.

Sophrona's heart beat faster, the sun warm on her face. Lifting her skirt off the toes of her traveling shoes, she hurried toward the sound of her mother's voice.

* * *

While Peter and Fenella said goodbye to their daughter, Thomas hugged his father. Isaac stuck out his hand, but Thomas grabbed hold, pulling him close to clap his back before turning him loose.

After he shook Peter's hand, Thomas moved closer to kiss his mother-in-law's cheek. With deeper lines in their faces than seemed possible since he had last seen them, Sophrona's parents boarded their wagon, starting their ride back to Baltimore Town.

Charm stepped up. "Which wagon do you want me responsible for?"

Thomas pointed to the small wagon. Charm tied his horse off back, climbing up in the seat.

Leading Sophrona and Penelope over, Thomas said, "Charm, my wife, Sophrona, with her friend, Penelope." He helped the ladies up on the narrow seat, Penelope in the middle. "They'll ride on this wagon, unless either of them wants to travel inside mine. I didn't find time to build a seat on my Conestoga."

After his wife got settled beside Penelope, he climbed up on the left wheel horse of the big Dutch wagon. Taking the reins, he looked back.

Father waved a hand. "The Lord travel with you, Lad."

Thomas nodded. He snapped his whip just above the horse's haunches, raising his voice. "Come on, now. We need to be somewhere."

Eight black horses, manes and backs gleaming in the sunlight, moved his oversized, loaded-down Conestoga up the road as though they pulled a chaise.

Thomas looked back to see Sophrona, twisted almost off the edge of her seat as she looked back, frantically waving to the family.

CHAPTER TWENTY-TWO

Thomas and Charm drove their wagons until twilight that first day, rarely stopping. The other wagons stayed up with them.

Thomas finally called for camp, insisting they circle the wagons and gather around a common campfire for protection. He intended to follow this procedure as long as the others accompanied them. He must keep his family, along with everyone else, safe.

The day had stretched long, the evening short, as Thomas, Sophrona, Penelope, and Charm hurried through a scant supper. Thomas took the first watch of the night, leaving the men to split up the other hours. His legs moved effortlessly as his feet discovered quiet ground to step on. Looking like little more than a fleeting shadow, he moved so silently, his mind filled with thoughts of Sophrona.

If only he had planned enough ahead to build a riding seat for his Conestoga, something quite possible. Sophrona could then sit next to him as he drove the wagon, the two talking and laughing as they covered the miles to their new home. If only he had done that.

* * *

Sophrona woke to Thomas' gentle touch in the dark hours of morning, finding he replaced Penelope, already gone from the wagon. She barely remembered eating supper the evening before or crawling into the wagon, sleep came so fast.

"Can I rest here with you?" He pulled her closer, nuzzling her neck. "I won't be missed for a while."

"I don't think so, Mr. Craighead. Married or not, I'm sleeping with Penelope on the trail." Heat shot up her face like a flame recalling her response to his touch. "There's a room of our own waiting at Aunt Elizabeth's house."

"Well, then, it looks like I'd better make myself useful before Charm grows tired of doing all that work himself." Thomas pulled her close, kissing her. "I don't need a nap. I'm plenty rested."

What nerve, getting up to leave like that. Of course, she practically insisted he go. Sophrona readied herself and joined Penelope, who prepared breakfast under a dark sky.

By the crack of dawn they got on the road, not stopping to water the animals until the afternoon. Once the wagons started rolling again, Sophrona went to clutch Thomas' hand as he walked, smiling up at him, gently fluttering her lashes against the light.

"I'm going to walk with you awhile," she said. She wore her green dress Penelope stitched together. The one dotted with small yellow flowers. Her skirt swayed gently each step she took.

Thomas strode next to her on the left side of the wagon, using the jerk line, along with a few verbal commands, to guide the team.

Sophrona enjoyed the cheery sound of tinkling bells, mounted on iron hoops above the collars of the lead horses. The sunlight warmed her face. It played across the top of Thomas' light brown hair, running down the length of his neck, picking out red traces. His broad chest strained at his shirt as he worked the line. No doubt, she needed a lifetime to express how much she loved him.

After a while, her steps slowed as her feet dragged. Thomas scrutinized her face before he sang out a short command, bringing the team to a stop. He pulled out the lazy board she could sit on, before placing his hands on her waist and swinging her up on the plank.

"It's time to ride. I don't want you so worn out, like last night. We still have a long way to travel."

169

* * *

Thomas showed Sophrona his old campsites as they passed, stopping at the ones that accommodated the six wagons. He marveled at the wonders of God, as he recalled the painful thoughts of losing her during his earlier travels with Father. Except for the intercession of his friend, Daniel Morgan, he may have hauled for General Braddock instead of going home to fight for her. He may have died like many others during that fight, hauling for the general.

They stopped at Owen's Ordinary to purchase feed for the animals. Then, sooner than he expected, they passed through Winchester, where Nathanial Radford's wagon left them. This time, instead of turning north toward Wills Creek, Thomas stayed on the great wagon road, also called the Carolina Road, traveling through Virginia.

"We'll arrive at Aunt Elizabeth's before the first day of September, Sophrona."

Thomas reached for her hand as they walked, grateful he decided to make this move with her. She smiled at him, her dark hair gleaming in the sunlight, her eyes reflecting the blue color of bonnet flowers before deepening.

"What a perfect way to celebrate our wedding anniversary."

"Do you mean seven years passed already?" Thomas cupped his chin with a hand.

Overcome with laughter, Sophrona slapped at him. "Five, Thomas. Five years."

Several days later he drove the Conestoga onto Looney's Ferry, crossing the Fluvanna River. His stomach lurched with the rock and sway of Fluvanna's rough water. On the other side, he waited for Sophrona's wagon to get ferried across, hoping Charm chocked the wheels well enough to keep it out of the river. His shoulders tensed at the thought of her getting hurt.

Early the next morning, as the sun's golden light broke through the clouds, Thomas started down the valley, drivers rolling in behind him. To the left were the Blue Ridge Mountains. On the right, they traveled beneath the towering Appalachians—mountains so tall they surely scraped the sky. In the late afternoon, as they continued on, Thomas thought the shadows of the Appalachians might reach them.

Arriving at the Staunton River, the wagons followed the river bed through a gap in the Blue Ridge until they came to the Blackwater River.

A few days later, they said goodbye to their fellow travelers, who continued on to North Carolina. Thomas turned his wagon onto little more than a wide trail.

Late in the afternoon of August twenty-second, he pulled his wagon onto cleared land in front of the log house his uncle built. He studied the rocks piled up beside the house, unique as the ones already embedded in the path leading to the door.

Charm stopped the second wagon a small distance from him.

Thomas hurried over to assist Sophrona in her climb down, before helping Penelope to the ground. He led Sophrona toward the house as his aunt and uncle hurried out to meet them.

"You must be worn out from traveling so long." Aunt Elizabeth hugged Thomas. Then she took Sophrona's hand, starting toward the house. "It looks like you've lost weight. Come on inside while I put some food on the table."

"It'll sure feel good to stir around a cook-place again," Penelope said as she followed behind, "after all those nights cooking over a campfire."

"We'll be in soon as we take care of the wagons, Elizabeth," Jonah called.

* * *

Thomas arched his back as he turned toward his uncle. "This here's Charm. Sophrona's father sent him along to drive the other wagon. He handles a team just fine."

"Are you going back to Baltimore Town, Charm?" Jonah said.

"Yes, but not for a while. Mr. Hackett told me to help Thomas build. Said his daughter needs a home of her own."

"No need to stay around for that. We'll help Thomas build his house. Should go up before winter starts, if nothing goes wrong." Uncle Jonah slid a shoe side to side as he talked. "Families around here are scattered so, some people hardly call us a community. Still, we all show up to raise a house for the new family. Same as the first few did for us."

"How long before you finish that?" Thomas nodded toward the rocks.

His uncle scratched a cheek. "Don't rightly know for sure, but maybe by next year. I scoured plenty of riverbeds, even a few creeks, to find those." Jonah cleared his throat. "I started that path after finishing the house. Only work on it when there's nothing else to do."

Thomas nodded. "That's going to make some walkway when you're through."

"We have that big open shed you can use for the wagons, Thomas. It's deep enough the rain won't soak your possessions." Jonah jerked his head toward a shed beyond the barn. "There's enough furnishings to sit on. Even have a room, but there's only an old bed for you to sleep on."

"Let's get those wagons in the shed, Charm. We need to pull out the bedstead. I'm especially partial to it."

"What'll I do about the animals when I'm through?" Charm said.

"Turn them loose in the stable out behind the barn." Jonah shifted his legs. "They'll get fodder along with the others."

172

"I assured Father I'd send him a post the day I arrived, Uncle Jonah."

"There's a neighbor riding with a freighter headed north. Get your message ready and we'll ride over there tonight."

A week later, after being assured they did not need him to raise a house, Charm left for Baltimore Town, his saddlebags loaded with food. He carried a letter to Sophrona's parents.

Thomas and Sophrona waved him off, as he disappeared into the forest.

They had started back to the house when the sound of pounding hooves spun Thomas around. Alex jumped from his horse, landing practically on top of him.

"Almost stopped my heart, Alex. I might die, yet. Hope you can stay awhile to revive me."

"Only tonight, but I'll come back every chance I get."

Alex crooked a finger at Sophrona. "Come on over here to give your handsome brother-in-law a kiss." Sophrona giggled as she reached up to peck his cheek.

Thomas stepped over to take Sophrona's arm, as the three turned toward the house.

* * *

The smell of blossoms permeated the warm morning air, as if a mischievous child wasted his mother's rosewater sprinkling it in the air. The birds flitted from tree to tree, chasing each other with calls. One filled the air with a warble so sweet, Thomas' thoughts turned to Sophrona.

A strong love for the Lord with all His grace seeped in, swelling Thomas's heart. He sighed, deeply contented.

His uncle walked their horses up from the barn. "Let's ride over for a close look at that land before you make a decision, Thomas."

Mounting his pacer, Thomas rode toward the narrow portion of the tributary that flowed into the Staunton River, about ten miles distant. After fording, they followed it to the beginning of the hundred and twenty acres, on down the waterfront side of the property.

"The spring's located about the middle of the land. Let's ride on over there."

Thomas followed him through the trees toward thick underbrush, where his uncle stopped.

"It's up ahead. You go on while I stay with the horses."

Thomas dropped to the ground, handing the reins of his horse to his uncle. He fought his way through the shrubs to a spring twice the size of most he'd seen, ringed with grasses and reeds. Clear water bubbled up. He was willing to get wet, even dirty, working his way through the lush vegetation to get a taste. He plunged his hand into the cold spring, cupping his palm to bring a stream of wetness to his mouth. The water tasted so sweet, he plunged his hand to pull up another drink. Smacking his lips, he started back to where his uncle waited.

"Straight over from the spring is a five acre piece that protrudes into this acreage. Since it's separate land, you may get a chance to buy it cheap." Jonah stopped to watch a speckled bird fly into a nearby tree. "I mean, who'd want to own only five acres surrounded by large tracts? Then have to worry about fencing it? It might turn out more of a nuisance than anything."

"I wonder how that happened." Thomas tried to imagine five small acres, cut out from a large block of acreage surrounding it, and then plugged into a bigger piece of land. Someone did not pay close attention when they started breaking up the original tract of forest.

Uncle Jonah pulled a sheet of linen paper from his saddlebag, showing Thomas the land's boundaries. After searching, they found three of the four markers.

"I don't see the small maple, do you?" Jonah said.

Thomas shook his head. He edged his pacer into the dense forest, toward a small cluster of trees. "Here it is, squeezed in the middle of these oaks. Looks like they outgrew the maple."

"Alright, then, is this what you want? Or should we ride over to that other piece we talked about?"

"No. I'm well satisfied with this place. The land's fairly close to your house and it borders the creek. Only thing is, I want to speak with Sophrona. See what she thinks."

Jonah scratched his head. "If you decide to take it, your brother may be close for a while, too. There's a young woman who attends his church. If he marries her, he'll stay around unless the church sends him elsewhere."

When they started back, Thomas pushed his horse faster toward the house where Sophrona waited. He wanted to tell her about the land. Getting closer, he reined in, keeping pace with his uncle.

"Where do I register the land once I've bought it, Uncle Jonah?"

"Over in New London. Benjamin Howard's clerk of the court for Bedford County. You'll take your bill of sale to him."

Thomas kept the pace slow. "I think we'd better have something to eat. Speaking of that, if I don't clear some land before winter, for a crop in the spring, we'll eat at your house often next year."

His uncle grunted. Thomas suspected, right now, that was the closest thing to a smile.

* * *

All day Sophrona thought about their anniversary and being alone with her husband to enjoy supper in their own room. The first of September finally came. She could hardly wait for his return.

She dropped her cleaning cloth on a table, walking to the window overlooking Elizabeth's front yard, hedged with lilac bushes. Happiness spread through her when Thomas rode in with his uncle. She shifted from foot to foot as she waited for him to enter, wondering what kept him.

175

"Oh, Thomas, I'm so glad to see you," she said as he approached.

"You mean to say you missed me?" He kissed her.

"I most certainly did. I always want you here with me."

"Come, let's go for a walk. It's a beautiful day."

When he took her arm, she glanced down, smiling. It was not possible for him to know just how much she loved him. She kept her eyes on him as they stepped down onto the stone path.

"Saw some promising land today. Would make a good home. What do you think?"

"I don't know why you ask me, Thomas. It's you who must be satisfied enough to work the land, along with setting up your freighting business."

"I want your opinion, too."

"What does it look like?" Gladness cast roots deep in Sophrona's soul. Thomas wanted her to help him pick their future home, even though she knew nothing about land.

"Well, a portion borders the river, while the forest is so full of God's creatures. The spring on it'll never go dry. The best thing of all is, it feels like we only need to build the house, 'cause it's already home."

"You must get that land if you want it. I trust it's the right place for us. I'm already impatient to see it."

He glanced away, then back at her.

"I'll ride out to see the owner tomorrow and do my best. I only hope my best is good enough to purchase us the land."

CHAPTER TWENTY-THREE

Thomas started out with his uncle at daybreak, covering the distance to the landowner's house in less than two hours. They slowed their horses to a walk as they approached the front of a plank house set back from the road. Trees surrounded the structure on three sides, and a heavy coil of smoke rose from the chimney.

A lean black dog appeared on the porch. The animal hesitated, but the raised hair on the ridge of its back running into its neck, suggested to Thomas it might fight to defend its master's property.

"Stay back, George," a man called as he exited the house, lumbered across the porch, then descended the steps. The dog slunk away, tail hung low between its hind legs.

Thomas slid off his pacer to stretch, as he waited for his uncle to speak.

"Robert, this here's my nephew Thomas. He's interested in some land."

"I'm pleased to make yer acquaintance, Thomas."

"The pleasure's mine." Thomas gripped Robert's hand before he stepped back. "I'm interested in that hundred and twenty acres. I understand you may have another five?"

The open expression on Robert's fleshy face disappeared, giving his jowls the mask-like appearance of smooth marble. His eyes were what Thomas noticed most—quick—calculating. The lids closed down to slits.

Robert nodded, then stepped back as he twisted to spit a stream of tobacco juice over his shoulder.

"How much you asking an acre?" Thomas smoothed the toe of his boot in a small half circle in the dirt.

"I'll need at least three pounds. I invested in this land to parse it out. Have to get my money back. It's prime land with plenty of trees for building."

Thomas' toe continued to grind.

"No doubt I'm interested in your land, but there's not a meadow in sight, Robert. Bringing down enough trees to clear a field might break a good man's back." He really wanted that land, but he needed to tread carefully. This man knew his business. "I'll consider one pound, ten shillings an acre. That's the best I can do."

Thomas moved to stand under a maple tree that cast a wide shadow. First his uncle, then Robert, joined him.

"I'll come down a little, not much—say two pounds, ten." The man's eyelids flickered.

He might be forced to walk away if Robert refused his best offer. That would sure be easier had he not tasted the water, or spilled the contents of his heart to Sophrona.

"My final offer is one pound, fifteen shillings an acre. Take it or leave it. We have a long ride home in front of us."

A shadow crossed the man's face. His eyes opened wider. "You'll need to give me two pounds. I'll throw in the five acres for the price of the hundred-twenty, if you want, but you must buy it today. That's my final offer."

Robert crossed his arms, his bottom lip swallowing his top one.

Sophrona's lovely face swirled in front of Thomas.

"All right. I'll take the land at that price."

He sealed the agreement with a shake.

"Come on in the house while I get the deeds ready. I'll have some of my wife's family witness the sale. She's cooking and it's almost done—no sense leaving here hungry."

The two followed Robert inside, where they took seats while he prepared the papers.

"There you are." Robert handed him the deeds.

Looking over the parchments for Robert's signature, Thomas said, "This looks good to me."

He handed the deeds to his uncle as he counted out the price of the land, the gold coin clicking softly as it mounded on the table.

After Thomas finished, Robert recounted as he removed the coin, then walked to a back room.

Thomas and his uncle rose when Robert's wife went to set pewter plates, then the food, on the table. They stood until Robert returned and said, "Sit down and eat while it's hot."

When Thomas stopped eating, Robert waved his hand toward the food. "Have some more of that roasted duck, another piece of bread. There's plenty."

"No, thanks," Thomas shook his head. "I've had enough. Sure do appreciate your hospitality."

When Robert's wife looked over from the cook fireplace, she smiled before looking down at the floor.

Thomas said, "Your wife's one fine cook, Robert."

Robert nodded. "She's the best around these parts."

Thomas rose, gathered his things, then left the table to wait for his uncle outside.

After Thomas cleared the steps, he threw the dog a few scraps he'd set aside. The cur hesitated, before it snatched up the food and disappeared around the house.

Thomas mounted up then patted the coat pocket that held the bills of sale, his money pouch, as well as the pistol he carried. Soon, Jonah left the house and mounted his horse, settling himself in the saddle.

"What do you think, Uncle Jonah? The price low enough?"

179

His uncle shrugged a shoulder. "From what I've heard, you did better than most. Robert's known for being tighter than the bark on any of his trees."

Nodding, Thomas kneed his horse. Except for a brief stop to stretch their legs, they traveled nonstop through the countryside, arriving back at the house before nightfall.

Thomas put up his animal before he hurried to the house, eager to see Sophrona. Entering the common room where she sat with Aunt Elizabeth, he smiled at her beauty, his heart filling with love. When she came to stand with him, he took her hand, leading her to their room.

* * *

"I thought about you today when I bargained for our land."

Sophrona moved toward him, arms circling his neck. "I'm proud of you. Was it hard?"

"Well, I'll say this about Robert. He's a shrewd businessman. He brought me to a place where it seemed almost impossible to offer any more."

"What happened to change that?" Sophrona gently swayed as she looked up in the face of her husband, his hair tousled, and a stray lock on his forehead.

Thomas' eyes brightened. "Well, I ended it. I couldn't justify paying any more for the land than I already offered. Just then, I envisioned your face."

"What did you do?" Sophrona's breathing slowed. He thought of her during negotiations?

He leaned down, kissing her. Straightening up, he ran fingers through his hair. "I did the only thing I could. When he made another offer, I took it."

"Mr. Craighead, tell me exactly what happened." Heart pounding, she moved closer.

"Well, I paid more than I intended to. I want us to live on that land, my lovely wife."

"Oh, Thomas, I love you so."

* * *

Sophrona went to the common room to help his aunt get supper on the table, while Thomas went to the front room. He glanced over the deeds again before handing the parchments to his uncle. "Everything seems in order to me."

"Well, then, we'll ride over to New London first thing tomorrow. The clerk...what's that, Elizabeth?"

"Supper's ready. Time to eat."

Thomas followed Jonah to the table, where he sat next to Sophrona. Later, with the sun barely down, he took her arm. "Let's retire for the night."

"Yes, such a long day."

Early the next morning, Thomas rode the thirty miles to New London with his uncle, following him into the court clerk's office.

Uncle Jonah shook the clerk's hand. "Ben, this here's my nephew, Thomas Craighead. He has some business with you." His uncle looked back toward Thomas. "This here's Benjamin Howard, Clerk of the Court."

"I'm pleased to meet you, Mr. Howard," Thomas said, as he moved up to shake his hand before passing him the documents.

He waited for the clerk to record the bills of sale in the court records. Mr. Howard signed the two deeds before he sealed them then handed them back.

"Here you are, young man."

Thomas counted out the recording fee. "I appreciate this. A pleasure doing business with you."

That afternoon he saddled a horse for Sophrona, then helped her mount, grateful for the short ride ahead. Once on the land, he helped her dismount, then pulled a wooden mug from his saddlebag and made his way to the spring. She needed to approve of the taste, as well. He knelt down for a drink, then filled the mug, taking it back to her.

"This is good water, Thomas. It's no wonder you haggled over the land."

"The water wasn't the only reason, Sophrona." He rubbed her cheek. "The extra five acres are just about perfect for building." He replaced the mug. "That will place the spring behind the house."

She smiled at him. "The air smells so good."

He nodded, breathing in the smells of a living forest. "Listen to that. There's nothing but silence except for the snap of twigs from our furry little squatters, or birds calling."

Taking a hatchet from his saddlebag, Thomas motioned Sophrona along as he began to notch his trees. He must clear enough land for a crop, using the timber to build their home.

* * *

Two months later, Thomas stepped back for a view of the porch being added to their house, his thoughts on living alone there with his wife. They had eaten nearly every meal with someone else ever since leaving Baltimore County. They only had a quiet supper alone on their anniversary. Before long, they would enjoy all the privacy they wanted. He smiled at the thought.

The neighbors who helped raise the house were skilled builders. After he worked beside Alexander and Uncle Jonah felling the trees, community members came to help square the timbers, using broadaxes.

December ended with a light snowfall. He worked hard to complete the inside of their home.

* * *

Thomas looked up as Alex arrived at full gallop, almost tumbling down as he dismounted.

"Guess I was expected here sooner. How's the work coming along?"

"It's good to see you, Alex. I'm all right with the house, but sure need your help working on an equipment barn." Thomas looked down. "I must finish that before starting my business. Can't run a freight business out of Uncle Jonah's shed—too far away, for one thing."

"I'll get more days off now. Cousin Alexander received a post from Father the other day. No doubt Father's received a report about what's going on with Murna." Alex paused. "Our Father may get an invitation to a wedding sooner than he expected."

"I knew you started courting a young woman attending your church, but I didn't know it progressed this far. What's Murna's last name? Sophrona will want to know."

"Duncan. Miss Murna Duncan. You'll meet her in the spring, provided her parents give permission for her to travel to meet our family. If everything goes well, I'll ask for her hand in the summertime. The wedding may take place in the fall."

A contented look crossed Alexander's face, prompting Thomas to say, "If she makes you happy, she'll be a blessing to our family."

* * *

Early 1760
Bedford County, Virginia

Thomas escorted Sophrona to their new home, where Penelope already worked.

Grasping her hand as he gazed into her eyes, he said. "Welcome to the place where we'll grow old together."

Sophrona giggled.

"I remember the night you promised me that if Father allowed us to marry, then—stop that. Penelope's looking."

"What's the matter? You act as if she's never seen a man kiss his wife before. I'll wager Penelope's husband once did that to her."

183

He bent his head for another kiss, hearing Penelope's laughter fade down the hall.

A few days later he finished trimming inside the house, using soft poplar wood from the tulip tree. After that, he worked with Alex each afternoon to build the freight shed.

One afternoon when he returned, Sophrona met him at the door. She took his hand, saying, "Come see the quilt I finished."

"That's some fine work." He admired the colorful blocks, inserted in circles, carefully stitched together on a wooden quilt frame. "Where did you get this design?"

"Aunt Elizabeth showed me."

He nodded. "I'm not surprised it's one of hers."

In the next few days, bed covers, then heavy drapes followed, as Thomas witnessed his wife's hard labor preparing the inside of their home.

* * *

On a sunny spring day, Sophrona shook tied rag rugs off the porch side as Alexander rode into view. He dismounted, tied his horse, then started up the steps.

"Where's that brother of mine? Hard at work, I trust."

Sophrona laughed softly. "You'll find him out at the freighting shed."

She looked Alex over. Something about him seemed different than at other times. Maybe happiness?

"Murna's coming to meet our family next week. She'll stay overnight as Aunt Elizabeth's guest. I'll tell Thomas when I leave. He'll be pleased to hear the good news." Alex stood at the top of the steps. "You'll like Murna. She's a gentle person."

"I'm sure of that. You always draw good people. Perhaps that's because of the joy in your life—your commitment to the Lord."

He started down the steps, turning to smile over his shoulder at her. Sophrona went back to work, her thoughts on Murna. She

184

grasped another rug, vigorously shaking it over the handrail, wondering about her. What did the woman look like? What if she did not like her? Sophrona took the rugs inside, realizing she had no choice. She must like Murna, her brother-in-law loved her. He was most important to them.

The following week Thomas saddled their horses for a ride to Aunt Elizabeth's. On arrival, he dismounted. Catching her by the waist, he helped her to the ground before tying the horses. They went inside where the family gathered.

Alex stood, helping a dark-haired young woman up from her seat. "Murna, meet my eldest brother, Thomas, and his wonderful wife, Sophrona."

Stepping closer, Alexander touched Thomas on the shoulder. "I'd like both of you to meet Murna Duncan." Softly he continued, "I know you'll soon grow to love her as I do."

Sophrona extended her hand. When she clasped Murna's fingers, a chill ran across her shoulders. "I'm so pleased to meet you, Murna." She knew, despite that fleeting feeling, he intended to marry a woman exactly right for him.

Alexander asked Murna's parents for her hand in marriage in the early part of summer. They set their wedding for the last week of August, which was no surprise to Sophrona. How did they manage to put it off that long, with the obvious feelings they had for each other?

The day before the wedding, Sophrona joined the Shepard household in their common room, preparing the couple's marital supper. Briefly recalling the foods at her and Thomas' wedding, it seemed past time to enjoy another feast.

The next morning, they returned to Aunt Elizabeth's. Thomas entered the house, as she followed. A hand reached out to clasp him on the shoulder. Startled, he whirled around, falling into his father's embrace.

"No need to unbridle yer temper, Lad. Didn't mean to startle you. I'm happy to see you, but thinking back I should have spoken first."

"I began to wonder if you'd make it in time for the wedding, Da."

"We arrived in the wee hours last night, worn out from traveling, and slept in the wagon." Cyrus glanced at her. "You'll need to excuse me, Lad. There's someone prettier than you I want to hug."

Sophrona forgot how much she missed his fatherly presence, when he hugged her. Even the way he included her in his love for Thomas.

Isaac stepped around his minister brother to shake Thomas' hand. "Nothing could keep Father from this wedding. Good thing he's getting married—Father needed a reason to visit."

Aunt Elizabeth called them to breakfast. Thomas escorted her to the trestle table, where his brothers took chairs on either side of their father. After the family finished, they left for the church.

Reverend Alexander Craighead met them at the door, where he must officiate this wedding without his assistant today. Their family crowded into the front, on one side. The Duncan family sat on the other.

Thomas' brother looked so handsome in his grey jacket over a white shirt, with dark brown breeches. Not as handsome as Thomas, but he ran close.

Murna's dark hair framed her face. The sprinkle of freckles over her nose gave her a youthful appearance. Sophrona studied her lacey yellow waist jacket, over a long dark gown. It brought out the gold in her light brown eyes.

After the ceremony ended, Sophrona realized she heard little of it, except when the two replied, "Yes", to the Reverend, gazing into each other's eyes. She approved of the way Alexander's manliness complemented Murna's delicate beauty.

When people began stirring around, she touched Thomas' arm. "I must leave with Aunt Elizabeth, to help set up their wedding dinner."

He kissed her cheek. "I'll see that everyone arrives."

Later, when the wedding guests sat down together, neither Murna nor Alexander touched their food more than a bite or two. They only finished a slice of their wedding cake before leaving. When the Duncan family finally departed, Elizabeth sent supper home for the newlyweds.

Sophrona sat with Thomas, listening while Cyrus reminisced about the days of his, Cousin Alexander's and Elizabeth's lives, growing up in Ulster. Laughter—and a few groans—followed, as he described the substance of their youth that bound them together.

The next day, Sophrona sipped coffee on the back porch, while Thomas spoke with his father.

"Your brother's made me proud, Lad. She's a fine woman for him. August—Alex picked a good month for marriage, if I must say so."

Thomas nodded.

"Now there's only Isaac. The way the lasses look at him, it won't take long before he has a wife."

"Tell me Da, how's Isaac handling business without his brothers around to help?"

"He's surprisingly good at competing for freighting jobs, with Gerald helping six days a week, sometimes, to stay up with the hauls. As Baltimore grows, Isaac's building a fine business."

His father extended his stay with them, traveling over the land Thomas purchased.

One evening on the porch, as the sun dipped below the horizon, Father said, "It's quite a feat bringing the owner down on the price for this land. It'd bring considerably more if you sold it now" His

187

father reared back, tipping the straight backed chair. "Built a good house and shed. I'm right proud a ya."

Happiness settled over Thomas. Father only spoke what he believed to be true.

Isaac finally complained about shoving their freighting business off onto Simon—now a freeman.

"I dread to see Father go, Sophrona." Thomas shoved his hands in his coat pockets.

"It has to be that way until he moves in with us. Then you'll be with your father again."

Several weeks after Cyrus left, Elizabeth lost another child.

Sophrona did her best to help her through the dark days. Both she and Thomas grieved the couple's loss.

Sitting on their back porch, Sophrona spoke to her husband.

"Aunt Elizabeth says that's the last time, Thomas. She's almost past her child-bearing years. She has lost too many already."

When Sophrona cried, Thomas held her. She wondered if her tears were not as much for her own lost children as for the Shepard's.

CHAPTER TWENTY-FOUR

Starlight, Virginia
Early spring, 1761

On a cold, overcast day, Thomas took Sophrona to supper at his Aunt Elizabeth's and Uncle Jonah's. It pleased him to see Alex, there with his wife Murna.

After they finished supper, the family moved to the front room. His brother guided Murna to a rose colored settee. Thomas sat on the camelback sofa with Sophrona on one side, his aunt on the other. Uncle Jonah poked up the dying fire in the cavernous fireplace, before he added more wood. He chose a cream colored wingback chair to sit on.

"Would you help me serve the dessert, Sophrona?" Aunt Elizabeth stood, shaking out her skirt before she offered Sophrona a hand. They disappeared into the common room.

"You seem unnerved tonight, Alex. Something wrong?" Thomas said.

Alexander averted his eyes. "Not now, Thomas."

Thomas' gaze swept his brother's face.

"It must be something important. I haven't seen you this jumpy since your last year at seminary."

"Just leave it alone for now," Alexander said, placing an arm around his wife.

Sophrona returned with his aunt, each bearing a tray. They handed out saucers of raisin cake with mugs of coffee. She swept a

189

hand behind the skirt of her dark blue dress before taking her seat next to him.

After taking a bite Sophrona said, "What good cake, Aunt Elizabeth. You must teach me the recipe."

"Come over the day before we get together next. You can help me bake this cake." Aunt Elizabeth patted her hair when Sophrona nodded.

Thomas looked toward his brother, whose wife dropped her head, concentrating on her cake.

In the ensuing silence, Alexander cleared his throat. "There's an announcement." His eyes grew shiny as he spoke. "I'm going to become a father. Murna's with child."

"Congratulations, little brother. I knew you kept something big from me." Thomas jumped up, crossing the room to clasp his hand.

"When is the child expected?" Uncle Jonah said.

Alexander looked uncomfortable. "Sometime in November, I think."

Sophrona went with Aunt Elizabeth to hug Murna. Alexander moved to the sofa with Thomas.

"If it's a boy, Uncle Jonah, I'm counting on you and my brother to help us raise him."

"You'll get plenty of help." His uncle's face brightened. "The women shall be a fine influence on the child if it's a girl."

"Another Craighead child entering our world—how good it will be to hear little feet on our floors again." Aunt Elizabeth's eyes glistened as she spoke.

Thomas wondered if she cried for the small footsteps coming, or the ones she no longer expected to hear on her own floors. His heart ached for her bout of long suffering.

Sophrona huddled with Murna, speaking quietly together and occasionally giggling, until Sophrona's voice rose. "What will you call the child?"

"That isn't decided yet, but his father shall choose a good name."
Murna placed a hand on her stomach.

"So, then, you think the child's a boy?" Sophrona said.

"We're praying for a son who'll grow up to help Alex with the crops. One who may get called by God one day." Murna sighed. "There's time enough for a girl."

Alex came to stand directly behind where his wife sat. "We may purchase land closer to here. Cousin Alexander's already agreed to keep me at his church. Hopefully, I'll become pastor to the next church that's built."

"Well then, I'm ready to help with your house." Thomas gestured for Sophrona to move back with him. "It's time for a place of your own. It's hard for two families living under one roof, especially when one family's practically newlyweds."

"We wanted to marry instead of waiting. Murna's parents were good enough to welcome us in." Alexander yawned. "We'll stay the night, Aunt Elizabeth, if you'll put up with us. It's too late to go home."

"Take the room you've always used. It's a pleasure to have you two with us. We haven't had many overnight guests since Thomas moved Sophrona into their new home." Elizabeth spread her hands. "Want to stay over—make it the whole family for breakfast, Thomas?"

"Well, maybe not tonight. You haven't enjoyed Alex's company lately. This'll give you time with him and Murna."

Sophrona trembled earlier, when he took her hand. He wanted to get her home. She carried a look he had not seen since they lost their children. It troubled him.

After bidding everyone goodnight, he took his wife's arm, walking her outside in the cool, damp air. Her bottom lip quivered as tears brimmed her eyes. He pulled her to him, whispering, "Don't cry. It will be all right."

191

He took her handkerchief, wiping her tears. Deciding to take the black horse she rode over, he helped her up on his, handing her the reins. He trusted his well-trained pacer to take her safely home, even if her emotions gave way. He swung up in the saddle, sinking a foot into the other stirrup.

Once home and barely in the house, she collapsed on a wingback chair. He went out to put away the animals. Hurrying back inside, he helped her into bed before blowing out the candle. For the first time since they'd left his father's house, she cried out in her sleep.

The next morning after they finished breakfast, Thomas said, "It's a lovely day. Care to take a stroll with me, while I fill some water buckets?"

Sophrona came back with a wrap she handed to him. He draped it around her shoulders, and leaned down to kiss her. Did she feel better than last night? He bent over, grasping the bail of a wooden bucket in each hand. They left the house following the well-defined path to the spring, new growth bursting into pale green color along the way. He stopped under a birch tree to set down the buckets before he took her hand.

"What's causing you so much distress?"

Sophrona looked down. "Murna being with child reminds me I lost two already. I can't give you…"

"No, don't say that." He pushed the hair from her face. "Just because you haven't birthed a child that's lived, doesn't mean you won't become a mother. Besides, it doesn't matter if we have children, as long as I'm with you."

Her face crumpled as he pulled her closer, gently pressing her head against his chest while stroking her hair.

"Yes, it does matter. It matters to me. I want a child from our marriage."

"We need faith in the Lord, Sophrona. He'll decide whether there are children or not."

She pulled back from him.

"Thomas, I'm terribly afraid He's already made that decision."

* * *

While spring turned to summer, Sophrona delighted in the fragrance of rosebuds, as well as other blooms. She stayed busy through the hot months of July and August while Thomas helped Alex build his house. As the days passed, she grew hopeful again, her thoughts never far from giving Thomas a child, a son she could almost see in her mind.

When the weather grew cool in September, she enjoyed the mornings, finding a splash of sunshine to sit in. During the evenings, she needed a light wrap on the porch, sitting with her husband.

One day, Thomas came in from the barn for a glass of water. He took a seat at the table in the common room, while she finished cooking.

"There's a cold snap coming in the next few days that I'm afraid will run into October, just before Indian summer." Thomas took a sip of water. "I'll bring in more logs for the cook-place. Uncle Jonah gave good advice, telling us to build on the sitting room. I'll use that room to season more wood until I get a proper wood shed built."

The cold period continued through the first week of October, just like her husband predicted. Little summer arrived, giving them sunny days.

Mid-morning warmed as birds took to the air. Perhaps they sensed the last of these lovely days before heavy snow descended, freezing the woodland. Sophrona rose, sighing as she listened to their songs, before gathering the skirt of her brown dress to start up the steps. She arrived at the top, only to sit on the thick wooden bench a while, not wanting to move.

Finally she stood, going inside to dress the turkey Thomas brought back from hunting just after daybreak. He already gutted the bird, leaving it on the sideboard in the common room. Hearing

Thomas come in, she hurried to get breakfast on the table. After washing up, he sat down with her for prayer before they ate.

"I'll be gone most of the day. If you want to visit my aunt, I'll ride over with you then continue on from there."

"No, I think I'll stay here."

"If you get lonesome for company, ride the pacer. I'll leave him saddled in the barn. Murna's visiting Aunt Elizabeth today. You've hardly seen her since back in the spring when we heard their news."

She nodded. "I'll wait to see how I feel."

"I'd stay home today, but we're trying to finish Alex's house before hard winter sets in."

They finished breakfast in silence. He kissed her before starting out the door. She followed him onto the porch, watching until he rode away. Alexander had chosen a building site a few miles from them, with about the same distance of travel to Elizabeth and Jonah's.

Later in the morning, she thought further about riding over to visit Elizabeth. She even started out toward the barn, but only reached the porch before resentment gripped her heart, turning her back. It was not Thomas's fault she had not seen Murna more. The blame belonged to her. She just could not stand to see her sister-in-law's happiness—not when she suffered so much torment.

Murna radiated a glow, touching her extended stomach often. This only served to remind Sophrona there was no big belly for her to stroke when she needed comforting. No descendent for Thomas. Not from her.

Next month Cyrus's grandchild was coming. The right to give Cyrus the first one belonged to Thomas, not Alexander. Their son would have been four years old this past June, their daughter three in May.

She set aside the memories of their dead children to drop a double handful of wild chopped onions into the cooking pot hanging off the iron crane's trammel. She added turkey legs, then wings, to the boiling water. Cooking the meat tender enough to fall apart, she would pick the bones clean before adding more vegetables, then leave it to simmer a while longer.

She took the remaining turkey down to the rock house Thomas built around the spring, leaving the covered pan inside where the meat stayed cool. She pulled the door closed, returning to the house to find another chore.

The cook-pot bubbled over, the liquid hissing as it dropped into the fire. She adjusted the crane, raising the pot. After she stirred the soup, she placed the wooden spoon on the sideboard.

Confusion quickly descended on her. She did not know what to do. The urge to see Murna came again, only this time stronger. She swirled, declaring to an empty room, "No. I'll not leave this house."

Penelope entered from the sewing room, a quilt cover draped over her arm. "What do you think about the top? Is it good enough?"

"Yes, you have some fine stitching skills. I like the pattern."

She followed Penelope back to the small room they used for sewing, caught up in her struggle over Murna and her dislike for her.

After laying aside the cover, Penelope turned to her. "Is anything wrong, Mistress?"

"It's just that I have the urge to visit Murna, but don't know why. If I go, you must keep the fire built up until the turkey's cooked."

"Yes, I'll do that while I clean. I'll help you mount up."

"I don't really want to go, but it feels like I should."

"Then are you going, Miss Sophrona?" Penelope looked deep into her eyes, startling Sophrona.

"Yes, I think so."

She crossed over the porch, clutching her skirt to descend the stairs. On the ground she hurried to the barn with Penelope beside her. The pacer neighed when she entered. She untied him, leading him out to the mounting steps Thomas placed in front of the barn.

"We're going for a ride." She stroked the pacer's muzzle before handing Penelope the reins. She climbed the steps, gathering up her skirt before she swung her leg over to settle both feet into the stirrups.

"I shouldn't be long," she said, as Penelope handed her the reins.

When she kneed the horse, he burst forward, galloping down the path at a rapid pace. The loose hairs around her temples wiggled in the breeze, tickling her face. She centered herself in the saddle, bracing for bumps as she rode, wondering why she felt so driven to see Murna. It wasn't as if they became good friends. She hardly knew her, so strong were her feelings of dislike over her sister-in-law's expected babe.

It seemed as if she just mounted the pacer when she rode into Elizabeth's yard, the animal's sides heaving. After she slid to the ground, she led the animal to water before she gathered her skirt and hurried to the house. She found Murna sitting on the porch.

"Hello. It's sure a pretty day to sit outside." She climbed the steps, taking a seat on a straight back chair next to her sister-in-law.

"I felt light-headed so I came out for some air." Murna rubbed her forehead. "Aunt Elizabeth went to gather herbs for her medicine box while I lay down, intending to return before I woke. But I couldn't sleep with my stomach aching."

"Does it still hurt?" Sophrona said.

"Well, yes. First my belly draws up hard then my back hurts. When my belly goes down, there's no pain for a little while."

Sophrona reached over to touch Murna's forehead. It was damp.

"Ohm…it's starting again." Murna groaned.

Sophrona laid a hand on her sister-in-law's stomach as it grew firm. She took Murna's arm, leading her to the door.

"Come inside. You're in travail."

"It's not time for the babe, yet. Not until next month." Murna sat on a wing-back chair. "Go find Aunt Elizabeth. She'll know what to do. Hurry, Sophrona."

She started out the door, spurred on by the desperation in Murna's voice. Once on the porch, Sophrona stood there. If she did not go after Elizabeth, then the baby might die. She might still give Thomas's father the first grandchild.

She heard Murna scream, "Hurry, hurry…"

CHAPTER TWENTY-FIVE

Lifting her skirt to avoid tripping, Sophrona raced down the steps as if pushed from behind. Murna could lose the child quickly. Something went wrong or she would not be laboring so early.

She came to an abrupt halt when she reached the bottom step. The urge to hide from her sister-in-law's view, as she fought against the dark thought, *Kill the child*, sent Sophrona backing up under the porch against the log house. Slivers of wood dug into her palm. The pain cleared her mind. Hand to her mouth, she fell on her knees on the dank earth.

Help me, Christ Jesus. The evil surrounds me so strong; I can't find my way out of this darkness.

As the struggle went on between heaven and hell, the cloud of confusion began to lift. She understood her anguish over the babe did not come from Murna choosing to hurt her. This woman only wanted to bare Alexander's child, and could never understand, or know, how much pain Sophrona was in.

She had told no one the depth of her true feelings, not even Thomas. As the tears spilled down her face, she realized God knew how much her heart broke. He knew everything about her.

Murna's screams reached a pitch that stirred her heart.

She's almost out of time. Hurry.

The Lord spoke to her. He had brought her here to help the babe. Sophrona rose from the ground. Fear grew, bile scalding the back of her throat as she started looking for Elizabeth. Her eyes streamed fresh tears so that she almost could not see where she ran.

198

"Aunt Elizabeth…"

She cut through the first field into the next one. A short distance away, Elizabeth hurried out from a clump of trees, running toward her.

"When did you get…what's wrong?"

"Murna's in labor," Sophrona gasped out.

Elizabeth's face went white. Her bag of herbs dropped to the ground as she ran past, arms swinging. Sophrona stooped to pick up the bag before stumbling after her. When they reached the house, she helped Elizabeth move Murna into a back bedroom.

"We need hot water," Elizabeth said.

After a brief nod, Sophrona hurried to the common room, where she poked up the fire before placing a kettle directly over the coals. As she set out a pan for the water, misery slowed her movements. She must speak to the Lord.

"Forgive me for not coming to You when my resentment began." She wiped her eyes, continuing softly. "All I ever wanted is to give Thomas a child…

She heard something, more a whisper. Her heart fluttered with hope—then uncertainty. Did she hear, *Soon*, or…

"Where are you?"

The urgency in Elizabeth's voice sent her to the kettle, then into the bedroom with a pan of hot water she set on a table. Murna lay curled up on the bed, clutching her stomach, moaning.

"Here, Sophrona, get in behind her. Wrap your arms around her ribs, dig your heels in then hold on. Keep her there. I don't want her sliding off the footboard while I'm birthing the babe." Elizabeth put a hand on her hip. "Hurry, girl. We don't have time for you to think about this."

Sophrona crouched down on the bed, pushing aside her skirt before she slid in behind Murna. She wrapped her arms around her sister-in-law's ribs, turning her face to the side so she could breathe. *Lord, help me.*

Elizabeth shook Murna's knee. "Push when I tell you. Stop if I say to. You'll still deliver this child if you listen to me."

The moaning started, growing louder, then Murna's body heaved as she screamed. Sophrona felt her slip toward the foot of the bed. Heels dug in, she reared backward toward the headboard, stopping Murna's slide.

"Stop pushing." Aunt Elizabeth moved her hands between Murna's knees. "The babe's almost ready".

It seemed to Sophrona her sister-in-law's entire body turned into a withering mass.

"Sophrona, get a good hold on her." Elizabeth blew out a breath. "Murna, when the next pain comes, push with all your might. Don't stop until it passes."

Murna grunted until it turned into screams. She gasped for air, slowing down. When she started grunting again, Elizabeth said, "Push. Push hard. The head's crowning. The babe's coming. Harder, it won't take long now."

Sophrona hung on as Murna's body bowed, then collapsed back onto her. The smell of blood and something pungent mingled in the air as Elizabeth worked between Murna's legs. When a thin little screech sounded, Sophrona felt Murna stiffen.

In a strangled voice Murna said, "Is the babe alright?"

"You have a son, and there's not a thing wrong with him from what I see."

Over Murna's hysterical laughter, Elizabeth said, "Come get the babe, Sophrona. Hurry."

She pushed Murna off her, then rolled aside. Once off the bed, she took the babe. Aunt Elizabeth cut the cord she had already tied. Squeezing the cheeks open, she ran a finger inside its tiny mouth to drag out what was left of the mucous, wiping it on a cloth. The weak cries continued until Elizabeth took the babe by the heels, whacking its behind. Enraged screams filled the room and caromed off the walls.

Elizabeth smiled as she reached for a large cloth to deftly wrap him tight. She dipped another soft piece into the pan, wetting it to gently wipe his face and head.

"You've given Alex a fine son. Take your child while I move the afterbirth along."

As Elizabeth placed the babe in his mother's arms, Sophrona rinsed her hands, wiping them on her skirt.

Massaging Murna's stomach, much like gently kneading bread dough, Elizabeth's hands traveled downward as she worked. Soft moans from Murna accompanied each squeeze. When the afterbirth came, she wrapped it in the blood-soaked blanket, then dropped it in a bucket.

After spreading a cover over Murna, who softly cradled her babe, Elizabeth urged Sophrona into the common room where they washed their hands and arms

"I don't know what I'd have done without you, Sophrona," Elizabeth said, while changing her apron. "The child wasn't due until next month, close to the end of November. I sure needed some help, today." Elizabeth stepped closer, giving Sophrona a hug.

Sophrona nodded as she dropped her gaze, stepping back. Elizabeth needed to return to Murna and the babe.

"Yes. Well, I'm glad to help, but I can't stay. Penelope expected me home sooner than this." She followed Elizabeth into the room and to the bedside, where Murna heaved in deep sleep. Touching the soft little stick of an arm, Sophrona whispered to the babe, "Despite what happened, I'm so grateful the Lord brought you through."

* * *

She met Thomas at the back door, wiping her hands on an apron.

201

"Murna delivered their child today, Thomas. I helped your aunt with the birthing."

"Yes, I know." He pulled her close in a tight embrace. "I stopped by there on my way home. My aunt said if you hadn't shown up, he might have died. Maybe Murna, too." He nodded as he spoke.

She stepped back, staring at her hands before looking into her husband's eyes.

"You were so determined not to go," he said. "What changed your mind?"

"The desire to see Murna grew strong. Then, to find her in labor...well, I..." She ducked her head to avoid his eyes. "I...God told me to help her, so I did."

"My beautiful Sophrona, I'm glad you listened to the Lord. They named him Cyrus Andrew, combining Father's name with one of our great-uncles. They're going to call him Andrew." He led her to the sofa, pulling her down next to him.

She couldn't tell him about her struggle. That it crossed her mind to let the babe die. Shame crept in to cloud her happiness. What if she had not...

* * *

Over supper, they decided to go see Murna and their new nephew the next day. No doubt, when she felt well enough to travel, Alex would take them both to her parents' home until he finished their new house.

Later at bedtime, lying under the covers, she whispered, "After I found Aunt Elizabeth to help Murna today, I told God I wanted to give you a child."

Thomas blew out the light then reached over for her. "I shall love you for my entire life," he said, voice husky as he pulled her into his arms.

The next afternoon they rode to his aunt's. Sophrona took a soft, colorful quilt she had pieced together for the son they lost. Murna's eyes brightened with pleasure as she unfolded it.

"This is a beautiful babe wrap. Would you like to hold Andrew?"

Murna wrapped him in the small quilt and, when Sophrona sat down, laid him in her arms. She rocked him, talking softly. A perfectly featured child, holding such a strong resemblance to the Craighead family, her heart ached to look at him. She silently thanked the Lord for placing her feet back on the right path.

She touched his smooth little face. When she traced his cheeks, he turned his mouth toward her finger and tried to suck.

"I believe he's hungry." Sophrona carefully stood up with the babe as Murna took the chair, and then handed him back to his mother to nurse.

She must never tell anyone about her struggle to end this child's life before he ever took a breath. No, ashamed as she felt for what almost happened, Thomas's God Almighty became her Lord, forgiving her for something which must always stay between them.

CHAPTER TWENTY-SIX

Golden sunlight scattered rays over the team as it pulled the empty Dutch wagon Thomas drove. The March day produced enough heat to thaw the ground in places. Warmth forced him to throw open his heavy coat as he stopped at the barn.

He picked a well-rested team, hitching it to a larger freight wagon, already loaded. He stepped back into the barn, saying to the new hired man, "Take the time to unhitch the team I drove in. Look them over. Then they need water and pasture."

He drove the loaded Conestoga on to the freight shed, where he climbed down off the wheel horse to wait. Ezra's wagon soon approached.

"Have any problems with today's delivery, other than a heavy load?" Thomas did not envy Ezra, who already finished a day's work, only to return for a second run. The deep lines etched in the man's face reflected the weariness he must feel.

"Nothing worth complaining about," Ezra said, wiping his brow.

"Well, it's a long way to travel with this one—clear to Salisbury. There's enough daylight left to take you down the road. Best get started. Sleep at an ordinary, but get on the road by daybreak."

Ezra grunted in agreement.

"This is a good team to use when the load's heavy, with the driver tired." Thomas patted the large black lead horse. "Don't startle easy, and they'll stay up with any wagon on the road."

Thomas reached over to tap the bells hung on the iron hoop above the lead horse's collar. "Arrive at Whitehead's Mill with bells on."

The driver nodded as he mounted the wheel horse. "I ain't ever lost my bells to another freighter, an' it won't be no different this time."

Thomas nodded. "Stay another day at Salisbury, if necessary, before starting back. Bring me the bill for your food." He studied his shoes before looking up. "And any stays at the ordinary, too. I'll see you get it back. Sure do appreciate your help, Ezra. I know you're tired."

"No need to worry. I'll take care of everything." The driver turned his head, spit, and wiped his mouth on a sleeve.

Thomas watched him drive away, satisfied his large freighter rested in capable hands for the next week. He backed the other wagon Ezra had driven into the shed, careful not to push it through the rear wall. Jumping down, he unhitched the animals. The bells tinkled as he walked the horses toward the barn. He recalled seeing more than one driver's team with extra bells, gained by using their team to pull out another's stuck wagon.

Once in the barn, he watched the new man look over the animals, searching for strained muscles or loose shoes. He wanted to make sure the new hire did not rush the job. Thomas then checked the harnesses for weak spots, hanging each one on a peg as he finished.

"Open the side door to give them pasture while you clean the barn. After you're through, brush them down." Thomas finished the last harness. "Secure both doors when you leave. You'll find supper ready in the common room."

"Yes, sir."

He clapped the man's shoulder as he headed out the barn door.

The sun's warmth touched his face. Thomas moved faster toward the house, aching to see Sophrona. He soon grew warm, shrugging out of his coat.

While freighting the previous day, he stopped to eat at a crowded tavern. Afterward, he joined other drivers on the floor in front of the fire, rolled up in his blanket. He finally slept after making a vow to be home with Sophrona every night, the Lord willing. This hinged on his business continuing to improve enough to hire more drivers. Soon he could purchase the indentures of two more men to work the farm, even freight for him.

Penelope, their main house servant now in charge of two other women, met him at the door and took his coat.

"Is it all right to serve supper in the dining room? I draped a white cloth over the table. Miss Sophrona so enjoys eating off your mother's rose-covered dishes."

He recalled the day Father insisted he take those dishes, along with the Welsh cupboard that held them.

"But I shouldn't, Da, they belong to you—not with me."

"Yes they do, Lad. It's just the matter of whether you take them now or later. As her first-born child, I think she'd want your wife setting the table with these dishes."

He honored his father's wish. He took the dishes.

"Yes Penelope, as if you hadn't already decided to do just that. Tell me, though. What ails my wife today?"

"Well, sir, I don't know of anything. She has stayed awfully quiet, and that's just not like her. Usually she laughs or talks, given the chance."

Thomas nodded. He hurried to their bedroom, where Sophrona stood facing the window. He came up behind her to slip his arm around her shoulder.

"Is everything alright, Mrs. Craighead? I've looked forward to being with you since I left yesterday."

* * *

Gazing out the window, Sophrona looked to spring's arrival now more than ever. She held news for Thomas close to her heart, wondering if his surprise would match hers. She heard their bedroom door creak—Penelope always knocked. Did he arrive home early? His arm went around her shoulder as he spoke. She sighed, warmth spreading through her as she turned to face him.

"It's a long two days, Thomas. I've waited for your return."

After he kissed her, he once again breathed near the hair at the back of her neck. The first time that ever happened, she asked him why.

"I like the way you smell," he had said.

"Shall we go down to supper now?" She reached for his arm.

Thomas escorted her to the dining room, where he held out her chair. He took his place at the head of the heavy oak table. She looked down then smiled. Penelope had set the table with his mother's bold, red-rose covered dishes.

"How do you feel, Sophrona? You look a bit peaked."

"It's nothing really, I…"

Mayre, a new servant girl, entered the room with a tray, setting its contents on the table. The servant left, to return with a platter holding leg of lamb, which she placed near Thomas' plate, along with some cutlery.

He stood, positioning the knife and fork. "One slice or two, Mrs. Craighead? Um, just what's 'nothing really' about?"

"Well, I…maybe give me two slices. One for me. The other for the son I'm carrying."

He dropped the carving knife in his haste to reach her chair. Taking her hand, he said, "You're sure, Sophrona? Really sure?" He pulled her up to where he stood, slipping his arms around her waist.

"Yes, Mr. Craighead, I'm sure I'm with child, but only the Lord truly knows if it's a son." She smiled up at him. He bent, kissing her on the forehead.

They sat down at the table again. She ate, contentment filling her heart at her husband's happiness over hearing about the child. She rose from the table to bring him rice pudding, one of his favorite desserts, but he let it be.

"When's our child coming, dearest?"

"Oh, I think somewhere near the end of summer." Hope swelled within her.

"What about…I mean do you know if…" He looked away.

"I'm in my fourth month, that's how I know. Besides that, I asked the Lord for a child, remember, a son? If He's given us a babe, it'll live."

"We're in March, so you conceived the child back in November, within a few weeks of Andrew's birth."

"Yes, it's true what you say, Thomas." Her face warmed as she studied her napkin.

Thomas cleared his throat. "Our children are going to grow up in the community. Aunt Elizabeth says one day our family shall call this town home."

"How many children do you want to have, Thomas?"

"Just one, for now. Then, the Lord may see fit to give us more. Today you've made me a happy man."

The lines on her husband's face smoothed out. He took a bite of pudding, placed the spoon in the bowl, and pushed the remainder away.

"It's a little cool outside," he said, "but I'd like us to take a stroll before dark sets in. Let the servants take care of all the clean-up."

He placed his napkin on the table before he stood offering his arm. In the front room, he draped a red cloak around her shoulders before they stepped out the front door. They slowly meandered down the path, into the timber line, losing view of the house. Thomas stopped her when they reached a cluster of oaks.

"We've waited seven years for this child." She pushed a lock of hair from her face. "What will we name him?"

Thomas placed his arm around her shoulder. "My father had a brother he loved, who died when only a few years old, named Starlyn. I'd like to call our child Starlyn, his middle name Peter, after your father."

"That's a perfect name—Starlyn Peter. I hope he looks like the Craigheads."

"Why do you say something like that? When you're so good to look at?"

"I think Andrew's so pretty. He looks like the Craigheads. I want our child to look like you, that's all." She touched his arm.

He leaned down to kiss her cheek. "Let's go back before they think we got lost and send a search party out for us."

* * *

The next day they rode over to visit his aunt and uncle. Thomas helped Sophrona off her horse. He let her ride today, but in a week or two he didn't want her on anything but a wagon seat. Maybe he needed to purchase a one-horse 'cheer', that sturdy shay, strong enough to take them down any road hitched to a good horse. Losing a child hurt terribly, but if she died too, he would never get over losing her.

He walked her into the house. "Aunt Elizabeth. Uncle Jonah. Anyone here?"

"We're in the common room," his aunt replied. When they entered, she said, "Where else do you expect to find me just about any time?"

Thomas laughed, as Sophrona went over where Aunt Elizabeth stirred a pot at the cook place and patted her shoulder. When she returned to Thomas's side, they sat at the trestle table, across from Jonah.

"Are you hungry?"

"No", Thomas said. He sniffed the savory smelling chicken soup that permeated the air. He relished his aunt's cooking any other time. He waited for Sophrona to speak, but she only shook her head.

"What brings you over here today, Thomas?" his uncle said, an eyebrow up. "You run out of work to do?"

Thomas glanced at Sophrona. The candle lamp glow, mingled with the red flames licking the pot, cast her ivory face in a golden glow.

"No, there's always plenty of work to do at home. We hurried over to give you some news."

CHAPTER TWENTY-SEVEN

"Aunt Elizabeth, Uncle Jonah, Sophrona's with child." Thomas rose from his seat, as the news overtook him again. He reached down, pulling Sophrona up into his arms, twirling her around, her long green skirt fluttering. Coming to a stop, he said, "I'm going to become a father!"

After they all stopped laughing, Uncle Jonah rose to shake his hand while Aunt Elizabeth took Sophrona's arm, leading her to the table.

"Let's celebrate," his aunt said, as she cut four slices of spice cake, then set out mugs of coffee.

"When's the child due, Sophrona?" Aunt Elizabeth sipped her coffee, concern reflected on her face.

"He's coming in late August, maybe early September. I'm past the difficult time." Sophrona took a bite of cake.

"So it's a boy, then?" Uncle Jonah turned toward Thomas, who nodded.

"Yes, sir, I believe so. But only because my pretty wife assured me this is true."

Soft laughter traveled the table. Thomas felt peace wedge deep down into his heart, knowing only the Lord could guarantee a son and also bring the babe into the world alive.

* * *

"Catch me that pretty butterfly," Sophrona said. "Hurry Thomas, before it flies away."

He chased her shiny blue butterfly with white spots on its upper back wings, but it flew swift and close to the ground. She laughed quietly when he turned too quickly, tangling his feet, going down on his knees in the soft dirt.

He stood, brushing off his breeches. "My dear wife, butterflies do not get captured—only admired." He crooked a finger at her. "Come here. I want a kiss for that, or I'll chase after you."

Sophrona came to him, smacking at the dirt he missed on the knees of his breeches, then offered him her cheek. Low trills of laughter still flowed from her lips at his gallant attempt to please her.

Thomas gathered her into his arms. "Oh, no, you won't get by with just a peck on your lovely cheek," he whispered. They clung together as he kissed her.

Sophrona stepped back. "May's almost over, Thomas, there's still so much to do. The garden isn't completely in…"

"Don't you plant anything. Not one thing. That's my job, or the servants', not yours. You are to be careful because of your condition." He ran fingers through his hair before cupping her face, his hold firm. "Promise me you won't take a chance on losing the babe for some plants we don't even need."

"Well, then, I won't think of doing that. I'll ask Penelope or one of the others to plant for me." Joy soared in her heart when she looked into his contented face.

* * *

The mild, warm days went by too fast. Then came the first of July. Thomas ran his freighting business with the hired men, but purchased the indentures of two new servants. Those two men mainly helped with his spreading farm.

Thomas especially liked Obediah Tune, the older of the two servants, with his quiet ways. He thought of his father's years, especially all the hard work Father was still capable of doing, when he decided on choosing Obediah. He felt this man's indenture a bargain, considering the roughness he witnessed with other, younger men.

* * *

Sophrona's belly grew bigger by the week. Her stomach extended so far out she needed to brace her legs when she rose from sitting. Her weight centered not on the balls, but on the frogs of her feet, even extending back on her heels.

She recalled first hearing frog used in conjunction with a foot. "Stop running through my vegetable garden, Sophrona. If you do that one more time, I'll roll you under the frog of my foot."

The fear of her mother's foot rolling her over stopped Sophrona. She crept out of the garden. Later that day, she took off a shoe to examine her foot, asking her mother, "Where's the frog of my foot?"

"It's that high part between the ball of the foot and the heel, where your foot doesn't touch the floor." Her mother had touched the spot then tickled the bottom of Sophrona's foot.

Early in July, her stomach shifted, riding lower. This seemed to take some of the strain off her back.

Penelope brought in a basin of water, placing it on a serving table in the dining room, where Sophrona sewed material into a tiny white gown. "You must rest, Miss Sophrona. The weather's hot. You're farther along, now." The servant wet a cloth then handed it to her. "This'll cool you off. Maybe you should lie down until supper."

"All right, but this gown must get finished. There's more to sew before the babe's born." She folded the garment, placing it on the sewing box before she wiped her face. "He'll need clothes, you know."

Penelope nodded as she took the cloth. "Yes, Miss Sophrona, and there's three of us to help, if you'll let us."

She rose to shuffle across the room when Penelope asked, "When did you say the child's due?"

"Next month—the end of August."

213

Penelope shook her head. "Unh-unh. I don't think you'll last that long. Maybe more toward the beginning of the month, I think. I had two children and I remember my babes dropped just before birth."

Sophrona waddled to the bedroom, where she eased herself onto a stuffed chair. Penelope followed her.

The servant had never talked about her family before. Curiosity grew in Sophrona. She wanted to know what brought Penelope to the new land, penniless, only to get indentured for her ship's fare. A woman so cultured. So talented in creating fine needlework, like the small pink roses she had sewn on Sophrona's wedding dress. No doubt, this skill earned Penelope a good living in England. Still, something put her on that boat to the new land.

"What happened to your family?" She rubbed her protruding stomach in a circular motion.

"The Crown arrested my husband without reason, then they took our property. He died in prison. They placed me, and our two children, on a ship to the colonies." A sob escaped Penelope's lips. "They died on the voyage—first my daughter, then my son. The captain threw their bodies into the water—said he 'buried them at sea'."

Sophrona gasped. Pain for this woman's loss overflowed her heart, as she blinked back tears. She pushed herself up from the chair, moving toward Penelope to take her hand.

"You shouldn't worry about me, Miss Sophrona. Not with your child due so soon. That's not good for you." Penelope wiped her face then patted Sophrona's shoulder. "Now, you ought to lie down. Get some rest."

Sophrona couldn't argue with a woman who thought of her welfare over the pain of losing her own children.

She slept until Thomas woke her for supper. Almost directly after eating, she returned to bed. Napping each afternoon, then early retirement for the night, continued on through July.

214

The first of August, a hot, humid day, fell on Sunday. An afternoon thunderstorm cooled the house, making supper a more pleasant time for her. Instead of going straight to bed after eating, she sewed. Later, she joined Thomas out on the porch, to enjoy the evening. At sunset, they watched the first faint colors appear in the sky.

"Do you believe God does what He says?" The constricted tone in her voice sounded harsh to her own ears.

"Why do you ask that question?" Thomas kept his eyes on her face.

"The babe's coming soon. I just pray he'll live through the birth."

He touched her hand. "The Lord's word is always good. He cannot tell a lie."

The tension in her shoulders slipped away as she let out a slow breath. She did not know how, but Thomas always knew what to say to help settle her inner turmoil. Like all the other times, was he right this time?

* * *

The following Sunday, after supper, Thomas escorted his wife to the porch. He studied her pale, angelic face, as he recalled her behavior the previous week. She took no naps during the day, nor did she go directly to bed after supper, but used that time to sew. Sometimes she stitched bedding to line the babe's cradle.

"Ooh...there's a sharp pain in my lower back. It hurts so much." She struggled to get up.

He rushed to help her stand. "Sophrona, what's wrong?"

"Oh." She swept a hand across the back of her dress. "My skirt's damp...Ooh, Thomas, the babe's coming."

"It's too early. Are you sure? Really sure about this?"

"Early or not, it's time."

He took her arm, starting toward the door, when a servant came around the side of the house.

215

"I've finished with the animals, sir. Is there anything else to do before I retire?"

"Yes, saddle my pacer. Hurry, the babe's coming."

"Yes, sir, right away." The man swung completely around as he broke into a run toward the barn.

The picture of his servant running fast as he could, stayed with Thomas. A horse restrained by a bit in its mouth might feel much the same as he did. He needed to go. As every emotion in him shouted "Ride," he could not. Not just yet.

He helped Sophrona inside the house. "Wait here until I get someone to stay with you. I'm going for Aunt Elizabeth."

He hurried back with Penelope, giving Sophrona a kiss before he rushed toward the door.

* * *

Sophrona grasped Penelope's arm as Thomas left. "Help me to the bedroom. I must get out of this dress."

"Yes, Miss Sophrona." Penelope patted her arm as they walked. "If you lay down, then put up your feet, it may slow the delivery. Give Elizabeth more time to get here."

When Sophrona moaned in pain, stopping to clutch her stomach, Penelope held onto her. Once in the bedroom, she helped her change into a shift before spreading a thick, older quilt on the bed.

"Lie down, Miss Sophrona. Don't worry about Master Thomas. He'll return soon."

"I know. It's just that I'm worried about the babe."

She started to cry and could not stop. A strong pain struck, rendering her incapable of thinking very clearly. When it passed, she remembered Murna's screams during her delivery. Fear froze Sophrona's mind, knowing she must experience full childbirth. Determination gripped her. She did not care how much it hurt. She would deliver their babe alive, the Lord willing.

To give Thomas a child—become a complete family. She did not allow her mind to think about anything except this babe being born. When thoughts of losing it came to taunt her, she drove them off with prayer. *Please Lord, let me have this one.*

* * *

Thomas hurried out to the servant, who handed him the bridle of his horse. He threw one boot in a stirrup, riding before he completely finished mounting. "Go, go." He slapped the stallion's flank. Sweat rolled down the sides of his face, as much from fear as the oppressive heat the August evening had not yet cast off.

Thomas already made this run twice before. The scenery just looked a little different than in Baltimore County, with Sophrona's midwife a relative this time instead of a neighbor woman. His heart froze in his chest thinking about losing another babe. She made it so far this time. If this child died, she might never accept it, like she eventually did the other two.

Sunset spurted out red across the sky like billowing smoke. How dare the heavens reflect such beauty on this night? He did not know what awaited his wife, life or death, as she tried to deliver their child. The sunset deepened as he drove the animal under him at a faster pace than he ever did before.

When Thomas reached the house, he dropped from his horse. Fear put flight to his feet as he cleared the steps and started pounding. One of their servants unlocked the door.

"I need help." The door slammed back against the wall behind him as he burst through the house.

"Where's every…"

"Thomas, what happened?" Jonah ran from the bedroom, face constricted in alarm and fingers digging through his hair.

His aunt hurried from the common room, flour clinging to her hands. "What's the trouble, lad?"

"It's Sophrona. Pain in her back—the water's broke. She's travailing…come help her." He paced as he pleaded, arms assaulting the air.

"I'll get the small wagon hitched." Jonah started toward the door.

"No, wait." Elizabeth wiped her hands on her apron. "The wagon's too slow. It's getting dark. I'll ride with Thomas. Saddle me a horse while I get my bag."

Jonah hurried out the door.

Thomas heard his aunt instructing the servants on her absence, as he left to give his horse water. The animal barely finished drinking when his uncle led a bay mare, with a stallion, up to the house.

After handing him the stallion's bridle Jonah said, "He's fast as lightning. Your horse is tired. I'll bring him over tomorrow."

The stallion nickered softly as Thomas mounted. A few moments later his aunt stepped out the door with her birthing bag. Uncle Jonah gave her a hand up and they rode for his house. He looked back once, worried she couldn't keep up in the fading light, but she stayed just behind him, holding her own.

The last rays of dull red light faded fast. Like a candle blown out, the evening sky turned pitch black as he rode up to the house, dropped to the ground, running to help his aunt off her horse.

"Run, run," he said, as she rushed toward the house, clutching her bag.

He stopped long enough to call for a servant to take care of their horses before he hurried into the house, then on to the bedroom.

CHAPTER TWENTY-EIGHT

"Miss Sophrona, I'll bring hot water." Penelope left, closing the door.

Sophrona raised her head as Elizabeth entered and set her brown, well-worn satchel on a straight-backed wooden chair. Her contractions still came far apart, but she felt relief with Elizabeth in the room.

"How do you feel?" Elizabeth said.

"I'm laboring, but it's slow. Not like when Murna birthed her child—so quick." She groaned. "One's coming now."

Penelope returned with a pan of water, set it on a table, and left.

Elizabeth rested a hand on Sophrona's stomach "That one didn't last long." She pushed the hair from Sophrona's face. "Are they all that weak?"

"Yes. They're short, but they hurt." Tears filled her eyes. "I'm worried. What if something's wrong—the babe won't come?"

"Don't be afraid. Let me see how you're doing." Elizabeth examined her. Finished, she washed her hands, then reached for a cloth. "You'll have this child. I don't see anything to stop you."

The door opened and Thomas stepped partway through. "Is it all right for me to come in?"

"You won't see anything new in here, Lad," Elizabeth said, her mouth pursed to one side.

Sophrona smiled at her remark, despite a pain coming on. This hurt, but she must not give in to fearful thoughts.

219

Her husband came to stand beside his aunt. "What do you think's happening?"

Elizabeth watched her a bit longer. "Well, she's in travail, but birth is a ways down the road. Go have some coffee before you take care of whatever needs done."

He nodded, pivoted toward the door, then turned back toward Sophrona.

She carefully hid any signs of pain as he searched her face. He leaned over, kissing her before he left the room.

* * *

Thomas reached for a mug of coffee Penelope set on the trestle table. A servant returned from replacing candles, laying the stubs aside for melting. She moved over to the cook place and raked the ashes from the hot oven readying it for the bread rising on the hearth.

Penelope moved to the cook fire, placed the loaves on a shovel, then twitched them off onto leaves that lined the bottom of the oven.

He left the common room to go back to his wife.

"How's she doing, Aunt Elizabeth?" He took Sophrona's hand. She seemed to attempt smiling, but her cheeks only puffed out with air. Groaning, she came partway off the bed.

"It's a slow delivery. Wouldn't surprise me if this child waited out midnight." Aunt Elizabeth clucked her tongue as she removed his uncle's pocket watch from her apron. "Eleven o'clock. Nothing seems to be wrong. She just has some work in front of her. You try to rest. You won't get any sleep tomorrow, not with all that needs done. I'll want some help when she's further along."

He kissed Sophrona's cheek then left for the front room, pacing the floor before settling on the sofa. Dozing off, he woke up around midnight. In the common room, he poured a glass of water. Penelope sat in a chair close to the cook-fireplace.

"Why don't you go see if Aunt Elizabeth needs anything?" he pushed the glass back. "She wants some assistance when the babe comes. You're the one to do that."

"I want to speak with you before I go, sir," Penelope said. "Could we do that now?"

"Yes, I think there's time to talk, unless Aunt Elizabeth calls."

Penelope nodded, emotion sweeping her face. "In three weeks my indenture is up. I'm not sure what to do." She wrung her hands.

Sympathy for this woman, who already went through so much at her age, touched him. She was almost old enough to be his mother.

"This may take longer than I thought. Why don't we wait until after the child's born? That'll give you more time."

Penelope stood. "If that's what you want to do."

"Well, if we talk about it now, it's only us. If later, we'll include Sophrona in our discussion."

"Yes, Master Thomas."

"Go see about your mistress, then talk with my aunt." He patted her on the shoulder.

He went to his office, lit a candle-lamp and looked over the schedule for the following days' deliveries. After he finished, restlessness sent him to the front porch, where he took a seat on a straight back chair to stare out at the night.

Such a soothing thing, all enveloped in darkness. The nothingness kept his worrisome thoughts at bay. He closed his eyes, enjoying the solitude.

The door flew open, whacking against a table.

Penelope stared his way, breathing hard. "The babe's coming, sir. Your Aunt Elizabeth said to hurry."

"Now...now?" Thomas shot up off the chair and pitched forward, sprawling half way over the porch rail.

"Yes sir. I'm going back. Miss Sophrona needs me."

221

Thomas sucked in air as he hurried after her. *Lord in heaven, let this child live. Please don't take the wife you gave me, either. I need her.*

* * *

"Waaah—Waaah…"

Thomas turned the knob, pushing open the door to see his aunt hand the babe to Penelope. How could the child breathe, so stricken with rage? Penelope smiled, holding out the naked babe, frail legs pumping like a frog.

She quickly enfolded the twitching little body, coated with a bloody whitish substance, in a linen cloth. Gently she wiped the mixture off the child's face and head. The tiny, puckered-up face turned a shade of purple as Thomas readied himself for another round of squalling.

"He's got some good lungs, that one," his aunt said as she gave him a tired smile. "Seems to me like he'll fit right in with our family."

He nodded as he moved over to grasp his wife's shoulders, covered with a damp, linsey-woolsey shift. When she smiled up at him, he stooped low to kiss her brow before patting her arm. "I'm so proud of you."

"You have a son, Thomas, one too stubborn for birth until the wee hours of the morning." Aunt Elizabeth sighed. "He wouldn't come on the eighth—oh, no—it had to be the ninth. Best keep your eyes on this child. He seems to have a mind all his own."

"Thank you for saving his life," Thomas said.

His aunt smiled back, her eyes gleaming. "Don't thank me. I only did what I'm supposed to do. Thank the Good Lord for your happiness."

She cleared her throat. "Go on now. Leave. There's a few things that still need done. Penelope shall bring him out after his mother counts his fingers and toes, admiring your handiwork."

With a smile, Thomas walked back to the porch, taking the same chair he sat in earlier. Happiness filled him as he watched the dawn cast streaks of light across a dark sky. The grey stains widened, but not enough to clearly see.

The knowledge that God Almighty gave him a son overtook his tired mind. He jumped up from the chair, stretching his hands toward the sky.

"You looked down on this miserable world of man and still saw fit to send Your only Son to die on the cross for mere little humans like me. That through His shed blood, I might gain eternal life. I don't deserve what You've given me tonight, but I am eternally grateful to You for Sophrona—for this child."

He pulled his fingers across his wet eyes, wringing out tears before wiping his hands on his breeches. "I won't forget You gave me the boy. I'll see that he's raised in Your presence."

Tears streamed down his upturned face as his words assaulted the sky, resonating into the silent night.

"I have a son. Thank you, Lord."

Drained of energy, he sat a while before stepping inside to the common room, where he took a seat at the table, heat from the cook-fireplace surrounding him.

Penelope brought in the babe, placing him in Thomas' arms. He studied the tiny face that looked so much like the child's grandfather, Cyrus. His hand engulfed the small fist.

"Starlyn Peter Craighead, you will turn into a fine young man one day, who'll make your mother proud."

He laid Starlyn on his shoulder, one hand supporting the neck and head, the other spread across his back, as he gently rocked his son. Placing a mug of coffee in front of him, Penelope reached for Starlyn, who already whimpered.

"I'll take him to his mother, sir."

On her return, Penelope went to the cook fireplace where she finished preparing breakfast. A servant filled platters with fried ham, biscuits plucked from the Dutch oven, and other foods that caused his stomach to growl. What a long night.

"Lord, we're grateful for all your blessings." Thomas raised his head then reached for a platter.

After eating, he went to the barn. By the time he returned, Jonah sat at the table with Elizabeth, having breakfast. Penelope handed her a cup of brewed tea. Elizabeth added dried herbs from a pouch she pulled from her pocket.

"Here, Thomas. Your wife needs this tea. Steady her when she sits up to sip it. Make sure she drinks it down to the dregs." His aunt pushed the cup toward him. "She did just fine delivering that babe. You know, he seems to favor Cyrus a bit."

Satisfaction stirred in Thomas. He wasn't the only one who thought Starlyn resembled his grandfather. He carried the tea in to Sophrona, supporting her back as she sipped it.

"Are you doing all right, then, darling?"

She nodded. Reaching down, she unfolded the child's covers.

"He's the son I asked for. The Lord made him pretty, like your family." She picked up a tiny fist, uncurling the fingers. She placed her curved baby finger next to the child's straight little one. She sighed. "See how his fingers are? He's perfect, isn't he?"

Thomas nodded. Why were Starlyn's straight fingers so important to her? He remembered first seeing her hands—usually hidden. The two littlest fingers curved inward, instead of straight like the others. He liked her hands the way they were, not how she wanted them. Besides, the babe had more than the Craighead blood. She was too beautiful to ever deliver an ugly child.

He slept in a different room the next few nights, while Sophrona recovered her strength. When she felt well enough to be up during the day, Penelope changed the bedding and cleaned the room.

His wife sat on the sofa as she nursed their child, softly stroking Starlyn's cheek with her fingertips. Her dark hair cascaded over a shoulder, brushing against the babe's head.

At nightfall they entered their bedroom.

"Hand me the child," he said. "I'll place him in the cradle."

Sophrona shook her head. "Not yet. He's too small to stay alone in that big cradle. Maybe he'll sleep there in a few weeks." She pulled the babe up on her bosom, whispering soft words to him.

Thomas kissed her before he nuzzled Starlyn's head. After blowing out the light, he crawled in next to them.

She awoke next morning when Thomas lit a candle.

"I almost forgot, in all the excitement. The night Starlyn was born, Penelope asked to speak with me about her indenture. She's soon a freewoman."

"Has it been that long since we married, Thomas? It doesn't seem like it to me."

He leaned over the bed to kiss her. "On September first it's seven years since we took our vows."

"Let's talk with her this evening." She slipped out of bed, covering the child before getting dressed. "I'm going to fix breakfast. It'll be on the table when you come from the barn."

Penelope built a roaring fire in the cook place, where she worked with another servant preparing food. Sophrona approached her after setting plates on the table.

"We'd like to speak with you after supper this evening, in the dining room."

"Yes, Miss Sophrona." Penelope took glasses and a pitcher of water to the table. "I'll set aside the men's breakfast.

Sophrona nodded. The indentured men lived in a two-room log house. They occasionally brought their clothes for wash or repair, when picking up their food.

She set pewter chargers filled with breakfast foods on the table, thinking about the years Penelope helped her. What if her friend wanted to leave now? She swallowed hard. The table was ready when Thomas returned.

After the blessing they both ate in silence until Thomas spoke.

"There's a load to haul—shouldn't take long."

Sophrona nodded she heard. When Thomas finished eating he leaned over, kissing her cheek before he left.

She stayed busy, cooking or cleaning while Starlyn slept. Some things had fallen by the wayside before his birth. Today, it seemed especially important to get all the dirt from the corners, even scrubbing the black smoke off the stones of her cook fireplace.

Someone tapped her shoulder, and she whirled around to find Thomas.

"I called your name three times. Whatever were you thinking, so distant from this world, Sophrona? You feeling all right?"

"Yes, things are on my mind, is all." Did he not see her fragile condition—with the possibility of losing Penelope? Like a shawl with a thread hanging loose, one good tug and she might unravel.

"That's my job—to worry." He touched her shoulders, searching her face.

"Supper's almost ready. I'll just see to Starlyn."

Thomas met her in the common room. He held their son while the servants helped put supper on the table. Then Penelope took Starlyn.

Thomas asked the blessing before they filled their plates, slowly eating, both lost in their thoughts. When Thomas finished, he stood.

"I'm going to speak with the men. When I return, we'll talk with Penelope."

Sophrona stood to take the child. Going to the front room, she sat down on the sofa. Starlyn fussed while she draped a lace-edged linen cloth over her shoulder, then adjusted her clothing. Soon he started nursing. She laid him down when Thomas returned.

"I'll ask Penelope to join us," she said.

After speaking with her, Sophrona went to the dining hall to sit with her husband.

Penelope came in with a tray holding bowls of rice pudding. She served the dessert before taking a chair.

"I married your mistress seven years ago this Wednesday," Thomas said. "On that day your indenture is over. What have you decided to do?"

Sophrona didn't trust herself to speak. She waited for Penelope to tell them.

"Master Thomas, there's no one in England to return to, nor money to pay my fare if there were. My mistress feels like family to me. May I stay on here to work? It'll cost you little more than my food and lodging. Besides, she'll need some help with the child."

Thomas rubbed his chin with a hand, occasionally nodding as Penelope spoke.

"I'll only ask enough money for my few small needs. When I grow too old to work, send me away."

Sophrona swallowed her sobs, as she listened to the older woman. Most likely, she would never live near her own mother again. She grew close enough to this servant, over time, to almost consider her a second mother. She cleared her throat.

"Thomas, I …let us consider this. I do need the help."

"I'll think on this, Penelope. After you become a freewoman, I'll give you an answer."

CHAPTER TWENTY-NINE

September 1, 1762
Bedford County, Virginia

Thomas and Sophrona sat down in the dining hall with Penelope. He reached for a quill, dipped it into an inkwell, where he signed both copies of her indentured servant's contracts. "I'll keep this for my records. Here's your copy."

Penelope stood as she reached for the parchment. "I'm most grateful, sir."

"Take care not to misplace your document," Thomas said.

"Yes, sir. I'll keep it somewhere safe." She folded the parchment, slipping it through a slit in the side of her skirt before sitting again.

Penelope Walters had completed her seven years of service to his wife. "In accordance with our contract, you'll receive a new set of clothes, as well as coin to start out on your own." Thomas cleared his throat. "Is it still your desire to stay with us, work for food, lodging, and a certain amount of coin?"

"Yes, sir," Penelope said, as Sophrona reached over to pat her hand.

"Then you may change your bed to a private room. You'll receive pay once a month."

"I'll not disappoint you or my mistress, sir."

"I don't expect you will, Penelope. We're pleased you're staying with us." Thomas rose from the table, going to the office.

* * *

October, 1762

Sophrona straightened after leaning over the bed, dressing the babe. "What's that? I didn't hear you."

Thomas cleared his throat. "Starlyn's two months old. Don't you think it's time he slept on his own? I don't want to roll over on him."

Uncertainty filled her as Thomas moved the cradle next to her side of the bed, but she ignored it. She could easily reach out to soothe the boy during the night, or take him into their bed for feeding. Still, it grew cold after they banked the evening fires.

Three months later, in deep winter, Thomas said, "What's wrong with our son? You've gotten up with him the last few nights. Sometimes he coughs so hard I'm afraid he'll stop breathing."

"He's come down with a bad chest cold from kicking off his covers at night. I can't keep him warm when he's in the cradle." Sophrona's voice wavered as she pushed back hair from her face. "I'm afraid this'll settle in his lungs—could turn into pneumonia. At least it isn't the boll hives."

"Boll hives might kill—run a fever then the hives don't break out?" He moved closer to her side. "I only wanted to protect him from being rolled on and smothered."

"I've applied cornmeal plasters for the last three days, but they don't seem to help." She fought back tears. "I meant to tell you, but each day I thought he'd get better."

The babe began to cry, then cough. His face turned red, his nostrils fanning out, as if searching for air. Sophrona fitted him up under her arm face down, as she hurried toward the front room, Thomas just behind her.

"Penelope, come quick," she called.

Penelope hurried into the room, a stricken look on her face. "What, mistress?"

"Take him; put him over your knees. He can't breathe." Sophrona handed him to Penelope, who sat down, placed his small body across her knees, face down, dropping his head slightly lower.

Getting a good hold on his ankles with one hand, she patted him between the shoulders in a soft, steady rhythm as she gently bounced him.

"Thomas, fill the washtub while I get linen to wrap him." Sophrona hurried to another room, where she grabbed some things.

She arrived in the common room with blankets and linen, to find Thomas scrubbing the wooden tub. "Rinse it. No time for cleaning. Then fill it straight from the water barrel," she said.

"That water's so cold. Shouldn't it be warm?"

She shook her head. "No. I want it cold enough to break the fever. I'll get the babe."

Shrieks assaulted her ears as she stopped in the front room to stare at globs of greenish mucous on the floor. "I'll take him, Penelope. You build up a roaring fire in the cook fireplace. Leave the floor. We'll take care of it later."

Back in the common room, she stripped her son, his body hot in her hands.

"Oh, Thomas, he's burning up."

She grasped him under the arms and plunged him into the tub up to his neck. Starlyn's bottom lip curled out as his face turned purplish red. Screams bleated from his mouth in waves.

"Lord help us, we can't do this alone," Thomas said, as he knelt on the floor, placing an arm around his son's upper chest to keep his head above water.

Sophrona wet a cloth, bathed Starlyn's face, then squeezed more water over his head.

"I'll take him, Thomas." She pulled him out, only to plunge him in several more times, as his little body bucked like a young mule. She pulled him out once more, wrapping him securely in one of his blankets. Soon the crying turned to whimpers. She removed the covering, swaddled him in linen, and then wrapped him in a heavier cover before pulling him close to her body.

Penelope continued to stoke the fire, chasing the draft from every corner.

Starlyn's eyelids drooped and he soon drifted into a fitful sleep. A servant held him while Sophrona left to change her clothes. She returned to find the tub removed, with supper waiting on the table.

They slowly ate while Penelope held Starlyn near the fireplace.

When they were through, Sophrona nursed him. He did not completely wake up, but only sucked in his sleep. She removed his covering after he finished, changing the damp, soiled linen. She ran her hands over his chest, up under his arms, then his neck, before dressing him.

"He's not so hot now. His fever's broken," she said, in an attempt to reassure his father. "Maybe he'll sleep better tonight."

* * *

Thomas filled the bed warmer with hot coals. Wiping off suet residue, he slid it between the covers several times, like he did each night. He blamed himself for Starlyn's illness. If he had not insisted on the babe sleeping alone, with it so cold, maybe he would not be sick.

"Should we move him back in our bed?" Sophrona said.

"Yes. He'll sleep with us. When he's better, we'll decide if he's going back to his cradle."

Thomas refused to dwell on whether their son got well. He pushed that thought away. "I'm sorry for removing him from our bed. I know better, now."

"You're a fine father, Thomas." Sophrona placed their son in his arms.

She changed into a shift before sliding under the covers. Thomas handed her Starlyn, whom she pulled close to her bosom.

He crawled into bed but could not sleep, only lay there listening to her shallow breathing and his son's little noises. Eventually, he drifted off, but awoke in fear when he heard Starlyn's fitful

231

movements. Sophrona shifted in the bed, and then he heard soft little sounds as the babe nursed.

In the still of the night, he turned to a more comfortable position, ready to fall back to sleep. His son seemed to breathe easier, now. *I'm grateful, Lord.*

* * *

May, 1766

Sophrona shook out quilts on their back porch, hanging them over the rail to air out in the sun, under a clear, robin's-egg-blue sky. The breeze blew around her face, cooling her brow as it brought the sweet smell of lilacs from out in the yard. She inhaled the flowers' perfume as her mind wandered back to that cold night when Starlyn became so sick they didn't know what might happen. He seemed better the next morning and never took sick like that again. Nearly four years old, she watched him out in the fields with Thomas.

"Look, Da…" Starlyn called. He waved an object.

It looked like an old bird's nest. His young legs took him through the middle of the field to catch his father. She stopped, expecting to witness the wrath leveled on their son for trampling down the young plants. Starlyn must learn to be careful and not destroy the source of their food.

Thomas turned in his direction, rushing toward him. She cringed when Thomas bent over, his back to her. Soon Starlyn swirled in the air, screaming with delight, Thomas' hands under his arms.

June crept in as the sun shone hot on the fields. Obediah would harvest some of their vegetable crops in July and August. With only a year of indenture left, becoming a free man, Obediah might go his own way. An older, more experienced workman, he sometimes drank a mug of coffee Penelope served him.

Their household became so involved in the joy of Starlyn's birth, then watching him grow; being with child again came as a surprise. John had entered the world on the last day of November, in 1764, with no time for Thomas to ride for his Aunt Elizabeth. He brought water before pacing the floor to wait out the event.

The child's birth came fast, forcing Penelope to catch him. She tied the navel cord, leaving it long when she clipped it. A sure sign to any visitors a male babe just arrived. Sophrona had smiled at that thought.

"Me, Da, me," little John called out.

Sophrona blinked as John came into view below, arms stretched toward his father. Penelope stood beside him, smiling proudly, as if the child's grandmother.

"Not this time, Jack. I must take care of the animals." Thomas headed down the incline toward the barn, Starlyn trotting behind him.

Why he insisted on referring to their youngest son by the informal name, Jack, remained a mystery to her. What if the boy grew up answering to that name?

John started to cry. The look of resentment on his face, as his older brother followed behind their father, caused her concern. She did not think it possible for a child under three to feel that way—not at his young age. No, too small.

"Maybe he's hungry, Penelope. Bring him in for some bread." Sophrona shook the last rug, reaching down to scoop up the rest. She handed them to a servant on her way through to the common room.

* * *

April, 1773

On a sunny afternoon, Sophrona took a basket filled with quilting materials out to the back porch. She pulled up a chair within reaching distance of the wooden table and close to the railing. She emptied the bundle of prospects on her lap, then set the basket on the floor.

Out in the field, every available man on the place worked with Thomas, forming the little hills to receive the transplanted tobacco seedlings. Alex, Uncle Jonah, and some neighbors also came to help.

Earlier, Sophrona helped the servants prepare a meal. They placed dinner on a table in the back yard, along with pitchers of water when the sun reached high overhead.

"We made custard pie, too," Sophrona had said to Thomas.

After the men finished eating, they returned to the field. Penelope handled the clean-up.

"Mmm—mmm." Sophrona placed cloth for quilting on the table, then reached for another scrap she recognized as material used for the boys shirts. She laid that scrap on the quilting pile then eyed the next one, placing it in the basket at her feet. She raised her head at the sound of Starlyn's and Andrews' voices.

"I made a bunch more hills than you, even transplanted the tobaccer," Andrew said.

Starlyn reached down, snatching a clump of dirt off the ground. He sliced the air with the clot, barely missing Andrew's head.

"Na, ya didn't. Ya couldn't hold me a light to go by."

"You're gonna need a light to find your way outta this." Andrew came at Starlyn, taking him to the ground where they wrestled. First one, then the other, took top position.

Sophrona absently stroked the piece of cloth a little faster as she watched. Big, strong boys for their age, Andrew already turned eleven, Starlyn in August. They looked like twin brothers in their faces, except gold touched Andrew's brown hair, his eyes bluish-gray. Starlyn's hair, a shade darker, reflected red highlights in the sun, his eyes blue.

When Andrew wrestled Starlyn into a headlock, Sophrona's shoulders tensed.

"I'll help ya, Star'n." John lunged toward Andrew, getting him by the foot. "Turn my brother loose or I'll twist your leg off."

234

"Leave me alone." Andrew pulled his leg back, kicking at John as he rolled off Starlyn. "You're too small to get into this."

Just as John went backward, Starlyn sat up, chest heaving. "I don't need your help, John. Leave us alone."

Once John gained his feet and hobbled away, Starlyn went after Andrew, plowing him to the ground. "Don't ever kick my brother like that again. He didn't mean any harm."

"I didn't intend to hurt him, but only wanted to get loose. Will you accept my apology?"

"That's alright. I know you're not one to mistreat people." Starlyn held him down.

Pride swelled in Sophrona as she watched her son defending his younger brother. She finished up sorting the material, standing to shake out her apron, when Thomas and Alex came around the corner.

"What's going on here?" Thomas said, fatigue evident in his slumped shoulders.

"Nothing, Da. Just…just wrestling." The boys stood up.

Sophrona removed the cloths from the table, picked up the half-filled basket, then went inside, taking the scraps to the common room. After she cut off the worn material, then sized the pieces, they would make a pretty quilt top.

* * *

Sophrona walked along with Thomas under the hot July sun. How she wished for autumn. Next month, the hottest time of the year, the heat became almost unbearable. She already stripped down to one petticoat, but the heat from her long dress still stifled her. Brazen as could be, she lifted her skirt to her knees, shaking her petticoat to cool off.

"Aunt Elizabeth believes our community needs a name," Thomas said. "She thinks it's small, but growing."

"What name do they want?" She shook her skirt again.

235

"Well, Aunt Elizabeth wants to bring families together next month to decide that. Especially those who traveled out with them, when the community first began. We'll start a round of harvesting at their house that day, helping Uncle Jonah bring in some of their tobacco plants."

"I'll take Penelope along to help Aunt Elizabeth. She'll want to visit, I imagine, while Obediah works with you." Sophrona smiled, remembering their courtship. "Penelope thought he would never marry her, but he did."

Thomas nodded. "He worked on the house he built her for a year after his indenture ended."

"It's sure pretty inside. She keeps it up while still managing to help me. I just don't know for how long, though"

"Don't grow too concerned about her. The home he built on our property is Penelope's and she'll always be taken care of like our family, whether she can work or not."

Sophrona nodded, her mind on the future. She did not want to think about losing Penelope.

Thomas rubbed his chin. "I'll work hard to bring in the other men's crops. When my fields are ready, they will help us."

"You work too hard. Sometimes I worry about that. Building your freighting business at the same time you farm. Our place looks more like a plantation."

"Nothing comes easy. Besides, I must work hard. It's good for me. That extra fifty acres I bought makes it possible to switch fields, so the tobacco crop doesn't wear out the soil. Father said that happens if the land doesn't rest." He glanced into the distance. "Let's turn back. I want the lads to go over the plants for tobaccer worms— they're especially bad right now." Thomas worked his fingers. "If they don't pinch off their heads, the worms destroy the plants. It's a good cash crop. We can't afford to lose it."

* * *

In August, Sophrona went with Thomas to help Jonah. After the men finished, she sat with him as the group discussed their community's name. Starlyn, John and Andrew went outside with the other children. The squall of an unhappy child carried inside the house, leaving her to hope their Craigheads were not responsible.

"After thinking on this, does anyone have a name in mind?" Jonah said.

Silence descended on the room until someone spoke.

"Let's call it Eagle, Virginia."

"No," another replied. "The name should be about our community. Every place has eagles."

Thomas spoke up. "We're not part of the original families like my aunt and uncle; still, I'd just like to know who the name is important to, here."

"Not me," a man said. "Whoever wants to name our community may do it, long as it's not something strange."

Nods followed his remark.

"I remember the first night we arrived," Elizabeth said. "Nothing around except that one room building a few older Scotch-Irish immigrants built. We turned it into a place to worship the Lord." She paused. After a breath, she continued. "We pulled our wagons together and cooked. I looked up at the stars that night, thinking how bright they shone, giving light enough to see by."

"That's right, Elizabeth," Jonah returned. "I remember you saying that."

"Yes. I remember it too," a neighbor woman said. "I was young then—a new wife. I thought we chose the right place to start over again."

Jonah glanced over. "Why don't we call it Starlight, like Elizabeth said that night?"

"Starlight. Starlight." Satisfied with the name's sound, the group agreed to call their Virginia community Starlight.

The name spread. Even the newest families knew what to call their home.

The crops came in on time for Thomas, Alex, and Jonah. The closely-knit family used their resources to assist whoever needed help, providing they worked.

It became known around the community; the Craighead-Shepard family helped anyone in trouble. Their reputation for kindness made Sophrona proud to be Thomas' wife and a part of Starlight.

CHAPTER THIRTY

Monday, June 10, 1776
Starlight, Virginia

Sophrona gathered her correspondence from the carved rosewood box on top of the chest of drawers. She entered the room, taking a seat at her maple desk in front of the window overlooking the yard. Her eyes filled with tears as she glanced over past letters from Father. How she wanted to see her parents. Sighing, she dipped a quill in the inkpot, and glided it across the tablet.

Dearest Father,

It is my desire this reaches you. The countryside is in such a state of upheaval. My slow response to your last post seems unforgivable, considering the pleasure you and Mother receive from news about your grandsons.

I hope you know how much I love you both.

Starlyn will be fourteen years this August. Where did the time go? He has become interested in a young lady. She seems more interested in his cousin Andrew. I'm most anxious to see how this ends. John shall turn twelve the following November.

Andrew and Starlyn are so competitive, they almost act like brothers. At times I think John feels left out of their friendship.

Sophrona paused to glance out the window. A black-capped chickadee landed on a limb. If only her life was as simple as the birds

239

that lived in their trees. Lonesome, she picked up the quill and dipped it in the ink well.

Penelope still resides with her husband in a house on our land, and treats the boys with love. They have flourished under her care.

How is Gerald? Having his children around must make Mother happy. How is her health? I worry terribly about both of you.

I'm concerned with the talk of war. The men all speak of freedom from the Crown. Thomas has become known as a reliable man in important circles.

I must end this as I see him and your grandsons coming up the path to the front door.

Tell Mother I love her dearly. Do answer soon.

I remain your loving daughter, Fronnie.

Sophrona placed the letter inside an outer leaf. Dripping hot wax on the two edges, she pressed a small wooden block into the wax, sealing the letter with a 'C'.

* * *

Removing ham from a spider skillet, Sophrona set the platter in front of Thomas. "I've written to Father."

He nodded, giving that smile she loved so much. "There's a load of freight leaving for Williamsburg today. I'll see that the driver posts it."

She filled his coffee mug, then sat next to him. She would get the letter after they finished. A servant placed the other dishes in front of them and Thomas asked the blessing before they started breakfast.

As they filled their plates, Penelope came into the room, placing a basket of eggs on the sideboard. She sat down at the table. "I'm so hungry this morning."

Thomas nodded, smiling. "I'll try to save enough food for everyone else. Where's Obediah?"

"He's working in the barn."

"What's taking Starlyn and John so long coming to the table?" Sophrona took a bite of pudding, finding a thin slice of apple. She must remember to add more sugar next time.

Penelope smiled. "I think something got settled this morning. Andrew rode up when Obediah walked me to the barn. Later, I passed John as he watched Starlyn wrestle with Andrew. They went at it real hard."

Thomas took a sip of coffee. "It's too early in the morning for problems—even for those two. What's going on?"

The older woman shook her head. "Don't know, but I heard Andrew say, 'who wants anything to do with her?' Then Starlyn said, 'Well, don't think you'll foist her off onto me.' All three boys were laughing when I reached your porch."

"You're smiling." Thomas touched Sophrona's hand.

She shrugged. "All that uproar must be over a girl."

Now she knew how Starlyn's first romance ended. She must remember to tell Father when she next wrote him.

"I need to leave soon for a short haul, if I'm going to make it home before dark." Thomas laid the napkin on his plate before rising from the table. "Maybe it's time for Jack to ride along with me. We haven't done that before. If he comes in, tell him to eat fast."

Obediah entered from the outside as Thomas started across the room.

"Morning, sir. The team's hitched up."

"You're one good man to have around, Obediah. Now all I need to do is get my freight manifest." Thomas strode past him toward his office.

Ducking her head, Sophrona smiled. How she loved her husband's manner of treatment toward the other men.

***

Sophrona sat on the back porch in her cotton shift, a thin blanket draped over her shoulders as dawn's first light slid across the dark sky. She had slept very little during the past week. A never-ending struggle lasted all night. She rolled in any direction but where she already lay, searching for sleep.

A pinkish red color began to light the eastern sky. Soon, coppery-colored streaks pushed against the darkness, the clouds like odd-shaped pillows, stitched around the edges with golden thread.

She jumped at a touch on her shoulder. "Thomas?"

"Do you feel all right?"

"Just restless. I think it's the weather—hottest first of July I remember in a while."

"You're up early," he said, pulling a chair close, taking her hand.

As they watched the sun rise over the trees, she leaned comfortably against his shoulder.

Nearby, a rooster crowed. Soon the backyard teemed with chickens scratching out bugs. Farther out, furry creatures scurried in the shadows of the tall grass as birds hopped through the tree tops filling the air with their morning songs.

"It's time to dress and fix breakfast." She stood, stretching. "The cook fire will heat up the common room more, the longer I wait. I'll wish for this cool air later today." Sophrona went to the door, going inside.

* * *

Second of September   Baltimore County, Maryland
Dear Thomas,

It's with greatest pleasure I write to say Isaac intends to take over the freighting business we've built up over the years since you departed. He and Mari are expecting a child in the spring. I want to give them room for as many children as they want.

242

Mari's mother, may God bless her soul, managed to secure a place for herself in our household, her husband being gone many years. She's a strong-willed woman who is almost as stubborn as Isaac. I suspect she'll soon choose another child to live with.

I do not want this to become common knowledge, Lad, so as not to hurt the dear woman's feelings, no—not for anything, but it's my desire to leave before she arrives.

It's the time we spoke of, so long ago, for me to come live with you. I hope you haven't changed your mind, as I'll be on my way before you receive this post. My wagon's loaded down, and it'll do me well to beat the coming bad weather. I will arrive there the first of November, with bells on.

Your father,
Cyrus Craighead.

Thomas stood and placed the letter on his desk.

"He's finally coming after all this time."

Sophrona came to him. "I'm so happy the boys shall know Cyrus—get to love him the way you do." He hugged her before she turned and left the room.

Thomas walked from the office, whistling as he strode out the back door and down into the barn. Now he would get the time with his father he missed after their move. Those times he wanted to discuss business with him, but could not, were over. The most experienced person he ever knew would give him advice on freighting or raising cash crops.

"Why are you whistling, Da?" Starlyn said.

Thomas laid aside the harness he had picked up and took his son by the shoulder, turning Starlyn to face him.

"I'm happy because your grandfather is coming to live with us. I've missed him so much. I can't remember being this pleased very many times in my life. Except when I married your mother, and then when you and your brother entered our lives. We're going to have a good time when he gets here."

* * *

The family gathered at Aunt Elizabeth's house for supper. After Jonah asked the blessing they began to eat.

"I have some news," Thomas said. "Da's on his way to Starlight."

"When did he leave Baltimore County?" Alex said, excitement in his voice.

Aunt Elizabeth gripped the sides of the table, partly rising. "My brother's finally going to live near me again. When shall he arrive?"

"Is he on horseback or driving a wagon?" Jonah looked across the table.

The room turned into a roar as everyone spoke at once. Andrew, Starlyn, John, and Alex's two youngest children, William and Katherine, all remained silent. They sat at the twelve foot, split-log trestle table Jonah built for the family years ago.

"All right, then." Thomas cleared his throat. "Da left last month, traveling over the Carolina Road. He expects to arrive around the first of November if nothing goes wrong."

Andrew said, "We'll finally get to meet Granda Craighead, Star'n. None of us know him yet."

"Who's Granda Craighead?" Katherine said.

"That's our Da's Da." William looked to his father for confirmation. "Girls are just dumb."

"That's right, William, he's my Da." Alex continued. "Lad, you shouldn't talk to your sister like that. There's nothing dumb about her."

Katherine stuck out her tongue at her brother, wiggling it, curls jiggling around her shoulders. William immediately returned the gesture before straightening his back, a superior look on his face as he glanced toward his father.

"May we be excused?" Starlyn said.

"Yes," Aunt Elizabeth said. The three older boys left the table. William and Katherine slowly followed them, leaving Thomas and the other adults to finish their coffee.

"If Da doesn't show up when he should," Thomas said, "one of us shall go look for him. That's a long way to travel alone."

A murmur of agreement went around the table. That didn't distract from the worry in his heart. After all the years he waited, nothing must happen to keep his father from the family.

"It's going to be all right," Sophrona whispered, pressing in close to his side.

Time would tell, but right now he needed to get away from the common room, maybe look in on the horses while Sophrona enjoyed his aunt's company a bit longer. They must leave before dark, or else stay the night.

* * *

Thomas looked up when Starlyn entered the storage shed.

"I just got back from Uncle Alex's. Didn't expect to stay gone this long, but Andrew wanted to break in a new colt." His son clutched his sides, bringing a knee up, as deep laugh rolled out, causing Thomas to smile. "That horse threw him so many times, Da, but he got up to crawl back on. You want some help with that?"

"I've finished scrubbing the board. Why don't you dump out the water?"

"Then—we're having company over?" Starlyn's face briefly changed as he touched the board. "This feels smooth as mother's face. I always liked the feel since real little."

245

Thomas reached for the cloth that went around the board. Starlyn had only seen it used as a platform for outdoor meals.

"No. Mr. Mathis borrowed the board to lay out his father. He said that he wanted to get him in the ground right away."

The board measured three feet wide, six and a half feet long, and over three inches thick. It came from heavy, solid cured oak, the two top corners rounded off.

Now old enough to hear about the board, he should tell Starlyn.

"They've used this board to prepare our family's bodies for burial, immediately after death, since long before I came into the world, Star'n. One day, someone will use it to bury us, as well."

"I don't like to think about death just yet, Da. It's too soon for me."

Thomas nodded. "Take a good look at our mark, down at the bottom."

Such a small mark for the size of the board, cut into the wood with precision. Thomas imagined the tools coming alive in the carver's hands. The man had dug out the excess wood, roundabout, leaving a deep, perfect mark.

Starlyn touched it. "Huh."

Thomas waited for him to remove his hand. "See how the bottom of the carved-out 'C' serves as the crosspiece in the middle of the 'H'? Then the rest of the 'C' curls over the 'H' completing the Craighead mark."

Starlyn nodded.

Thomas pointed toward an oval carving further down that ran almost the width of the board. Those details took exceptional talent to cut. The oval's left side resembled a jagged hill and, at the top, a fortress. On the opposite side of the oval, a two-masted ship tipped backward, starboard side up, masts pointing toward the fortress. Waves that once curled crisply in the oval's middle had become worn down.

"What about this?" Starlyn's fingers caressed the oval.

"I'm not sure." Thomas scratched his head. "My Da said his uncle Andrew brought the board home from Scotland."

"But what did he tell you about this?" Starlyn gently tapped the oval.

"Well, Father said his Uncle Andrew went to Scotland to see his Granda Ranald Muirhead, when the nearby Crowley family sent young James to Grandfather Ranald for help. Margaret, their ailing mother, needed money for good food and care."

"Did he give them the money, Da?"

"No. Granda had a land dispute going with the Crowleys."

"How did Andrew get the board, then?"

"Andrew caught James when he left, giving the boy money for his mother. She recovered. The night before Andrew left his Granda, returning to their new home in Ireland, James brought him the board containing the carving. Andrew said James told him 'The Scots won't be indebted, and certainly not me to you, Andrew.'"

Thomas looked out into the distance, before he continued. "Rumor said this lad did his carvings at the mouth of a cave in early morning light. No one outside his family ever saw him carve—only the results."

"Remember anything else?"

"Da told me Uncle Andrew lost the board to his brother in a bet he thought sure ta win. After the bloody row came, his brother John turned it into a cooling board for family burials. Someone else carved the family mark." Thomas searched his memory. "John and Andrew, his uncles, gave Da the board. He used it to tote his relatives' possessions onto the ship that brought the family from Ireland to North America."

"Then, was that the last of it?" Starlyn straightened his shoulders.

"Only one other thing. Da recalled their Granda saying, 'Always keep the board.'"

Patricia Reece

Starlyn pushed the hair off his forehead. "I hope they won't need to use it for you or me anytime soon."

CHAPTER THIRTY-ONE

Snowfall already covered the front path. Thomas went to the back porch for a look at the sky. The lowering sun cast a glow on floating, large white flakes, cloaking the earth in a delicate covering.

He turned toward Starlyn and John as they walked to the barn for the evening chores. "It won't take long to get this done, three of us working together. Not like it took Obediah, alone. We may be doing everything for a while, with him not feeling good."

After they finished in the barn, Thomas headed toward the door, turning to say, "When you two finish, bring in some wood."

He had not traveled far when a snowball whizzed by his ear.

Thomas turned around. "All right, who threw that?"

"It wasn't me, Da," John looked down.

"Me neither." Starlyn fumbled with his coat collar.

"Since it wasn't either of you, then it must be both." Thomas worked his face into an 'uh-huh' look. He swiftly scooped soft snow off the ground, packing it hard as he could. His first ball caught John just under the chin. The next one rained down snow off Starlyn's head.

"Get him, John. He can't take us both." His sons went to work, forming snowballs faster than he thought possible. Their strong nimble hands soon filled the air with icy retribution.

After several minutes of back-and-forth, Thomas gave up.

"I'm going in. Don't stay out here too long."

He glanced back at John, who already turned on Starlyn, launching snowball after snowball. Grunts filled the air. He shook his

249

head as he continued to the house. At times that boy sure reeked of stubbornness, as he tried to best Starlyn in everything they did.

Thomas hung his coat on a wooden peg. Going directly to the front room fireplace, he poked up the fire and spread his hands in front of the flames. After he sat down, Sophrona came in to sit by him. Around bedtime, he banked the fire. Taking her hand, he said. "It's getting late. Let's go to bed."

He tried to fall asleep, but only tossed in the bed. Tomorrow was the first of November, the day he had long waited for. It made no sense to place all his trust in a date, but still he expected his father to arrive on time. He had met schedules for many years.

* * *

Sophrona muttered in her sleep as Thomas carefully inched his way out of bed. He dressed and went to the common room. Shoveling ash to the side, he stirred up the coals, coaxing a weak flame with some tinder. His fingers aching from the cold, he worked faster, building a roaring fire.

What if something happened to Father? Extending his hands behind him, he backed up to the fireplace. When his back grew too warm, he pivoted, facing the fire. Should he go look for him? Father could die in weather like this.

He turned as Sophrona entered the room, a wrap clutched around her shoulders, blue skirt not quite touching the floor as she came to him.

"I disturbed you when I left the bedroom." He leaned down to kiss her cheek.

"No, it wasn't that. I just couldn't sleep. I'll make us a cup of tea."

While Sophrona hung a pot of water on the trammel hanging over the fire, Thomas picked up the keys from the table, usually kept in her pocket. He unlocked the small tea caddy, taking out a pressed block of tea.

"Then is everything all right?"

She nodded, but Thomas did not feel convinced. He unlocked the sugar chest, removing a piece of beehive-shaped sugarloaf to place with the tea. Setting out the sugar cutter his wife used to snip off chunks, he moved on to the fireplace to add more wood.

Sophrona brewed their tea. They sat at the table, slowly sipping the hot liquid as the fire drove the cold from the corners of the room.

"Why couldn't you sleep?" He yawned, an arm bent back, elbow poking the air.

"I don't exactly know, but for the last few weeks I've worried about Mother. In his last letter, Father said she didn't feel well. That troubles me."

"Surely your father would let you know if anything happened, don't you think?"

"Yes, I suppose so. It's just not easy getting news from family." Sophrona looked down, and then up. "Even though your freighting helps us get our correspondence, I'm never certain our posts always get received." Pausing, she tucked some hair back under the lacy dust cap she occasionally wore to bed. "It seems like you had trouble sleeping, too."

"I'm anxious for Da to get here. I won't sleep well until he does, not with Indians and Tories roaming around and the colonies at war. The snowfall reminds me we're closer to winter. Could get a big storm. Remember our third year here?"

Sophrona nodded as silence descended on the table. Thomas looked past her, his eyes fixed on the wooden box he built several years earlier. Her containers of medicinal herbs lined one shelf, with various liniments and salves filling the upper portion. He stood to stretch.

"The fire's burned low." Thomas added more wood before he returned to the table. A rooster crowed, reminding him the chores

251

waited. "Obediah's not getting up quite as early these days. I'll wake Starlyn to help. No doubt John will come, too. Try not to worry."

"After kissing her, it seemed to him that her face softened, color returning. He left her humming as she began breakfast.

* * *

Thomas had finished with the animals when pounding on the barn door resounded through the building. Someone hollered. The voice sounded muffled, impossible to understand. Thomas' heart beat faster as the pounding grew louder.

What if a band of Tories waited out there? Sophrona and the other women worked alone in the house. His sons turned to him, their eyes big in tight faces. He slipped off his coat and rolled up his sleeves, before reaching for a wooden pitchfork.

"If I don't come through this, get to your mother. Protect the women any way you can."

Thomas slipped to the door, grasping the handle. *Please, Lord, let it be all right.* He threw it open and rushed outside, slicing the air with his pitchfork. Starlyn and John came out behind him, circling the man there. One with a mallet, the other a piece of iron.

"Woo there, Lads. Would ya work over a hungry ole man before he gets to eat?" Father stood before him. His body shook, head thrown back in laugher.

Thomas swallowed hard. "I might have hurt you. What did you think you were doing, Da?"

"Well, methinks I should be expected today. It's the first of November then, isn't it? I didn't think having a little fun might cause so much excitement."

Thomas laughed so hard his body went limp. He slid to one knee, clutching his belly.

"Get up Lad. You'll catch yer death a cold. That might force me to go back and live at Isaac's—face his mother-in-law. Then what's a man ta do?"

Starlyn and John started laughing as Thomas pulled himself off the ground. He clutched his father close, tears filling the corners of his eyes.

"Starlyn, John, this here's your Granda. Come say 'Hello'."

Father brushed at something in his eye as he reached to embrace his grandsons. "I've waited a long time to meet the two ah you."

"Granda, that a new freighter? It's bigger than almost anything we have." Starlyn stood next to him. The four turned toward the wagon sitting up above the house.

Granda turned toward Starlyn.

"That's a new Conestoga. Four talented men worked on that wagon for a good two months. I didn't know if they'd get it ready in time for me to leave, but they did. Just like they said."

Thomas admired the wagon body's blue paint, standing out against the sun's gold cast on the mounds of snow. Red covered the remainder of the wagon, the canvas white. His own freighters had the same colors, but not as bright as his father's new wagon. Not for a long time.

"Are you hungry?" John touched his sleeve.

"Yes, John. After a long, miserable journey, I'm sure to enjoy some of your mother's good cooking."

"Let's get a look up close, Granda," Starlyn said.

"But he's hungry." A fierce look spread over John's face.

Shivering, Thomas stepped just inside the barn to get his coat. Shrugging it on, he dug cold hands into his pockets. "Did you stop at the house?"

"No, Lad, I came directly to the barn."

"How'd you know to find us in the barn, Granda?" John tugged his collar up.

"Well then, John, where else might you be this time of morning?"

Thomas smiled but Starlyn laughed, reddening John's face.

"Let's go eat something, Da." Thomas touched his father's arm.

"Yes, John's right. I'm hungry. We'll look over the new wagon after breakfast."

When they came through the door to the common room, Sophrona hurried forward.

"Cyrus, I'm so happy to see you again." She hugged him then turned toward a servant. "Pour water for their hands. Hurry, the food will get cold."

"Where's Obediah?" Thomas turned toward Penelope.

"He's not coming up this morning. Something's got him down with a fever."

Sophrona turned to her. "Soon as we're through, take him some soup and bread. That's sure to make him feel better."

* * *

Thomas, his sons and his father rose from the table after eating.

"Let's take a walk, Lad." Father headed to the door.

Starlyn went out to the wagon with them. John trailed behind.

"Where'd they first come from, Granda?" Starlyn's face creased in earnestness.

"Well, they build these particular wagons in Pennsylvania, down in the Conestoga Valley of Lancaster County. The Dutch make them strong enough to freight around hills or mountains. I may have lost my load on the way out here, if not for the wagon's deep center keeping it from shifting."

Thomas stood back as his father spoke to the boys. He was so pleased their grandfather arrived in time to influence Starlyn and John's lives.

"Granda, this one's big," John said.

"Yes. Twenty-four feet long, four feet wide, four feet deep. The oak wood's a good inch thick. The top spreads over sixteen bows. I insisted on white canvas for the top. No homespun fer me. The puckered ends sure kept the rain and snow outa the wagon bed."

Thomas stepped aside, as his father moved closer to the wagon and removed something, wrapped in a blanket. "Let's walk back to the house. After that I need to empty this wagon."

John ran ahead, opening the door.

The two men went into the front room, where Thomas stoked the fire, adding more wood.

"Well then, where's Sophrona?" His father said.

"No doubt in the common room. Let's find her and have something warm to drink."

Father followed him, clutching the object, setting it down on the table before taking a seat.

* * *

Sophrona glanced over her shoulder from the cook fireplace. She laid down her wooden spoon. The soup would go good with the bread baked last night.

"Please put on the water for some tea," she said to a servant.

She unlocked the tea caddy and took out the exact amount needed while being careful not to waste a leaf. She did the same with the sugar safe, not wanting their new young indentured servant to think her careless.

"We've had tea once today, but we'll drink some with you, Cyrus." Sophrona reached for cups. "When the tea's used up, we won't purchase any more. Thomas refuses to pay the Crown's exorbitant prices. Besides, I find myself anticipating a good mug of coffee."

As she reached for a platter of cookies, Cyrus said, "Sophrona, please sit down with us."

Placing the cookies on the table, she sat across from Cyrus, noticing he held a blanket covering something.

He reached into the blanket and pulled out a small, reddish-brown cherry-wood box. "This is for you." Standing, he passed it across.

"Where did this come from?" She took the box.

"Your mother and father came by the day before I left Baltimore County. They asked me to bring this along for you."

She ran her hand over the smooth wood, her heart filled with hope. Then Mother was feeling better.

"You'll need this, lass, or ya won't get it open." Cyrus held a tiny notch key between his thumb and forefinger. He passed it to her.

Carefully she inserted the key, unlocking the box. On top lay a note that she unfolded.

Dearest daughter,

> I have sent you a present too beautiful just to be laid aside, instead of worn. That's what will happen if I keep them. I have thought about you so much lately. I pray for your happiness. I send you these with much love.

> I hope you like the wrap. It is sure to keep you warm. Your father paid a goodly price for it coming from the East Indies. I wondered if the neighbors heard him protest when he read the receipt. Oh my, daughter, but he loves you so.

> Give my love to Starlyn, John, and Thomas.

> Mother

Sophrona blinked her eyes and sniffled before she laid aside the letter. Picking up the needlepoint handkerchief she forgot about making at seven years old, she carefully unfolded the corners and took out a gold-colored silk bag. Reaching in, she pulled out a square of white material and removed the string of pearls she'd worn on her wedding day. With excitement over marrying Thomas, and Mother fastening the pearls at her neck, she had not noticed the large diamond embedded in the clasp. Blinking back tears, she placed everything back in the carved box, setting it on the table before slipping the key into her pocket.

"This also belongs to you, lass." Cyrus handed her the white linen bundle.

She pushed her cup away, unfolded the linen piece, and gasped.

"Wrap? This isn't just a wrap, it's a shawl. A paisley cashmere shawl. It's so beautiful. I just love it."

She stood, draping the multicolored wrap over her back and shoulders before crooking her arms, drawing them close to her sides. The shawl ends reached down toward her hem, spreading out the paisley pattern against her dress. She arched her shoulders, drawing the wrap closer. Mother would laugh at her preening, now, like a fine peacock. After turning in several directions, she removed the shawl and carefully folded it, wrapping the linen cover around it.

"Would you place this on the desk in the front room for me?" She handed the bundle to John.

She rose from the table going to her father-in-law.

"That's a lovely thing you've done, Cyrus, bringing their gifts all this way to me." Bending down, she kissed his cheek.

"Well then, you're happy. That's what your parents wanted. Along with my furniture and the chair I made for Thomas's mother, there's several iron bars and other items in the wagon that your father said Thomas might find useful."

"I'm glad Peter sent that iron," Thomas said. "I can use it about now."

"Lad, I'd like to unload the freighter and get it under cover."

Thomas, his father and Starlyn stood, going toward the door.

As they left, Sophrona reached down to brush her hand over the satiny wood of her box.

The pleasant feeling she experienced earlier diminished, though, as if something was not right. She pulled her hand back.

257

CHAPTER THIRTY-TWO

The family traveled to Aunt Elizabeth's for supper after services. Thomas breathed in clear, sweet air as he guided the one-horse chaise down the road. Father, Starlyn and Jack rode horses. The boys urged their mounts ahead in a fierce neck-to-neck race. His father adjusted speed to ride alongside Thomas.

"How old is Blackwater Valley Church, Lad?"

"I believe they built it before 1750. It was here when Aunt Elizabeth and Uncle Jonah arrived." Thomas gently tugged the reins. "A few Scots built it as a residence until they put up houses—then later used it for worship. Most of them have moved on, with some buried in the graveyard on the hill, behind the church."

"Well, Lad, the name fits, so close to Blackwater River. Maybe it's time to rebuild the church, with several more families here now. I wouldn't want to tell the good folks of Starlight what to do, of course, only being here a short time, myself. I'd sure help with it, though."

Thomas picked up the pace, as his father lengthened the distance between them.

"Let's talk about it at supper. Uncle Jonah gets along well with the other first families. He wouldn't hesitate to make a suggestion to them."

Several hours later, after everyone finished eating, Sophrona helped Elizabeth serve cinnamon-baked apples and rice pudding. Thomas noticed the two women enjoyed their friendship, sharing a laugh as they served coffee or set glasses of water on the table.

Uncle Jonah worked his way deep into his rice pudding, when Father cleared his throat.

"Tell me, Jonah, is it just me or did the church room seem crowded, today?"

"Seemed crowded to me, but that building's what we have to meet in. There's not a soul interested in tearing that church down for a new one." Jonah turned his attention back to his pudding.

Father poked at his baked apple before he put down the spoon. "No, it wouldn't do to tear that fine church down, but maybe add onto the room. It's as tight a building as I've seen. The pine logs'll certainly fit well with some brick." He picked up the spoon again, only to continue. "I'd be proud to build the kilns for firing the bricks—even use my Conestoga to haul them. But then, maybe I just need to mind me own business."

Aunt Elizabeth dipped her head several times. "Why, I've thought about that very thing, myself. It seems that building's getting smaller by the meeting. The other families might want a bigger place to worship, what with all the children born lately." She blotted her lips with a napkin, as she looked up at her husband and continued.

"Then again, maybe it's not worth bothering with, Jonah. Maybe Cyrus should just forget about this." She carefully folded her napkin, placing it on the table, her head tilted to the side, as though she expected an answer.

"Oh, no, Elizabeth. I think that's a splendid idea Cyrus has." Jonah ran a hand across his hair. "Why didn't I think about that?"

He turned to Cyrus. "I'll ask around, see if the men are interested in this."

Thomas struggled to keep a smile off his face as he watched Father quietly nod.

"Do you have some thoughts about it?" Jonah said.

Cyrus scratched his head. "Well then, the one room's a fine area for adding a larger pulpit as well as a baptismal. Then take down the

259

back wall where the door is, to extend the building with brick. Hang a large, heavy outside door going into the church, the pews going up through the brick addition almost to the pulpit, the stove moved back to the side of the addition. I'd suggest making the addition even wider to accommodate more pews."

When Cyrus ducked his head, Aunt Elizabeth's face brightened as she smiled, nodding at her husband.

Thomas stirred his spoon through his bowl again, as he listened to his father, aunt and uncle. He had no doubt his uncle's love for his aunt included her brother as well.

Alex remained silent during most of supper, and all of the discussion. He occasionally spoke softly to Murna.

The three older boys did not speak, but from the looks on their faces, Thomas suspected they knew something unusual transpired. They just did not know what.

* * *

January, 1777

Sophrona turned from the cook-place as Thomas came in from a two day freighting trip. "I ran into a wagoner I worked with from Baltimore Town. He gave me a post for you."

She set down the bowl, wiping her hands on her apron before she took the letter.

"I'm surprised to receive this from Father. It's so soon after I wrote that Cyrus arrived with their gifts. It seems like only last week that I asked you to post his letter."

"It was only last week. We have a little tea left. Why don't you sit down in the front room while I get someone to make you a cup? I'll be in there directly."

Sophrona sat on the sofa, shoulders swaying, contented. She flicked her wrist, the letter waving. What good news did he send? Perhaps they planned to visit in the spring.

Thomas brought in the tea. She took a sip and set the cup on a side table before she broke the seal on the letter. She looked up to see him eye her with concern. Her hand trembled as she unfolded the post.

Baltimore Town
December the 27th, 1776

My dearest daughter, it breaks my heart to tell you, your mother passed on late last evening. She became ill, but I thought she was improving.

Gerald is having a difficult time with her death. It seems to help, having his family.

No need to come back for her funeral. She will be buried before you receive this post.

More later, when I see clearly enough to write.

Father

Her chest constricted as she sobbed. Thomas sat down beside her.

"My mother died." Wiping at her face with a hand, she gasped, unable to catch her breath. "I can't stand it…she's gone…wasn't at the funeral."

He held her until the crying slowed. She dabbed at her eyes. When she stood, grief washed over her. Mother gone? Her body swayed.

"I'm going to lie down for a while. I don't feel well."

"I'll walk with you." Thomas took her arm, guiding her to their room. When she lay on the bed, he spread a light cover over her.

"I will come get you before suppertime."

Thomas woke her several hours later. She rose, changed her dress then ran a damp cloth over her face. They walked to the table, taking seats. Sophrona looked down before she spoke.

"Starlyn, John, your grandmother passed away on December 26th. The news came in a letter today from your grandfather. I already miss her so."

"I'm sorry, Mother. I hoped to go see her one day. Spend time with her." Lips pressed together, Starlyn carried the look of a small, bewildered child. His pain cut through her like a knife blade. She might get over her suffering, but she would find it more difficult to get past his.

"Me too, Mother—what Starlyn said." Jack's eyes glistened before he looked down.

"Join me in giving thanks for our food." Thomas took her hand. "Father we're grateful for Your provision and Your mercy, in Christ's name."

As the family raised their heads, Cyrus spoke in a low tone. "I'm sorry she's gone, Sophrona."

Penelope nodded, Obediah beside her. "She always treated me good, right from the first."

"Thank you, Penelope. I know she liked you." She gazed away before saying, "Mother wouldn't want us so unhappy. Let's eat, everyone, before the food gets cold. She never would have allowed that to happen."

Sophrona pushed the food around on her plate as she watched her sons, so full of life as they overcame her mother's death. She did her best to enjoy their quick wit as they engaged their father or grandfather, then laughed with Obediah. Her tears must wait. Without doubt, she would cry in bed this evening and for many nights to come, but for now, their cheerfulness drove back the shadow of despair that threatened to overtake her.

* * *

The new year brought harsh weather conditions that didn't end until April. Then the daisies, along with other wild flowers, pushed up from the sundrenched earth, spreading colors only God could have painted on their petals.

Several men worked on the church, as others rode along to help Thomas and his father load or unload bricks. By June, all that remained was the inside of the building.

The morning after completion, as they put the finishing touches on the building's outside, several wagons came to a stop. Children stepped down, pushing to get ahead of others as they hurried toward the church.

Thomas stood on the top step with his father. "We're finally through with the addition. Now everyone shall worship together without being so crowded."

"What do you think about our work, Lad?"

"Well, it's sure good to look at, although we didn't build it for that."

Just then, John grabbed his grandfather's elbow as he pointed. "See that girl in the blue dress, Granda? Who's that man she's standing next to in the brown vest? I sort of remember her, but she's changed. I don't recall her name."

"Well now, let me think, John." Father scratched his head. "I believe that's Will Thompson's young daughter, Rebecca. Seems like he said their family came from Ulster."

"Hold on, now, John," Thomas said. "Isn't that the girl who sat on you after service years ago?"

"No, Da. Not at first she didn't. She just got me down."

"Well, how'd that happen?"

John looked down. "Her friend Sarah came up from behind and they wrestled me down to the ground. Then she sat on me. I couldn't get up. I remember her friend's name cause she kept saying, 'No, Sarah, I'm not through with him yet.'"

"Da, don't tell Starlyn about this. Maybe he's already forgotten it happened."

263

"All right, son, but you did good to ask your Granda, since he talks to many of the men around here." Thomas scratched his head. "I sure don't remember her name. Plenty's happened since then. Besides, I wasn't the one who pulled her off of you."

CHAPTER THIRTY-THREE

August 27th

Sophrona's heart jumped into her throat when Penelope hurried into the common room, her shoes dripping water from the downpour outside. "Mistress, there's something wrong with my Obediah. I can't wake him."

Sophrona reached for her hand, pulling Penelope down beside her at the table. Years had passed since Penelope called her "Mistress".

Somehow, she must help Penelope remain her friend, not tumble back into a servant role. She looked toward Thomas for understanding on how to comfort her friend and former servant. He gently shook his head, a look of alarm on his face.

"Someone get her water," she said. Starlyn brought Penelope a glass and she took a sip.

"Is he still alive?" She rubbed the older woman's arm. "Tell me what happened."

"He acted like his usual self last night, except he drank some sugar water and whiskey, for the cough he's fought so long." She burst out crying. "This morning when I shook him, he wouldn't wake up."

"But...but he's still breathing?" Sophrona gripped Penelope's arm, a sinking feeling inside.

Penelope nodded. "He's warm. He just won't wake up."

"Starlyn," Thomas said, "ride for Aunt Elizabeth. Tell her we need help quickly."

Sophrona rose, touching Penelope's arm. "Come. Let us take a look."

"Elizabeth shouldn't be long," Thomas said. "I'll send her down when she gets here. I must appoint the freighting runs, and I'm set to take the short one. I'll hurry back before nightfall. If you need help before I return, ask Da."

Sophrona nodded as she continued through the house, putting on a shawl before stepping through the front door. The rain had slowed a little. When they reached the small house, she stood back until Penelope opened the door. Sophrona followed her to the bed where Penelope shook her husband calling, "Obediah, Obediah, wake up."

Sophrona heard him speak, but she could not understand him. She reached over to lay a hand on his forehead. "He's a little warm, Penelope. Think we should uncover him? Maybe use a cloth on his forehead?"

Rolling back the bedding, Penelope said, "I don't know what he's doing with all those covers. It wasn't that cold last night, rain or no rain."

Penelope left the room, brought back a pan of water, and reached in her pocket for a cloth. She dipped it in the pan, wrung it out and wiped her husband's face.

"What do you think's wrong with him?"

Sophrona shook her head. "I'd better wait for Aunt Elizabeth. She'll know more than me." She wouldn't say anything to hurt Penelope. He didn't look good, but, still, he could recover.

As Penelope stepped closer, he moaned. She grasped his shoulder. "What is it, Obediah?"

He did not answer.

She pushed his thick gray hair away from his forehead and wiped his face. Aside from the rain softly hitting the roof, the only sounds in the room were the rhythmic sloshing of the cloth and the dripping of the water, as Penelope wrung the cloth back in the pan before laying it on his forehead.

Sophrona avoided looking at her, as if words were the great enemy, not his illness. When she finally did, Penelope darted her eyes away, feverishly working with the cloth as she tried to cool his forehead. Bound up in silence, they both jumped when Elizabeth called from the doorway.

"It's me."

"Back here, Elizabeth," Sophrona said. "We're in the bedroom."

"I rode as quickly as I could without breaking my neck on that slippery ground," the older woman said as she entered the room, removing a leather cape.

"I'd better change the water." Penelope grasped Elizabeth's cape. "Maybe put another stick of wood on the fire to keep the soup pot warm. He may wake up hungry." She leveled the pan between the cape and her other hand, then left the room.

Elizabeth pushed back her hair, casting a sympathetic glance at Sophrona.

When Penelope returned with a linen cloth draped over her arm, the pan in her hands, Elizabeth said, "How long has he been like this, Penelope?"

"When I got up this morning, I tried to wake him." Penelope rinsed the cloth, placing it on his forehead. "He told me he loved me when we went to bed last night, gave me a kiss, then..."

"I'd like to rinse my hands," Elizabeth said.

"Go ahead." Penelope handed her a dry cloth when she finished.

Elizabeth carefully raised Obediah's eyelid with a finger. She laid her ear to his chest. "How long's he been congested?"

Penelope looked down. "Well, I want to say early winter, but it seems longer than that. Could go even further—all the way back to September or October."

267

Obediah gasped for air. Elizabeth reached for his hand. "He's growing cool and damp. Let's cover him."

Sophrona helped Penelope spread the quilt up to his chin. She glanced at Elizabeth's face but couldn't tell her thoughts. Obediah's breath sounded different, like the clattering sound of a child's rattle, or hail softly spraying the roof—before silence.

"Quick, get your mirror, Penelope," Elizabeth said.

Penelope hurried to a chest of drawers in the corner, returning with a small wood-framed mirror.

Holding it down to his lips, Elizabeth continued, "He's not clouding up the mirror. At least not that I can tell."

Penelope clutched her hands below her throat. "How much time does he have?"

Elizabeth's face softened. "Is he a child of the Lord?"

"Yes, for many years. Even before he met me."

"It's time to pray, Penelope." Relief flickered over Elizabeth's face as she said, "He's already begun his journey home."

After the three took hands, Penelope bowed her head. "Lord, we thank you for sending Obediah into our lives, into my life…giving us so many years together…"

Sophrona cried with Penelope, who then overcame her burst of grief to continue.

"Merciful God, I ask Your hand of protection on Obediah, as he passes through the Shadow of Death on his way home to You…"

After that only a strangling sound came from Penelope.

Elizabeth said, "Praise you Father. We give you glory, in Jesus' name."

Dropping hands, the women wiped their faces. Elizabeth checked the mirror again, only to shake her head.

"He's in God's hands, now."

Sophrona's heart squeezed with pain as Penelope cried out, "Not this soon."

She moved to hold her friend, whose tears continued to flow. They slowed when Penelope picked up the pan and hurried from the room.

"I don't know where Thomas intends to bury him," Elizabeth said, "but let's get him ready before the cold death sets in."

When Penelope returned Sophrona left them, finding Starlyn.

"You and John take the cooling board to Penelope's house."

When she reached the barn, Cyrus met her at the door. "He's gone?"

She nodded.

He passed a hand across his face before he said, "I'll have the coffin ready by the time Thomas gets home. He'll need to go in the ground today. Won't keep until tomorrow."

* * *

Thomas drove his team toward the barn, stopping when his father stepped out to meet him, the women standing just behind him. "Obediah's ready to go into the coffin, Lad. He's on the cooling board, dressed in his very best. The coppers I put on his eyes can stay."

Thomas looked into the distance before meeting his father's eyes. "So, then, it's over. Obediah's race is run."

Father nodded.

Sadness touched his heart. "If we're going to get him buried before the sun goes down, we'd better get to it. August isn't a good keeping month."

"Lad, the coffin's already at Penelope's. We are only waiting for you."

Jonah rode up and swung down off his horse. "I'd say from the looks on your faces, it didn't turn out good."

"No. We're waiting for Thomas to show us where the graveyard is," Cyrus said.

269

"There's the small meadow on the hill, with some scattered trees, Da. I intended to turn that into the graveyard, one day, but there wasn't a need, yet. I was so glad for that, I just kept putting it off." Thomas cleared his throat and looked over at Starlyn.

"Go choose a good place under a shade tree, and start digging. The rain's softened the surface, but that's still hard ground. So take the new iron pick-ax along with the shovel."

"Yes, Da." Starlyn turned toward the barn.

"John, you find a rock to mark Obediah's grave, until we get a proper headstone. Hurry."

"What size?"

Thomas rubbed his chin. "Well, a big one. Or at least several smaller stones.

John looked over his shoulder. "Yes, sir. Do ya want me to swing the pick-ax to soften up the ground ahead of Starlyn shoveling?"

"Well, as long as your brother doesn't object."

Starlyn came past. John said, "Give me the pick-ax. Da said I can break up the ground."

"Better work fast to stay out in front of me. Here." Starlyn handed it to him.

After Starlyn headed toward the hill, John shifted the pick-ax to his other shoulder. Running, he passed his brother.

Thomas glanced at his father before shaking his head.

"Well then, a wee bit of competition is healthy for a boy. Remember Alex trying to stay up with you, Lad? It didn't hurt him any. I think part of this is Obediah's death."

Thomas said. "I suppose the boys had to see death face to face, sooner or later."

He put away the wagon before he went to Penelope's house, where they removed the strips binding the body to the board. Cyrus undid the knot on top of the head, removing the strip of cloth to hold the jaw shut until the cold death set in. After the men laid the body in the coffin, Cyrus nailed down the lid.

"I'll go help the boys dig," Thomas said. "Then bring them to help move the coffin."

A little later he returned with Starlyn and John. "We'd better get him buried now, or we'll work by lamplight. Could be mighty dark up on that hill."

* * *

"I'm going back to the house" Sophrona said. She returned with the Bible and took Penelope's left arm. Elizabeth walked on Penelope's right. They followed behind the little procession, careful to stay on the cleared path up the hill to the burial site.

After they lowered the coffin into the ground, the small group stood silent as Thomas opened the Bible.

"The Lord is my Shepherd; I shall not want…"

Sophrona squeezed Penelope's arm, whispering. "We're all going to miss him."

"…Yea, though I walk through the valley of the shadow of death, I will fear no evil: For thou art with me; thy rod and thy staff they comfort me…"

Sophrona reached down to scrape up a large lump of wet dirt, molding it into two portions before placing one in Penelope's hand. Penelope just stood there. She nudged Penelope. "It's time to honor his passing."

"Go ahead, Penelope, he was your husband," Thomas said. "You must go first."

Time passed; no one spoke. Rays of gold touched the sides of the hill, while rose red mingled with the ever-darkening night sky. Penelope finally started toward the open grave, moving as if on burdened feet.

"I'm here, Penelope." Sophrona stayed close by her friend's side, breathing in the acrid smell of the deep green piney woods. Penelope

271

approached the ruptured ground, hesitated, then swung her arm forward, releasing the clot. The sound of it hitting the boards of the coffin rang through the quiet.

Sophrona reached out to catch her when Penelope teetered on the brink of the hole, before regaining her balance. The woman had one last thing to say.

"I'll miss you every day, Obediah, until it's my time."

Releasing her lump, Sophrona ran hands down her skirt before taking Penelope's arm.

"We must leave, Thomas," Jonah said, as he and Elizabeth moved up to drop some dirt in the grave. "It will soon get dark." Elizabeth patted Penelope on the hand when they went by, hurrying toward the crest of the hill.

One by one, the others stepped up to the grave to drop their handful of dirt on the coffin.

"I'm keeping Starlyn to help fill this in, Da." Thomas brushed the soil off his hands. "Would you escort the women down while there's still enough light to see? Take John to help you in the barn."

"We'll take care of the evening chores, Sophrona. Then we'll come up," Cyrus said when they reached the bottom of the hill. He turned to follow John, who walked toward the barn.

"Let's put supper on the table," Sophrona said. "Martha June must have it fixed by now."

"Maybe it's a good thing I'm still here to help you," Penelope said, laughing so hard she needed to wipe her eyes. "Her name's Martha Jane, not June."

Sophrona gripped her arm. It must be Penelope's nerves. Why else would she have a fit of laughter after just burying her husband?

"I'd find it hard to do without you, my friend. Maybe I'll only call her Martha, for now."

They stopped near Penelope's house. "I'll just go in to lay out a few things for later tonight, before I go to sleep. Then I'll come up to help you."

"Why don't you get something to sleep in while I wait, Penelope? Then stay with us tonight. Tomorrow after breakfast, we'll both come down to your house. I'll have Starlyn bring in your wood, to cook, but we'd like you to eat with us. Well, at least breakfast and supper."

"All right, then. I won't take long." When Penelope returned, they continued on.

Supper was ready and they set the table. Cyrus and John came in from the barn. When Sophrona heard Thomas and Starlyn enter the house, she sighed in relief, happy they made it off the hill. Thank you, Lord. That cemetery land had never been disturbed. How many snakes did they barely miss, coming through the brush and weeds in the deep twilight?

CHAPTER THIRTY-FOUR

Starlight, Virginia
September, 1777

After rising, Thomas carried a mug of coffee to the front room. Father poked up the fire as he stepped over to the window. A few wisps of darkness clung to a pale sky. He studied the morning as Alex's wagon pulled into view, with Andrew trailing behind on horseback. His stomach tightened. Something must be wrong.

He turned from the window. "Da, Alex is here."

"What's important enough to take him away from Cousin Alexander's church this Sabbath?" Father said.

"I don't know." Thomas set the mug down then pivoted back to the window. As Alex helped Murna step down from the wagon, their son William jumped. Dismounting, Andrew went to the wagon and swung down his sister Katherine.

Thomas pulled on his boots to follow his father out on the porch. A rooster crowed as the sun crested the hill, showering sunlight over the front yard and their family.

"Come on in. You must have left early to arrive at dawn." Thomas started back inside.

After entering the house, Andrew said, "Starlyn down at the barn, Granda?"

"Yes, with John. Go on down."

As Andrew left, Murna ushered William and Katherine toward the common room.

Drawing close, Alex threw an arm around Thomas. He moved over to their father, embracing him.

"Can't remember the last time you got in a hugging mood, brother."

"We came to attend services with the family," Alex said, looking away from Thomas.

While their father poked up the slow-burning fire, Thomas sat on the sofa with Alex.

Sophrona entered the room with three coffee mugs on a tray. She went to the fireplace, where Father replaced the poker, then took a mug, before stepping over to Thomas.

"Have you eaten yet?" Sophrona said, handing the last cup to Alex. "We'll cook plenty."

"If making breakfast for five more isn't too much trouble, we'd sure appreciate the food. We left so early no one ate, unless the children took something on the way out."

"You and Murna are our family—cooking for family is never too much." She turned, hurrying toward the common room.

Father cleared his throat. "All right then, tell us what's so important you left before dawn to get here."

"We have unexpected news." Alex's voice deepened. "I'm called to replace the Presbyterian pastor in Salisbury, North Carolina." He pursed his lips. "I'd prefer leaving the following fall, but the man's age, along with an injury, makes it impossible to care for his church past April of next year."

"Does my cousin favor the position?" Father said.

"Yes, sir. Cousin Alexander wielded some of his influence. He said I'm as good a pastor as himself, therefore I should accept the position." Alex ran a hand over his hair. "Said he wouldn't always be around, therefore I must take the help while he is."

A shadow passed over Father's face. Early in marriage, his Cousin Alexander's wife and only babe died during childbirth. Thomas tried not to think about his father's death.

"Three Alexanders—all ministers—only you and my first cousin still alive." Father glanced away. "Second cousin Alexander, with his strong love of liberty and freedom, moved to Mecklenburg County, in North Carolina, where he sank deep roots." Father's voice grew thick. "One of the finest ministers to ever lay claim to Scottish blood—gone from this earth over eleven years, now. I regret not seeing him again before he died."

"Why didn't you?" Alex said.

Father pulled at his face with a hand. "Couldn't help it. You and Thomas already gone, left Isaac at the house. He just didn't know enough about freighting ta leave while I made the trip."

"Are you all right?" Thomas said.

Father nodded, wiping his eyes. "Never mind that any. Just remembering a painful time."

The room grew quiet as the men finished their coffee.

"So then, Alex, when do you leave?" Thomas said.

"I'm expected in Salisbury by May first of next year. The Lord's people shouldn't be without a shepherd more than a day or two." Alex rubbed his neck. "I'm told we'll make it there in a fortnight."

"What does Andrew think about going?" Father said. "Starlyn's his cousin, but also his best friend."

"He's telling Starlyn now," Alex said. "He doesn't want to go, but wants to stay with us."

Thomas rose, going to the window. "Here come the boys now. I expect the women will soon be finished."

"We intended to visit Murna's parents this Sabbath," Alex said, "but finding I'd been accepted in Salisbury changed that. After services, we'll go to Aunt Elizabeth and Uncle Jonah's with all of you, where I'll tell them we're leaving."

Martha, a young servant, set the trestle table with plates. Sophrona filled platters with ham, while Penelope sliced still-warm bread pulled from the cook-place oven. Stewed apples, as well as rice pudding, went into bowls.

The family stood at their chairs to hold hands as Father said, "Dear God, we're thankful for this provision, and for Alexander's guidance. You alone know what he must do before he leaves this earth. In Christ Jesus' name, Amen."

* * *

The most beautiful fall Thomas remembered ended after the deciduous trees blushed, dotting the piney-wood forest with scarlet, orange-red, and the cottonwood's molten gold leaves.

In late December, he watched the weather. When it snowed, most of it melted soon. He turned from the window when Father came into the front room, carrying two mugs of coffee.

"Don't let it trouble ya, Lad, but we'd better get the seed beds in the ground by February. They must be ready to transplant on time, if we want a tobaccer crop."

Thomas nodded as he reached for his coffee.

Father glanced at him. "That former store proprietor in Williamsburg, selling two of his best indentures last December, seemed a stroke of luck, eh lad?"

Thomas thought about their good fortune. "Much as we needed good men, I'd say it was providence, Da." He released a deep breath. "With us not getting indentured servants from England after the British blockaded the ports."

He already sensed the dread that came each year. A fear the beds might not get put in on time, only easing up after they went in, releasing the knot in his stomach. If he failed that task, they would lose their cash crop. Funds that carried them over when freighting customers ran behind paying their bill.

The first of February, winter died off. Around the supper table one evening, Thomas said, "Anyone who's not working on freight is needed to build the seed beds. Get a good night's sleep. We start before daybreak."

The next morning Father helped him mix the tobacco seeds with soil to spread over the seed beds. Then, with his sons' help, they staked the shelter area and helped place a covering of linen on top to protect the sprouting seedlings.

Each day Thomas had his drivers hauling to stay up with his growing business.

One morning he said, "I'm keeping one of the new indentures off the wagons, Da. There's enough men to haul our freight for now. Baxter will help break up the fields so they're ready when the tobacco seeds need transplanting." He shifted position. "I'd like to get that done as soon as possible. Maybe even start by the first of April, this year."

"Well then, better get to it soon as possible, Lad. Neither Alex nor Andrew can help. They'll be packing the wagons for their move. We may even need to give them some assistance."

Thomas tried not to think about the move. It was difficult enough to watch Starlyn's face when Andrew came around.

"Be sure Baxter's in the lean-to, Da, when he's not in the fields. A new blacksmith, who lacks experience, needs some. We'll want him producing tools by summer time."

"I'll see he build's everything we need, Lad."

Nodding, Thomas said. "Later in the year, when he's not smithing, I will put him on long distance hauls with a seasoned driver."

* * *

Two weeks later Father joined him in the front room.

"Lad, watch who you put on the militia's loads. It doesn't look good for George Washington, with his men coming through a bad

278

winter and all. We don't want the Tories getting wind that you're moving arms or ammunition."

"I let that one man go. He just didn't seem right, Da. I didn't feel good about catching him sneaking around some rifles. I believe the Lord sent me in there so quietly, to stop him before he opened that crate."

"If they discover what we're doing, they'll raid your freight wagons. Maybe bring the fight to our land, storage sheds, barns— even our home." Father rubbed his chin. "They're just a few right now, but they've already started burning down places that don't favor the Crown."

"I'll be careful, Da."

They left his office and went to breakfast. Sophrona's face reflected that look, the one she wore when he worried. Must be instinct. He never told her anything significant about his work with the militia or those wooden crates his freighters hauled. Still, she knew something. War raged in the north, and the threat of fighting moved southward. He must be careful not to show concern around her.

Meanwhile, Thomas worked long days, transplanting the tobacco crop. He put the new servants busting up soil until late evening, every day, between hauling.

He thought about Starlyn's care for last year's crop. The lad had learned all the steps for harvesting, then finishing, the tobacco leaves. He knew how to grade, bundle, and flatten the hands of tobacco for freighting. It wasn't their only money, but it added to their wealth.

One evening Thomas said, "Well then, Starlyn, how about managing the crop this year?"

"Which crop, Da?"

"The cash crop."

Starlyn's face brightened, before looking down. "A man must be careful working tobaccer."

279

Thomas held back a smile. "Maybe you can talk your Granda into helping you this year. If it goes well, you'll take over the crop."

"Yes, sir. I'll make you proud of me, Da."

They finished transplanting the tobacco seedlings before putting in their food crops.

* * *

April 15, 1778

At daybreak, Andrew rode up to the house.

"Is everything all right then, Andrew?" Thomas called from the front porch. His nephew slipped off his horse.

"They're on the way, Uncle Thomas. Da said tell you we can't stay long. I came early to see Starlyn."

"You'll find the boys in the barn with your Granda. They should be finished soon. We'll set more places at the table."

"No need to do that. We've already eaten." Andrew turned toward the barn.

Thomas hurried to the common room. "They're on the way, Sophrona, but won't be staying long."

"Breakfast is almost ready." He took a seat at the table, while she brought him coffee.

"Martha, put together a box of food." Sophrona placed a hand on her waist. "Use all the bread we baked last night, the beef roast, the cookies and the cake we just baked." She hesitated, pushing back her hair. "Slice the beef. They'll be on the road two long, hard weeks. Soon as they're gone you may stir up another cake and mix more dough. Tonight we'll bake bread."

"Yes, Mistress."

Penelope put on water to boil before she set out mugs.

After breakfast, Thomas went to the front porch to wait. Before long, Alex drove his large Conestoga up by the freighting shed. Their younger son, William, brought the smaller wagon in behind, jumping down to check the ropes that tethered their cow and calf to the back of the wagon.

Starlyn, Andrew and John came out of the barn. They walked up the path toward the house.

"So then, you're off for Carolina, Thomas said. "Can you visit for a while?"

"No. We must get on the road soon. It's a long way to travel."

"Well then, let's go to the packing shed."

Alex and Father followed him in, where Thomas took a bundle off the shelf. He placed it on a work table, laying aside the blanket to reveal four Pennsylvania rifles.

"It's getting worse with the Tories out of control, Alex. Now they're doing anything they want."

"I have a pistol, Thomas, but it's not the same as a good rifle. God willing, we won't need these, but I'll fight to the last drop of blood before I'll let anything happen to my family."

Thomas added some ammunition, rewrapped the arms, then handed the bundle to his brother, who carried them out to the larger wagon.

* * *

Sophrona placed a tray of hot coffee on a table outside. Penelope followed her with more mugs and dishes of pudding for the children. While they sipped hot drinks, she took Starlyn inside for the wooden box of food. He packed it toward the wagon, refusing his cousin William's offer to help.

"I'm going to miss you something terrible, Sophrona." Tears ran down Murna's face. "Who else but you would prepare our family extra provisions for the road? We'll enjoy some of this tonight. I'll think of you when we eat."

Sophrona gave her a handkerchief. "One day we'll see each other again, Lord willing." Years ago, who would have thought her capable of growing to love Murna as she did.

281

"Let's go, Murna." Alex put down his mug. "The journey's still in front of us."

They all walked toward the wagons, Sophrona holding Murna's hand.

While the children milled around saying their goodbyes, Thomas and Cyrus escorted Alex to the wagon, where he embraced them both. The two men stepped back while he helped his wife and daughter into the wagon.

Andrew mounted his horse to take the lead.

"I'll return soon," Starlyn said. He joined Andrew in front to lead the way.

Reacting as if one, Starlyn and Andrew looked over their shoulders, backs straight. The sun picked out red in Starlyn's dark hair, while Andrew's light brown already reflected the summer's customary threads of gold. Both faces watched for Alex's signal, one with blue eyes, the other blue-green. Starlyn and Andrew could have been their fathers twenty years before, the resemblance being so strong. Sophrona swallowed the lump in her throat, batting her lashes to clear the moisture, unwilling to break down in tears.

William's wagon followed Andrew and Starlyn. Alex brought up the rear.

They disappeared from sight. Thomas took Sophrona's arm as they strolled in the direction of the house, Sophrona gripping her blue skirt to keep it from swinging each step.

"I'm going to miss not having them close by," he said.

"It'll be lonesome tonight, Lad." Cyrus moved up to Thomas's other side.

Thomas turned to John, walking behind them. "Why didn't you ride along with them?"

"It's Starlyn's last time with Andrew, maybe for a long time. Besides, I'll be with him every day from now on."

When they reached the house Sophrona waited next to Thomas.

"I'm going to check the freight load for tomorrow, Da."

"Well, Lad, Penelope said her roof leaks. I'll see if I can fix that. I'm taking John to help me."

Sophrona followed Thomas toward the house, when the pounding of hooves turned them around. Starlyn reined his horse in hard, the animal's sides heaving, as he practically tumbled to the ground.

"They're gone now. On their way to North Carolina."

Thomas nodded, while she studied their eldest son's face.

"Don't worry about the evening chores. I'll take care of that, soon as I take care of my horse." Moisture pooled in the corners of his eyes as Starlyn tucked his chin toward his chest, swiping at his face. He turned toward the barn.

Once inside, Sophrona slipped away to their room. She did not dwell on the pain from the family's loss. She already knew what grief felt like. She lay on the bed, overcome with sadness over her son's broken heart. Starlyn grew up with his cousin Andrew, enjoying his company just about every day unless one of them took sick. Sometimes even illness did not keep them apart.

Starlyn had stood tall through their departure. Tomorrow he would feel the loss of his best friend. If she knew her son at all, that would be his most difficult day.

CHAPTER THIRTY-FIVE

Sophrona enjoyed autumn's mild days, as she picked berries or searched for medicinal herbs to refill her containers. When Thomas, Cyrus and Jonah brought in a bear, dividing out the meat, she used some of the grease to make salves for winter.

Afterward, she turned her attention to sewing. Penelope worked alongside her, piecing new quilt tops.

While September provided plenty of dry days, October brought some rain. The nights grew cool, but did not freeze. The leaves started turning in the hills around the middle of the month. Nearer the house, autumn became more evident toward the end of the month. The season produced a crisp, pronounced blend of red, gold and yellows leaves.

Penelope became ill near the end of October.

Sophrona carried down soup. She swung out the crane, hanging the pot on the fireplace trammel before starting a fire to warm its contents. She rinsed a glass and filled the water pitcher, placing both on the small table next to Penelope's bed.

She moved quietly, but found no need for concern. The older woman slept on, while she straightened the house. She cleaned off the small sideboard near the eating table, filled a soup bowl, then took it to her friend's bedside table.

Gently shaking Penelope, she asked, "Are you hungry?"

"Thirsty...so thirsty."

She helped her sit up for water before feeding her some soup. After Penelope finished eating all she could, Sophrona eased her back down, covering her with a quilt.

"You've come down every day since my illness, taking care of me. The cough's better now. I'll get up tomorrow."

"There's no need for that until you feel better." Sophrona patted her hand.

"The wood box will run out soon. I'll need to fill it. You know, the nights are too cool anymore." She turned her head sideways, coughing. "Can't take the cold like I used to. Must be my age."

Penelope had lost weight since Obediah passed, her drooping cheeks crosshatched with age lines and her hair almost white. The texture of her friend's hair felt coarse to the touch, the ends frizzled. Sophrona had failed to notice all the changes. Why had it taken an illness to show her the poor woman's condition?

"Don't worry about gathering wood, Penelope. I'll have Starlyn bring some in later today. Just let him know when the box needs filled again."

The next morning, when Sophrona entered the common room, Penelope was stoking the cook-fire while Martha sliced ham for the three-legged spider skillet.

Sophrona patted her shoulder. "You feel better than yesterday?" She searched Penelope's face. "We'll manage breakfast. If you want to lie down, I'll wake you when it is on the table."

"No. I'm fine now." Penelope mounded the coals for the skillet. "I'll just dress the turkey Starlyn brought in for the soup pot. Don't you worry any about me. I feel better than I have in days."

Sophrona watched Penelope step across the room, her movements as quick as they always were. The thought filled her with a quiet joy. No need to worry now about the woman she grew almost as close to as her own mother.

* * *

"It's not like Penelope to miss a good breakfast." Sophrona clasped her hands. "I wonder what's keeping her down at the house. I stopped by there yesterday and she seemed fine."

"I'll stop at her place after I drop this off, Miss Sophrona." Martha hurried toward the door, carrying a pan of ham, biscuits, and other foods to the men servants' quarters.

At the table, Thomas spoke to his father. "The good weather's running out—there are crops to worry about." He took a drink of water. "We're hauling more freight this year than before. That new contract will keep us busy for several years, even if freighting for the militia wanes."

Father wiped his mouth. "Working out a deal with John Donelson's Bloomery iron furnace seems more than luck, Lad. The Good Lord had something to do with that contract to freight his iron to a foundry."

Thomas nodded. Then he turned toward Starlyn.

"Those logs we felled in the springtime are fairly dry, now. After the tobacco chores, take Jack down to the woodpile. Get the crosscut saw for the older, seasoned logs. Work out a good rhythm. It would be a bad time to ruin the saw with winter coming on."

"Yes, sir—and if he'll let me take the lead, we won't have any problems."

Thomas nodded as he looked at his younger son. "Jack will work with you. He doesn't want our family facing any more hardships than we already do."

Jack stood. "No sir, Da. I'll work with him. I'll do a good job, too."

Martha returned to the common room, the empty pan in her hand. When Sophrona caught her attention, the servant nodded. "Said she'll come up later. She has something to do."

Sophrona poured more coffee before sitting down.

After Thomas finished his cup, he rose from the table to stand. "All right, now, let's go. There's plenty to keep us busy."

After they left, she shoveled out ashes in the cook fireplace before doing other chores.

* * *

Thomas smelled supper when he entered the house. No time to eat, now. In the common room, Sophrona slid molasses cookies onto a large pewter plate. Dark curls pushed back from her face, ivory skin flushed pink from the heat, she looked as beautiful as the day he married her.

"I didn't expect you back this early. Supper shouldn't be long, once I finish here."

She brought him some water. After he took a long drink, he set the glass on the table and reached out for her hand.

"Sit down with me, Sophrona. There's something I must tell you."

"What's happened? You look so serious."

"Starlyn found Penelope in the wood shed when he went in for the saw."

"She shouldn't be in that shed." She picked at the cloth of her sleeve. "I told her Starlyn would bring in the wood. How is she?"

"A timber rattler bit her. No doubt the snake crawled up under the stacked firewood like they do. She likely disturbed it when she went for an armful." Thomas shook his head. "It looks like she struggled with it, maybe even after it bit her. Pieces of wood strewn everywhere. A block of wood lay on top of the snake, with its head pretty well mangled. I tell you that took some maneuvering. I think it bit her more than once before she killed it."

He paused, slowly shaking his head. "It looks like she tried to crawl out, but the venom in a five foot snake is powerful. If she got help after the first bite, instead of taking time to kill it, she may have lived." Thomas passed a hand over his face. "Happened around mid-day. I had sent a man for a block of wood this morning, and she wasn't in there then."

Thomas put his arm around her as she cried. Sophrona laid her head on his shoulder. After a while she pulled back, wiping her tears.

"I'm sorry she's passed on." He swallowed. "If she hadn't gone in there, Starlyn would have entered the shed next for the saw. I don't know how, but she managed to kill that snake before it got away."

Sophrona sniffled. "I already miss her."

"Try thinking about this as Penelope looking after our eldest son, one last time."

"Thomas, it'll be difficult without her. She was the last grandmother and the only one the boys knew."

He nodded. "John's helping Da build the coffin. Starlyn rode for Aunt Elizabeth. I thought you'd like her here. We placed Penelope's body in her house on the bed."

"I'd better take care of her before the cold death comes." Sophrona stood as Thomas took her hand.

"Are you sure you want to do this instead of waiting for Aunt Elizabeth?"

"Yes. I wouldn't turn that over to someone else—treat her as a stranger."

He walked her to Penelope's little house.

* * *

Sorrow gripped Sophrona's heart as she crept into the small, neatly kept home. The front room did not feel warm without Penelope alive to greet her. Small cobwebs, not so obvious before, now stood out. Dust, floating in the beam of sunlight shining through a small window, reminded her it would soon be on the surfaces and floor. She never noticed these things while Penelope's presence filled the house.

She poured water into the pan Penelope used for Obediah and set it on the table in the bedroom, going to the bed where Penelope's body lay in her old, faded work dress. She blinked back tears as overwhelming sadness filled her. No time to cry—too much work. Later she would find a way to grieve this death. Her friend always felt like family, although she did not have a drop of Hackett blood running through her veins.

Removing the well-worn shoes first, then the dress, Sophrona gasped at the condition of Penelope's body. The snake had struck her three times, one bite on her lower leg, one on a forearm, and one in the area just below her shoulder. The flesh around the bites had lost its shape, almost like it melted. The angry black-red bruising looked raw.

Sophrona washed Penelope's body. How very painful to go after that snake as it continued to strike at her. She had only so much time to kill it and still get help. Sophrona might never know exactly what happened, but when the venom from the snake slowed Penelope's body, did she make a decision to finish the job despite her time running out?

Deep sobs racked her body as she tried to envision the last minutes of Penelope's life, the poison racing through her. Dying, old, alone, with no one to hear her call for help, hold her hand.

* * *

Starlyn returned with Aunt Elizabeth and Uncle Jonah. Thomas stood on Penelope's porch where Sophrona worked inside. His uncle walked his aunt down. She pushed by him, patting his arm as she went. Before entering the house, she said, "You have a strong wife. Don't worry too much about this."

Thomas walked down to the barn with his uncle. "Let's get this coffin moved, Da. We're using time we don't have this late in the day."

Thomas and John took the front, his father and uncle the back, packing the coffin up to the small house.

Penelope had on a long blue dress she usually wore to services, along with her good shoes. They placed the body inside, with some assistance from Aunt Elizabeth. Before Father nailed down the coffin lid, Sophrona straightened out the dress collar, crying as she worked.

"Better hurry, Sophrona. Starlyn may need help to break up the ground, with this being the first of November."

"I'm finished now," she said.

"Nail it down, then grab hold, Da. We need to hurry," Thomas said.

The four each took a corner, packing the coffin out and up the hill.

Thomas glanced over his shoulder to see Sophrona coming up behind him, the Bible in the crook of her arm, his aunt walking beside her.

Starlyn almost had the grave dug when they arrived at the graveyard. After they lowered the coffin into the ground, Thomas took the Bible and opened it to the twenty-third Psalm. He read all six verses.

Sophrona lingered at the gravesite after dropping her handful of dirt. He stood beside her when she moved back.

Soon Starlyn came to stand on her other side, tears in his eyes. "I'm going to miss her too, Mother."

When Starlyn moved over to his grandfather, John came to stand with her. He hugged her before going to stand by Starlyn.

Aunt Elizabeth and Uncle Jonah paid their respects, then started toward the path going down. Elizabeth said, "We're going home, Cyrus."

Walking back to the house, Thomas took his wife's hand. Sophrona looked up, eyes shiny, as she spoke.

"I'll miss her something awful. She made my life bearable before we left Maryland. After we arrived here, she managed to improve my rather happy existence. She became the mother I brought to Virginia—and another grandmother for our children."

"Well, if you asked her, I believe Penelope might have said she felt like our children's grandmother." Thomas squeezed Sophrona's hand when she smiled at him. "I don't think it mattered she wasn't a blood relative, at least not to her. I know it didn't matter to you."

* * *

February 1779

Thomas worked alone in the barn when John entered.

"Sarah McClure and her friend Rebecca Thompson are having guests over. Sarah's mother will play the harpsichord. I'd like to ride over to Starlight town. I'll try to get back before dark."

"I don't think Starlight's a town. Not yet."

"But it has several establishments, an attorney, a store that receives goods from the Atlantic ports and Europe. Even though not much arrives now, what with the war on." John stood there, a fist on his waist much like his Granda.

"Well, when put like that, I could see where Starlight looks more like a town to you," Thomas said.

The boy nodded, a serious look on his face.

"Go ahead, Jack. Be careful riding over there. These are strange times we live in."

His son smiled as he reached for a bridle.

"Da, I would appreciate you not telling Starlyn where I'm going. It's only my concern, not his."

"No. No, I wouldn't want to tell him anything about your affairs. Not unless you said to."

Maybe John's reluctance had more to do with Starlyn finding out which girl interested him, than for any personal reasons. Still, he gave his word. As he finished, John worked on saddling a horse.

Thomas went to the house, where Sophrona stirred a pot of turkey soup. She stopped to pour him coffee.

"Don't expect your younger son to eat with us." He leaned against the sideboard with his steaming mug, "You'll need to set something aside. He's off visiting Miss Sarah McClure."

Sophrona nodded. "Isn't that the girl he tussled with?"

"Well, I think maybe a part of it. Her friend Rebecca truly led the charge. All three were small children, then."

"I don't remember John being interested in anyone, except possibly that one young girl, Lydia," Sophrona paused, "but it seemed to me she cared more for him."

"I'd better see what Da and Starlyn are doing about the tobacco seedbeds." Thomas set his mug down, turning toward the doorway.

He strolled through to the front door, going out as a horse raced by. John crouched over the neck, his knees buried in the animal's sides, its legs a blur. He must soon speak with that boy.

* * *

A few weeks later, at the end of March, Thomas returned at evening after delivering a freighting order. Sophrona stirred a pot at the cook-place, putting down the spoon to glide across the common room, her blue skirt barely skimming the floor. He kissed her, pulling her closer as she whispered, "I missed you."

He nodded, smiling. "Starlyn received a post from Andrew. A wagoner hauling leather goods from North Carolina recognized my name, where we both stopped. He thought it a stroke of luck he'd run into me, after agreeing to deliver the post."

Thomas went to the table while Sophrona filled him a plate.

Starlyn came in, taking a seat across from him. "I rubbed down your team before I threw them fodder. After they ate, I looked them over. Seems like one of the bigger lead horses developed a limp during your run—may be close to throwing a shoe." His son rubbed a jowl. "Lamplight's not that good. I'll take another look tomorrow."

"You know, the wagon didn't roll so straight. Kept drifting to one side, probably what caused the problem." He took out the post, handing it to Starlyn. "You're a good man. Don't miss much, either. Now, what does your cousin say?"

Sophrona placed his supper plate on the table with a goblet of water, before sitting next to him.

Starlyn broke the seal, read, then laid down the post.

"Andrew says he's signed up with the North Carolina militia. He wants me to join him, Da."

"Well, they're looking for young men to join the Continentals or the militia. You'll turn eighteen August the ninth. If you're inclined to join up, then go ahead. Four months won't determine whether you're a man or not."

Thomas took a sip as his wife sucked in her breath. He glanced to see her face lose color. He patted her on the back before turning to face his son.

"Don't know what to do, right now." Starlyn sighed. "Maybe I'll just think it over a while." He left the table, clutching Andrew's letter.

* * *

May arrived. The plants Sophrona brought from Baltimore County thrived. The lilac and rose bushes grew taller in this new land, it seemed. Soon, their blooms would scent the air with fragrance.

Their forest trees offset the nodding clusters of bluebells, hanging off one or two foot stems in the open areas. The pink buds, among proud blue trumpets, changed to a soft blue when they blossomed. The bluebells had become numerous since she came to call Virginia home.

"It's a shame bluebells don't possess the healing properties of lungwort, since they look so similar," Elizabeth said.

"I'd think they're good for something, otherwise why did the Good Lord give them a beauty that attracts everyone, Aunt Elizabeth?"

"The Cherokee medicine men use them for whooping cough. So, they're beautiful as well as useful." Elizabeth leaned over a cluster, cupping her hands before pulling them toward her face, bringing the fragrance closer to her nostrils.

Sophrona giggled as they continued their walk, skirting around the next pocket of bluebells in the direction back toward the house.

"You know, our quilting group's getting smaller," she said. "Minnie's sister-in-law wasn't there last time."

"Her sister-in-law didn't come because she's down with a cold," Elizabeth said, "but she'll return soon as she can."

"Well, I guess there's no need for concern, then."

"I wouldn't say that, Sophrona. The two newest women said they'll stay at home for now, since their husbands are Tories. They won't be back unless we patriots lose the war. I think their men fear our influence on their wives, somehow."

"The men are making their women's work harder than it needs to be," Sophrona said.

Elizabeth nodded. "At our last quilting, one of the women said everyone will soon become a Loyalist, or not be here. Says the King's attention has turned to the southern colonies, getting ready to take control."

They arrived back at the house. Sophrona said, "Come on in. I'll cut you a piece of that walnut cake you enjoy so well."

"Maybe next time. I really need to get home. I'll see you at services on Sabbath."

Sophrona waited until Elizabeth mounted her horse before she climbed the steps going inside. She admired Elizabeth's agility. It had not slowed with age.

She wished that for herself.

CHAPTER THIRTY-SIX

Thomas stepped outside. The afternoon temperature seemed mild for November, the wind tolerable, more like the time between late winter and early spring. He sniffed the air. A sprinkle of bumps rose on his arms. What was wrong? Trouble surely came. He just did not know from where.

Harland, an indentured servant, left the tobacco barn, whistling as he came. After arriving at the steps, he took a seat on one, then rubbed an ear.

"It looks like Starlyn's got a good head for raising tobaccer. He put us re-chinking the curing barn. He's already started planning for next year's crop." He laughed, showing a mouthful of wide, white teeth, with a gap between the front two.

Thomas fought a smile at the man's words. The tug at a corner of his top lip told him he might lose that battle.

Tilting his head back, Harland said, "You want me to do anything?"

"Have you eaten yet?" Thomas watched the man's face. He looked hungry.

The servant shook his head, sighing as he rose from the step. Brushing off the back of his homespuns, he said, "I'd better tell Starlyn I'm going to eat. He may want me for something." He waved a hand as he turned to leave.

Thomas looked past Harland, strolling toward the tobacco shed. Father, Starlyn, and another servant walked from the building, headed toward the house. He turned to go up the steps, when the

295

sound of pounding hooves echoed through the hollow. He pivoted so fast he almost stumbled, dread flooding his mind.

"It's John—riding hard—stranger on his tail," Harland shouted.

"Get to the barn. Grab a rifle." Thomas ran toward the barn, thankful several horses were saddled.

Harland came through the door, holding it open as Thomas grabbed a rifle, mounted his horse, then rode out, heart pounding so that he could hardly think. He must help his son.

John raced past him clinging to the saddle, fear evident in the position of his body, perched over the heaving mount. Thomas turned his horse to block the stranger's way, his flintlock held close to his body.

"Get off my property." He breathed deep, anger filling his words. "Don't ever come back here looking for trouble."

The man sneered. His thin face sprouted a few days' whiskers, a black hat jammed on his head. "I ordered him to halt, but he tried to outrun me."

"If he doesn't want to stop, you'd better not expect him to."

The man jerked his head, looking over his shoulder. At least four other riders came toward them.

"The Crown gave me all the authority I need. They already took Savannah, and they're just getting started. Now, I want that boy…"

"Leave now." Thomas's stomach churned when the riders moved in behind the man. He gripped the stock, raised his rifle high, leveling it over his forearm. They would take John over his dead body.

"You may get one of us, but you're going to d…" The rider stiffened, his gaze fixed on something past Thomas.

He heard movement behind him as a horse snorted.

"Well, then," Father said, "you'd better turn around. Ride away while ya can. The Crown won't help ya, today."

Thomas glanced over his shoulder to find Father side by side with Starlyn. Every man on the place behind them, all mounted, all armed.

"What happened today, Jack?" he called.

His son walked his horse up abreast of him. "Don't really know for sure. I started home from Uncle Jonah's when I passed these men. He called for me to stop," John nodded toward the first man, "I didn't like the way he acted toward me so I kept going."

"You shouldn't bother my son. You were wrong to do that. Come see me next time you want something."

Thomas steadied his flintlock as he shot above the man's head, parting the top of his hat. He slid from his horse and, opening the brass box in the stock of his gun, took out a patch before removing a lead ball and powder packet from his shirt pocket. He stuck the packet between his teeth, wrapped a ball of lead in the patch, while his eyes never left the stranger, who clutched at his hat while gasping for air.

Before Thomas could ram the rod down the barrel, the man yanked on the reins, turned his horse, and cut a trail across the field. He rode far out in front of his friends, who followed.

Thomas waited to make sure they did not turn back before he walked his horse into the barn. He decided to leave him saddled a while longer.

He waited for the others to enter, then said, "Losing Savannah's just the beginning of our problems. Things may get worse before it's over. If anything looks suspicious, grab a firearm first, then find out what's wrong."

* * *

Sophrona turned from the window as her husband entered the front room, holding a rifle.

"What happened? Who's John running from?" She rang her hands.

"There were Tories on the prowl. One of them wanted to question our son."

"He needs to stay home or he'll get hurt. You must tell him." She stepped toward him.

He leaned the weapon against the corner of the fireplace before pulling her into his arms, rubbing her back.

"I can't possibly do that. He's too old to protect like a child. No matter what happens in this war, even if he joins the militia, you're not to treat him like one."

She trembled. "You don't think he'd join the war. Don't know what I'd do if he got hurt."

"Other young men, more like boys, joined our cause where the fighting's heaviest. Some are younger than John. He hasn't said anything about wanting to fight, and most likely only wants to stay here to worm his way into control of whatever Starlyn's doing."

Sophrona slumped against him, relief flowing through her. They laughed at the thought of John passing up war just to outpace his older brother at home.

* * *

Late March, 1780

Winter passed without major incidents. Those who called themselves Loyalists left the Craighead household alone. On a few occasions Thomas joined forces with Uncle Jonah and others, who rode out to help families harassed by a band of roaming Tories.

A light wrap on her shoulders, Sophrona sat on the back porch with Thomas and Cyrus. The approaching full moon shone down, casting luminous shadows on the trees and buildings.

Thomas shifted position. "What's the outlook for Charlestown, Da? You think the town's going to withstand the Crown's soldiers?"

"Don't rightly know, Lad. Since the news came to us, the British have taken the two forts at the approach. I'd say it doesn't bode well for Charlestown. If the town falls, best expect the Crown to move north toward us."

"How long before we know if Charlestown fell?" Starlyn said.

Her firstborn's voice filled the night, startling Sophrona. A chill moved up her shoulders as if a sharp breeze swept the porch. She turned toward the door where he stood. He moved so silently, she did not know he stood there until he spoke. She drew her wrap closer.

"That news may be two or three weeks off, coming from so far," Cyrus said, "but eventually we'll hear the outcome."

Thomas grunted in agreement.

"You've been so quiet the last few days. Something troubling you?" Thomas said.

Starlyn stepped onto the porch, closer to Thomas.

"Well, John's trying to take over the hand peg position from me. I don't want him doing that. I know exactly where I want the hole for the plant to go before I stick the peg into the ground. It's easy for a servant to follow me dropping in the plant, then John comes after him to add the water and fertilizer. I'm fast growing tired of arguing with him."

"He's younger than you." Thomas leaned back. "Try being patient with him."

"That's not all, Da. He wants to top the flower buds and sucker, instead of killing the tobacco worms. Says he's not going to pinch off their heads anymore because that's child's work. They'll eat up the crop real quick, if he doesn't. Then all our hard work is for nothing."

Thomas cleared his throat. "Starlyn, it's your tobacco crop. Do what you think's best."

"Well, he's not going to wrestle this crop from me, no matter what. He's not in the barn. I haven't seen him. Where is he going lately, anyway, with all those Tories on the road?"

Thomas gave her a quick glance.

"He's out there somewhere. I wouldn't worry about him. He has the ability to outride most of those men."

"All I'll say is he has a hard day's work in front of him, tomorrow. Well then, I'm going to bed." Starlyn came over and kissed her cheek.

Cyrus stood. "I'm taking my leave for the night, as well, Lad."

Sophrona stayed with Thomas, silence building. In the distance, an owl hooted.

When she heard the sound of a lone horse ride in, she sighed softly. A little later she said, "I'm ready to go in, Thomas. Now that John's home."

He took her elbow as she rose, walking her inside. She waited while he barred the porch door, something he'd started after riders crossing their property awakened them.

* * *

The wagons rolled day after day. Thomas hired more help to stay up with his regular freighting contracts, as he hauled ammunition, food, or other items the Virginia militia needed.

He entered the common room where Sophrona stirred a large kettle of stew hanging on a trammel. It bothered him that she worked alongside the servant women, with the summer so hot.

"I'm hungry. Is that stew ready?"

She turned, her face flushed pink with a faint smile on her lips, her sleeves rolled up. The lavender dress brought out her dark hair, plastered to her forehead. The curls fringing her temples seemed lighter than the rest, giving her a soft, angelic look.

"I'll bring you a bowl with some fresh bread. Let's go on the back porch. It's cooler."

Thomas walked to the porch where he leaned over the railing, taking a look at his sons far out in the tobacco fields.

She brought him a glass of water. He circled her waist, pulling her close enough to kiss before he sat down. She went back inside, soon returning with his stew and a plate of bread, placing both dishes on the well-worn table before she sat with him.

"I am grateful, Lord," he said. Then he took a bite. "It's good enough again for supper."

"I made enough to have all you want, especially the boys. Both are building an appetite."

They sat in silence as he finished the food, along with a second slice of bread.

"I don't like to haul on the Sabbath, nor the men who attend church, either. Regardless, we all need to do what we must until the war ends. Maybe then things will change."

"What will happen if General Washington loses?" She flipped hair off the back of her neck.

"We mustn't think about that. Just pray the Lord gives us victory over the Crown."

Thomas gazed out over the fields. "In a few more days, I expect Starlyn to begin the tobacco harvest. It looks like he worked out the problems with his brother."

Sophrona sighed, a gentle smile on her lips. "I can't believe it's the end of July. I—oh, I almost forgot! A girl came to the house today. A man driving a wagon waited for her as she brought me a note for one of the boys."

"Which one?"

"Well, it's for John, but she asked for Jack. That's what's written on the note, too."

"Sophrona, the only one who ever calls our son 'Jack' is me. Where's the note?"

He finished his water. When she returned, he reached for the letter. "It does say Jack. I'll give it to him later, when he comes in. Did you recognize her?"

"I'm not sure, but she looked like the Thompsons' daughter."

* * *

301

A few days later when the men returned from the fields to eat, the servants placed dinner on tables set under the shade trees. Thomas admired his wife's quick movements as she brought pitchers of water and milk from the house. She did not waste a step as she worked. Father, Starlyn, and John joined him at a table. They waited for Sophrona to sit down before eating.

Afterwards, Starlyn followed Thomas into the common room.

"I'll need to hire a few men to bring in the crop. It's about the best we've ever grown—too big for me and John to handle. The servants are only available when you're not working them."

"Go ahead, but don't forget about the shipping embargo that's on. Starlyn, we may not get as much for our crop as in previous times. The agent may even want to offer you less than what it's worth."

Starlyn nodded. "Then I'll hire two men instead of the four I'd planned on. I'll use them in the morning hours when it's cooler. Maybe we'll get more work done that way. Besides, a bigger crop could average out to what we earned last year."

"Yes, that could be right. If you need any help with the new men, let your Granda know. I'll keep the servants busy only a portion of the day, for the next few days. You may use them for a couple of hours in the afternoon until you hire the help."

"Yes, sir." Starlyn left the room.

Later, his younger son found him. "I'll help in the barn tonight; take care of my chores—even Starlyn's. There's no need for him to come down. He has other things to do."

"All right, then. But remember, we clean out the barn today."

"I don't mind hard work."

When Thomas nodded, John left.

Later, after supper, Thomas walked with him to the barn. They worked until his son broke the silence.

"Rebecca's note invited me to a get-together, after services. I may be home late."

"You're out late often these days. Anything going on I should know about?"

"No, it's just that I'm interested in someone. She's the one who brought the invitation. It'd be good if Starlyn didn't find out. It's my business, not his."

"As I told you before, I'll let you tell your brother what you want him to know. As your parents, we shall stay silent on the matter. The sun's going down soon. We're not finished yet."

"Yes, sir." John whistled as he worked.

* * *

The next day after supper, as they lingered over apple pie, John spoke to his family.

"From here on out, I'd like you to address me as 'Jack', instead of 'John'."

Thomas held his tongue, but Starlyn got to the matter rather quickly.

"Why? Did you tell some girls that Father named you Jack?"

Thomas noticed how dark blue his younger son's eyes were, as they glistened in his strained face.

"No! Who told you that? Even if I had, it's the truth, because Da's always called me Jack."

Thomas glanced at his wife, before turning to John.

"Is your brother right? Did you tell someone your name's Jack, not John?"

He looked down. "Yes, Da, I did. I like what you call me better than my given name."

Father glanced at Thomas. "That's a fine name. I think Jack fits him, now that he's older."

Patricia Reece

"All right, little brother, if that's what you want. It'll be easy to call you Jack. I've heard it most of my life." Starlyn took another bite of his pie.

Thomas stayed at the table when the others left. Sophrona brought him a mug of coffee before she sat next to him.

"What's going on with Joh…I mean Jack?" She pushed hair out of her face. "Might as well start calling him the name you always have. It seems he's chosen it."

He touched her cheek with the back of his hand.

"I don't rightly know, but it has something to do with that Thompson girl. I just hope it's nothing to worry about."

CHAPTER THIRTY-SEVEN

November, 1780

Thomas's freighting business continued to bring in a reasonable profit. Despite the bleak prospects the war brought on, the Craighead household sold their cash crop, suffering little loss.

"I'm not going over that barn looking for any more cracks we might have overlooked." Jack's lips came together in a thin line as he reared back, chin jutted out, arms dangling at his sides.

"The auction warehouse just closed, Jack. This is our time to get that work done, like every year." Starlyn moved closer. "November's almost over. There's time in December to chase whichever girl you're dead set on catching. For now, you'll work like the rest of us."

Tired as he was, Thomas appreciated Starlyn's insistence on being thorough. His eldest son wanted them to start over, despite already chinking every log of the big curing barn. He expected them to do what Starlyn asked, even Jack. His eldest son's decisions led to good crops.

"It's none of your business what I'm doing on my time. Tell him, Father."

Much as it troubled Thomas to watch his sons argue, he would not get in the middle of their struggle. They must figure this out on their own.

"That's enough, Jack. He's in charge of this operation."

Jack grunted, as they began to pour over the barn, applying mud to anything that resembled a crack. They finished chinking and put the ladders away as the sun lowered in the western sky.

"Let's go see what Sophrona's prepared for supper," Granda said. "Surprising how fast a full stomach can change a man's outlook on situations."

* * *

December 1st

The day brought unusual cold. Sophrona went to the front room, where she wiped off the tables. She swept ashes off the hearth, poked up the fire, then settled a log onto the flames—one almost too big to lift. A noise outside sent her hurrying to a window. She pushed back the material, being careful not to be seen. A horse snorted. She trembled, as she strained to make out who climbed the steps.

Fear pushed at her when a knock sounded at the door. Silently she moved from the window, unsure whether to answer. Her hand wavered before reaching to twist the door latch.

"Is Starlyn here?" A familiar-looking young man stood there.

"No. He's gone."

"Would you give him this?" He held out a folded note.

"I'll see that he gets it."

He emitted a string of hacking sounds through the fuzz of his tattered beard. His threadbare coat looked inadequate.

Touched with concern, she said, "Care to have something to eat or warm up?"

"No, ma'am. I live just over the ridge. I'm heading back to North Carolina as soon as I can. We got to stop them British soldiers before…"

Distress registered on his face as his words trailed off. Remembering him as a neighbor's son, sympathy squeezed her heart.

"Be careful on the road. Tories are brazen troublemakers."

"Yes, ma'am."

The young man, looking more a boy as he turned, weaved his way down the steps, groaning himself up on the horse. Clutching the reins, he kneed his stallion. She waited until he disappeared before closing the door.

She sat in front of the fire, smoothing the paper between her fingers. Once used to advertise a slave sale, someone turned it into a message for Starlyn. They wrote his name on a blank patch along the paper's edge.

The note troubled her. She thrust it deep into a pocket of her skirt as if that would quell her anxiety. Restless, she hurried to the common room, where she absently stirred a pot of beef and vegetables at the cook fireplace.

Just about dusk the servants filled dishes. They had barely finished when she heard Thomas's laughter echo from the front room. He, Cyrus, and the boys would soon have supper with her.

"What a long day. I'm hungry enough to eat anything," Thomas said, as he pulled her to him, kissing her cheek.

"Enough of that. I want something to eat." Jack's face twisted up, his blue eyes glinting. "Doesn't anyone care Starlyn tried to work me to death?"

"You don't know hard work, yet." Starlyn raked a hand through his hair, fingers lifting the brown mane off his forehead and pushed it back. Red highlights danced along the thick locks. "Just wait until tomorrow ends. Then see how you feel about getting worked to death."

Sophrona sat down next to her husband, joining Cyrus's laughter at the bickering.

Leveling a firm look at his sons, Thomas cleared his throat before the family bowed their heads. "We're thankful for Your provision, in Jesus' name."

Thomas raised his head then studied the table. "I noticed strange horseshoe marks in front of the house. Did we have company?"

Sophrona patted her pocket, the paper crinkling.

"Yes. A neighbor boy from over the hill dropped a note off for Starlyn." She pulled the letter from her pocket and handed it across the table.

Starlyn turned it over. "It's late in the year for correspondence about a sale. Besides, we're not interested in owning slaves. Who sent this?"

"Open it." Thomas reached for a bowl.

Starlyn broke the seal, unfolded the paper and looked at the note, his face losing color.

"What's wrong, son?" Sophrona's heart beat faster.

"It's from Andrew, Mother. I'll read it.

"'Starlyn, I hope this finds everyone well. You did not join me when I first signed up with the militia. I pray you find it in your patriotic heart to now do so. My regiment just won a great victory at King's Mountain. The Redcoats are on the run. I did not fight in that battle, but I shall in the next. Our local militia wants you in the company. I beseech you cousin, join me in Salisbury before the fifteenth of December. Do not wait. Our cause needs your help and I need you fighting alongside me.

To freedom from the King—your cousin, Andrew.'"

"That's it, then." Starlyn swiped at his eyes with a hand before looking up.

Sophrona swallowed hard, her throat so tight she dared not speak.

Thomas set down his mug. "What do you have a mind to do, lad?"

Starlyn did not answer, only shrugged a shoulder as he rose and left the room.

* * *

The next morning Thomas sipped coffee in the common room, the day's freighting roster on the table under the lamplight. He looked up when his sons entered.

"Let me think on this a while." Jack scratched his neck.

Starlyn sat down across from Thomas. "You can't take too long…"

"Well, just give me some time." Jack went to the sideboard where he poured a glass of water, bringing it to the table.

Thomas recognized the stubborn look settling on his younger son's face. He wondered if Starlyn could budge him anytime soon.

Blowing on his hands, Father entered the room. Sophrona poured him a mug of coffee as he took a seat.

"It's a cold day out there. The lads helped me give the horses plenty ah feed and fodder."

"They'll need it today, Da," Thomas said. "We'll start at day break, hauling until dark."

"You'd better make a decision, little brother, before I drag it out of you." Starlyn went as if to rise.

"What are you two in contention over this time?" Thomas said.

The boys stared at each other. Starlyn broke the silence.

"If I go to North Carolina, someone needs to oversee the tobacco crop—at least until I return. It may only be a short while. You and Granda are burdened with enough to do. You shouldn't need to worry about that."

Sophrona left the room as a servant placed food platters on the table. She returned, taking a place next to Thomas, her face splotched red. He reached under the table and held her hand as he asked the blessing.

They finished breakfast as daylight broke, the meal eaten almost in silence. The sun shone through a window, lighting up the room, reflecting off the far wall. Thomas drank another quick cup as the others hurried to get their coats.

Sophrona stood, shook out her skirt and moved to the cook fire. He rose to join her.

"How can you stand the thought of him going away?" She wiped her eyes. "To think he might die on a battlefield, far from home. I...I'll never recover if something happens to him."

"He hasn't made up his mind yet." He placed a hand on her back as she buried her face in his chest. "Maybe you're worrying for nothing."

He pulled back to wipe her tears. Taking her hands, he gently rubbed her two curved end fingers. "He's a man, who will now make his own decisions. We need to trust the Lord to take care of him in this matter, as we did in all others."

"Yes, Thomas, you're right about this."

"It's late." He leaned down and kissed her. "I must go. Try not to fret."

She nodded.

Thomas left. He did not feel very confident about their firstborn child going off to war.

That evening, his younger son joined him in the barn. They removed the waste from the barn floor in silence, until he stopped to rest.

Jack leaned against his shovel. "I'd like to attend a party at Sarah McClure's house tomorrow evening. I'll be late coming home."

"Feel free to go. Then, is it Rebecca you're still interested in?"

"Well, yes, but sometimes I find myself next to Lydia, only I don't understand how that happens. I prefer Rebecca, but she's difficult to stay close to. Sometimes I get so mad that I leave. What's a good way to tell Rebecca it's her I want? I mean, how would you do that?"

"You just need to say what's on your mind, but bide your time. Make sure you're completely honest with yourself, son."

"All right, then. I'll wait for the right opportunity to do that."

When they finished, they hauled the waste to the field, spreading it around. They returned to the barn, where Jack strawed the floor while Thomas pitched fodder to the animals.

They started toward the house. "So then, you going to help your brother with the crop?"

Jack stopped to turn toward him, chewing his bottom lip. "Don't know. I haven't completely made up my mind."

* * *

December third, Starlyn sat across from Jack during supper. After they'd eaten, Sophrona served apple cake.

Starlyn poked at his slice. "So—are you gonna to do this for me?"

When Jack didn't answer, Starlyn kicked at his brother under the table.

"Say 'yes' or 'no', but don't ignore me. That's downright mean. I deserve an answer."

"You've had time to make a decision," Sophrona said. "Now tell your brother what it is."

Jack nodded toward his mother. "Starlyn, I don't want to work the crop, only for you to take it back when you return."

"Are you saying just give you the crop?"

Jack nodded. "Yes, if you want me to work it while you're gone."

"I can't. I already put so much into it, you'll only need to worry about doing the work." Starlyn pushed a hand through his hair, lips a thin white line. "Besides, you wouldn't even make the effort to do the job right, last time we chinked the barn. Not until Father made you. I'll get back in time to see you don't run it into the ground."

Jack frowned. "If you want me to take the crop, give it to me. Else I'm not doing it."

"He can't do that." Starlyn stared at the wall. "I'll only be gone a while. Besides, he has to work, doing something."

311

Thomas glanced at his wife before turning to Starlyn. "No, he can't. You've worked hard these past years, making our family a profitable crop."

Jack looked at him. "But he can't make me take it, then give it back to him."

"If you ever take over the tobacco crop, then Starlyn must give it to you." Thomas paused, eyes on a window pane needing another glaze.

Finally he said, "I won't force you to do the right thing, Jack. Me and your Granda will work the crop, handle the fields, and run the business. Never mind doing that for your brother. I'll hire extra help, if I must."

"No, Da, you won't need to do that." Jack glanced down. "Starlyn, I'll take the crop. When you come home—it's yours."

"Thank you little brother. You may find it will help you become a better businessman, when you're all grown up." Starlyn stretched out his hand in a formal bid to seal the agreement.

Jack ignored the gesture as he jumped up, leaving the room.

A look akin to disgust had crossed his younger son's face. Thomas wasn't indifferent to the disappointed look that briefly crossed Starlyn's tight face, either.

He feared Jack might find resistance to such an attitude, if he continued on that path later in his life.

After Jack left, silence settled over the table.

"When ya leaving, then, Starlyn?" Father broke his silence.

"I'm riding with a couple of other volunteers, day after tomorrow."

* * *

December the fifth came, dark and bitter cold. Thomas studied the freighting roster. Father and Jack worked in the barn while Sophrona cooked, leaving Starlyn to pack his personal effects in his saddlebags. Finally, the family sat down to breakfast. Sophrona's face held strain he could not remember seeing since they left Maryland. The previous night, he woke each time she turned in bed. They both finally slept.

Starlyn laid his napkin on the table before he stood. He went to kiss his mother's cheek.

"There isn't much time before I must go. It's a difficult thing leaving the people I love, to fight a war we didn't start—but must surely win or forever lose our freedoms."

Thomas called Starlyn's name, as the rest of the family moved to the front room. He harbored a premonition of dread as he clasped his firstborn's shoulders in a strong embrace.

"God go with you, son." He choked as Starlyn moved from the safety of his arms into a dangerous war.

A cold blast of air filled the front room. Starlyn started down the stairs toward his horse, Thomas's thick, supple long-coat draping his son's body, the stiff collar hugging his neck. Leather gloves covered his hands.

Sophrona left the room, her face stricken with too much grief for Thomas to comprehend.

Unexpectedly, Jack yanked the door open.

"Wait, Starlyn."

He rushed down the stairs, grabbed Starlyn's arm and they talked a while. Jack hugged his brother for so long, Thomas wondered if he'd ever turn loose to come back inside.

Starlyn mounted his horse. Still looking over his shoulder at the house, he brought both knees together, driving his mount forward. That decisive moment imprinted itself in Thomas's mind. He swallowed hard. His son carried the stuff that made good men, of that he had no doubt.

Jack didn't come in, but walked toward the barn, shoulders hunched, his head down.

Father watched Starlyn depart the house from the doorway, too.

313

"Well then, Lad, it's done. I'll help Jack with the animals. Maybe he could use the company right now. Find your wife. It's my opinion she needs some company, as well."

CHAPTER THIRTY-EIGHT

Thomas entered the common room. Sophrona struggled to cut away the charred parts of the pheasant she burned, which included most of it.

He shrugged. "Don't waste your time fretting over this. The Lord provided for us. I trust He shall again."

"I should pay more attention to my work, difficult as it is for you to bring home meat."

Thomas worried about her. Starlyn seemed ever present in her thoughts and most of his, too, their son's whereabouts unspoken between them. If one of them brought up his name in conversation, they quickly moved on. As though both were afraid to fling open that door.

Then he thought about Jack, who seemed to drive his mother to madness. The lad moved around the house in slow motion, his face so fastened on the floor, as if he lost something valuable down there.

Finished with her work, Sophrona came over to sit with him.

"Jack is going over to Sarah McClure's house again this evening. I don't know what goes on with that boy, visiting Sarah but talking about Rebecca. Guess I should be happy he's finally telling me."

Thomas cleared his throat. "Rebecca is Sarah's friend. When he goes to Sarah's house, it's to see Rebecca."

They both looked up when Father entered the common room. He sat down at the trestle table across from them.

"Things don't look so good between Jack and those two girls. Almost seems they're against him, like you said happened when the three were young." Father shook his head. "If that's true, he is sure to come undone before long."

"You must talk to him, Thomas. Find out how to help him," Sophrona said.

"No, I'll not do that. Neither must you. Not if he's ever to become a man."

"But he's not a man. He's just a boy. We've already lost one…"

"Don't say anything like that again." He encircled her shoulder with an arm. "I know you're worried about Starlyn's safety, but don't put voice to a tragedy that hasn't happened. If Jack's ever to work out his problems, we must let him do that without our interference."

"Are you sure that's best?" She patted at her eyes with her apron.

Thomas nodded as he tilted his face toward the ceiling, hoping that was so.

* * *

Sophrona heard coughing as she entered the front room, where Thomas sat with Cyrus and Jack.

"It's time for supp…"

"You all right, Da?" Thomas reached around to clap his father between the shoulders.

"Well then, you took care of my problem, Lad."

Thomas touched his shoulder. "Does that happen often?"

"Often enough—seems to come with age."

"Why do you worry about him? It's me who's dying." Jack jumped up, wheezing as he stomped back and forth in front of the fireplace. "I can't stand it anymore."

Startled, she moved toward her son.

Thomas grasped her arm. "Don't—not yet."

A high-pitched moan from Jack sent fear mounting inside her. What was wrong with him? When tears rolled down his face, she understood it as something new. He had replaced the soft tears a young John might display with raging emotion, it seemed.

316

"Mama, she didn't mean it when she asked me to come see…visit…her so beautiful. A pretense is what it was…"

"What do you mean?" Thomas said, as he turned loose of her arm.

Cyrus moved to a chair when Sophrona took Jack's hand and led him to the sofa, seating him between her and his father.

"Rebecca invites me to their socials, but each time I try to sit with her, she moves. Usually Lydia comes to sit by me. Then I'm stuck beside her, too embarrassed to say anything to Rebecca."

"You must find a way to clear this up." Thomas scratched his head. "It isn't like you not to speak your mind."

"Well, I don't, because Sarah always gets between us when she sees me coming. It isn't private when everyone hears what you say."

Pain seeped into Sophrona's heart when she realized how much her son wanted Rebecca's attention. "What will you do?"

Jack rose, starting for the door.

"Don't hold supper for me. I'm going down to the barn."

"Hold up there. I'll go with you." Cyrus stood to follow him out.

Sophrona went to the common room, where a servant helped her reheat the food before setting it on the table. When Thomas entered, they ate in silence. Spreading cloths over the food bowls, she left them for Jack and Cyrus.

Dishing out two bowls of cinnamon-stewed apples, she followed Thomas to the front room sofa where they ate in front of the fire. Sophrona thought she'd choke on the last bite, if she didn't say something.

"Do you think he'll be all right, now that he's talked about it?"

"Oh, I don't know about that. But, if you want an answer, I'd have to say there's more to come out, if he'll only let it."

"I don't know how much more I can take. Our oldest son is in the war. We don't know if he's alive or not. Our youngest son is so

317

eaten up with unhappiness, who knows what he'll do. May the Good Lord help us all."

* * *

January 1st, 1781

A bitter cold blew in, unlike anything Sophrona remembered in the last few winters. One of Thomas's men started long before dawn clearing the pathways to the barn, then to the freighting sheds.

The sun rose, casting a golden glow over the deep blanket of white snow that fell through the night, giving it a pearly color.

"Soon as I'm through, take this pan of food down to the men-servant's house," Sophrona said to Tessa, a stout female servant.

"Yes, ma'am."

Sophrona tucked a cloth over the pan.

The woman slipped into a heavy wrap, grasped the pan, and heaved it up in front of her.

Sophrona looked around as Tessa disappeared out the door. The woman moved so fast, she must remember to caution her about the slippery snow.

Thomas entered the common room with Cyrus. "How soon before we eat? Time's getting away." Jack walked behind them.

"Sit down while I put breakfast on the table."

She moved a stack of pewter plates to the table's edge, then spread them around. A servant brought bowls and then glasses. Sophrona placed rice pudding on the table. She filled a charger with fried meat, placing it next to the pudding. She heaped biscuits from the Dutch oven on a platter, taking them to the table. Finally, she took a seat.

After Thomas asked the blessing, they filled their plates and concentrated on the food.

"Jack, move split wood, along with several large logs, from the woodshed onto the back porch." Thomas briefly paused. "Stack some in the woodbins in the house. It's going to take plenty of fuel to keep us warm the next few days."

"Yes sir, I'll take care of that when we're through." Jack ate his rice pudding.

Before long, Thomas left with Cyrus. Jack pulled on a warm coat to follow them.

Sophrona grasped one side as she helped Tessa lift a pot. They hung the bail on the trammel, poured in some water then swung the crane back over the fire.

"Maybe bring in some meat. Be sure to take a sharp knife, and watch out for slick spots," Sophrona said.

Nodding, the servant reached for a cape, swung it around her shoulders, buttoned it and pulled on mittens. She took a big pan off the wall before going out in the cold. Tessa might take a while to separate some of that hanging meat.

Sophrona built up the fire in the cook fireplace before she lowered the pot. The water needed a strong blaze to boil. After that she would reduce the heat, letting it simmer through the day.

Tessa, who came to them through the death of her former master, returned with the meat.

Sophrona cut it into small pieces, sliding it off the wooden board into the water. Later, after the meat was tender enough to practically be cut with a spoon, she would go to the root cellar for the vegetables.

The morning progressed as her thoughts turned to Starlyn. When fear for him made her nauseous, she gave it to the Lord. Only He had the ability to help their son. She had great faith that He would. The next time, she must ask Him sooner.

In the late afternoon, when Thomas, Cyrus and Jack returned, they sat down to supper.

After a second bowl of stewed beef, Thomas said, "This may be the best pot of stew you've made."

"Thomas, you say this every time I cook it,"

They barely finished eating when Jack excused himself and left the table. Cyrus left shortly after, declining her invitation for dessert. Sophrona sliced two pieces of apple cake, placed them on saucers, then filled Thomas's mug with coffee.

They had finished their cake when Jack strode into the room. Sophrona slid a critical eye over his blue, fitted jacket. His trimmed hair, parted on the left, hung just below the collar of his beechnut colored shirt.

"You're so handsome. Where are you going all dressed up?" she said.

"Now leave the boy alone," Thomas turned to smile at her. "He's old enough to handle his own affairs. That is, unless he wants to tell you."

"I've made up my mind. Rebecca owes me an explanation—an answer—maybe both. I'll probably come home late this evening."

He walked toward the front room. Sophrona followed behind as he reached for his coat, shrugging it on. Thomas came in next.

"Jack, the weather's bad. Must you leave the house tonight?" She waited for his answer.

Thomas touched her shoulder. "There's something important he must do."

They followed him to the door. He went down the steps, where Cyrus stood holding his horse's bridle. Jack slid a black boot in the stirrup and pushed up, swinging over his other leg, settling into the saddle. He glanced back at them as he rode away.

Sophrona turned to Thomas. "Do you think he'll do all right out on the road?"

"The good Lord willing."

* * *

Thomas waited for his son to tell him about Rebecca. He expected Jack to say something about the outcome, but he remained silent on the matter.

"How's Jack managing the procedures for this year's tobacco crop, Da?"

"Truth is, I'm right proud ah him." Father nodded as he spoke. "Busy as he is courting the lasses, he's prepared the seedbeds on time for planting, even stepped into Starlyn's place driving the freight wagons. Well then, he'll make a good business man one day."

"Why do you say that, other than being one yourself?"

"It's the way he directs the loads—knows the routes."

"It sounds as if he's doing well. Not at all like when he worked under his brother."

"Ya mustn't forget the boy's only seventeen, Lad. After Starlyn joined the war, well, that let Jack out from under his shadow. At least until Starlyn comes home."

Father looked in the direction of the common room. "It appears yer wandering lad has returned home."

"Da." Jack called.

"I'm up front with your Granda," Thomas said.

Jack entered the room, his steps confident. "I finally got an answer from Rebecca. It wasn't easy, but I forced her to speak with me."

"If you're satisfied, I'm interested in hearing what she said."

"I'm not all that pleased. Rebecca told me straight out she's looking for a suitor, but she's not sure it's me. Said I'm a little young. Even though she said I'm welcome to see her again."

"Are you going to court her, then?"

"Maybe. Maybe not."

CHAPTER THIRTY-NINE

The days grew milder. Thomas appreciated he would be home early. He had the day's light load. His father took a larger Conestoga for the long route, with a servant accompanying him. Jack drove the smaller wagon, sure to return him home by the afternoon.

They planned to finish the tobacco seedbeds for tomorrow's planting, using more help.

"Where are Starlyn and Andrew today?" Sophrona's brow showed a trace of flour.

"You mustn't worry about that," he said. "The good Lord knows."

Sophrona gave the bread-making over to a servant. She brought Thomas a mug of coffee, then sat next to him.

"It seems like a hint of spring in the air, the last few days. Wouldn't surprise me if…"

Thomas stood at the sound of hoof beats drumming down the road.

The sound of a wagon sent him to the front room, Sophrona behind him. Dread grew as he wondered what brought Father back early. Did something go wrong with the load?

Pounding echoed through the house, followed by a shout.

"Anybody here?"

He placed a finger on his lips, motioning her to follow as he entered the bedroom for a rifle. He signaled for her to stay there while he cautiously made his way toward the front room.

"Hey, anybody there?" a male voice shouted.

322

He sidled up to the window panes in the door, but couldn't see out without pulling back the curtain. "Who is it? You trying to break down my door?"

Thomas thought he heard a stream of laughter. Did his nerves just give way?

"Open up. Someone here wants to see you."

Thomas gripped his rifle closer as he called out. "Identify yourself."

"You've got one more chance to open up before we come in."

Faint laughter billowed through the door. Once before, Father pounded on the barn door when he came to live with them. But today his father did not pound on the door. Thomas suddenly felt his knees grow weak.

He crept to the common room to open the door, but heard a rifle cock on the other side.

Returning to the front room, he shouted. "I'm coming out. If you're on my property, I'll put a bullet through you."

A wave of laughter forced him to wonder who was addled enough to laugh at death.

Thomas opened the door, dropped on his knees, positioning his rifle upwards as he shot.

The smoke from his gun cleared. A man in a blue and red Continental uniform stood sideways, his face white as the color of his breeches. A spot of his long facial hair looked singed. Another soldier stood backed up flat against the wall.

Laughter rang out from a different direction.

"General Morgan declared him reasonable. But almost taking the fullness of my beard, maybe even my life, isn't the act of a rational man."

The fog in Thomas' mind cleared, as Daniel Morgan received help getting out of a wagon. Daniel, still laughing, suddenly winced as his legs buckled when his feet touched the ground. He might have fallen, but for the shoulders of two young men bracing him.

A big square freight wagon rolled up with two men perched on the seat, followed by four horsemen Thomas recognized as Virginia militiamen. They stopped behind the first wagon.

"Daniel, what in the world brings you here?"

Thomas waited as the men helped Daniel get to the porch and up the stairs.

"I've stopped to visit one of my oldest friends. Can't stand long Thomas—it's my sciatica."

Thomas held the door open as the men helped Daniel into the front room, where the big man took a seat on the sofa.

"Daniel, I'm going for my wife. She thinks we're having trouble."

He went to the bedroom, where Sophrona huddled on the bed. He put an arm around her.

"It's all right, now. There's nothing to worry about." He helped her stand. "Come into the front room. I want you to meet Daniel Morgan."

"Is that who knocked?" She patted hands over her hair before straightening her skirt.

"Yes, his men. Strange, I don't remember Daniel indulging in such humor." He shook his head.

"Thomas, you are the good friend of his youth, but you were not around him long. Years have passed." Sophrona tilted her head. "You said the men in camp liked him exceptionally well. Maybe things like this made him easy to stay around."

He took her hand, pulling her close before leading her to the front room.

"Daniel, I'd like you to meet Sophrona, my wife. Meet General Morgan."

"Now I understand why you hurried back to Baltimore Town, Thomas—a woman as pretty as her. You're fortunate to have married her." Daniel stretched his legs out as he spoke.

"I'm so pleased to finally meet you, General Morgan. Thomas spoke often of you."

"Now, you mustn't call me that. I much rather prefer Daniel."

"Yes, Daniel."

A captain entered the room. "General Morgan, the men want to know if they're leaving soon or you want them to set up camp. I don't know what to tell them."

"Why don't you stay? Your men should move my freight wagons out of the open shed, then stay there. Plenty of fuel in the wood shed." Thomas shifted his legs. "There are enough supplies to make their stay enjoyable. Also, the barn sleeps well when a person's tired."

"Sure this won't put you out? These men don't mind the ground."

"It's no problem. We'll enjoy your company. My youngest son Jack's coming home soon. My father lives with us now. He'll get back from a delivery before nightfall."

Daniel spoke to the captain. "Captain Tate, tell the men to settle in. We'll stay the night."

"Yes, sir." He went out the front door.

Thomas turned toward Sophrona, who stood at the door resting a hand on the jamb.

She removed her hand, placing her fingers at the base of her neck. "Gener…I mean Daniel, you must pardon me. There are some things I need to attend to." She left.

Thomas moved to the sofa, taking a seat next to Daniel and facing him full on. "What in the world possessed you to let them trifle with me today? What if I killed someone?"

Daniel smiled. "These men need the experience. Besides, anything but death might only bring them a holiday."

325

Thomas nodded. "What else brings you this way?"

Daniel groaned as he arched his feet. "My sciatica's killing me, Thomas. You know? Hip-gout. I'm going home to Winchester, to recover. General Greene knows I'm not worth much this way."

"Well, that explains why you needed help to get from your wagon into the house." Thomas rose to stoke the fire, briefly hesitating to question Daniel. "That doesn't explain what happened to your face. It sure looks painful, even for someone as hardy as you."

Daniel laughed, causing the sunken crease on the left side of his face to stretch out.

"It's an old wound that's healed well, now. Just a few years after our affair with General Braddock, I got ambushed running messages from one fort to another. I took a musket ball through the neck, mouth and jaw. I streamed blood, spitting out some teeth, but I managed to hang on as my horse carried me to safety."

It pained Thomas when Daniel's face twisted up. "Sure seems to me like you cheated death."

"That fast Indian running alongside my horse wanted to kill me, but I outdistanced him. Sure didn't want to get mutilated." Daniel reached to rub a hip. "I avoiding his tomahawk, as I hung onto that filly's neck while she carried me back to the fort I'd just left." He let out a long groan. "They killed the two militia with me, taking their scalps. I lived—but don't know how."

A servant entered with a tray. She set out cups of coffee, then saucers of cake. Thomas took a sip of his coffee. He set the cup down, when the door burst open and Jack rushed in.

"Someone tell these people my name," Jack demanded. "I don't think they believe me."

The captain threw up his hands. "I'm sorry, General. He wasn't very cooperative."

"I don't need to be," Jack blurted out. "I live here."

Thomas nodded toward Daniel. "This here's General Morgan. He's an old friend of mine and your Granda. His men have the task of protecting him as he travels."

"Don't go too hard on your son." Daniel motioned to the captain, who went back outside. "I would react the same way at his age."

Thomas pursed his lips before reaching for his cup.

Daniel turned toward Jack. "Tell me, young man, what is keeping you busy these days?"

"Well, today I need to finish up the seedbeds—plant the tobacco seed before I stake and cover the beds. I don't know that it'll all get done today." Jack placed a hand at his waist.

Daniel nodded. "Yes, it will. Mind telling the good captain I'll speak with him, Jack?"

When Captain Tate came in, Daniel said, "He needs men to assist him. See that he gets enough help so it doesn't take all day putting in those seedbeds."

"Yes, sir, General Morgan."

"I appreciate the help, sir." Jack left the room.

Daniel heaved himself up. "I need a breath of air to clear my head, Thomas. You care to step outside?"

Thomas stood. "Some chairs are on the back porch, and you'll get a good view of your men helping with the seedbeds."

"Maybe we'll sit on the porch for a while. Then I'll need to walk, so my legs don't cramp up in my wagon, tonight."

They went to the back porch. Thomas upended two chairs, clearing out debris before setting them upright. He left the most comfortable seat for his guest, who sat there briefly before moving from side to side, shifting his legs in various positions.

"I believe we'd better take that walk so my legs limber up. I have either sat, or lain, in that wagon for too many miles."

Thomas rose to lead him down the back stairs. They walked around the house to the front. Daniel winced with each step he took, making it painful for Thomas to watch.

"General Morgan." Several men moved toward Daniel. Thomas stepped aside to allow him privacy while he talked with his soldiers.

After the men finished speaking, Thomas rejoined Daniel for their walk.

"We have a room for you." Thomas looked over Daniel's exceptional frame as he spoke. "The bed is big enough for two people. That'll just about fit you."

"I don't want to put you out. I'm used to my wagon."

"Actually, if you don't sleep in the bed, no one will. It's empty with Starlyn in the war."

"Oh, yes! That's the name…but I had no idea just who…"

"There's a stranger moving fast toward the house," a guard called out.

"Grab him. You—stop right there," the captain instructed. Several men moved to intercept the stranger.

In the middle of this, Thomas and Daniel started laughing.

Daniel caught his breath. "Leave him alone, before he loses his temper. That's no stranger, that's my friend, Mr. Cyrus Craighead."

The men backed away. Father met Daniel in front of the house. After they shook hands, Thomas, Daniel and Father walked to the house, where they took coffee in the front room.

* * *

After all this time Sophrona finally met the man who, aside from Cyrus, played the most influential part in Thomas's decision to return for her. If Daniel had not fallen in with them while freighting, Thomas may not have fought for her. No happy marriage. No Starlyn or Jack.

Her heart ached anew at the thought something may have happened to Starlyn. *Please Lord, keep our child safe.*

Sophrona turned to Tessa. "The day's growing long for General Morgan. Let's put on supper."

"Yes, Miss Sophrona. How many places do I set in the dining room?"

"Six of us shall eat in there, including the General with his captain." Sophrona brushed her hands down her apron, then reached for a tray of pewter chargers filled with food, as Jack came in the back way.

"We're eating in the dining room. You must clean up if you expect to sit at my table."

"Yes, Mother." A contented look settled on his face.

"You look so happy. Something I should know about?"

"Yes, but I'll tell you when Father is present. After you two aren't so busy."

She nodded as her younger son left the room.

"Please set the pitchers on the table," Sophrona instructed a servant.

"Yes Mistress. I'll take care of that right away."

Sophrona lifted the tray, taking it to the dining room, where she placed the food on the table. After that, she went to the front room.

"Supper is served in the dining room, Daniel. Would you and the captain join us?"

"We'd be honored to sit down at your table, Mrs. Craighead."

She gathered their cups on a tray, taking them to the common room.

Arriving in the dining room, Thomas pulled out her chair. After her, the men took their places. Cyrus asked the blessing.

"We're grateful for this food, Lord, as well as the presence of our good friend, Daniel. We ask your hand of protection on him and his men, in Jesus' name."

The beef platter went around the table, followed by other dishes.

"Pass Daniel the bread," Thomas said as he reached for some beef.

"About that bedroom. I'm looking forward to a good night's sleep," Daniel said.

"You'll sleep well enough to think you're already home." Thomas handed his glass to Sophrona, who filled it with water.

Cyrus stopped eating. "I guess Daniel's staying in the empty bedroom?"

"No, I thought he'd fit better in Starlyn's bed," Thomas said.

"We talked about that bedroom earlier," Daniel said, addressing the table, "and I started to tell Thomas about Starlyn. We got interrupted when Cyrus came home."

Sophrona's breath caught, making it hard to breathe. Thomas reached for her hand.

"A young man named Starlyn helped organize the wagons we captured from Tarleton, the morning we won the battle at Cowpens. I had moved my troops up to meet General Greene that day." Daniel scratched his scar. "When I heard a militia sergeant say 'Move that wagon, Craighead,' I asked him who he was."

"What did he say?" Cyrus said.

"He said his father's name was Thomas Craighead, and Cyrus was his Granda. After I asked about your residence, Starlyn gave me the directions to Starlight."

"What about Andrew Craighead?" Thomas said.

Daniel's brow wrinkled. "No, no, I didn't meet him. Starlyn did a fine job organizing those wagons. It didn't surprise me to learn he came from this family. That young man knows how to handle freighting."

"That's Starlyn, all right. Always wants to outwork everyone else." Jack snorted before turning back to his food."

Daniel scratched his sunken left cheek. "Now that I think about it, Cyrus, he favors you."

"Well then, Daniel, I've heard that since his birth." Cyrus straightened his shoulders.

Silence descended as they finished eating. A servant brought out bowls of stewed apples.

"This is a fine supper, Mrs. Craighead. I can't remember when I had anything as good."

She slowly rubbed her hands together, his compliment lifting her spirits. "It's been a pleasure having you with us. I'm so pleased to hear about Starlyn. Do you think he'll come through the war all right?" Was she ready for his answer?

"Well, I can't promise he'll come home, but the battle has turned. More of our troops are surviving, while more of the Crown's are not."

Sophrona found comfort in Daniel's words. She clutched them close to her heart.

"I think it's time to give my sciatica a long rest. Don't expect me for breakfast, Mrs. Craighead. We'll get on the road before dawn." Daniel wiped his mouth and placed the napkin on his plate before he stood. Thomas, Cyrus and Jack stood also.

"I'll meet you on the porch," Thomas said. "Then when you're ready, I'll show you to Starlyn's room. Captain Tate's welcome to take the spare bedroom."

"Need to speak with my aide before I retire." Daniel turned to leave the room, accompanied by the captain.

"I need to take care of some things in the barn," Cyrus said as he left.

After the others left, Jack sat down.

Sophrona gazed into her younger son's eyes. "Did you want to speak with us tonight?"

"No, we'll talk another time. What I want to say is far too important to rush."

CHAPTER FORTY

Tuesday, February 13, 1781

Tossing until almost midnight, Thomas awoke with a start. Daniel Morgan's upcoming departure had kept him awake. Thomas had no doubt he would miss him. The man grew as easy to be around as slipping on a pair of favorite old, worn slippers.

Living in such dangerous times for their country as these, something could happen to his friend, and Thomas might not know for a while. Father also enjoyed Daniel's company, always speaking highly of him.

He crawled out of bed, dressed in the dark, being careful not to disturb Sophrona. He closed the door as he left. Golden light from a roaring fire in the cook-place lit up the common room. A servant moved around the hearth stirring a pot, then took the lid off a Dutch oven, inspecting the contents. Several candle lamps helped brighten the corners of the large room.

Thomas sat at the trestle table, where Daniel joined him. Tessa brought them hot coffee.

Captain Tate came to stand by them, refusing coffee from a servant. "We're almost ready to leave, sir. I'll wait outside while you finish."

The captain turned to Thomas. "Thank you for the hospitality. Can't remember the last time I tasted a supper like the one your wife set on the table last night."

Thomas nodded as Tate pivoted to leave.

After they finished, Daniel pushed his cup aside and rose from the table. "It's about that time, much as I'd rather stay here a few more days."

"Glad you finally found time to stop by. Been so long." Thomas stood, following Daniel out onto the porch.

He sucked in crisp air. A trace of musk from winter's damp leaves found its way to his nostrils. A sure sign spring was at the door. A waning half-moon illuminated the dark night sky. It shed the welcoming light each man needed to do his job.

"Whooo—whooo."

Thomas glanced up as a shadow passed overhead. He shivered at the ominous call.

The men lined up, ready to go, as two soldiers moved to wait by Daniel's wagon.

The captain moved closer. "The men are ready to assist you into the wagon, sir."

Looking down, Daniel replied. "I'll ride in the carriage those two slaves we took from Tarleton are driving."

The captain nodded, then strode toward Daniel's wagon, directing the men to the carriage.

"Thomas, how's the condition of that road going from the Great Road to Petersburg? You heard any bad news?"

"No. You should make it to Petersburg without any problems. My freighters notify me immediately if there's any difficulty traveling that stretch."

Daniel spoke low, his words measured. "I'd like to stay longer. However, I'm sorely pressed to speak with General Lawson, so I must take the long way home."

Thomas nodded as he reached out to grip Daniel's hand. When Father stepped forward to clap Daniel on the shoulder, Thomas realized he had stood in the background all along, waiting until the right moment to say goodbye.

Daniel stepped off the porch, walking toward the carriage, before turning back toward them. "I'll see you again Thomas—and you, too, Cyrus Craighead."

Thomas raised his hand in farewell. "God willing, Daniel, God willing."

* * *

Thomas rose when Sophrona entered the common room. She poured a glass of water before coming to the trestle table.

"Daniel's already left." Thomas gazed at her face. She seemed contented this morning, the lines around her eyes faint, almost unnoticeable. He stretched his arm around her shoulder as she sat next to him, pulling her close.

"I hoped to get up early enough to say goodbye," she said.

He patted her arm, then reached for his coffee.

Across the table, Jack sat beside Father. They stayed silent, as though lost in thoughts of their own.

"We have animals to take care of." Thomas finished his cup. "Then there's the hauling."

"Figure out the work roster for the day, Lad, while we take care ah the barn." Father stood and walked toward the door. Jack followed him.

When the servants entered the room, Sophrona rose to join them. Soon the common room filled with the sounds of food being prepared. The women talked and laughed as they worked.

"I will be in my office," Thomas said, as he headed toward the doorway.

* * *

Sophrona found herself humming as she bustled from one chore to another. Unlike other mornings since her eldest son went to war, she awoke rested, her mind free of worry. Starlyn might come home. Daniel almost said as much at supper last night.

334

She shook out her skirt and went to the kitchen to rinse her hands before starting supper. A servant poked up the cook-place fire, adding more wood, then swept off the hearth.

"Maybe slice up some bread, too."

"Yes, Miss Sophrona." The servant reached for the bread board.

She stirred the pot hanging off a trammel with a wooden spoon, before tasting the contents. Much like she watched Mother do all those years at home. She sighed in satisfaction. The pot tasted about as perfect as any soup she ever made. Thomas savored her turkey soup. He never left any, eating every bite she served him.

He came in and changed his shirt before sitting with her.

"Jack's so quiet today. It's not like him."

"Is there anything wrong?" She glanced toward the cook place, dread growing. What if their only son still at home had a bigger problem than his feeling for Rebecca?

"No, everything seems all right. Just wondering why he's so quiet."

Just then, their son followed his Granda through the door. She rose to dish up supper, a servant helping to get it on the table.

Thomas asked the blessing. The table stayed silent as they ate. Sophrona watched her son take a few bites of his bread. He dipped his spoon in his bowl, as if to play with his soup like when a boy. Back then he really did play. Now he just stirred it around. She chewed on the inside of her lip, not eating either.

Jack cleared his throat.

"I want to...that is, I'm bringing Lydia over to meet the family this week, if that is all right." His cobalt blue eyes grew bright as he spoke, looking much like his father's.

Feeling relieved, Sophrona almost jumped up to hug him, but stopped herself.

"Now, I thought you were interested in Rebecca." Thomas drummed the table.

Cyrus's eyes narrowed, looking at Thomas. "The lad has a right to change his mind, I'd say."

Thomas nodded. "Yes sir, Da, right up to the time he takes his vows."

Sophrona gazed into her son's eyes. "Yes, you did say Rebecca—now Lydia?"

"Lydia's liked me since childhood, but I didn't appreciate her. At least not until Rebecca turned me away."

Sophrona glanced at Thomas. Did he see Jack's face light up speaking Lydia's name? Should she get ready to meet her future daughter-in-law? The thought of gaining a daughter stirred a feeling inside akin to the first appearance of small, yellow and blue wild flowers after a long, harsh winter.

"She's anxious for you to like her, Mother. If we become betrothed, I'd like us to live here after the wedding, until I'm successful enough to build us a home. Is this all right with you and Father?" Jack gave her a charming smile as he reached for his water glass.

Sophrona met Thomas's eyes before he addressed their son. "It's your home. If your relationship with Lydia leads to posting marriage banns, then after the wedding you're welcome to live here as long as you wish."

* * *

Hitching the horse to the lightweight, two-person chaise, Jack packed out a stack of covers, placing them on the seat. He stepped into the carriage and took the reins.

"I'll return soon, Da."

Thomas watched him roll out of sight, before going inside to hang his coat on a wooden peg. Sophrona put the servants straightening the house or helping cook, as she roasted a goose he brought down with the first shot just after daybreak.

She poured two mugs of coffee, which he took to the front room. Handing Father one he sat next to him on the sofa, beginning to appreciate the warmth from the fireplace.

"Well then, Lad. Think she's the one for our Jack?" Father took a sip of his coffee, setting the mug down to slowly massage his shoulder.

"Seeing them together may tell us something. Even if we don't know how they feel toward each other, his mother will. She'll know if they're thinking about posting their banns."

When did Father age so much? Busy with the daily tasks of farming, hauling for the war, even just plain living, he had failed to notice. Pain rolled over him as the knowledge settled in his mind that Father grew older. He immediately dismissed the thoughts.

The warmth of the fire, peppered with sparks from the burning wood, took Thomas to a peaceful place in his spirit only God ever allowed.

Father rose, adding more wood, then turned his head toward the outer wall of the front room. "I do believe that is young master Jack, returning with his new love."

Faintly, Thomas heard a horse neigh.

Sophrona came into the room smoothing back her hair, as Thomas rose to get the door. He opened it, moving aside to allow the young woman entry. She carried a covered glass cake plate in her hands. When Jack stepped through, he pulled the door closed, before reaching to take the cake server. She shook her head.

"Lydia, meet my mother, Sophrona; my father, Thomas; and Granda Cyrus. My brother Starlyn's off fighting against the Crown."

Lydia took the cake plate over to Sophrona, handing it to her. "I hope this taste's alright. I...I'm still learning to bake."

"I'm sure it will, Lydia. It smells so good." Sophrona took the cake. "Come with me to the common room. We'll taste it before we set out coffee. The men may join us when they please."

Delight touched Thomas's heart when Lydia smiled at Sophrona, falling into step behind her. He would give his wife and their prospective daughter-in-law time to ready the table before suggesting they join them.

* * *

"I think there's too much salt in the cake, Mrs. Craighead," Lydia said, biting her lip.

Sophrona looked into the gold-flecked brown eyes of the young woman who finally succeeded in getting her youngest son's attention. Dark brown hair framed her face to tumble down her back. Lydia seemed sincere, as well as lovely to look upon. Her son chose well.

"Let's just get a taste of what you brought."

Sophrona sliced off a piece of the molasses cake dusted with brown sugar. It was filled with raisins. She cut it in two parts, offering the saucer to Lydia before she took the other piece.

"Mmm, that's so good. Maybe a little salty, but it's not enough to ruin the cake. Now we need cups for the coffee." Sophrona took another bite.

Thomas, Cyrus and Jack entered the room. The men took seats at the trestle table, where Sophrona served them cake with their coffee.

"Will you join us for supper, Lydia?" Thomas said.

"Yes. We need time to…and supper is…I mean…." Confusion crossed the young woman's face as she looked toward Jack.

Jack cleared his throat. "I'll handle this, Lydia."

Briefly looking down, Lydia folded her hands, a contented look on her face.

"We planned on discussing our betrothal during supper, while everyone's here." Jack tugged his pursed lips to the side of his mouth. His chin scrunched up as he looked around the table then up toward the ceiling, while the silence deepened.

* * *

"Well then, go ahead, lad. Everyone sure wants to hear what's on your mind." Thomas took a sip of his coffee, carefully placing the mug on the table.

"We're planning to wed in the summer. Then Lydia shall move in with us, as we previously discussed."

Jack took Lydia's hand. She glanced down, a gentle smile on her face, before looking up at Jack, eyelashes fluttering. Thomas had no doubt his son found a woman to love him through his life. She reminded him of Sophrona, in ways, a pretty woman who always let him take the lead—trusting his judgment. He didn't know anything about that other girl, Rebecca, but his son would need to search far and wide to find a woman any better for him than Lydia Brown.

"...and I would so enjoy you helping Mother prepare for our wedding," Lydia said. "Your opinion's important to us."

Sophrona's eyes lit up in that way Thomas loved, sparkling blue and so full of happiness.

"Yes, I'll help your mother prepare for this."

"Do you think Starlyn's coming home by summer?" Jack's shoulders straightened. "I'd like for him to attend."

Thomas looked at his father, then at Jack.

"I don't think so, but only the Good Lord knows for sure what's going to happen. If not, then your mother shall contact him when we know where he's located, to give him the good news."

He looked into Sophrona's pretty face, aglow with happiness. They lived through so much during their lives together. Taking her hand, he thought of the years they still had left, trusting the Lord they would be good. Years busy with the grandchildren from Jack, and then Starlyn, as they enjoyed many times together as a family.

Thomas wasn't concerned about death, it being the Good Lord's plan. Both of them trusted Him in everything.

Thoughts of Starlyn crossed his mind. He remembered the night his eldest son came into the world. The Lord gave Starlyn to them.

He might take him back, now. All according to His will for Starlyn and their family. He turned, then, to join in the conversation as they celebrated their younger son Jack's happiness.

THE END

www.ingramcontent.com/pod-product-compliance
Lightning Source LLC
Chambersburg PA
CBHW051329250626
47155CB00007B/2520